W9-CLW-330

CHANCES ARE

RICHARD RUSSO

CHANCES ARE

ALLEN&UNWIN

First published in Great Britain in 2019 by Allen & Unwin

First published in the United States in 2019 by Alfred A. Knopf, a division of Penguin Random House LLC, New York

Allen & Unwin
c/o Atlantic Books
Ormond House
26–27 Boswell Street
London WC1N 3JZ

Phone: 020 7269 1610
Fax: 020 7430 0916
Email: UK@allenandunwin.com
Web: www.allenandunwin.com/uk

A CIP catalogue record for this book is available from the British Library.

Hardback ISBN 978 1 91163 036 4
Trade paperback ISBN 978 1 91163 037 1
E-Book ISBN 978 1 76087 168 0

Printed in Great Britain by Bell and Bain Ltd, Glasgow

10 9 8 7 6 5 4 3 2 1

For those whose names are on the wall

For a second there we won.
Yeah, we were innocent and young.

"Miss Atomic Bomb," The Killers

CHANCES ARE

Prologue

The three old friends arrived on the island in reverse order, from farthest to nearest: Lincoln, a commercial real estate broker, practically cross-country from Las Vegas; Teddy, a small-press publisher, from Syracuse; Mickey, a musician and sound engineer, from nearby Cape Cod. All were sixty-six years old and had attended the same small liberal arts college in Connecticut where they'd slung hash at a campus sorority. The other hashers, mostly frat boys, claimed to be there by choice, because so many of the Thetas were hot, whereas Lincoln, Teddy and Mickey were scholarship students doing the job out of varying degrees of economic necessity. Lincoln, as good-looking as any of the frat boys, was immediately made a "face man," which meant donning a scratchy white waist-length jacket to serve the girls in the sorority's large dining room. Teddy, who'd worked at a restaurant during his junior and senior years of high school, became a cook's helper, making salads, stirring sauces, plating entrées and desserts. Mickey? They took one look and escorted him over to the sink where a mountain of dirty pots sat piled alongside a large cardboard box of off-brand steel scrubbers. Such was their freshman year. By the time they were seniors, Lincoln had been made head hasher and could offer both his friends positions in the dining room. Teddy, who'd had enough of the kitchen, promptly accepted, but Mickey said he doubted there was a serving jacket big enough to fit him. Anyway, he preferred remaining a kitchen slave to making nice with the fancy girls out front, since at least the galley was his own.

Converging on the island forty-four years later, all three were grateful for the educations they'd received at Minerva, where classes had been small, their professors available and attentive. To the naked eye, it had looked like most other colleges did in the late sixties and early seventies. The boys had long hair and wore faded jeans and psychedelic T-shirts. In dorm rooms kids smoked dope, covered the smell with incense, listened to the Doors and Buffalo Springfield. But these were mere matters of style. To most of their classmates, the war seemed a long way off, something that was going on in Southeast Asia and Berkeley and on TV, not coastal Connecticut. Editorials in the *Minerva Echo* were forever lamenting the lack of any real activism. "Nothin's happenin' here," one said, riffing on the famous song lyrics. "Why that is ain't exactly clear."

No place on campus was less rebellious than the Theta house. A few of the girls smoked weed and went braless, but otherwise the sorority was a protective bubble. Yet it was here, far more than in their classes, that the real world began to reveal itself conspicuously enough that even nineteen-year-olds like Lincoln and Teddy and Mickey couldn't ignore it. The cars parked out back of the Theta house were not only nicer than those in the regular student lots but also the faculty's. Stranger still, at least to young men who didn't come from wealth, the owners of the vehicles in the Theta lot didn't feel particularly lucky to be at Minerva, or even to have parents who could afford the staggering tuition. Where they came from, Minerva was the natural extension of the first eighteen years of their lives. Indeed, for many, this had been a safety school, and they spent their freshman year getting over the disappointment of not getting into Wesleyan or Williams or one of the Ivies. Though they'd known the statistics on the grades and SATs required to get into such elite institutions, they were used to having other factors count, too, things you could neither talk about nor quantify but that still caused doors to magically open. Anyway, Minerva was fine. At least they'd gotten into the Theta house was how they looked at it. Otherwise, they might as well have gone to UConn.

On December 1, 1969, the evening of the nation's first draft lottery, Lincoln convinced the house mother to let the hashers serve dinner half an hour early so they could all crowd around a tiny black-and-white TV in the back room where they ate their meals. Given that their fates hung in the balance, the mood was strangely buoyant, at least at the beginning. Of the eight hashers' birthdays, Mickey's came up first, 9th out of 366 possibilities, causing the others to break into a chorus of "O, Canada," which might've gone over better if they'd known more than the first two words of the song. Of the three friends Lincoln's came next at 189; better, but not safe enough, and impossible to make plans around.

As the lottery continued, a relentless drumbeat of birthdays— April 1st, September 23rd, September 21st—the mood in the room grew more somber. Earlier, while serving the girls' dinner, they'd all been in the same boat, but now their birthdays made individuals of them, people with singular destinies, and one by one they drifted away, back to their dorm rooms and apartments, where they would call their parents and girlfriends and discuss the fact that their lives had just changed, some for the better, others for the worse, their grades and SATs and popularity suddenly beside the point. By the time Teddy's birthday finally came up, he and Lincoln and Mickey were the only guys left in the hasher room. Passionately opposed to the war, Teddy had told his friends earlier in the day that he would go to Canada or jail rather than get drafted, so to him the lottery was meaningless. But of course that wasn't really true. He didn't want to go to Canada and wasn't sure that when push came to shove he'd have the necessary courage of his convictions to actually go to jail in protest. Distracted by these thoughts, by the time only twenty-odd unannounced birthdays remained, he was convinced that his had already been read out and he'd somehow missed it, maybe when they were adjusting the TV's rabbit ears. But then there it was, 322nd out of 366. He was beyond safe. Reaching to turn off the TV, he realized his hand was shaking.

There were a dozen or so Thetas they counted as friends, but only Jacy Calloway, with whom all three were in love, was waiting outside the sorority's back entrance when they finally emerged into the frigid dark. Once Mickey told her—with that big, goofy grin plastered on his face—that it looked like he was headed for Southeast Asia, she slid down off the hood of the car she'd been sitting on, buried her face in his chest, hugged him close and said, into his shirt, "Those fuckers." Lincoln and Teddy, both luckier on a night when that—not smart, not rich—was what you wanted desperately to be, managed nevertheless to feel intense jealousy when they saw the girl of their collective dreams in Mickey's arms, never mind the uncomfortable truth that she was already engaged to another young man entirely. As if Mickey's good fortune in this brief moment somehow mattered more than the short straw he'd drawn an hour earlier. Then, as his birthday was announced, both Lincoln and Teddy had the same sickening reaction: that two years ago the people in charge had taken one look at Mickey and assigned him the shittiest hasher duty in the Theta house, and when he reported for duty, he would again be sized up at a glance and sent straight to the front lines, a target no sniper could miss.

Right this minute, though, with Jacy nestled in his arms, they couldn't believe his incredible good fortune. This is called youth.

LINCOLN HAILED FROM Arizona, where his father was minority owner of a small, mostly played-out copper mine. His mother was from Wellesley, the only child of a once well-to-do family, though, unbeknownst to her, not much of that wealth remained when her parents were killed in a car accident while she was a senior at Minerva College. Another daughter might've resented how little was left of the family fortune after their debts were squared, but Trudy was too devastated by sheer grief for anything else to really register. A quiet, solitary girl who didn't make friends easily, she was suddenly all alone in the world, untethered from love and hope, and terrified that tragedy might befall her as suddenly as it had her parents. How else to explain her decision to marry Wolfgang Amadeus (W. A.) Moser, a small, domineering man who had little to recommend him besides his absolute conviction that he was right about anything and everything.

Not that she was the only one he managed to bamboozle. Until his sixteenth birthday, Lincoln actually believed his father, whose outsize personality was in stark contrast to his diminutive stature, had done his mother a favor by marrying her. Neither attractive nor unattractive, she seemed to disappear so completely in large gatherings that people afterward couldn't remember whether or not she'd been present. She seldom objected, even gently, to anything her husband said or did, not even after they returned from their honeymoon and he informed her that *of course* she would forsake her Roman Catholic faith and join the fundamentalist Christian sect to which he belonged. When she accepted his proposal of marriage, she'd taken for granted they would live in the small desert town of Dunbar, where the Moser mine was; but she'd also assumed they'd take vacations from time to time, if not in New England—which her husband confessed to loathing—then maybe California, except it turned out he had no use for that coast, either. He was a firm believer—as he explained it to her—in "learning to love what you have," by which he seemed to mean Dunbar and himself.

To Trudy, everything about Dunbar and the man she'd married felt foreign, at least at first. The town itself, hot and flat and dusty, was unapologetically segregated, whites on one side of literal railroad tracks and "Mexicans," as they were called, even those who'd resided there legally for over a century, on the other. Though it was, to her way of thinking, a nothing town, Dunbar seemed to have everything W. A. (Dub-Yay, to his friends) Moser required: the house they lived in, the church they attended, the shabby little country club where he played golf. At home he ruled the roost, his word law. *Her* parents had discussed things, so she was surprised to learn that her own marriage would operate on a different model altogether. They'd been married for several years before Lincoln came along, so it was possible they had argued occasionally about how things would play out—his father gradually bending Trudy to his will—but Lincoln's impression was that while his mother might've been surprised by her new life, she accepted it from the moment she set foot in Dunbar. The first time he remembered her digging in her heels was when it came time for him to apply to colleges. Dub-Yay meant for him to attend the University of Arizona, his own alma mater, but Trudy, who'd gone to live in Tucson with a maiden aunt after her parents died and finished her degree there as well, was determined that their son would be educated back East. And not at a big state university, either, but a small liberal arts college like Minerva, the school she'd dropped out of a semester shy of her degree.

The argument began at the dinner table with his father proclaiming in his high, whiny voice, "You know, do you not, that for any such thing to happen, I would have to be dead?" A statement that was clearly designed to end this conversation, so Lincoln was surprised to see on his mother's face an unfamiliar expression that suggested she'd contemplated her husband's mortality with equanimity and was undeterred. "Nevertheless," she said, and this in fact did end the discussion, at least for the time being. It resumed later in his parents' bedroom. Though they kept their voices down, Lincoln heard them going at it in there through the thin wall that separated his room from theirs, and it continued long after his father, who always went to the mine early, was usually asleep. It was still ongoing when Lincoln himself finally drifted off.

The next morning, after his father, bleary-eyed from lack of sleep and unaccustomed domestic discord, headed off to work, Lincoln lay in bed mulling things over. What on earth had come over his mother? Why was she waging this particular battle? As far as he was concerned, the University of Arizona was perfectly fine. His father had gone there and several of his classmates were heading there, too, so he'd know people. After tiny Dunbar he was looking forward to life in Tucson, a big city. And if he got homesick, he could easily make the short journey back to Dunbar for the weekend. A couple other classmates would attend colleges in California, but nobody he knew was moving to the East. Did his mother imagine he wanted to be on the other side of the country, where he didn't know anybody? And going to classes with kids who'd all graduated from fancy prep schools? Well, what did it matter? At some point after Lincoln fell asleep, his mother had no doubt come to her senses and realized the futility of openly opposing his father on this or any related subject of significance. Order, by now, had surely been restored.

So he was surprised again to find her in the kitchen humming a jaunty tune and not at all sheepish about what had transpired the night before. She was still in her robe and slippers, like most mornings, but also seemed to be in unusually high spirits, as if she were about to go on a long-anticipated vacation to an exotic port of call. It was all extremely disconcerting.

"I think Dad's right," Lincoln told her, pouring himself a bowl of cereal.

She stopped humming and looked him in the eye. "What else is new?"

Which brought him up short. After all, it wasn't like she and his father argued all the time and he always took his father's part. Last night's was, in fact, the first real argument he could remember. Now here she was spoiling for yet another fight, this time with him. "Why spend all that money?" he continued, trying to sound reasonable and unbiased as he poured milk on his cereal and grabbed a spoon from the drawer. It was his intention to eat standing up as usual, leaning against the counter.

"Sit," she told him. "There are things you don't understand, and it's high time you did."

Grabbing the step stool from between the fridge and the kitchen counter, his mother climbed up onto the highest step. What she was after was on the top shelf of the cupboard, and far in the back. Lincoln watched, amazed and, yes, a little frightened. Had she hidden something up there where his father wouldn't find it? What? A ledger of some sort, or maybe a book of photographs, something secret that would shed light on these things he supposedly didn't understand? But no. She was reaching for a bottle of whiskey. Since he hadn't moved away from the counter, she handed it down to him.

"Mom?" he said, because it was seven in the morning and, really, who was this strange woman? What had she done with his mother?

"*Sit*," she repeated, and this time he was glad to obey, because his knees had jellied. He watched as she poured a slug of amber liquid into her coffee. Taking a seat across from him, she set the bottle on the table, as if to suggest she wasn't done with it. He half expected her to offer *him* some. Instead she just sat there staring at him until, for some reason, he felt guilty and looked down at his cereal, which was getting soggy.

The gist of it was this. There were several facts about their lives of which he was ignorant, starting with the mine. Sure, he'd known that it was slipping, and that over the last several years the price of copper had tanked. Each year there were more layoffs, and the workers had again threatened to unionize, as if *that* would ever happen in Arizona. Eventually the mine would close, and the lives of all these men would be shaken. None of this was news. No, the news was that *their* lives might be shaken. Indeed, they already had been. Many of the extras—things they had that many of their neighbors didn't, the in-ground pool, the groundskeeper, membership in the country club, a new car every other year—were thanks to her, she explained, to the money she'd brought to the marriage.

"But I thought—" he began.

"I know you did," she told him. "You'll just have to learn to think differently. Starting now."

The night before, his father had attempted, as usual, to lay down the law. He refused to pay for any son of his to get educated in a part of the country he scorned for its snobbery and elitism; he'd come back a damn Democrat or, worse, as one of those long-haired Vietnam protesters who were on the TV every night. A private, liberal arts education back East would cost them five times what a "perfectly good" education could be had for right here in Arizona. To which his mother had replied that he was wrong—imagine her actually telling him any such thing!—because it would cost *ten* times more. She'd telephoned the admissions office at Minerva College and knew whereof she spoke. Not that cost was any concern of his, since *she* meant to pay for it. Furthermore, she continued—imagine, *continuing!*—she hoped their son *would* protest against a war that was stupid and immoral and, *finally*, that if Lincoln voted Democratic he wouldn't be the only one in their tiny family to do so. So there.

Though Lincoln loved his mother, he was reluctant to accept these new economic claims as factual, mostly because they cast his father in such an unfavorable light. If she, not he, was responsible for the "extras" they'd so long enjoyed, why had his father allowed him to believe that W. A. Moser alone was the source of their relative comfort? Nor did this new maternal narrative align with what he'd been told since he was a child—that, yes, once upon a time his mother's family had been wealthy, but that her parents' death had exposed an economic house of cards: bad investments, covered up by improvident loans, dwindling assets leveraged again and again. That even once the money ran out, they'd continued living the high life, summering on the Cape, taking expensive midwinter vacations in the Caribbean, bundling off to Europe whenever the mood was upon them. Partygoers and heavy drinkers, they had probably been drinking the night of the accident. They were . . . yes, don't deny it . . . like the *Kennedys*. To his father's way of thinking it was a morality tale about foolish, decadent people who hailed from an arrogant, snobby corner of the country, people who didn't know the meaning of hard work and had finally got their long-overdue comeuppance. He'd stopped short of claiming he'd rescued Lincoln's mother from a dissolute life, but the inference was there for the taking. Was his mother now insisting this familiar narrative, so long unchallenged, was a lie?

Not entirely, she conceded, but neither was it the whole truth. Yes, her parents had been improvident and, when the financial dust settled, the family fortune had been all but wiped out, but a small house in Chilmark, on the island of Martha's Vineyard, had somehow been saved from creditors and placed in a trust for her until she turned twenty-one. Why had Lincoln never heard about the place? Because when his father learned of its existence shortly after they were married, he'd wanted to sell it—out of spite, according to his mother, to further cut her off from her past and thereby keep her tethered more securely to himself. For the first time in their marriage, she'd refused to meet his demand, and her intransigence in the matter had surprised and perturbed W. A. Moser so profoundly that he'd refused, again out of spite, to ever visit the damn place. His obstinacy was why, year after year, the house had been rented during the summer season, the rates going up each year as the island became increasingly fashionable; and this money was placed in an interest-earning account they dipped into from time to time for all those extras. She now meant to use what remained on Lincoln's education.

Ah, the Chilmark house. When she was a girl, she told him, her eyes moist at the memory, there was no place in the world she'd loved more. They arrived on the island on Memorial Day and didn't return to Wellesley until Labor Day, she and her mother in residence all week, her father joining them on weekends, when there would be parties—Yes, Lincoln, there was *drinking* and *laughter* and *fun*—people crowding onto the tiny deck that from a distant hill overlooked the Atlantic. Her parents' friends always made a great fuss over her, and she didn't mind that there were few other children around because for three long months she had her mother's full attention. All summer long they went barefoot, their lives full of salt air and clean-smelling sheets and gulls circling overhead. The floors got sandy and nobody minded. Not once all summer did they go to church, and no one suggested that this was a sin, because it wasn't. *Summer* was what it was.

She hoped Lincoln would one day come to feel the same way about the Chilmark house, and to that end she'd already made the necessary arrangements for him, not his father, to inherit it. She just wanted him to promise that he wouldn't sell the property except out of some grave necessity, and promise, too, that if he *did* have to sell it, he wouldn't share the proceeds with his father, who would hand over the money to his church. It was one thing, she said, for her to give up her sole true faith, but she had no intention of allowing Dub-Yay to permanently endow a bunch of damn snake handlers, not with *her* money.

It took his mother most of the morning and several whiskey-laced coffees to impart all this new information to her slack-jawed son, who listened with a sinking heart, his entire reality having been violently altered. When her voice finally fell, she rose to her feet, wobbled, said "Whoa!" and grabbed the table for support before ferrying his cereal bowl and her coffee mug over to the drainboard and announcing that she thought she'd take a nap. She was still napping when his father returned from the mine that evening, and when Dub-Yay roused her to inquire about dinner, she told him to cook it himself. Lincoln had rehidden the whiskey bottle in the cupboard, but his father seemed to intuit what had transpired in his absence. Returning to the kitchen, he regarded his son, sighed deeply and said, "Mexican?" There were only four restaurants in Dunbar, three of them Mexican. At their favorite they ate chile rellenos in profound silence that was interrupted only once, when his father said, "Your mother is a fine woman," as if he wanted that entered into the official record.

Gradually things returned to normal, or what had been normal for the Mosers. Lincoln's mother, having momentarily located her voice, went back to being quiet and submissive, for which Lincoln was grateful. He had friends who lived in houses ruled by discord. When all was said and done, he supposed he had every reason to feel fortunate. For one thing, he'd just come into property. For another, though it would be a financial strain on his parents, he'd apparently be heading off to an elite East Coast liberal arts college next year, something nobody from Dunbar had ever done before. He would think of it as an adventure. But listening to his mother explain the facts of their existence had shaken him profoundly. The solid earth beneath his feet had turned to sand, and his parents, the two most familiar people in his life, into strangers. In time he would regain his footing, but he would never again entirely trust it.

———

TEDDY NOVAK, also an only child, grew up in the Midwest, the son of two harried high-school English teachers. He knew his parents loved him because they told him so whenever he asked, but sometimes he got the impression that their lives had already been chockfull of kids before he came along, and suddenly here *he* was, quite possibly the kid that would break their spirits. They were forever grading papers and preparing lessons, and when he interrupted these pursuits, their expressions conveyed unspoken questions like *Why do you always ask me and not your father?* and *Isn't it your mother's turn? I did the last one.*

As a boy Teddy had been small, fine boned and unathletic. He liked the *idea* of sports, but when he tried to play baseball or football or even dodgeball he invariably limped home bruised and battered, his fingers bent at odd angles. He came by this naturally. His father was tall but skeletal, all elbows and knees and thin skin. His Adam's apple looked like it had been borrowed from another, much-larger man, and his clothes never seemed to fit. When his shirtsleeves were the right length, there was enough room in the collar for a second neck; if the collar was snug, his cuffs ended midway between elbow and wrist. His waist was twenty-eight inches, his inseam thirty-four, so pants had to be ordered special. In the middle of his forehead there grew a luxuriant tuft of coarse hair that was surrounded by a wide moat of pale, mottled skin. No surprise, his students called him Ichabod, though no one could say for certain whether the nickname derived from his appearance or from his special fondness for "The Legend of Sleepy Hollow," the first text students encountered in The American Character, his signature senior lit course. What Teddy's father liked best about the story was that his students could be depended on to miss its point, which he would then clarify for them. They enjoyed the supernatural element of the Headless Horseman, and when he turned out not to be supernatural at all, they were disappointed. Still, they found the story's ending—in which the all-American Brom Bones triumphed and the pretentious schoolteacher

Ichabod Crane was made a fool of and run out of town—deeply satisfying. It took some heavy lifting to convince them that the story was actually an indictment of American anti-intellectualism, which Washington Irving had recognized as central to the American character. By arriving at precisely the wrong conclusion about the story's purpose and meaning, they had unwittingly made themselves the butt of the joke, or so Teddy's father maintained. Particularly hard to convince were the school's athletes, who naturally identified with Brom Bones, who was strong and good-looking, cocky and cunning and dim-witted, and he ended up with the prettiest girl in town, just as they themselves did with the cheerleaders. Where was the satire in that? To them, the story was about natural selection. Even if it *had* been satirical, Teddy's father—ridiculous-looking man that he was—was the wrong messenger. He deserved, the jocks believed, a fate not unlike Ichabod Crane's.

Teddy's mother was also tall and loose limbed and bony, and when she and her husband stood together, they were often mistaken for brother and sister, sometimes for twins. Her most pronounced feature was an exaggerated sternum that she was forever tapping, as if heartburn were her constant, chronic companion. Witnessing this, people often leaned away from her, lest whatever she was attempting to tamp down suddenly erupt. Worse than any of this, for Teddy, was that his parents appeared to see each other much as the world did, though Teddy's very existence hinted that there must've been a time when this was not true. All too aware they were physically ungifted, they seemed to take whatever solace they could from their superior sensibilities, their ability to articulate with wonderful disdain their various strong opinions, alas the exact talent that had doomed poor Ichabod Crane.

From an early age Teddy sensed how different he was from other kids and accepted his lonely lot in life without complaint. "They don't like you because you're smart," his parents explained, though he hadn't told them that he was disliked, only that he felt odd, as if some kind of instructional handbook on boyhood had been distributed to all the other boys. Because he so often ended up getting hurt when he tried to act like one of them, he mostly stayed safely at home and read books, which pleased his parents, who were disinclined to chase after him or even to wonder where he might be. "He *loves* to read," they always remarked to other parents, who marveled at Teddy's straight A's. *Did* he love to read? Teddy wasn't sure. His parents were proud not to own a television, so in the absence of companions, what else was there to do? Sure, he preferred reading to spraining his ankles and breaking his fingers, but that hardly made reading a passion. His mother and father looked forward to the day when they could retire from teaching and grading papers and do nothing *except* read, whereas Teddy kept hoping that some new activity would present itself that would be enjoyable without resulting in injury. Until then, sure, he'd read.

His freshman year of high school, a strange thing happened: an unexpected growth spurt by which he shot up several inches and put on thirty pounds. Overnight, he was half a head taller, with far-broader shoulders, than his father. Even more astonishing, he discovered himself to be a fluid, graceful basketball player. By junior year he could dunk the ball—the only boy on the team who could—and he had a fadeaway jumper that at his height was virtually impossible to block. He made the varsity squad and was the leading scorer until word got around that he didn't like to mix it up. When shoved, Teddy would back off, and a well-placed elbow to the ribs discouraged him from entering the paint, where, as a forward, he was told he belonged. All of this made his coach so livid he even derided as cowardly Teddy's fadeaway jumper, which the team depended on for anywhere from twelve to fifteen points a game. "You have to *bang* with them," he'd yell when Teddy hung around at the top of the key, waiting patiently for his shot. "Be a man, you damn sissy." When Teddy still showed little inclination to bang, the coach tasked one of Teddy's teammates to play him aggressively in practice in the hopes of toughening him up. Nelson was a head shorter but built like a tank, and he derived great satisfaction from sending Teddy sprawling when he knifed through the lane on designed plays. When Teddy complained that Nelson was fouling him, the coach snapped, "Foul him back!" Of course Teddy refused.

Indeed, Nelson so enjoyed his hardball duties that he also took to putting a shoulder into Teddy's ribs in the corridors between classes, knocking him into the lockers and scattering his books. "Brom Bones!" his father said, recognizing life from literature, when Teddy described what was going on. The remedy, as his old man saw it, was obvious: quit the team and thereby reject the stereotype of the American male as a brainless jock. Teddy didn't see it like that. He loved basketball and wanted to play it as the noncontact sport he felt it truly was. He wanted to receive the ball at the top of the key, give any defender a shoulder fake, spin and take his fadeaway jumper. The sound the ball made when it went through the net without touching the rim was as perfect as anything he'd experienced in his young life.

His varsity career ended predictably, though had Teddy predicted it, he probably would've taken his father's advice and just quit. One afternoon in practice, when he went up for a rebound, Nelson undercut him, sending Teddy crashing to the floor on his tailbone. The result was a hairline fracture of a vertebra that according to doctors could've been much more serious. Even so, it sidelined him for the rest of the season. Among the dozens of books he plowed through during his convalescence that spring and summer was Thomas Merton's *The Seven Storey Mountain*, which for some reason gave him the same feeling as swishing his jumper. When he finished the book, he asked his parents, neither of whom was religious, if he could attend church. Their characteristic response was that they had no objection unless he expected them to go with him. Sunday morning was when they read the *New York Times*.

Because Merton was a Trappist monk, Teddy tried the Catholic church first, but the priest there was what his father would've instantly identified as an anti-intellectual, a moron, really, as far removed from the monastic ideal as you could imagine, so next Teddy tried the Unitarian church a block farther away. There the minister was a Princeton-educated woman. In many respects she reminded Teddy of his parents, except that she seemed genuinely interested in him. She was pretty and not at all bony, so of course he fell in love with her. Still under Merton's spell, he tried to keep that love pure, but most nights he fell asleep imagining what she might look like under her robe and stole, something he doubted Merton would've done. He was both heartbroken and relieved when she was transferred to another parish.

Senior year he was cleared to return to basketball, but he didn't turn out, which compelled the coach to mutter *sissy* under his breath every time they passed in the hall. Either that or *pussy*, Teddy couldn't be sure which. To his surprise, he discovered that he didn't much care what Coach thought of him, though he must've cared a little, because that summer, just before Teddy headed off to Minerva, the coach, attempting to free a stick that had become wedged between the blade and the frame of his lawnmower without first turning the motor off, managed to slice off the top joint of what he always referred to as his pussy finger. Teddy, when he heard about it, couldn't help smiling, though he felt guilty, too. He'd written his college entrance essay on Merton and doubted the monk would've taken pleasure in the suffering of another human being any more than he would've spent long nights, as Teddy recently had, imagining what a pretty Unitarian minister looked like under her vestments. On the other hand, Merton never met the minister in question and had apparently been a bit of a rake before his conversion. Also, Teddy thought, there was no reason to suppose that God lacked a sense of humor. He didn't meddle in the affairs of men, Teddy had been told, or *cause* them to behave in a certain way, but so far as Teddy was concerned, Coach losing the tip of his pussy finger like that had to have tickled Him.

MICKEY GIRARDI WAS FROM a rough, working-class neighborhood in West Haven, Connecticut, famous for bodybuilders, Harleys and ethnic block parties. His parents were Irish and Italian, his old man a construction worker, his mother a secretary at an insurance agency, both deeply committed to assimilation. They flew the flag and not just on the Fourth. A veteran of the Second World War, his father could've taken advantage of the G.I. Bill but knew a guy who could get him into the pipefitters union, which he figured was better. Mickey was the youngest of eight, the other seven all girls, and he was spoiled rotten in so many respects—clothes bought especially for him, his own room right from the start. Okay, it was about the size of a closet, but so what? The family's house was large, as it needed to be, but modest, only three blocks from the beach, great in the summer when cool breezes came in off the water. When the wind changed direction, though, you felt like you were living under the nearby interstate, the traffic noise was so loud. Sunday dinners, you were home and no excuses. Spaghetti with sausage and meatballs and pork shoulder braising in tomato sauce. Michael Sr.'s mother's recipe, handed down reluctantly to her Irish daughter-in-law, with one or two key ingredients left out for the sake of contrast. Family first, America second—or maybe vice versa these days, with so many grubby longhairs always flashing their imbecilic peace signs—everything else a distant third.

For Mickey, music came first. His first job was sweeping up the mall music store where he'd seen a Fender Stratocaster in the window and fallen in love. After the guitar came an amp. In a band at age thirteen. By sixteen, sneaking into raunchy New Haven bars and sitting in with older guys whose girlfriends didn't wear bras and seemed to enjoy revealing this fact by bending over in front of Mickey, who would later joke with Lincoln and Teddy that he had a hard-on for all of 1965. "I catch you doing drugs with those guys," his father warned, "you're gonna be the first kid in America ever beaten to death with a Fenson guitar."

"Fender," Mickey corrected him.

"Bring it here then, smart-ass. We'll do it right now. Save time."

About the last thing in the world Mickey wanted to do was go to college. In school he'd always hovered between mediocre and piss-poor, but all his sisters had gone or were going, and college was what his mother wanted. Community college, live at home, was the plan. Mr. Easy, his mother called him. Always the path of least resistance. Mickey supposed she was right. He wasn't terribly ambitious. But he failed to see what was so wrong with staying in West Haven. With his sisters gone, there was plenty of room, except on Sundays and holidays.

Unfortunately, even to go to the community college, you had to take the SAT, so one Saturday morning Mickey did. Not wanting to disappoint his mother by being the only kid ever rejected by a community college because of his SATs, he'd declined a gig the night before and actually gotten a good night's sleep. He figured it wouldn't kill him to try for once. Tuition was cheap, and if he did well enough to snag a few bucks to help with books and expenses, it'd put him in good with the old man.

When the results came back, his mother met his father at the door. "Have a look at this," she said, pointing to their son's score, which was in the top two percent. "The kid's brilliant."

Since Mickey was the only kid in the room, his father looked around to make sure another wasn't hiding somewhere. "Which kid?"

"This one," his mother said. "Your son."

His father scratched his head. "This one right here?"

"Yes. Our Michael."

His father studied the SAT results, then his wife, then Mickey, then his wife again. "Okay," he said finally. "Who's the father? I've always wondered."

The next day, Michael Sr. was still trying to work it out. "Take a walk with me," he said, grabbing Mickey's shoulder with a meaty paw. When they were down the block and out of earshot, he said, "All right, come clean and I promise I won't be mad. Who'd you get to take that test for you?"

Mickey felt his left eye twitch. "You know what, Pop?" he began.

"Don't say it," his father warned.

"Fuck you," Mickey said, completing his thought.

Senior stopped walking and threw up his hands. "You said it." Then he cuffed his son on the back of the head, hard enough to make his eyes water. "Help me out here, because I want to understand. You're saying this test is on the up-and-up?"

Mickey nodded.

"You're telling me you're smart."

"I'm not telling you anything," Mickey said.

"You're telling me that all this time you could've done good in school and made your mother proud?"

Mickey felt that seeing things in this light took some of the luster off the near-perfect SAT. He shrugged.

"What were we thinking?" his father said, more to himself than his son. "We were doing so good with girls."

"Sorry," Mickey said.

"Okay, listen up, 'cause this is what's gonna happen. You're gonna go to college and you're gonna do good. No discussion. You either make your mother proud or you don't come home."

Mickey started to object, only to discover he wasn't sure he wanted to. He himself was still processing the remarkable SAT results and had begun thinking beyond community college. At West Haven High, when word got around about his SATs, several of his former teachers stopped him in the hall. "Hey, what've we been telling you?" was what they all wanted to know. So instead of objecting to his old man's command, he said, "Can I major in music?"

His father looked at the sky, then at him. "Why do you *always* have to push your luck?"

"So I can major in music?"

"Fine," Senior said. "Major in Fenson guitars for all I care."

Mickey thought about correcting him, but his father did have a point. He *was* always pushing his luck.

WHAT WERE THE ODDS these three would end up assigned to the same freshman-dorm suite at Minerva College on the Connecticut coast? Because yank out one thread from the fabric of human destiny, and everything unravels. Though it could also be said that things have a tendency to unravel regardless.

Lincoln

September was the best month on the island. The crowds were gone, the beaches empty, the ocean still warm. No need for restaurant reservations. After Labor Day, the politicians had all returned to D.C., the left-wing Hollywood/media types to L.A. and New York. Also gone were the smug, privileged frat boys, many of whom imagined themselves Democrats but who in the fullness of time would become mainstream Republicans. Half of Lincoln's Las Vegas agency—or what was left of it after the Great Recession—was made up of Sigma Chis who'd been long-haired pot smokers and war protesters in the sixties and seventies. Now they were hard-line conservatives, or anyway harder than Lincoln. These days, a lifelong Republican himself, Lincoln had a difficult time finding comfort anywhere on the political spectrum. Voting for Hillary was out of the question, but if not her, then who? A baker's dozen of GOP candidates were still in the race—some legitimately stupid, others acting like it—at least through Iowa. So Kasich, maybe. Bland wouldn't be so bad. Think Eisenhower.

Anyway, a relief to shelve politics for a few days. Lincoln had little doubt that Teddy, who would arrive tomorrow, was still a raging lib, though there was no way of telling whether he'd be in the Clinton or the Sanders camp. Mickey? Did he even vote? Probably not a bad idea to give Vietnam a conversational miss, as well. The war had been over for decades, except not really, not for men their age. It had been their war, whether or not they'd served. Though his memory was increasingly porous these days, Lincoln still remembered that evening back in 1969 when all the hashers had gathered in the back room of the Theta house to watch the draft lottery on a tiny black-and-white TV someone had brought in for the occasion. Had they asked permission to watch on the big TV in the front room? Probably not. The social boundaries of sororities, like so much else in the culture, had started eroding, as evidenced by their regular Friday afternoon hasher parties, but they could still crop up unexpectedly. Hashers still entered the house through the rear. Anyway, the draft wasn't about the Thetas, it was about Lincoln and Teddy and Mickey and the others. Eight young men whose fortunes that night hung in the balance. A couple were dating Thetas, as Lincoln would the following year with Anita, and planned to see them later in the evening, but they'd watch the lottery on the crappy little set in the back room, not the big color one in the front room, because they belonged there, as did the war itself.

They'd made a party of it, everybody chipping in for a case of beer—strictly against the rules, but Cook wouldn't squeal, not that night. The rule was that you couldn't start drinking until your birthday had been drawn and you knew your fate. Mickey's came first, shockingly early. Number 9. How was it that Lincoln could recall this detail, when time had relegated so much else to memory's dustbin? He remembered, too, how his friend had risen to his feet, his arms raised like a victorious boxer, as if he'd been hoping for precisely this eventuality. Going over to the aluminum tub, he'd pulled a beer out of the ice, popped the top and chugged half of it. Then, wiping his mouth on his sleeve, he'd grinned and said, "You boys must be feeling pretty dry in the mouth right about now." The other thing Lincoln recalled was glancing over at Teddy and seeing that all the blood had drained out of his face.

Absent from these vivid memories, though, was how he'd comported himself. Had he joined the others in serenading Mickey with the Canadian national anthem? Had he laughed at the god-awful jokes ("Been nice knowin' ya, Mick")? He had a dim, perhaps false, memory of taking Mickey aside at some point and saying, "Hey, man, it's a long way off." Because even those who'd drawn low numbers probably wouldn't hear from their draft boards for months, and college students were allowed to finish that academic year. Most juniors in good standing—as Lincoln, Teddy and Mickey were—would get one-year deferments to complete their degrees before reporting for duty. Maybe by then the war would be over or, failing that, winding down.

Later that evening Lincoln called home, hoping his mother would answer, though naturally it was his father who picked up. "We watched," he said, his nasal, high-pitched voice exaggerated by the tinny, long-distance connection. "Like I told your mother, they won't go beyond one-fifty." As with all his father's opinions, this one was expressed as fact.

"Unless you're wrong and they do," Lincoln said, emboldened, perhaps, by being three thousand miles away.

"But I'm not and they won't," Dub-Yay had assured him, probably to allay Lincoln's fear, though he sometimes wondered if his father's pronouncements served some other, more obscure purpose. Ever since his mother let him in on the truth about their family finances, his father's declarations had begun to tick him off. "How did the other Stooges make out?" Dub-Yay wanted to know. (Lincoln had told his parents that he and Teddy and Mickey, so unlike the preppy Minerva boys with rich parents, had come to think of themselves as the Three Musketeers, to which his father had immediately responded, "Three Stooges would be more like it.")

Lincoln swallowed hard. "Mickey got nailed. Number nine."

"It's a foolish war," his father conceded. "But you don't get to hold out for a just one."

Lincoln supposed he agreed, but it still annoyed him that his father would be so cavalier where his friends were concerned. "What would you say if I went to Canada?" Lincoln ventured.

"Not one blessed thing." This statement was delivered without hesitation, as if Dub-Yay had been anticipating the question, given it some serious thought and was anxious, as always, to share his conclusions. "The moment you did that, you would no longer be my son, and we wouldn't be speaking. I didn't name you after Abraham Lincoln so you could become a draft dodger. How fared Brother Edward?"

That was his nickname for Teddy, who'd visited them in Dunbar that summer. Lincoln's mother had liked him immediately, but Dub-Yay hadn't been impressed. It was W. A. Moser's deeply held conviction that a single round of golf would reveal everything you needed to know about a man's character, and he had made up his mind about Teddy on the first tee when he failed to remove his wristwatch. Nothing pleased Wolfgang Amadeus more than to extrapolate the world from a grain of sand. In retrospect, though, Lincoln doubted the wristwatch incident had anything to do with his misgivings about his friend. More likely Teddy had said something provocative about the war or remarked that all the members of the Dunbar Country Club were white and the staff Latino.

"Teddy's safe," Lincoln said. "Three hundred–something."

"Just as well. I can't imagine what earthly use that boy would be in combat." *Or anything else*, he seemed to be saying.

Had Lincoln even spoken to his mother that evening? Here again, memory, like a conscientious objector, refused to serve.

What *was* etched vividly in Lincoln's brain, however, was the moment when all three Musketeers emerged from the Theta house and found their beautiful d'Artagnan shivering in the December cold out back. Just as he remembered the shameful thought that had entered his head unbidden—*You lucky dog!*—when she took a surprised Mickey in her arms and hugged him tight. You had only to glance at Teddy to know he was thinking the same thing.

Jacy. Vanished from this very island. Memorial Day weekend, 1971.

IT WAS STILL EARLY when the ferry docked in Vineyard Haven on Friday. Lincoln was supposed to have gotten there the night before, but thunderstorms at O'Hare had put him into Boston late; by the time he'd picked up his rental car and driven to Woods Hole he'd missed the last boat. He thought about calling Mickey, who lived somewhere nearby, but he'd mentioned his band had a gig that night, so there was nothing to do but check into a motel near the ferry landing. After e-mailing Anita to let her know he'd arrived safely, he considered walking into town to see if there was someplace still open for dinner, but he was exhausted, and his lower back was stiff with travel, so he decided instead to go to bed hungry. More weary than sleepy, he lay awake in the musty room, wondering what further ravages merciless time had wrought upon his friends and, sure, how he'd look to them. It'd been—what, a *decade* since he'd last seen them? No, not quite, because everybody at the Minerva reunion had been discussing the astonishing fact that America had elected a black president. *Thank God for name tags*, he remembered thinking. And for Anita, who never had any trouble recognizing people across eternities, though it was possible she'd followed them on Facebook or Googled them in advance. Every time she introduced Lincoln to one of her Theta sorority sisters, it was all he could do not to say, *You're kidding. Really?* The men seemed to have fared better, though the years had punished them, too. The athletes in particular had gone to seed. At the last sighting Teddy was still trim, his face unlined except for crow's-feet at the corners of his eyes, but his hair had thinned and his face appeared gaunt after an illness he seemed reluctant to name. No surprise there. He'd always been protective of his privacy. Mickey still had a head full of dark, curly hair that was only just starting to fleck with salt, and he still wore it relatively long, but he was working a beer gut that would've been his defining physical characteristic if he hadn't been nearly six foot six. His good looks had always been of the rugged variety, but to Lincoln it looked like he'd been in a series of bar fights. And maybe he *had* been. Though usually the gentlest of giants, his temper would inexplicably flare up, and when it did, watch out.

Like that time they'd gone over to the SAE house. What, junior year? Three SAE pledges, as part of some initiation ritual, had crashed their hasher party with the Thetas that Friday afternoon, and in gratitude for not being tossed out they'd invited the whole crew to a bash at their frat that evening. Mickey had advised against going. "If we do," he warned, "there'll be trouble." Which made no sense. The SAEs hadn't caused any problems that afternoon, and their invitation had sounded genuine enough. But Mickey, who'd already drunk so much beer that he kept dropping soapy pots on the kitchen floor, would not be talked out of his mark-my-words prophecy. In the end, despite his dark misgivings, the others had convinced him to go along, just in case he was right and there *was* trouble. If things headed south, it would be smart to have Mickey on hand.

To screw up their courage Lincoln, Teddy, Mickey and the other hashers had returned to their apartment and drained the rest of the keg before heading over, en masse, to the frat. Only Teddy had stayed behind, claiming that Cook's disgusting beef Stroganoff had set his stomach roiling, though Lincoln suspected a more likely cause was the possibility of a brawl. The SAE's front door was flanked by two large stone lions, and Mickey, swaying on his feet, had set an empty beer can on the head of the nearest one. They could hear loud music pumping inside and wondered how anyone would be able to hear the bell when they rang it. Someone did, though—happily a pledge who'd been at the party that afternoon. He was a big kid, almost Mickey's size, and looked like he'd been drinking ever since. It took him an inebriated moment to place them, but then he flung the door wide open and cried, "Gentlemen! Enter!" At which point Mickey stepped forward and punched him in the face. Unless Lincoln was misremembering, they'd all just stood there in the entryway, staring stupidly down at the coldcocked kid, until finally one of the other hashers put a hand on Mickey's shoulder and said, "Well, you *did* warn us."

By the following morning everyone at the Theta house had heard about the incident, and there was talk of firing the lot of them. Jacy, herself furious, arrived at their apartment midmorning and commenced pounding on the door. Lincoln and Teddy, groggy and hungover, had only just gotten up, but the sight of a livid Jacy brought them fully awake. "Where is he?" she said, pushing past them, and then, when they didn't answer quickly enough, "Never mind. I'll find him myself."

Mickey's dark, smelly bear den of a bedroom wasn't the sort of place your average Theta would've willingly entered, but then Jacy wasn't your average anything. If she was the least bit squeamish, she gave no sign, even when she discovered Mickey lying facedown on top of the blanket, clad only in his boxers. Instead of speaking, she kicked the bed, hard, causing its occupant to groan but not wake up. The second kick, even harder, did the trick. "Jesus." Mickey blinked up at her in the dark. "Who let you in?"

"Give us a minute," she told Lincoln and Teddy, and when they backed sheepishly into the hall, she kicked the door shut.

All too happy to be excused, he and Teddy had gone out onto the patio, where yesterday's empty aluminum keg floated on its side in the metal tub. "We should return this," Teddy said, as if this duty, in the context of the moment, were of primary importance. "Get our deposit back."

"Right," Lincoln agreed, but neither moved.

A few minutes later Jacy emerged with a very pale, contrite Mickey in tow. (Had she watched him get dressed? Lincoln wondered.) "Let's go," she said.

"Where?" Lincoln had felt obliged to ask.

"You're going to the SAE house and apologize."

They both focused on Mickey, who shrugged as if to concede they had no choice in the matter. As if, admit it, there was no chance the three of them together could take this girl in a fair fight.

"I wasn't even there," Teddy pointed out.

"All for one," Jacy told him. "One for all."

When they arrived at the SAE house, the beer can that Mickey had set on the lion's head was still there. Lincoln remembered climbing up the porch steps and ringing the bell, but after that came a memory glitch. They must've muttered their apology, but to whom? The kid Mickey had punched? The house president? Had Mickey even spoken, or had Lincoln, as head hasher, assumed responsibility? Had the apology been accepted?

It must've been, because on the walk back to the apartment Jacy's anger had leaked away, like air from a balloon. "Actually, it *is* kind of funny," she admitted, sharply elbowing Mickey. "You really didn't even say hello? You just hit him in the face?"

Mickey shrugged again. "So I'm told."

"And then you all just slunk off? Left the poor kid lying there in the foyer?"

"It seemed best," Lincoln explained. "The party was down in the basement and the music was up really loud."

Mickey snorted, his memory jogged. "Cat Stevens. Who but a bunch of faggot SAEs would listen to fucking Cat Stevens?"

"You wanted to go down there and fight them all," Lincoln continued, "but we talked you out of it."

Jacy shook her head. "What I don't understand is what got you so pissed off in the first place."

"I don't know," Mickey admitted. "But I remember really objecting to those fucking lions." All three of them had stopped and just stared at him until he shrugged, shamefaced. "Or it could've been the Cat Stevens. Hard to say."

At this Jacy had burst out laughing, which gave them all permission. They'd howled all the way back to the apartment, their shared hilarity putting the whole episode behind them. On the patio Mickey righted the keg, picked up a used cup from where it bobbed in the water, poured out the dregs and put it under the tap, causing the others to wince. When nothing but air hissed out, he sighed and dropped the cup back in the water. "I guess we should start cleaning up," he said. Clearly, he was including Jacy in this imperative. "Everybody pick a room." Because, as always after hasher parties, every room in the house was littered with plastic cups and shards of potato chips, every flat surface discolored with beer rings.

"Why should I help clean this disgusting pigsty?" Jacy said.

"All for one," Mickey explained. He'd apparently chosen the patio as *his* "room" and was picking up plastic cups.

"One for all," Teddy and Lincoln had chimed in on cue.

"On one condition," she said.

Mickey shook his head. "No fucking conditions."

"One condition," she insisted.

"Okay, one." Where Jacy was concerned, Mickey always caved in quickly.

"No more punching people."

"Just me or all three of us?"

"Just you."

Mickey brooded on the unfairness of this arrangement, but finally said, "All right."

"Promise me."

"I promise."

"Okay, then," she said, bending over to pick up a cup.

"Peace train soundin' louder," sang Teddy, who actually *liked* Cat Stevens.

"Gliiiide on the peace train," the others chimed in, Musketeers once more.

How *young* they'd all been. How foolish. What would Jacy think if she could see them now? Lincoln wondered. Three goddamn old men.

DESPITE THE EARLY HOUR, he decided to drive into Edgartown before heading up island. Maybe Martin was one of those realtors who arrived at the office early. If he wasn't in yet, Lincoln could get breakfast in town—having skipped dinner the night before, he was famished—and then grab some provisions at the package store: wine for Teddy, beer for Mickey, a good single-malt scotch for himself, though he wasn't much of a drinker anymore.

The town was surprisingly busy, and the harbor parking lot full, but he got lucky, someone backing out of a space just as he pulled in. Island Realty was dark, a CLOSED sign on the door, though Lincoln cupped his hands around his eyes and peered inside. *Don't do that*, Anita advised him from the other side of the country. *If the place is closed, it's closed.* In his wife's opinion Lincoln was always refusing to take no for an answer. *Come back later, when it's* open. *Don't be like your father, always looking for special treatment. If there's somebody inside, sitting in the dark, it's because he doesn't want to be disturbed.*

And someone *was* in the back of the office, a man who looked to be about Lincoln's age. Seated with a newspaper spread out across his desk, a steaming cup of coffee in his left hand, he was probably the very man he'd come to see. *Let him read his paper,* Anita insisted. *You can see the* CLOSED *sign, right? The office doesn't open for another forty-five minutes.* Don't, *for heaven's sake, knock on the glass.*

Lincoln knocked. Of course he did. Okay, maybe that meant he *was* his father's son. Had Anita truly been here, he would've felt obliged to dispute this claim, but she wasn't. He was alone, which meant he could be anybody he wanted, including the only progeny of Wolfgang Amadeus Moser, of Dunbar, Arizona.

Startled by the knock *(See? You scared him. Explain to me again why you're like this.)*, the man inside looked up, saw Lincoln and rose to his feet, even managing a smile as he weaved his way among the desks. Unlocking and opening the door, he said, "You look like a man who might be named Lincoln Moser."

"And that," Lincoln said, shaking his hand, "would make you Martin."

The other man acknowledged this was indeed the case. "Actually," he said, switching on the overhead lights, "I Googled you."

"There was only one Lincoln Moser?"

"Two in Greater Las Vegas, but the other was a black high-school principal."

"Yeah, quite a few black men are named Lincoln. I don't think my father knew any in rural Arizona, though."

"Would it have changed his mind?"

"Not much does."

"How about a cup of coffee?"

"I had one on the ferry."

"Doesn't mean you can't have another."

"With me it does, actually." In fact, it was distinctly possible that the near-constant state of gastric distress Lincoln suffered these days was a symptom of an as-yet-undetected ulcer traceable to the 2008 financial meltdown. On the other hand, it might be nothing more than acid reflux, which came with the territory of getting old. His wife, being a woman, wanted clarity on this issue, whereas Lincoln himself, not being one, was content to dwell in uncertainty a while longer.

"I thought you were getting in yesterday," Martin said.

"I was supposed to, but one of my flights was delayed and I missed the last boat."

"Hate when that happens. Anyhow, you're here. You didn't come in to tell me you changed your mind about listing your place, I hope?"

"No, I just thought I'd stop and introduce myself. But the town's still pretty busy."

Martin nodded. "Season runs later every year. Busloads of old folks from all over. Families with children who haven't reached school age. Weekenders, when the weather's nice like this. The whole island used to lock down Labor Day weekend. Now it's Columbus Day."

"Good for the locals."

"I suppose," he said, as if he had doubts on that score. "Anyway, I was in Chilmark a couple days ago, so I did a quick drive-by. Sweet little place you've got. Priced right, it should sell in about two seconds flat."

"You can tell that without going inside?"

"Honestly? Out there? Almost to Aquinnah, on a lot that size? Many buyers will consider it a teardown."

Lincoln felt himself wince. "You just hurt my mother's feelings, and she's been dead for years."

"Sorry."

Lincoln waved him off. "No need to apologize. I'm in the business."

"Commercial, did I read? Things still bad out West?"

"We're starting to turn around in Vegas. Just not fast enough."

"None of my business, but are you selling because you need to?"

"No, because I *might* need to. And if I do, I might need to in about two seconds flat."

"I only ask because the revenue stream must be decent out there. I gather you rent the place in season?"

Lincoln said they did and told him the name of the management company that handled things.

"You and your family don't use it?"

Lincoln shook his head. "We've got six kids. For Catholics, three bedrooms and one bath just don't cut it."

"Any of those kids still home?"

"The youngest graduated last year."

"Okay, so you're basically free. You and the wife could retire here."

"Nah, we're confirmed westerners." *One of us, anyway,* he heard Anita say, clear as a bell. Lincoln's being one of these, in his wife's view, was yet another way that he was Dub-Yay's son. An unfair criticism, surely. Anita herself might be an eastern transplant, but their kids—the older ones married, with kids of their own—were spread up and down the West Coast from San Diego to Seattle. Fond as Anita had been of the island back when they used to visit, there was no chance she'd ever live three thousand miles from her children and grandchildren. Until the recession, they'd planned to hold on to the place, steal a couple weeks' vacation from time to time. Anita still had family in western Massachusetts and she remained close to a couple of her Theta sorority sisters who'd settled in New England. Anyway, the best-laid plans.

"When I got back to the office," Martin was saying, "there was a message from one of your neighbors wanting to know if you were putting the place on the market. Must've seen the logo on my car. A guy named—"

"Mason Troyer," Lincoln finished. "He's been pestering me to sell for years. No idea why. His place is already twice the size it was when his parents owned it."

"Wild guess? He wants to turn your Cape into a guesthouse, then sell both. They're worth more together than separately. Which could be good for you."

Lincoln hadn't thought of that. Too long in commercial real estate. "Can I ask if he's a friend of yours?"

"Never met the man. Know of him."

"He's an asshole."

Martin chuckled. "That's the conventional wisdom. He'll probably come at you with an offer before we list it. To avoid paying commissions."

This, Lincoln recognized, was probably a trial balloon: the other man gauging if Lincoln was the sort who'd be susceptible to such an offer.

"Like I said. An asshole."

Instead of looking relieved, Martin frowned.

"What?"

"Stay on his good side would be my advice. He has a reputation."

"You Googled him, too?"

"Didn't have to. It's a small island. People out in Chilmark steer well clear of him."

"I intend to do the same," Lincoln assured him.

"What time do your friends get in?"

"One later today. The other tomorrow morning."

"And leave?"

"Sunday or Monday."

"But Monday morning's still good for us?"

Lincoln said it was. When they rose and shook hands, Anita piped in again: *Apologize at least.* "Sorry to interrupt your morning coffee," he said as they headed for the door.

"That's all right. Time the day got started."

"My wife sometimes accuses me of inconsideration. Among other things."

"Well, enjoy her while you can. Mine died last year."

Lincoln sighed. "That's another thing she accuses me of. Putting my foot in my mouth."

Martin smiled. "I suppose we could all be priests."

THE CHILMARK HOUSE SAT perched on a hummocky, picturesque two-acre plot of land that sloped down toward State Road and beyond that the Atlantic, perfectly blue today under a cloudless sky. As he stood on the back deck, from which all this was visible, Lincoln's first thought was, *Nope. Only an idiot would ever sell this.* Setting down his two bags of provisions on the warped picnic table, he took a seat on the top step and soaked up the view for a long moment, then called Anita. "We can't sell this," he told her when she picked up.

"Okay," she said.

"What do you *mean*, 'okay'? We have to." After all, it wasn't just a question of them getting back on their feet after the recession. Their children had also needed assistance getting back on theirs. He and Anita had been glad to help, but doing so had made their own finances precarious. They'd probably be okay unless something else went wrong, but something else might. "We agreed."

"And now I'm agreeing again."

Which made him grumpy. "Where are you?" Because there was shouting in the background.

"At the courthouse. Cooling my heels. I may have to hang up in a hurry."

"You think we should risk it and not sell? Just hope the worst won't happen?"

"Wasn't that exactly what we were doing when the worst happened?"

"True," he admitted.

"How's the weather?"

"Sunny. Seventy-two degrees. We're supposed to have a full week of it. You should come join me for a few days."

"I wish I could."

"Weren't we supposed to retire, both of us, like, two years ago?"

"Days like today, I'm ready."

"Martin says that's what we should do. Retire here, in this very house. If the kids want to see us, they can jump on a plane. Time for us to start thinking about ourselves, Martin says."

"Who's Martin?"

"Our realtor. A wise man."

"And would I be correct in assuming that Martin said exactly none of that?"

"Not *exactly*. Was that a gunshot?"

"Somebody knocked over a stanchion. I have to go, Lincoln."

The sound of his name on his wife's lips was, as always, something to savor. Like most married couples, they spoke to each other mostly in diminutives. Anita seemed to save his actual name for small but intimate moments. Its curated use seemed to imply that, in her view at least, he was still the same man he was when she said, "I, Anita, take you, Lincoln." White hair, acid reflux and a stiff lower back notwithstanding.

"Okay, I'll talk to you later."

"We don't *have* to sell, but we probably should."

"I know."

And yet, hanging up, he couldn't help but think about his mother, how she'd loved summers here as a girl. *There was* drinking *and* laughter *and* fun . . . *We went barefoot all summer long . . . The floors got sandy and nobody minded . . . We didn't go to church all summer.*

Would selling it be a betrayal? She certainly wouldn't want him to lose his company or put his loved ones—that large and still-growing brood—at risk. But wasn't it also possible she'd meant the inheritance as a test? She'd no doubt observed, as Anita had, that with each passing year he was, goddammit, becoming more like his father. Not so much that they agreed on everything, but rather in terms of temperament and instinct. What if the house was intended as a reminder that he was her son, too, not just a clone of Wolfgang Amadeus Moser? That he was not entirely unrelated to a woman who'd moved about the world like a breeze you couldn't be sure was there, barely strong enough to sound the wind chimes? This thought, he realized, sitting on the steps of the house she'd refused to part with, was probably occasioned by the fact that wind chimes were actually hanging from the eaves here, stirring in the gentle breeze. As a rule Lincoln was not a fanciful man, but he couldn't help wondering—had his mother just spoken to him?

In the distance a screen door screeched open on an unoiled hinge. Farther down the slope and off to the right sat Mason Troyer's huge, gray-shingled "cottage," its deck easily double what it had been back in 1971. His parents were nice, modest and decent people who never would've approved of their son's ostentatious renovation. But that was the thing. The elder Troyers were dead and gone, and whether they'd been nice people or not was beside the point. They'd left the house to Mason, presumably to do with as he pleased.

A naked woman—too far away for him to tell her age, but probably in her forties—had come out onto the deck with a tall glass of something and stretched out on a chaise lounge. A moment later a large, older man—Troyer himself, Lincoln was certain—emerged, also naked, the door again snapping shut behind him, the bang arriving a split second later. Something about his posture, how he was angling his body, suggested that he was aware of being watched, or maybe just hoped he was. He stood perfectly motionless for a beat, then turned and looked up the hill. When it occurred to Lincoln that he might be about to wave, he quickly got to his feet and gathered his two bags of supplies, the sound of distant laughter following him inside his mother's house.

Teddy

Teddy thought about heading out onto the ferry's upper deck and soaking up some of the warm September sun but opted for a booth in the air-conditioned snack bar where the Wi-Fi signal would be stronger and he could get some work done. Most of his decisions these days were similarly utilitarian and estranged from the pleasure principle. An even keel, he knew from long experience, was always best. Avoid Sturm und Drang. Highs not too high, lows not too low. In this manner he was sometimes able to ward off his spells—he didn't know what else to call them—before they gained purchase. Sometimes they manifested as full-blown panic attacks, hurricanes that battered him for a day or two before blowing out to sea, while others descended like fugue states and could linger, like an area of low pressure, for a week or more. And then there were the ones that were preceded by a kind of euphoria, a profound sense that something wonderful was about to happen, a promise of heightened understanding, even wisdom. These were the spells he feared most, because in their aftermath—with reality restored and the promised insight having failed to materialize—they felt like genuine mental illness.

Fearing that one of those might be in the offing, he'd seriously considered declining Lincoln's invitation and paying a visit to the monastery instead. Brother John was always glad to see him, and he had a complete set of Marx Brothers movies, which Teddy suspected were probably more therapeutic than prayer and fasting combined. He knew for certain, though, that over the years the monastery had seen him through some rough patches, maybe even kept him out of the loony bin. Lately, however, he'd begun doubting the efficacy of his periodic retreats. When he was younger, they had provided a contrast to his life out in the world. Yet over the years a secular monasticism had crept into his everyday life, so the two worlds weren't quite so different anymore.

No doubt about it, this trip to the island—in the company of old friends and recollected youth—was risky, a potential threat to his hard-won equilibrium. Jesus, sixty-six years old. He'd hoped that by now he wouldn't have to be so vigilant, that given enough time the madness—because that's what his spells amounted to—would ebb. After all, diminishment seemed to be the order of the day. Wouldn't you think the spirit, unshackled at last from so many of the body's youthful imperatives and bolstered by the wisdom of experience, would finally become ascendant? Wasn't memory, that bully and oppressor, supposed to become soft and spongy?

But it was only for the weekend, and he would likely survive. Its pleasures would be modest enough. Morning walks among Chilmark's rolling hills. Afternoon bike rides. Beer and white wine chilling in the fridge, though he'd do well to go light on alcohol. Lincoln might want to sneak in nine holes of golf at some point. On Saturday night Mickey apparently meant to drag them to some joint in Oak Bluffs to hear a local blues band, but otherwise it didn't seem that much had been planned. Time would pass quickly. There was nothing to fear, as the saying went, but fear itself.

Still, best to keep vigilant, so instead of going outside and watching the distant island grow until it filled reality's frame, he would put those forty-five minutes to good use. The manuscript he was editing was deeply flawed. Even when accepting the book for publication, he'd known he would come to regret the decision; that even if he could mitigate its flaws, the book would do little to advance Seven Storey Books, his beleaguered small press, which, as the name suggested, specialized in religious and "spiritual" titles, roughly half a dozen a year. The venture had been birthed a decade earlier when a colleague named Everett asked Teddy to look at a monograph he was having trouble finding a publisher for. When Teddy read it, he immediately saw why. The book was poorly organized, with its most original and compelling chapter buried in the middle, and like most academics, Everett wasn't a gifted stylist. Still, it was smart in its curious fashion, and what was wrong with it struck Teddy as fixable.

"Tell me how," Everett had pleaded when so informed. He was coming up for tenure that year at St. Joseph's, their small Catholic college, and his case was hardly strong. By his own admission he was a mediocre teacher, though his students seemed to think he'd have to improve significantly to achieve mediocrity. He'd avoided serving on committees the past four years by claiming he was writing a book. If it didn't get published . . .

But here was the problem: the book might be fixable, but Teddy doubted Everett was the man for the job. There were technical flaws, lots of them, and those could be addressed easily enough, but what was *really* wrong was deeply rooted in his colleague's education and experience, the classes he'd taken and avoided, his natural aptitudes, his blind spots. In a word, his character. Teddy felt this was far more often the case than writers realized. Sure, he could point out the more glaring lapses in judgment and maybe give Everett a few tips, and if he followed Teddy's advice and worked hard, by this time next year the book would be better, if probably still not good enough. And anyway, what difference did it make? The guy didn't *have* a year. Nine months from now he'd be out on his ass.

"Give it to me for a month," Teddy suggested. It was then the end of July and he had no plans for August. Worse, he'd noticed his personal barometric pressure dropping of late. He needed a task, something that would require his full attention for thirty days but no longer.

"*Give* it to you?" said Everett.

"Right," Teddy said. "Download it onto a disk."

Everett's eyes narrowed suspiciously. "I can't pay—"

"I don't want your money," Teddy assured him.

"Then what *do* you want?"

That, strangely enough, was the exact question Teddy had been asking himself most of his adult life and for which he'd found no compelling answer. The first person to ask it, though, had been his academic adviser at Minerva College, who'd wanted to know what Teddy intended to major in. Unable to decide, he opted for general studies, a curriculum designed not so much to answer the question as to postpone it. According to the registrar, by the time Teddy graduated he'd taken more courses in more academic disciplines than any student in Minerva College's history. Tom Ford, his favorite professor there, had told him not to worry about that, but of course Tom had been cut from the same bolt of cloth. Referring to himself as "the last of the generalists," he was the chair of the humanities program, where he taught a class in Great Books, but he also taught "special topics" classes in English, philosophy, history, art and even the sciences. Mostly he invented classes he wished had been offered when he'd been an undergraduate. Teddy had taken so many of them that Mickey joked that he was the only Minerva student who was majoring in Ford. Not until his senior year did Teddy catch wind of how poorly his mentor was regarded by his colleagues. He'd never advanced beyond the rank of associate professor, because he not only never published anything himself but also took a dim view of anyone who did. Their books, he claimed, were proof of how little they knew, how narrow the sphere of their knowledge was. More than anyone, it was Tom Ford who'd given Teddy permission to indulge his curiosity without expecting it to pay dividends in terms of professional success. *Someday*, he wrote at the bottom of one of Teddy's essays, *you might actually write something worth reading. My advice would be to put that day off as long as possible.*

The idea that he might write a book worth reading had appealed to Teddy, and he imagined that if he followed Tom's advice and example, then one day the right subject would present itself. Except somehow it never did. The problem was that no single interest felt more urgent than the next, and a good case could always be made for both. Maybe for him the right subject didn't exist, or, conversely, they all were right, which ironically amounted to the same thing. Over time he came to suspect that what he lacked was an obsession, and apparently there was no cure for that. Had he been a horse, his trainer would've put blinders on him, narrowed his field of vision. Intellectual curiosity, moreover, was not the same as talent, and he gradually came to understand that his own particular aptitude was for fixing things. From an early age he'd possessed an intuitive grasp of how and why things went off the rails, as well as how to get them back on again. He enjoyed taking things apart and putting them back together. Whereas most people hated assigned tasks, especially complex ones, Teddy in fact enjoyed them. For this reason, the notion of fixing Everett's botched job was appealing.

It had taken him the whole month of August. Once finished, he slipped the manuscript into Everett's department mailbox on a Friday afternoon; on Monday morning, when Teddy arrived on campus, Everett was sitting on the floor outside Teddy's office, staring off into the middle distance with the book in his lap. When he looked up, Teddy could see the man was crestfallen. At the sweeping changes Teddy had wrought? At how little of himself remained in the text? Probably both. "Wow," Everett said. "I really suck, don't I?"

Standing over him, Teddy felt surprisingly little empathy. He'd agreed to fix the book and he'd done so. Was he expected to shield its author from self-knowledge as well? "How about you come into my office, Everett," he said. "You're scaring the kids."

Inside, the man slumped into the chair provided for students, and on his face was the same mixture of bewilderment, fear and anger that Teddy associated with undergraduates who wanted their grades explained. To complete the picture, Everett said what they always did: "It was *really* that bad?"

"Well—"

"No, I mean . . . you did an amazing job," he said, riffling the manuscript's pages. "Your title is much better than mine. The whole thing's a lot better. It's just . . . I don't know . . . not *mine* anymore."

"Of course it is," Teddy assured him.

Everett looked up hopefully. "Yeah?"

"Send it out."

"To publishers? I'm not sure I can."

"You did before."

"I know, but they'll think—"

"They'll think you revised it. That's what it needed. Revision. It's what we tell our students, right? Revise, revise, revise."

"I guess," Everett said, though Teddy couldn't tell whether he was agreeing that, yes, he also told his students this, or if it was finally occurring to him that the advice might actually be true. "Anyway," he went on, "I owe you . . ."

Teddy waited for him to complete his thought—a bottle of wine? dinner at a good restaurant? a horsewhipping?—but he seemed unable to. Finally, he got to his feet and just stood there with his manuscript over the wastebasket, and for a moment Teddy thought he meant to chuck it in. "You know, it's funny," he said, though you needed only to glance at the man to know that whatever he said next wouldn't be funny at all. "When I got my PhD, I thought I was all done feeling like this."

"Like what?"

"Inadequate."

"You'll feel better when it's published," Teddy told him.

"You think?"

"Yes, I do. Your name will be on the cover. You'll get your tenure. That's what matters, right?" Okay, it wasn't what Tom Ford thought mattered, but he'd been an outlier, even back in the seventies. As anachronistic then as Teddy was now.

By the end of the week Everett seemed to have gotten over his dejection at least enough to take Teddy's advice and resubmit the book. Unfortunately, it came back by return mail with a note from the publisher saying that, having already rejected the book, they were unwilling to reconsider their decision. In the ensuing weeks half a dozen others followed suit, and Everett was crestfallen all over again. "I feel awful," he told Teddy. "After all your hard work."

Teddy felt bad, too, though for him there was a silver lining. As he saw it, even if *The God Project* (Teddy's title) never saw the light of day, the month he spent whipping it into shape hadn't been wasted. He'd discovered something about himself. He'd both enjoyed fixing what was wrong with the book at the macro level and also the micro work of editing, the phrase-to-phrase, comma-to-comma fine-tuning that most people found brain scalding. Tom Ford, who'd encouraged Teddy to consider a career in journalism, also told him that in addition to being a good writer, he possessed excellent diagnostic and editorial skills. Until now he hadn't had anything to apply them to.

Later that same autumn Teddy went to a college fund-raiser held in the ballroom of a large downtown hotel, the sort of event where faculty are encouraged to mingle with influential alums and donors. The featured speaker was St. Joseph's new president, Theresa Whittier, an attractive middle-aged woman of clearly mixed race, whom Teddy had not yet met. The first ever layperson to lead the college, she'd been hired to come to grips with its finances, which for decades had been in a slow but relentless decline. In her brief remarks she told her audience that she'd spent the first two months of the semester getting feedback from faculty, staff and alumni about bold new initiatives the college might undertake without— and here she got a laugh—breaking what was left of the bank. Institutions, she claimed, were like individuals. They got into ruts.

Copy that, Teddy thought. He'd come to the event in the hopes of getting out of a rut of his own. His daily routine of teaching classes and holding office hours, going out for long walks in the late afternoon, opening a bottle of wine in the early evening and finishing it over a solitary dinner, then settling in for the rest of the evening with a novel or an old movie on TV, was comfortable, even pleasurable, if unexciting, the even keel he'd always sought. Lately, though, several friends, noting how often he turned down social invitations, had begun asking if he was depressed. Was it his imagination, or did these inquiries trail an implied criticism? Were these people suggesting that in his shoes *they'd* certainly be depressed? Or were they genuinely concerned? *Was* he depressed?

Okay, but in the entire history of the world, name a single person whose spirits were ever lifted by attending a fund-raiser. As he stood in the coat-check line at the end of the evening, trying to think of one, Teddy felt a tap on his shoulder, and when he turned around, there stood Theresa Whittier. "Okay," she said, "so what's *your* big idea?"

He'd had three glasses of wine, so he said, without hesitation, "Seven Storey Books, a small publishing house that specializes in smart books on religious topics."

"And you are?"

Teddy took out and showed her the lanyard he'd put in his jacket pocket as soon as he was admitted to the ballroom.

"I thought I'd met all the regular faculty, Teddy."

"I'm irregular faculty," he explained.

"What? Like seconds in a clothing store?" she asked, an eyebrow arched.

"Sort of. Adjunct faculty."

"Ah, right. The dirty little secret of the academy. A series of one-year appointments?"

"Depending on need."

The eyebrow arched again. "You don't seem bitter."

"I don't have to attend department meetings. What's that worth?"

"Point taken. So, describe these books we're going to publish."

"Theology aimed at the layman. Nothing too heavy. The intersection of faith and good works. Memoir."

"Like Merton."

He nodded. "Maybe the occasional novel. Even a book of poems, if it's the right book of poems."

"And who would know whether it is or isn't?"

"Me. Actually, I have a book in mind for our first title. It's called *The God Project*."

"Can I read it?"

"I'll drop it by your office."

"Work up a budget while you're at it."

When her coat came, he held it out for her to slip on. "Been a while since anyone's done that," she noted, sliding her arms through the sleeves.

"You're not offended, I hope?" Because these days nearly everything offended someone.

"No," she smiled, "but holding the door might be overdoing it."

"Right. Gotcha, no door."

The following week she sent for him. "Okay," she said, handing back *The God Project* manuscript.

"Okay?"

"Okay, St. Joe's will fund Seven Storey Books, with you as its general editor."

"Wow."

"I spoke with your author," Theresa went on, grinning now. "He's *regular* faculty. I gather you roughed him up a bit with your critique?"

"There was a good book in there. I just helped him find it."

She seemed to accept this explanation without necessarily buying it. After discussing some practical details and procedures, she told him he could get to work setting up the press. When they shook hands, she regarded him quizzically and said, "You're an odd man, Teddy."

He considered telling her that this was a fairly odd thing to say about anyone she'd met so recently. "In what respect?"

"Is it your usual MO, going through life with your badge in your pocket? Not wanting people to know who you are?"

"Pretty much."

"So I've gathered. When I made inquiries, nobody seemed to really know you. I believe the phrase was, 'He keeps to himself.'"

"And you think maybe I'm a serial killer?"

"No, I'm just wondering if Seven Storey Books will end up biting me on the keister."

"I hope not," he said, trying as best he could to match her rueful smile and to not look at the keister in question.

"Me too," Theresa said, playfully. "Because if it does, mine will not be the only keister bit."

That night, halfway through a bottle of chardonnay, he recalled her remark. *Was* he odd? If so, had he always been, or was it a recent development, the result of having lived alone for so long? Was this oddness obvious to everybody? If so, why was someone pointing it out only now?

Teddy also remembered that at the door to Theresa's office, when they shook hands, hers had been warm. And when she turned around to go back to her desk, he'd noted there was nothing wrong with her keister. What was odder? he wondered. For him to have noticed these things? Or to have acknowledged, even in the moment, that he would not act on them?

He also wondered if she too was eating alone.

FOR AN ACADEMIC TITLE *The God Project* had done well, winning a small but significant award and bringing the college some welcome attention. Also, an onslaught of manuscript submissions. To Teddy, it seemed that almost as many people were writing books about faith as were reading them. Most of the submissions were dreck, but a few small gems were mixed in. No new Thomas Merton, of course, but then he hadn't expected there would be. What flagged during those early years, even as the press's reputation grew, was Teddy's enthusiasm. Gradually, he came to understand that he was unlikely ever again to replicate the experience of *The God Project*. Most writers weren't desperate enough to just hand over their book and let Teddy revise it, free of authorial griping and interference. Having written the damn thing, they tended to think of it as theirs. Moreover, the possibility that they themselves sucked, no matter how richly warranted, never seemed to occur to them, as it had to poor Everett. Indeed, many were arrogant dickweeds who refused to accept criticism, no matter how carefully and sympathetically couched. They openly flouted Teddy's most reasonable suggestions, and a few even called him names for making them. Mostly, though, they were like the author of the book he was editing on the ferry, hopelessly trapped, without realizing it, in a contemporary idiom that was ill suited to their timeless subject matter. What this particular guy was writing about, whether he knew it or not, was *sin* and *redemption*, but those words had gone out of fashion, so he refused to use them. The books Teddy had been publishing for the last decade weren't bad, but neither were they the kind of books Tom Ford would've approved of. They weren't urgent or necessary. They flowed with the cultural current, never against it, because the men and women who wrote them weren't on fire.

Anyway, this would probably be Seven Storey's last year. After a decade as president of St. Joseph's, Theresa, the press's primary champion, had been offered the position of provost at a large Catholic university out West and was stepping down. When Teddy half-heartedly floated the idea of moving the press to her new school, she'd been less than enthusiastic, perhaps because it meant that he, and not just Seven Storey Books, would be following her there. It was hardly that they weren't fond of each other, and over the years there'd been talk about them. They'd gone out a few times, to dinner or the occasional concert, and enjoyed each other's company, but that had been it. Teddy didn't doubt that Theresa was disappointed when their relationship hadn't evolved into something more intimate, but he didn't know this for a fact and couldn't think how to ask. Before her arrival on campus, the conventional wisdom had been that he was gay. It was possible she'd heard that rumor and, when he didn't try to get her in bed, concluded it must be true. It was also possible that their friendship had cost her politically. After all, she was the college president and he a lowly adjunct who'd been given a cushy position that many "regular" faculty were envious of. If they weren't having sex and he wasn't giving her free drugs, then what on earth did she *want* with him? Whatever her reasoning, she seemed to desire a clean break.

Probably just as well for him, too, though he had to admit he was sorry to see Theresa go. In addition to mutual attraction—he hadn't imagined that, had he?—they had a fair amount in common. As a young woman, she also had thought she might have a vocation and had flirted with the convent much as Teddy had with divinity school. And he sensed that somewhere in Theresa's past there dwelt a profound sadness or disappointment that she never spoke of, something she'd either prevailed over or fought to an honorable draw. Did it have something to do with her being biracial? Had she been made fun of as a child? He'd thought about inquiring, but if she was generous and trusting enough to confide in him, he would've needed to decide on the spot whether to reciprocate, and he was pretty sure he wouldn't be able to.

Of course this worm had been in the apple long before Theresa appeared on the scene. Maybe it'd been there from the start. Fixing Everett's book, helping him get tenure, had looked so much like acts of kindness that Teddy had almost convinced himself they really were. But face it, he hadn't even liked the guy. Genuine kindness would've involved sitting down with Everett and helping him understand what he was doing wrong, showing him how to fix everything that required fixing. Teddy had told himself there wasn't time for any of that, but truthfully he'd just been impatient, and this, when examined honestly, looked a lot like contempt, maybe even misanthropy. Worse, he knew all too well how he came by it. How many times as a boy had he asked his parents for help only to have them snatch the paper or pen out of his hand and just *do* whatever it was he needed help with, as if his presence in their lives and incessant demands on their time were just too exhausting for words. Clearly, he wasn't worth their effort. If he had been, they'd gladly have spent that time with him.

Apparently, *this* was the kind of man he'd become. Not just odd—Theresa's verdict—but the sort of person who snatched things. Definitely not the kind you take with you on a new adventure.

So, what next? Retire? With only himself to provide for, he could afford to. Maybe move someplace warmer and nicer than Syracuse. He had no desire to return to teaching when the press went under, which was probably just as well. His department chair had long been resentful of Teddy's cushy editing job, and with Theresa gone there was nothing to prevent the man from terminating his contract. If that happened, he'd have to find some other way of keeping busy. Possibly as a freelance copyeditor. A lot of books he read these days needed one, and copyeditors weren't expected to work *with* writers, just to correct their mistakes and pick the spinach out of their teeth. Necessary work. But was it necessary for *him*? A whole new endeavor would make better sense, but what? How could he decide? It would be like being asked to choose a college major all over again at age sixty-six. Maybe life didn't allow you to remain a generalist forever.

When the announcement came over the speaker that the ferry would be docking shortly and that drivers should return to their vehicles, Teddy discovered that he'd edited less than a page since leaving Woods Hole. He might as well've gone out on the deck and basked in the soul-warming sunlight. Why the hell hadn't he?

Outside, the glare was so intense that Teddy, emerging from the relative dark of the snack bar, had to shut his eyes tight. Could it really be *this* bright, or was the intensity a harbinger of nasty things to come? Sometimes his spells were preceded by general heightening of the senses. At the railing, with one hand shading his eyes, he squinted down at the crowded pier, hoping to spy Lincoln, who'd promised to meet his boat. He'd just about concluded that his old friend must've been delayed when he spotted him among the throng. In the nearly a decade since they'd last laid eyes on each other, Lincoln's hair had gone completely white, and his posture was ever so slightly stooped. The real shock, though, was his companion, the dark-haired young woman whose shoulder he had his arm around. Jacy! Was it the sight of her after all these years or the side of the ferry nudging the slip that caused Teddy to momentarily lose his equilibrium and grab on to the rail for support?

It's not her, he told himself, shutting his eyes once more against the blinding sunlight. *It's not.* Because it *couldn't* be. The girl on the pier below was in her twenties, and Jacy would be in her mid-sixties now, on the cusp of old age. Before such irrefutable logic he reminded himself that his brain would have little choice but to genuflect, yet he was afraid to open his eyes. When he finally did, the world was still intensely bright but less painfully so, and he now saw that the girl in question wasn't really *with* Lincoln, just standing next to him. And of course he didn't have his arm around her. That had been a trick of light and shadow. Nor, once he really looked at her, did she resemble Jacy at all. No, it was the island that had conjured her up. That, plus the girl's physical proximity to his old friend, and bingo! His too-susceptible mind had been tricked into believing the impossible.

And tomorrow, to this volatile mix, add Mickey. Was it possible that the three of them here on the Vineyard again after so many years might just blend a magic potion powerful enough to summon her? If so, he thought, feeling panic rise in his throat, he should just stay on the boat. Return to Woods Hole. He could be back in gray Syracuse by early evening.

But it was too late. Lincoln had seen him, too, and was waving. There was nothing to do but wave back.

The girl who wasn't Jacy was also waving, and for a moment she seemed to be waving at him, but, no, it was the boy at Teddy's elbow, whose presence he felt before turning to verify it, before the kid called "Hey, babe!" and began prancing down the gangplank toward this girl who was clearly the love of his young life. He would lose her, of course, because that's how these things worked. What you can't afford to lose is precisely what the world robs you of. How it knew what you needed the most, just so it could deny you that very thing, was a question for philosophers. Answer it and you'd have the kind of book Tom Ford would've considered worth writing: urgent and new and absolutely necessary. To write it, though, you'd have to be on fire.

"JEEZ," TEDDY SAID, studying the photo of Lincoln's family, the sun less intense on the deck of a tavern overlooking Oak Bluffs Harbor, with their cold pints of beer sweating on the wide railing. Teddy couldn't remember the last time he'd had a beer. Their server had recommended a local IPA, and the first taste was so bitter he thought he should send it back. Now, the pint half gone, he'd revised his opinion. Somehow the bitterness had become almost pleasant. In his experience, bitterness had a tendency to do that.

The photo in question was on Lincoln's iPad, which allowed Teddy to expand each face with his thumb and forefinger. Three girls, three boys, all medium height, slender, the girls strikingly beautiful, the boys all grinning, sandy-haired Robert Redfords. Their grandkids radiating health. "It's like you and Anita have made it your personal mission to eradicate ugliness from the species."

"Blame her, then," Lincoln said, though he was clearly proud of his handsome brood. And it was true. The girls, especially, did take after their mother, who'd been a Minerva beauty herself. Yet Lincoln's genes were also on display with the boys, their relaxed postures reeking of athleticism, probably tennis. They weren't tall enough for basketball or brutish enough for football. Maybe baseball. And, knowing Lincoln, golf.

"Where's Wolfgang Amadeus?" Teddy wondered, returning the iPad. He'd met Lincoln's father only a handful of times, but he'd certainly made an impression and not just because of his name. "I'm surprised he allows family photos that he's not part of."

"We generally don't show 'em to him for fear he'll photo-shop himself in," Lincoln said. "He's lost some ground since Mom died, but he's still Dub-Yay. Couple years ago we flew him up to Vegas for Clara's wedding, and he stood up to give a speech at the rehearsal dinner. Nobody'd asked him to. He just assumed that people would want to hear what he had to say, even if most of them were strangers. Cody had to practically tackle him to get him to shut up and sit down."

Teddy chuckled. He could see it all in his mind's eye, the damned old fool.

"Anita's the only person I've ever known to have the slightest effect on him. Maybe because she's a lawyer. Most of the time he'll do what she says."

They continued to stare out over the water as a small freighter backed into the now-empty slip, the ferry Teddy had come in on already steaming back to the mainland.

"How about your folks? Are they still in Ann Arbor?"

"Madison," Teddy corrected him. Somehow, despite being high-school teachers, they had managed to worm themselves into a retirement community named Burnt Hills that catered to Wisconsin faculty, the main draws being weekly lectures on a variety of topics given by still-active professors, free bus transportation to concerts and other campus events that were open to the public, as well as on-site classes in computer science and poetry writing that could be taken for academic credit, though Teddy couldn't imagine what people their age would want with that. They'd started out in an apartment of their own, then transitioned into a larger communal building that offered varying degrees of assistance; two years ago they'd graduated, if that was the word, to something akin to a nursing home. Teddy had always assumed the day would come when they'd regret not making more room for him, but the quality of their lives in Burnt Hills had rendered any such regret unnecessary. In old age they remained brutally self-sufficient, a closed emotional loop, apparently content with each other's company, the daily *New York Times* and all those books they hadn't had a chance to read because they were always grading papers. Quite a few former students visited them there, and Teddy sometimes ran into them. His parents always greeted him warmly, though no more so, it seemed, than their other guests. Even when they knew he was coming, they looked puzzled when he actually appeared, almost as if they were trying to place him. What year had he been in their homeroom? What had he written his senior essay on?

"I have to say I'm disappointed in him," Lincoln mused, back on the subject of his father.

"How so?" Teddy wondered, genuinely curious. How could you be disappointed in a man who'd exhibited so few admirable traits? Wouldn't the *Good Ship Disappointment* have set sail long ago? His own certainly had.

"I don't know. I guess after Mom died, I expected him to be lost.

You know how old married couples are sometimes? One dies and the other rapidly declines? Becomes disinterested in the world around them? I kind've thought Dub-Yay might be like that. Maybe they weren't the most affectionate couple you ever saw, but they shared a bedroom for forty-five years. I figured there had to be more to their marriage than met the eye. But no, he came home from the cemetery and hired a housekeeper. As if that was all Mom had meant to him. Someone to feed him, clean up after him."

"All marriages are mysterious," Teddy offered, though he was actually thinking more about Lincoln's marriage to Anita than Dub-Yay's to Lincoln's mother. They weren't mismatched, exactly, but Anita had always struck Teddy as being more interesting. It wasn't so much that she was smarter than Lincoln, though she probably was. Rather that she'd always seemed more open to life's possibilities. She had more room to grow, to become. Lincoln was more fixed. Even back at Minerva, the shape of the man he would become was already visible, his husk already hardening. Like, well, his father. Though Teddy supposed he was hardly one to talk.

"Anyway," Lincoln continued, "Anita's pretty sure he's seeing some woman."

"Seriously? How old is he?"

Lincoln scratched his chin. "Ninety? Ninety-one? Maybe he's just tired of paying for a housekeeper, but who knows?"

"You think it might be the sex?"

"Nah. He'd be bragging if that's what it was."

"You must be coming into some property when he dies, though, no?" Not that it was any of Teddy's business.

Lincoln chuckled. "*If* he dies, you mean. Yeah, there's a split-level ranch in Dunbar that hasn't been updated since he bought it in 1950. Whatever that would bring."

"And the Chilmark house."

"That's already mine," he said. Was it Teddy's imagination or was there some reluctance in this admission? "It belonged to my mother."

"Really?" Though, yeah, now that he thought about it, he did remember hearing something about this.

"You?" Lincoln said. "Any inheritance in your future?"

Teddy shook his head. "I'm not privy to the details, but when my folks sold their place I'm pretty sure they turned over the proceeds, plus their social security and retirement accounts, to Burnt Hills, that nightmare they're in."

Lincoln nodded. "That's how it worked with Anita's folks."

"The good news is I don't really need anything. Over the years I've squirreled away some savings, and there's just me."

"I doubt Mick's got much coming, either, not with seven sisters and him the youngest sibling."

"I was reading the other day where the transfer of wealth from our parents' generation to ours is the largest in history," Teddy said. "How'd we manage to miss out on that?"

"Good question. It's true, though. There's a lot of money out there, even after the recession. If you read between the lines of the *Minervan*, most of the people we knew there are one-percenters now."

"I don't even read the lines, much less between them." This wasn't entirely true. It was in the alumni magazine that he'd learned of Tom Ford's death from AIDS in the mideighties. And he generally glanced at the class notes section for their year, wondering if maybe this would be the issue where Jacy surfaced, when he would learn where she'd gone, who she'd married and what she'd done with her life. Did Lincoln and Mickey do the same thing? he wondered.

They'd come to the end of their beers, and when their server came over to ask if they wanted another, Lincoln said, "What do you think?"

"I've got no place to get to." This weekend or any other, actually.

When their fresh pints came, they clinked glasses. "To old friends," Teddy said, enjoying the moment, more relaxed and at peace than he'd felt in a while. Maybe that panic on the ferry had been a false alarm, because those too-bright, pulsing primary colors had turned into muted pastels. Who knew? Maybe this weekend would be just what the doctor ordered. Maybe.

A breeze with September in it blew in off the water. Teddy inhaled deeply. Autumn, even in his childhood, had always been his favorite season. When you're a kid and your parents are teachers, it's September, not January, that marks the beginning of a year. He'd always been the first one back to Minerva and loved having the campus all to himself for a day or two before the other students and faculty began trickling back in. Lincoln always arrived next, and then Mickey, since his band usually played somewhere in town the first weekend before classes started. Jacy was always last, coming as late as the middle of the first week of classes. Things couldn't *really* begin until then.

"You know who I was thinking about on the ferry?" Teddy ventured.

"Yep," Lincoln said. "I do."

And they left it at that.

Lincoln

On Saturday Lincoln awoke with the distinct impression that Mason Troyer had featured in his dreams. If so, it made sense. Yesterday, after he and Teddy returned to Chilmark, the message light had been blinking—Troyer, saying he'd heard they planned to list the house and they needed to talk.

"You're selling the place?" Teddy had asked, surprised.

"We haven't decided yet," Lincoln explained, the statement feeling oddly true, as if he and Anita had somehow *agreed* to sell without exactly *deciding* to. It hadn't been his intention to say anything to Teddy or Mickey about putting the house on the market, because they'd want to know why and he didn't really want to go into it. As a successful commercial realtor, he'd always made more money than they did, not that he'd ever lorded this over them. And why would he? Teddy clearly defined success differently, and it never would've occurred to Mickey to define it in the first place. Was it shame at having come so close to financial ruin that he was feeling? He didn't want to think so, but what else could it be? In the Christmas cards and e-mails he exchanged with Teddy and Mickey since the 2008 crash, he hadn't let on that anything was amiss. If they were paying attention, they probably knew that Las Vegas was the epicenter of the subprime financial storm, but since he'd given them no hint that he himself was in jeopardy, they'd no doubt assumed he was okay. Even now that it looked like the agency had finally turned a corner, he had no desire for them to know how close he'd come to going under. Not that they would've secretly gloated. On the contrary, they'd have felt terrible for him. Still, the membrane separating sympathy from pity could be paper-thin, and Lincoln—here again his father's son—wanted no part of the latter.

Later in the evening, recalling Martin's dark hints about Troyer, Lincoln had Googled him, and the asshole did indeed have a colorful island history: numerous entries in the *Vineyard Gazette* and *Martha's Vineyard Times* for DUI, failures to appear in court when summoned, repeated noise complaints from neighbors. But there were darker stories, too. In the late nineties, an accusation of sexual harassment by an unnamed woman that was settled out of court before it could come to trial, and another woman had been granted a restraining order against him. When Troyer promptly violated it, he'd been jailed, and by the time he got out, she'd left the Vineyard. During Lincoln's search, other websites popped up, promising more details for a fee, but for the moment he decided against going down that particular rabbit hole.

Now, lying in bed, the early morning light streaming in the window, he remembered something else.

Anita's voice was thick with sleep when she picked up. "Is everything okay?"

"Crap," he said, realizing why she was groggy. "I forgot about the time difference."

"It's okay," she said. "My alarm was about to go off anyway. What's up?"

"Mason Troyer. Do you remember the day—"

"Yeah."

"What do you mean, 'yeah'? I haven't told which—"

"The afternoon he came over when you were gone?"

"Right. Remind me what happened, exactly?"

"There was something we needed, and you were going to drive into Vineyard Haven. But then it occurred to you they might have it at the little store in Chilmark, and they did. So instead of being gone an hour, you were back in like fifteen minutes."

"When I came in, you two were in the kitchen," he said, the incident coming into focus now. They'd been standing on opposite sides of the kitchen table. Something about their stiff, awkward postures had reminded him of Freeze Tag, the children's game where everybody'd run around until somebody yelled "Freeze!" and they'd have to stop in their tracks. That's what his wife and Troyer had looked like, standing there with the table between you—as if his unexpected return had frozen them.

"He claimed he'd come over because he wanted to make an offer on the house," Anita was saying, "but something felt off. I mean, you no sooner drove off than he was there at the door. Like he'd been watching the house and waiting for you to leave."

"He didn't—"

"No, he didn't touch me or anything. And the conversation itself was benign. But he still gave me the creeps. It was more like he was weighing possibilities in his head. Risk-assessment stuff. Trying to gauge how strong I was, how much trouble I'd give him. What I remember most is how happy I was to hear your tires on the gravel outside. And *he* looked startled, that's for sure. Like he was as surprised as I was that you were back so soon, which he wouldn't have been if he hadn't watched you leave."

"How come you didn't tell me any of this then?"

"I almost did, but by the time he left I'd convinced myself I must've been imagining things."

"You did precisely what we warned our daughters never to do."

"God, you're right. We always told them to trust their instincts." They were both silent for a long beat. "So, what's this about, Lincoln?"

"I don't know. I really don't."

"Are you expecting trouble?"

"He won't come around, not if he sees Mickey." There was that day in the kitchen when the asshole cornered Jacy, and Mickey made short work of him, a crisp uppercut to the chin, right on the button. They'd heard the thunderous crash out on the deck.

"Promise me you won't mess with him?" Anita said.

"I don't even intend to return his call," he told her. If he dropped by, Lincoln would deal with it. Martin was probably right. Troyer no doubt wanted to make a direct offer and screw the realtor out of his commission.

"Did the guys get in okay?"

"Teddy arrived yesterday afternoon. Mickey's due any time now."

"Give them my love."

"Why don't you hop on a plane? You could be in Woods Hole in time to catch the last ferry. The boys would love to see you."

"I'd love to see them, but I have to be in court bright and early on Monday. And later today I'm driving to Arizona to check on Wolfgang Amadeus, remember?"

"Choosing my father over me, eh?"

"Don't guilt me, buster. This is *your* job I'm doing."

Yes, and dealing with his father fell to her far too often. What he'd told Teddy yesterday was true, though. If good outcomes were what you were after, Anita was the ideal person for the job.

Hanging up, he massaged his temples with his thumbs. Had he really dreamed about Troyer last night? Somewhere between his thumbs a dark thought was coalescing.

IN THE SHOWER, he made a mental list of things that required his attention after Teddy and Mickey left on Monday. The place was beginning to look shabby, inside *and* out. Too many of the exterior shingles had transitioned from weathered to warped, and the interior walls all needed a fresh coat of paint. The wooden deck railings were going punky with rot. Anita had instructed him to make a cellphone video of every room in the house so she didn't have to rely on his own assessment. In her opinion he was, like most men, blind to what was right in front of his face. Lincoln supposed she was right, but in his view too many gender insults were getting lobbed in his direction of late. Whenever he was foolish enough to generalize about women, he himself could count on a chorus of outrage from his wife and daughters. So how was it that men remained fair game? More to the point, if Martin was right and the place was a teardown, the video he'd been told to make would be a waste of time. For that matter, so would a paint job and new shingles.

He was toweling off when he heard a low, throaty rumbling outside and felt the floor vibrate under his bare feet. Knowing what this heralded, he quickly pulled on gym shorts and a T-shirt and hollered to Teddy, who was out on the deck working on some manuscript.

The big Harley shuddered into silence just as Lincoln emerged. Mickey—dressed in jeans, cowboy boots and a leather jacket—pulled off his helmet and just sat there, staring off into deep space, his expression uncharacteristic, unreadable. Longing, Lincoln speculated, or regret? Whatever, it vanished so quickly when Mickey noticed him standing there that Lincoln wondered if he'd imagined it.

"Face Man," Mickey said, breaking into his old, familiar grin.

"Big Mick on Pots," Lincoln responded as he stepped gingerly across the gravel in his bare feet. Their old nicknames—avatars of younger selves—were a long-established ritual of greeting.

"What the hell's wrong with you?" Mickey said, frowning. "You're all bent over like some old man."

"Stiff lower back," Lincoln admitted. "I straighten up as the day goes on."

They shook hands, Mickey still astride the Harley like he was deciding whether or not to stay. The screen door squeaked open on its rusty hinge as Teddy, dressed in a bathing suit, flip-flops and a threadbare Minerva sweatshirt, came through.

"Tedioski," said Mickey, who had at least one nickname for everybody he knew. Others for Teddy included Teduski and Tedmarek. "So, come over here and let me have a look at you. You're not wearing socks with your sandals, anyway."

"You thought I would be?"

"I figured this could be the year."

"You look the same," Teddy said. "Or at least the sixty-six-year-old version of the same. Are you able to get off that thing, or do you just sit there looking like Brando?"

Slipping out from under his backpack, he handed it off to Lincoln, who was surprised by its weight. "What's in here? Rocks?"

"Vodka, tomato juice, Tabasco sauce, vodka, celery and vodka," Mickey informed him, swinging a big leg over the Harley to release the kickstand. "We had a gig last night. I didn't get home till three."

When he wedged his helmet under the bike's seat, Teddy rapped it with his knuckles. "You've started wearing one of these at last."

"It's the law," he said. "Also, there's this." He parted his longish rocker hair to reveal a long, angry pink scar.

"Jesus," said Teddy, the blood draining out of his face.

Mickey chuckled, all too aware of Teddy's lifelong horror of bodily affliction. "Anyway," he sighed, shouldering his pack again, "it's Bloody Mary time." He regarded Lincoln dubiously. "You think you can make it back inside, old man, or do we need to carry you?"

"Good to see you, too, Mick," Lincoln told him. "I can't think of why, but it is."

Mickey clapped him on the shoulder. "Come on. It's the abuse you miss."

"That must be it."

At the door they heard a metallic groaning behind them and turned just as Mickey's Harley lost its purchase in the gravel and tipped over. His freed helmet rolled lopsidedly down the grade, coming to rest at their feet. "Be like that," Mickey said, addressing the unruly bike, then went inside.

Teddy picked up the helmet, raised an eyebrow at Lincoln, then hung it on the nearby lamppost.

Lincoln held the door wide open. "Let the games begin."

"SWEET, ROLLICKIN' JESUS," Mickey said, peering down the slope. He'd taken off his leather jacket and was sitting with his boots up on the railing. "Is that a naked woman down there?"

All three were drinking Bloody Marys. Mickey had rooted

around in the kitchen cabinets until he found a pitcher to mix them in. Where had the pitcher come from? Lincoln wondered. That was the thing about renters who could afford Chilmark in July and August. Once they discovered the place didn't have something they required, they just drove into town and bought it, then nine times out of ten left it behind. The kitchen was full of bizarre gadgets Lincoln couldn't even guess the purpose of. Several summers ago, back when Keurig coffee makers were brand-new, some August renters had purchased one and just left it there on the counter along with a list of suggested upgrades that included a Bose radio, a cell-phone-charger dock, a Wi-Fi router and a video-game console. Lincoln had been for ignoring the list, but Anita immediately went online, bought every single item and had everything delivered to the management company that handled their rentals.

Lincoln assured Mickey that, no, his eyes weren't deceiving him, though it was unclear whether this was the same naked woman he'd seen yesterday. They were about the same build—big breasted, thick in the middle—but the other had been a blonde, hadn't she? This one's hair—at least the hair on her head—was darker, though maybe it was just the hour of the day, the angle of the sun.

"No wonder you were out here grading papers," Mickey said to Teddy, who was now sitting with his back to the scene below, the manuscript beneath his chair, out of harm's way.

"I'm editing a book, not grading papers," he clarified.

"You'll have to explain the difference to me sometime when there's nothing more interesting going on. Binoculars, is what we need right now."

Down the slope another door banged, and Troyer, again naked himself, came out onto the deck. He said something to the woman—they were too far away to hear what—but her laughter wafted up the slope on the breeze.

"Okay, never mind the binoculars," Mickey said, angling his chair so he wouldn't have to look. "Tell me that's not the same jerk-off from back in the day. The fuck was *his* name? The guy who groped Jacy?"

"Mason Troyer."

"Right. Troyer."

"He owns the place now. His folks died a while back."

"For rich people, they were pretty nice," Teddy recalled.

"What do you mean, 'for rich people'?" Mickey snorted. "There's some law that says *they* can't be nice?"

Teddy munched his celery stalk thoughtfully. "I believe there is, actually. And those particular people were in violation."

"Ah, here we go," Mickey sighed. "Will this be one of your lectures from 1969, Mr. Marx? Or do you have new material?"

"Outside of a dog," Teddy said, wiggling his eyebrows and puffing on an imaginary Groucho cigar, a whole other Marx than the one Mickey alluded to, "a book is man's best friend. Inside of a dog, it's too dark to read."

The Troyers *had* been nice folks, Lincoln recalled. They seemed as baffled as everyone else that they'd somehow managed to produce a bad seed like Mason.

"Okay, impress me," Mickey said to Teddy. "What're you listening to?"

"Mostly alt rock."

"Like what?"

"The Decemberists. Belle and Sebastian. Mumford and Sons."

"Faggot music."

"We're using that term now?" Teddy said. "College-educated guys like us?"

Mickey ignored this protest. "That's hipster shit. People who listen to crap like that drink pumpkin-spice lattes. Come on. What else? You must listen to *some* real music."

Teddy shrugged. "Some singer-songwriters. Tom Waits. Leonard Cohen. Josh Ritter. The Boss, of course."

"Okay," Mickey conceded. "These I can respect."

"Who's the Boss?" Lincoln said.

Both men stared at him.

"The thing is," Mickey said to Teddy, "I never know when he's kidding. Can you tell?"

"Not when the subject's music," Teddy admitted.

"Okay, your turn." Mickey was now pointing at Lincoln with his celery stick. "I assume you're still devoted to Montovani."

"Don't start."

"Teduski. What do you want to bet he's got a Montovani Pandora station?"

"What's a Pandora station?" Lincoln said.

"You're shitting me, right?"

"I am, actually."

"Let me see your phone," Mickey said.

"No."

"Give it here. This is serious. Don't make me take it away from you."

Lincoln sighed, handed it over.

Mickey scrolled through the icons. "Here we go," he said. "Pandora. My God, this is terrifying. Herb Alpert and the Tijuana Brass. Nat King Cole."

Teddy was beet red now, his shoulders shaking.

"And yep. Here it is. I knew it. Johnny Fucking Mathis. *Chances are . . .*," he crooned, "*'cause I wear that silly grin . . .*"

Lincoln grabbed the phone back and slipped it into his pocket.

"Please tell me you and Anita never had sex after listening to Johnny Mathis. Because I've always had this image of her as a classy lady."

From down the slope came a whoop of female hilarity. Reluctantly, all three turned to look. Troyer seemed to be nuzzling the naked woman's midriff. At least that's what they hoped he was nuzzling.

Mickey rose to his feet and grabbed his leather jacket. "I gotta go inside," he said. "That's making me queasy."

"Why do you think I've got my back to it?" Teddy said.

At the sliding door, Mickey said, "You guys didn't make plans for tonight, right? There's a band playing down on Circuit Ave that I keep hearing good things about."

"If we must," Lincoln sighed.

When the door slid closed behind him, Lincoln, in spite of himself, peered down the slope again. Troyer had taken a seat now, and the woman had rolled over on her stomach.

"Question," he said when Teddy retrieved his manuscript from under his chair and prepared to go back to work. "Do you remember that history class we both took at Minerva?"

"Civil War and Reconstruction," Teddy replied without hesitation, as if for some inexplicable reason he too had been thinking about that very class. "Professor Ford."

"First day of class he gave us the final-exam question."

Teddy nodded. "What caused the war."

In addition to the regular blackboards, there'd been a large portable one on which, as the semester progressed, they'd listed possible causes, some proximate, some remote. Though he'd been pretty sure Ford disagreed, Lincoln had ended up arguing that it was fought over economics—the industrial North versus the agrarian South. Teddy had argued that it had been fought over slavery, a moral issue. Both their theses, now that Lincoln thought about it, had been predictable. Which begged a question: had his and Teddy's characters already been formed? At the time, college had appeared to offer an endless smorgasbord of possibilities and it felt like they were engaged in the act of *becoming*. Had that been an illusion? Had they already, by that point, *become*?

Teddy was grinning. "Remember how pissed off we were at the end? After we turned in our finals, we went to see him and demanded to know what the right answer was? What *he* thought caused the war?"

Lincoln had forgotten this, but the details now came flooding back. "And he just smiled and asked us what we thought had caused the *Vietnam* War. The whole point of the course had been for us to examine one war in light of the other, and neither of us ever made that connection. He should've flunked us both."

Teddy was studying him quizzically. "Odd train of thought."

"Happens more and more these days," Lincoln admitted, not

really wanting to go into what had steered him down this particular path. Grabbing the pitcher, he held it up. "Want any more?"

"God, no. I've got half a buzz on already and it's not even noon."

Inside, Mickey lay stretched out on the sofa. He'd turned on a college football pregame show with the sound down low. A good, long nap was clearly on the horizon.

Lincoln held up the pitcher. "Finish this off?"

"Why not?"

He poured what was left into Mickey's glass. "Mind if I ask a question?"

"Shoot."

"When you pulled in earlier? You just kind of sat there and stared off into the distance for a minute. The look on your face made me wonder what you were thinking about."

Mickey was silent so long, his eyes on the TV, that Lincoln wondered if he meant not to answer, but he finally said, "She's more real here for some reason."

"I know what you mean," Lincoln said. "And I'm pretty sure Teddy feels the same way. What do you think happened to her, Mick?"

He shook his head, still looking at the TV. "All I know is she's gone."

"Gone as in . . . ?"

Only then did he turn to look at Lincoln. "Gone as in *long*."

Teddy

Teddy worked awhile longer, until the sun, directly overhead now, made it uncomfortably warm. He was shoving the manuscript pages into his shoulder bag when Lincoln, now dressed in chinos, a Ralph Lauren polo shirt and loafers, came back out onto the deck. Teddy noticed him glance down the slope toward Troyer's place, and saw his expression darken, even though the neighbor and his woman had gone inside. "Where you off to?" Teddy ventured.

"Edgartown," Lincoln said. "You're welcome to join me."

But he was fidgeting with his keys, obviously anxious to leave. If he'd really wanted company, he would've extended the invitation sooner. "I'll pass, but thanks. What's Mick up to?"

"Fast asleep on the sofa," Lincoln chuckled. "One arm behind his head, under the cushion."

"He always slept like that," Teddy smiled. "He's changed the least of any of us, don't you think?"

"Is that a good or a bad thing?"

"Beats me," Teddy admitted, though he'd meant the observation as a compliment. Earlier, seeing Mickey astraddle his Harley had occasioned a surge of . . . what? Affection? Yes, but more than that. Something more selfish. Like, how bad could things really be if Mickey was still alive and kicking, still his old confident self, oblivious to politics and current events, giving them shit about their musical taste. Was this what we wanted from our oldest friends? Reassurance that the world we remember so fondly still exists? That it hasn't been replaced by a reality we're less fully committed to? "I don't think any of us has changed very much, actually."

"We all got old," Lincoln pointed out. "Be honest. Can *you* imagine playing rock and roll until two in the morning—at our age?"

"Oh, I don't know," Teddy said. "I'm often up at two. And again at four."

Lincoln chuckled at that, though Teddy could tell his thoughts had drifted away. He was studying the Troyer place again, as if it posed some sort of riddle. But after a moment he snapped out of it. "If you get hungry, there's deli meat and cheese for sandwiches in the fridge."

"Okay," Teddy said. "Would you happen to have a bicycle around?"

"There's one in the shed. I'll unlock it."

"Thanks. I might go for a ride." When his friend started down the steps, Teddy said, "Lincoln?"

"Yeah?"

"I might need to leave the island early."

Lincoln cocked his head. "Everything okay?"

"Remember those . . . spells I used to have?"

"You're still having them?"

"Not often. I haven't had one in a while, in fact. I've gotten pretty good at recognizing them, and sometimes I can head them off. Not always, though."

Lincoln nodded. "What's it feel like? When they come on."

"Depends. Sometimes it's gradual, like a migraine aura. Colors intensify. Everything feels slightly off. Other times—wham, all at once." Yesterday, when he'd hallucinated Jacy on the Oak Bluffs pier, he wondered if it might be one of those episodes, but apparently not. More likely he'd been experiencing a tremor, a small adjustment of his emotional tectonic plates brought on by a change in the routine he counted on to maintain his equilibrium. "They can be pretty weird. Sometimes I even have these . . . premonitions? About what's going to happen next?"

"We should go to the track, then," Lincoln suggested.

Which dislodged a pleasant memory. The four of them. A Saturday night. Senior year. Mickey's band was supposed to play, but at the last minute the gig got canceled and they were all at loose ends, so they'd piled into Teddy's beater and driven to the dog track in Bridgeport, the sleaziest, most depressing place any of them had ever stepped foot, including Mickey, who as a musician had a far-deeper experience of disreputable venues. All night long they'd lost, bet after bet, until the last race when Jacy, attracted by the ridiculously long odds, bet an exacta composed of the two longest shots in the field. The prohibitive favorite came out of the gate like a shot. Normally, race over. But on the first turn the dog suddenly went down in the dirt, howling—in the stands you could hear the poor thing shrieking, its leg having snapped like a twig. Teddy remembered feeling faint at the sight. There was far worse on the news each night, boys his age being sliced to ribbons in the jungle, but this animal's awful, caterwauling misery was only fifty yards away, and the proximity was sickening. What finally drew his attention back to the race was seeing Jacy climb up onto the table for a better view. On the backstretch her two long shots were somehow in the lead, in the wrong order, but still. "Run!" she was screaming at the top of her lungs, "run, you mother*fuckerrrrrrrrr*!"

Lincoln was grinning now. "I can still see all those geezers watching her jumping up and down, practically drooling."

"She wasn't wearing a bra," Teddy said. "And those old coots? Same age as we are now."

"True," Lincoln said sadly.

"How much did she win?" Teddy said. "Do you remember?"

Lincoln shook his head. "I don't. Hundreds, probably. Anyway, a lot for back then." Here he paused. "Do you take anything?"

"Some pills for anxiety. I don't like to take them, though. They make me stupid."

"I'm sorry, Teddy. I thought all that was in the past. But do what you need to. Mickey will understand."

"I'm hoping it won't come to that. Sometimes exercise does the trick."

He's going to glance at the Troyer place again, Teddy thought, and sure enough, Lincoln did. Did it qualify as a premonition when you've known someone for forty-five years?

Odd, Teddy realized, once Lincoln had left, that he should also be thinking about Tom Ford across the decades. Proximate and remote causes. Don't give too much credit to the former, Tom had warned them. The deeper and longer something remained buried, the more power it had when it finally rose to the surface. So it had been with Ford himself, in the closet all those years. A secret that, when finally brought out into the light, was lethal to its keeper.

Teddy put on sunglasses. In the distance the ocean was impossibly blue.

VANCE, TEDDY THOUGHT, pedaling out of the gravel drive and onto the road. That'd been Jacy's fiancé's name. Either that or Lance. Or maybe Chance. He'd been two years older. If memory served, his and Jacy's parents were best friends and belonged to the same country club. All very Greenwich, Connecticut. They hadn't started dating until the summer between her sophomore and junior years, mostly, at least in the beginning, as a favor to Jacy's parents. She'd been smoking a lot of dope and protesting the war, and they feared she was running completely wild. Vance, who'd just graduated from Dartmouth, was headed for Duke law school in the fall. A straight arrow, he wore his hair short and parted at the side, and evidently had missed the memo about never trusting anyone over thirty. He called every man his parents' age "sir," and every woman "ma'am." For sure, he and Jacy made an odd couple, and everyone had been pretty surprised to learn they'd become engaged by the end of that summer.

What he and Lincoln and Mickey found even stranger was that

Jacy didn't seem to miss him when he was in Durham, nor did she visit him there as other engaged Thetas often did their fiancés. He called her several times a week, but did she ever call him? His name never came up in conversation unless one of her sorority sisters mentioned him, which they frequently did—not-so-subtle reminders that she was spoken for and should behave accordingly. In her fiancé's absence the Thetas took seriously their duty to guard their sister's virtue. For some reason, though she couldn't go on dates, she was permitted to hang out with the Musketeers on weekends when Mickey's band performed, even to sing with them on songs that required a female vocalist. She did a particularly mean Grace Slick.

Why had the Thetas trusted them? Teddy wondered as he pedaled his borrowed bike down the dirt road past Troyer's place. Had they really seemed so harmless? Was that how Jacy herself had characterized them to her sorority sisters so they would relax their vigilance? Did the fact that there were three of them somehow render them less dangerous than a lone ranger would've seemed? Or did it all come down to class? Jacy might be wild, but she wouldn't throw away a future with a real catch like Vance—Lance? Chance?—not for a fucking hasher. Had that been the thinking?

Only Jacy's roommate, a girl named Christine, the house president, had acted suspicious, and the night they all returned from the dog track she'd been waiting for them in the front room. On the drive back from Bridgeport, flush with Jacy's winnings, they'd hit bars in Milford, New Haven and Madison, and by the time they arrived at Minerva they were all giddy with drink.

"So what's the deal here?" Christine said when they staggered in the front door, four abreast, elbows interlocked, as if they'd been off to see the wizard.

As hashers, Teddy and Lincoln and Mickey entered through the back, so when the house president demanded to know what the deal was, Teddy's first thought had been that she was talking just to them, putting them in their place. But no, it was Jacy she was addressing. "Are you doing all three of these clowns, or what?"

Mickey stiffened at this, but Jacy stepped in front of him and got right in the other girl's face. *"Nooooo,"* she said, "but what a great fucking idea!"

Christine took a step back, ostentatiously fanning away the alcohol fumes. "Your fiancé would be absolutely heartbroken if he could see you now," she said.

"And wouldn't *you* love to comfort him!" Jacy said, poking the girl in the chest with her index finger.

"Hey," Christine objected, slapping her hand away. *"I'm* not the slut here."

"Too true!" Jacy told her. "Watch and learn, bitch." Then, turning to her terrified companions, she said, "And just where do you think *you're* going?"

Though she'd failed utterly at shaming Jacy, Christine was having better luck with Teddy, Lincoln and Mickey, all of whom had begun backing toward the open door.

"Come *here,*" Jacy ordered, so of course they obeyed, lining up in front of her, as if this were a military exercise and she meant to inspect their uniforms.

She kissed them in order, Lincoln first, full on the lips, then Teddy, her breath somehow sweet despite all the beer, and finally Mickey, whose knees buckled. With alcohol, sure, but not only alcohol. "Steady, big fella," she told him, and in his mind's eye Teddy could still see the goofy grin that bloomed across Mickey's face.

"Disgusting," Christine said. "Forgive me if I don't stick around for the blow jobs."

Later, back in the car, Teddy's keys dangling from the ignition, all three friends had sat in silence, stunned into sobriety by Jacy's kisses. Mickey spoke first. "Okay, we draw straws," he said. "I don't see any way around it. One of us is going to have to murder the prick."

"Fine," Lincoln said, seemingly for the sake of argument, "but then what? There's still three of us and only one of her."

"Good point," Mickey conceded. "And you know what? If there *were* three of her, I'd want all three."

Had it really happened like that? Teddy wondered. The clarity of this memory made him dubious. Could something that happened so long ago *be* that vivid now? Or had he and Mickey and Lincoln burnished the memory's details by recalling it so fondly over the years?

At the State Road T-intersection, Teddy faced a choice. Turn left and he'd be headed toward Menemsha, a quaint fishing village where he could eat greasy fried clams out of a paper boat. Right meant the Gay Head cliffs, the one place on the island he should avoid at all costs. *Why risk it?* he thought, even as he turned right.

Lincoln

The newspaper office, located on a quiet, tree-lined street, was locked up tight, and why not? Labor Day had come and gone, and the *Vineyard Gazette* was a sleepy weekly newspaper, not the *New York Times*. Served him right, Lincoln thought, returning to his curb-parked rental. Instead of chasing phantoms in Edgartown he belonged back in Chilmark, doing the job he'd come here to do, though the more he thought about it, the more he feared the whole trip was misbegotten.

The case he'd made to Anita for coming to the island in person was so persuasive that Lincoln had ended up persuading himself. It *had* been almost a decade since they'd visited, and who knew what kind of damage ten years' worth of seasonal renters had inflicted? Did it just need a little sprucing up? A fresh coat of paint? Or something more serious, like a new roof? How could they settle on a listing price without seeing firsthand what needed to be done?

Yet what the trip was really about—and part of him had known this from the start—was his need to say goodbye to the Chilmark house. He owed his mother that much, surely. Nor, if he was honest, was this all. He had, it seemed, unfinished business here, the precise nature of which continued to elude him, though it seemed to involve his friends. Because no sooner had the idea of coming to the island in person occurred to him than he'd invited Teddy and Mickey to join him. And if the three of them were there, how could

Jacy not be, at least in spirit? It was her ghostly presence that made the symmetry between this weekend and the one on Memorial Day back in 1971 inescapable.

Whose idea had *that* weekend been? Strange that Lincoln couldn't recall how it had come about. Had his mother suggested it? It always pleased Trudy whenever he and his friends visited, so maybe. Or had it been one of those group decisions? As graduation neared, it had dawned on all of them that everything was about to change. Jacy would marry her straight-arrow fiancé in June. Mickey had already contacted his draft board and completed his physical; he'd be reporting for basic training in a matter of weeks. Teddy, still in his Thomas Merton phase and protected by his high draft number, was considering divinity school. Minerva had been their refuge, and now they were about to lose both it and one another. Had they been comparing notes and realized none of them had plans for the holiday weekend and thought, *Hey, why not spend it together?* Also possible.

What didn't make sense about either of these scenarios was that by then he and Anita had become serious, were even talking about maybe getting married, though given how broke they were, and that their futures—his draft status, her heading off to law school—were so up in the air, marriage didn't make a whole lot of sense. Still, they kept returning to the possibility over and over. They'd both enjoyed their relatively carefree undergraduate lives, but they were also anxious to get started on more serious adult postgraduate ones. Those last few months at Minerva, Lincoln had spent less and less time with Teddy and Mickey, choosing instead to study with Anita in her library carrel (though they often ended these study sessions by turning the lights off and groping each other in the dark). On weekends, when Mickey's band generally played, they remained behind in the front room of the Theta house and watched old *Perry Mason* reruns on TV. "If you're this boring now," Mickey had observed, "what are you going to be like at fifty?"

Boring, maybe, but if they were ever to get married, they needed to start saving, or Lincoln did, anyway. Toward that end Lincoln

had even considered, albeit briefly, returning to Dunbar after graduation to await the call-up that might or might not come later in the
year. He could have his old bedroom, wait tables at the country
club and put the money he would've spent on rent in the bank. His
mother would love having him around, and Wolfgang Amadeus
always liked having somebody else handy to share his many opinions with. But spending twelve whole months in Dunbar had been
too dispiriting to contemplate seriously, as was the idea of him and
Anita being apart for so long.

Instead they'd come up with a geographical compromise that
was somehow both practical and borderline insane. Lincoln would
take a job at an upscale resort in Scottsdale where the tips would be
good enough to make paying rent doable if he could find a roommate or two. Mornings he could take some real estate courses, and
if he didn't get called up, maybe he'd begin an MBA at nearby ASU.
Anita, who'd been admitted to Stanford, would instead attend law
school in Tucson. Two hours away seemed about right, distance-
wise. Any closer would be torture, really. Anita was from a large,
devout Catholic family, which meant that in an era of free love
Lincoln had somehow managed to fall for one of the few girls in
America who still believed in abstinence before marriage. (Though
he shared no such conviction, Lincoln would discover that his
Church of God upbringing had prepared him admirably to with-
stand sexual deprivation.)

Also, though he didn't want to live in Dunbar, he liked the idea
of being close enough to drop in occasionally. His mother had few
friends, and he knew how much his visits meant to her. And he had
little doubt that she and Anita would soon become fast friends.
His father was a different story. He was still having a tough time
adjusting to the idea of his son marrying a non-Christian. (By Dub-
Yay's strict definition, Catholics didn't qualify.) When Lincoln had
broken the news that he'd fallen in love with and hoped to marry a
Catholic girl, Wolfgang Amadeus had repeated the word, as if its
meaning were obscure. "Catholic," he mused in his helium voice.
"*Roman* Catholic?"

At any rate, this was the new adult life he and Anita had been preparing themselves for during those final months at Minerva. Why would he have agreed to a long holiday weekend on the island with his friends that would've postponed, psychologically, at least, the very future he and Anita were so keen to occupy?

"You again," said his wife, her voice abruptly there on the line even before his cell registered a ring. "What's going on now?"

"Okay, it's 1971. May."

"This is getting weird, Lincoln."

"Bear with me. Whose idea was it for us to spend Memorial Day on the island?"

"Yours."

"Mine?"

"Yes."

"Are you sure? That makes no sense. Weren't we trying to save money? Flying back East, even on standby, would've been expensive."

"Except you didn't, remember? You and Teddy stayed in Connecticut after graduation. Your rent was paid through the end of May, and he had that internship at the *Globe* that started in June. You'd wanted us to head west right after graduation, but I had a family reunion over Memorial Day, and we couldn't leave until after that."

"Right," Lincoln said, these details coming back to him now, as they so often did, on the wings of Anita's certainty.

"How come Teddy and I didn't just go to the island after graduation?"

"Your parents were supposed to be there. Your mom talked Dub-Yay into spending a couple weeks in the Chilmark house before returning to Arizona. But then he reneged and they flew straight back."

Fucking Dub-Yay, Lincoln thought now. Still chafing over the fact that Lincoln had sided with his mother and attended Minerva instead of enrolling at the University of Arizona, he'd basically attended graduation under protest, complaining that the trip back

East would cost a small fortune and when they got there they'd have to turn right around and fly home again. To which his mother replied that if he was interested in getting his money's worth, they should spend a week or two in Chilmark. They had no renters lined up until early July, so why not? Unable to think of a plausible excuse not to off the top of his head, the old boy had given in. But later, when push came to shove, he changed his mind, just as Anita remembered, offering some cockamamy excuse about trouble at the mine, the workers again threatening to unionize, that obliged him to head straight back to Dunbar. Lincoln felt his throat constrict. His mother never saw the island again.

"Anyway," Anita was saying. "When you found out the house would be empty, that's when you floated the idea. We argued about it, if you recall."

"Why?"

"Because you were supposed to be with *me* that weekend. At the family reunion. You didn't want to come because you wouldn't know anybody."

"Your family terrified me. The way they all talked at once, always getting louder and louder. I grew up an only child."

"I *wanted* to introduce them all to the man I was going to marry."

Lincoln felt the sting of his selfishness, so like his father's, across the decades.

"*And* on Monday, after everybody left, you and I were supposed to rent a U-Haul truck and load it up. But *you* were still on the island, which meant that job fell to my brothers and me."

"What an asshole. Why would you marry a man who did something like that?"

She ignored him. "You finally waltzed in late Tuesday morning determined to hit the road, right that minute. My mother had fixed us a nice lunch, but *you* said we needed to leave if we were going to make it to Buffalo by nightfall. God only knows how you decided on Buffalo, but you made it sound as if the sky would fall if we only got as far as Albany. We said goodbye to my parents and drove off within half an hour of your arrival."

"Not that you're holding a grudge or anything."

"Hey, don't blame me, buster. You're the one reminding me about what a brat you were." But then her voice softened. "Mostly I remember the trip itself."

Lincoln chuckled. "Right. All those Motel Sixes. No AC. Us not having sex."

"Lying to our parents. Telling them we had enough money for separate rooms. A quarter for the Magic Fingers was a splurge."

"Seems like another lifetime."

"There's another thing you're conveniently forgetting. You originally pitched the Vineyard weekend as being just you and Teddy and Mickey. Then, *after* I reluctantly agreed, I find out Jacy's going to be there."

"Teddy's the one who talked her into coming," he said, the memory suddenly there for the taking.

"Ah," she said. "That you *do* remember."

She was right, of course. His memory, when it wasn't failing him utterly, was suspiciously selective.

"So what's all this about?"

"I wish I knew," he admitted. "Guilt, probably. Martin says the Chilmark house is probably a teardown."

"And you feel like you're betraying your mother."

"Silly, huh?"

"No. You miss her. It hasn't been that long." When he didn't respond, she said, "So, did Mickey get in okay?"

"Shortly after I talked with you. He arrived with the makings for Bloody Marys. Even celery."

"Huh, imagine that. Mickey not changing."

"It's Teddy I'm worried about, actually. He's having those spells again."

"Really?"

"Not as bad as before, but still."

"Remember that time we visited him in the psych ward?"

"Are you making this up?"

"Junior year. Not long after you all got your draft numbers.

Finals week, I think. He had a meltdown and checked himself into the campus infirmary, and they transferred him to Yale/New Haven. Don't you remember how awful he looked, how he just kept repeating that he felt really sad."

Yes, and one of the doctors taking Lincoln out into the corridor and asking him if Teddy had ever talked about suicide. If he owned or had access to a gun. How in the world had he managed to forget all this?

"Tell me something," he said, abruptly shifting gears. "Do you ever regret not going to Stanford?"

"That would be like regretting us. Our kids. Our grandkids."

"I should've made you go. It wasn't right for you to give that up."

"Lincoln." That feeling again, of his name on her lips. This time conveying forgiveness.

"Yeah?"

"I really need to get on the road. Your dad isn't known for his patience."

"Of course," he said. "Go."

Now it was her turn to pause. "I'm pretty sure there was one other reason you wanted that one last weekend on the island," she said, and Lincoln felt a dark foreboding. "You were trying to decide."

"Decide what?"

"Between me and Jacy."

WOLFGANG AMADEUS MOSER. Ridiculous name, ridiculous man.

That very first summer when Lincoln returned home to Dunbar from Minerva College, he'd begun to see his father with new eyes. His parents were waiting at the gate to greet him, and his first thought was *Who's the little pip-squeak standing next to my mother?* Somehow his father had shrunk. Had he been ill? But, no, on closer inspection, he looked hale and hearty, full of his usual piss and vinegar, just . . . smaller. Not that he'd ever been a giant, of course. As a high-school freshman Lincoln had surpassed him in actual height, yet for some reason the fact that he was literally looking down at the man hadn't registered. Why hadn't he noticed when he was home over Christmas?

Of course this sudden perception was probably linked in Lincoln's mind to other things entirely. As a boy he'd never questioned his father's importance. After all, he was not only a minority owner of a mine that employed half the men in town but also a deacon of the church, which made him seem essential to the community. Ministers and mayors and country-club presidents came and went in Dunbar, whereas W. A. Moser was a constant, and until Lincoln went away to college, it never once occurred to him that he wasn't universally revered, that some people saw him as judgmental and unyielding, a figure out of the Old Testament, more to be feared than admired, more tolerated than loved. One day that first summer, coming out of a shop on Main Street, Lincoln had fallen in step behind two men who were deep in conversation. "The reason he's so upright," one said, "is that he's got a stick up his ass." A year earlier it never would've occurred to Lincoln that they might be talking about his father, while now, without any identifying clues, he was sure of it. As the summer progressed, he began noticing other things as well. Even Dub-Yay's friends willingly conceded that he was the oddest of ducks, and his high-pitched whine was often imitated to devastating comic effect. At the country club, where Lincoln served as a waiter, some of the higher-ups from the mine, their tongues loosened by alcohol, offered him unasked-for sympathy, marveling that he'd lived eighteen years in the same house with Wolfgang Amadeus Moser without murdering him.

Despite now regarding him differently, Lincoln continued to get along with his father well enough, mostly by avoiding politics. The war weighed on Dub-Yay or, rather, the nightly news did, with its constant coverage of student unrest, especially protests taking place in regions of the country he didn't approve of to begin with, like the East and Northern California. It wasn't that he approved of the war; he didn't. But neither did he think you had to endorse something in order to support it. It was more a question of whom you chose to align yourself with: on the one hand, a known liar and crook like Nixon; on the other, a bunch of grubby, long-haired protesters and pot smokers who didn't have an ounce of ambition, unless it was to take up the sitar. "Give peace a chance to *what*?" his father liked to ask whenever someone waved that particular sign on TV. If *any son of his* felt the urge to carry such a poster in public, he proclaimed—as if he'd fathered a great many sons in addition to the one sitting there in the dark living room with him—he hoped that son would do him the favor of shooting him in the head so he wouldn't have to watch him prancing around on television. "And shoot your mother, too, while you're at it," he advised. "She should be spared that sight, as well."

Lincoln also began to see his parents' marriage differently. Why had he not noticed before that they never invited people over for dinner or even a get-together on the patio? Why, outside of church, did they appear to have no intimate friends, especially given how starved his mother seemed for companionship? Why, whenever Trudy was on the verge of becoming friends with some woman in the neighborhood, did his father always find some fault with her? And why, when they sat next to each other on the sofa, did his parents seldom touch? For the first time he wondered if his mother might be unhappy. Each new, unwanted epiphany further untethered him.

Indeed, on every occasion he returned home from college, he found new reasons to rethink the first eighteen years of his life—the house he'd grown up in, the neighborhood he'd explored on his bike as a kid, the town of Dunbar itself. Things that had always felt solid, familiar and reassuring suddenly seemed not just peculiar but somehow diminished. Evenings, when he wasn't working at the club, he and Dub-Yay would sneak in nine holes of golf after dinner as the desert cooled in the dusk. He'd always loved their quirky little country-club course, but after playing the lush green courses back East, where errant shots went into the water or deep in the woods, he saw how little real challenge this one offered. It was flat as a pancake, and a well-struck ball rolled forever on its parched

fairways. Was that what his father liked about it? That the par fives
were all easily reachable in two, allowing you to believe you were
a big hitter?

Everything felt bewildering. Time itself seemed to operate differently; instead of poking along languorously, it began moving at
warp speed. Free will, which more than one of his Minerva professors had suggested might be an illusion, appeared to genuflect
before grim fate. Two of his classmates were killed in Vietnam, and
several others died of overdoses. At least two girls, including one
Lincoln had dated, were rumored to have had abortions. Boys he'd
sworn to remain friends with forever now seemed like strangers, and
they clearly felt the same about him. "I don't remember you being so
stuck-up," one told him. Others had gotten jobs at the mine, which
meant frequent layoffs, sitting around in local bars and collecting
unemployment, drinking cheap beer and waiting to get rehired.
Still others, having flunked out of college, moved back in with their
parents and were working at minimum-wage jobs, their dreams—
assuming they'd had any—gone bust that quickly.

Early one August morning, the summer of his junior year, Lincoln's mother joined him on the patio where it was shady and he
was reading a book for a class he'd be taking that fall. "I bet you're
real anxious to get back," she said, pulling up a chair and setting a
tall glass of ice tea in front of him. His mother's sun tea was among
a very few things about his life in Dunbar that remained exactly as
he remembered.

"I am," he admitted, though saying so felt like a betrayal. After
all, he wasn't exactly suffering. He made decent money at the club,
and waiting tables there wasn't so different from slinging hash at
the Theta house. He took as many shifts as management would give
him so the summer would pass more quickly.

"You shouldn't feel guilty," she said, reading his mind. "You have
your friends. You're getting a good education. There's nothing for
you here."

"You and Dad are here."

"You know what I mean." They were quiet, then, though clearly there was something on her mind. "You think you'll marry that girl?" she said. "The one you mentioned?"

"Jacy? We've never even been on a date. Also, of the three of us, she seems to like Mickey best. And anyway," he continued, "she's wild as the wind. I don't think she's really in love with any of us."

"Maybe she's waiting to see which of you has the courage to declare himself."

Then they fell quiet again, until Lincoln chuckled.

"What's so funny?"

"I was just trying to imagine introducing her to Dad," he admitted.

She regarded him sadly. "In matters of the heart that is not where your mind should go." But she seemed to understand that that's where it *did* go, and probably *would* go for a very long time. Eventually, he might come to repudiate his father's doctrine, but the man himself would be tougher to exorcise.

"THE THING TO UNDERSTAND about your father," Lincoln's mother had once explained when he was in high school, "is that you always have a choice. You can do things his way, or you can wish you had."

At the time he'd seen her remark as defeatist, but gradually understood that she wasn't advocating capitulation so much as making sure he fully comprehended the consequences of confrontation. Her husband's perseverance, she knew better than anyone, wasn't just dogged; it was positively tidal. And how right she'd been. Arguing with his father was like trying to put a cat in a bag: there was always a limb left over, and at the end of that limb a claw. Not one to be intimidated, especially in front of Anita, Lincoln often questioned and on occasion even repudiated the Gospel according to W. A. Moser, but he never achieved anything like victory because the man refused to admit defeat and never, ever quit the field. "Back when you were a Christian," Dub-Yay would say, apropos of nothing beyond reminding him that his conversion to Catholicism, decades earlier, was still in play. When Lincoln had explained that he and Anita both felt it was important to present a united front to their children when it came to religion, his father, who would've made a fine country lawyer, responded that he couldn't agree more. However, he pointed out, if Anita had converted to Church of God, the front they would be presenting to their children would be both united and *correct* instead of just united. Whenever he and his father disagreed, Lincoln was simply wrong.

That he should remain so stubbornly committed to finding a third path—some strategy that halved the distance between angry confrontation and meek acquiescence—was perplexing even to Lincoln. His mother had already pointed out that he only had the two choices. Why couldn't he quit looking for the third that she'd assured him—and she would know—didn't exist. Even now, at sixty-six, he was still trying to square the Dub-Yay circle, to reconcile what never could be—that his two very different parents wanted very different things from their son. When he pleased one, he of necessity displeased the other. When his mother died, he thought maybe that would put an end to the struggle, but no. Though she might be dead and buried, she continued at odd moments to plead her posthumous case, especially here on the island, the place she'd loved most. Wasn't that what her quiet fifth-column insurgency had been about all along? Her need for him to understand that even though his father was a force of nature, he was her son, too? By refusing to relinquish the Chilmark house, she was declaring, in terms her husband had no choice but to accept, that there was some part of his wife over which he'd never hold sway. Clearly, to her the Chilmark house wasn't just wood and glass and shingle. That it represented a time when her parents were still alive, when she felt happy and safe in a world they'd created, long before W. A. Moser turned up? Had his father, Lincoln wondered, understood all that?

How could selling *not* be a betrayal? Wouldn't it hand his mother a posthumous defeat and imply another triumph for the Moser genes, all the more satisfying because it would be transacted by their son, not himself? What saddened Lincoln most was the very real possibility that his mother had known from the start how all of this would eventually play out. Hadn't she said as much? *You can do things his way, or you can wish you had.*

How ironic that in the end Anita herself had proved to be the elusive third path. In her, though Dub-Yay would never admit it, he'd finally met his match. Even more astonishing was that he didn't really seem to mind all that much. It was as if he'd been waiting his whole life for a woman capable of swatting him off his perch. "I do worry about you, Son," he said one day after Anita had put her foot down about something, "overmatched as you are by that woman. I don't see how this ends well."

"Did it end well for you, Dad?" Lincoln inquired.

"Your mother was a fine woman, if that's what you're getting at."

Which had made Lincoln feel very small indeed, because that *was* what he'd been getting at. That his father had bullied his mother into becoming the docile, obedient woman that his own content-ment seemed to require. That getting her to surrender her own Catholic faith hadn't shamed him in the least; on the contrary, he was proud to have converted an idolater.

In this one respect, at least, by converting to Catholicism and thereby repudiating his father's arrogance and moral certainty, he could plausibly congratulate himself that he'd behaved honorably. But had he? Had he truly spurned the Gospel according to W. A. Moser or just tweaked the man's manipulative techniques by using them more subtly? Maybe Anita was telling the truth when she claimed she didn't regret not going to Stanford, but so what? The point was he hadn't really encouraged her to do what was clearly in her own self-interest. Why hadn't he put in a genuine good-faith effort? Well, love was part of it. They hadn't, either of them, wanted to be apart for a whole year. But hadn't he also feared that if she went to Palo Alto, she might never rejoin him? That at Stanford she'd find someone more worthy of her than he was? Which in turn made him wonder if it had been fear that caused Dub-Yay to renege on his promise to go with Trudy to Chilmark after Lincoln's gradua-tion. Had he sensed that if his wife ever returned to the place she'd loved as a girl, she might just stay there? That she might remember who she'd been before they met, before he'd made her into who he wanted her to be?

THE DEEPER PUZZLE, of course, was what all this had to do with Jacy. Anita's suggestion that he'd invited his friends to the Chilmark house because he'd been trying to decide whether it was herself or Jacy that he was in love with echoed in his mind. He didn't want it to be true, and he didn't believe it was, at least not literally. Unless he'd gotten this all wrong, the actual purpose of that final Vineyard get-together had been to set his mind at ease about the choice he'd made months before, perhaps on the night they'd all returned from the dog track and Jacy brashly kissed them there in the Theta house. He still recalled palpably how that kiss made him feel—both lost and free, terrified and exhilarated. And later, when Mickey joked about murdering her fiancé, he'd felt something dark and reptilian stir inside him, though he tried his best to deny it. No, of course they wouldn't *murder* her fiancé. All they were doing was acknowledging that if any girl in the world was *worth* killing for, Jacy was the one. And yet . . .

In the weeks and months that followed, as the exhilaration of Jacy's kiss began to fade, his sense of being untethered by it actually grew, as did his fear that if he somehow ended up with Jacy he would be *truly* lost, unknown to himself or at least to the person he'd always believed himself to be. It was not long after this kiss that he and Anita started going out, and part of the reason they became so serious, so fast, was that with her Lincoln knew he *wouldn't* feel lost and that whatever reptilian thing in him that Jacy had stirred into wakefulness could go back to sleep. In choosing Anita, he'd felt like he was not just declaring his love for her but also testifying as to the man he intended one day to become, as well as to the kind of life he meant to live. Strange that his mother, who knew Jacy only from his glancing descriptions, had advised him not to rule her out. If Anita was right, apparently part of him hadn't wanted to, either.

A block up the street, a middle-aged woman with a canvas tote over her shoulder was striding purposefully toward him. When she arrived at the *Vineyard Gazette*, this woman would, he felt certain, climb the porch steps, unlock the door and let herself in. If he was wrong, he told himself, he would take it as a sign that he was also wrong about this new reptilian stirring in his brain that had caused him to Google Troyer.

But already the woman was digging in her bag for her keys.

Teddy

Teddy had forgotten how steep State Road got near the Gay Head cliffs. By the time the lighthouse at the tip of the promontory came into view, he was exhausted and breathless. At the edge of the parking area sat an empty bicycle rack. His bike didn't have a lock, but it was old and its fenders rusty. Hard to imagine anyone swiping it. Nearby, an enormous coach marked CHRISTIAN TOURS idled, empty except for its driver, who was eating a sandwich outside the open door.

Up the slope stood the same cluster of gray-shingled shacks that Teddy recognized from 1971, still selling cheap souvenirs and sunscreen, overpriced T-shirts, sandals and pashmina scarves. Also postcards of the famous red-clay cliffs. Jacy had bought one that day, so he bought another now. Maybe he'd send it to Brother John with a note: *Headed your way. Cue up the Marx Brothers.* At the small takeout restaurant atop the cliffs, he ordered a clam roll and a diet soda and took them out onto a patio where half a dozen picnic tables were chock-full of seniors, several of the men wearing loud Bermuda shorts and dark socks under their sandals. He made a mental note to tell Mickey.

Seeing Teddy with his clam roll and no place to sit, a woman who looked to be in her early seventies waved him over. "Come join us," she said, her accent deeply southern. Her companions dutifully scooted down to make room. "Where you been hidin'?" she asked. For some reason she was wearing a green visor, as if expecting a poker game to break out any minute and she meant to deal the first hand. "I don't think we even met yet."

"No, I don't believe we have," Teddy said, sliding onto the bench across from her.

"Oh," she said, registering his accent and drawing the appropriate inference. "You're not with the tour. You looked like you might be one of us."

"Now, Ruthie," said the fellow at her chubby elbow, no doubt her husband, "don't go insultin' the man. You don't even know his name yet."

"I'm Teddy," he said, offering his hand.

"How'd you get all sweaty?" the woman seated next to him wanted to know, leaning ever so slightly away from him.

Back in Chilmark, there hadn't seemed to be much point in taking a shower before a long bike ride. "Well, I didn't come here on an air-conditioned bus."

"So, how'd you come?"

"On a bicycle."

"Where from?"

"Chilmark."

"You pedaled up that big hill?" said a large man wearing a John Deere cap. "See, now that's just showin' off."

"All downhill on the way back, though," Teddy pointed out.

"We were just talkin' about the election," the woman called Ruthie said abruptly. "We got us a Bush, two Rubios, three Cruzes, a Carson and a Trump. Where you at, Teddy?"

"None of the above, I'm afraid."

"Lock her up," said the woman's husband, grinning broadly now, as if he'd just made a joke.

"A *Trump*?" Teddy said. "Isn't yours a Christian tour?"

"He claims he *is* a Christian," the man said. "Maybe he just don't wear it on his sleeve like them others."

"So, where does he wear it, then?" John Deere wondered.

"No place visible to the naked eye," said the woman next to Teddy, leaning even farther away from him now.

"Speakin' of naked," said another old crone. "Is it true what the bus driver said? That the beach down below is nudist?"

"Used to be."

"Used to be *when*?"

"The seventies."

"Everybody used to run around half naked back then."

"This was both halves," Teddy said around a bite of clam roll.

"Damn," said a woman who'd been silent to this point. "How do you get down there?"

"You got sex on the brain, Wilma."

"It's gotta go somewhere."

When a horn sounded out in the parking lot, people at the other tables began gathering up their trash. These benches didn't push back, so it took a while for the older folks to extricate themselves. "Our driver's got us on a real tight schedule," Ruthie said. "Keeps threatenin' to leave and go back home without us."

"Well," Teddy offered, "there are worse places to get stranded."

"Anyhow, nice talkin' to you," she said. "I wasn't sure if I was going to like people up north, but so far they've all been nice. Not like home, but nice."

"Nantucket's next," said the man who'd suggested locking Hillary up. "Basically the same thing as here, or so they tell us."

Teddy smiled innocently. "Right. Like Georgia and Alabama."

"Actually, those two are nothing alike," said John Deere, sounding as if he must be from one or the other.

"I believe that was Teddy's point," said Ruthie, and just that quickly her veil of sociability fell away. "I believe he was having some fun at our expense, Roger. After we were nice enough to make room for him." Give her credit, too. She met Teddy's eye and didn't look away. "Don't make like that wasn't what you were doing, either, because I know better."

"Plus, you smell," said the woman sitting next to him.

Along one shingled wall of the restaurant there were separate rubber barrels for trash, aluminum cans and paper, but the old people just shoved everything into the nearest receptacle until there was no more room, then moved on to the others and filled those up. When they were gone, a waitress came out of the restaurant and surveyed the situation. She regarded Teddy as if the mess were something he might've prevented. "Not my people," he assured her. He was still a bit unnerved by how quickly the whole table had turned on him.

"Assholes," she said.

"Christians," Teddy clarified.

The woman shrugged, evidently willing to split the difference.

Ruthie had been right, though, Teddy had to admit: he *had* been making fun of them. Gentle fun, but still. No doubt they'd feared running into snobs here in New England and he'd proved them right. Theresa, at St. Joe's, had more than once accused him of elitism. "You think people don't catch on, but they do."

"What do they catch on to, exactly?" he'd inquired, genuinely curious.

"That you take a dim view of people in general and them in particular. And yourself most of all."

"I'm supposed to think *better* of myself? Wouldn't that make me *more* of a snob?"

"No, you're supposed to cut everybody some slack."

She had a point. Though outwardly courteous, he was sometimes privately and, it seemed, transparently judgmental. When their metaphorical bus tooted, the people he took a dim view of quickly gathered their belongings, like these Christians had done, and moved on, relieved to be shut of him.

There was, however, an upside. Right now, for instance, he had the whole patio to himself, and from it the most stunning views on the island, sparkling blue water and cloudless sky stretching all the way to Cuttyhunk. He'd stopped sweating, and the breeze, which atop the cliffs seemed to come from several different directions at once, lifted his hair pleasantly, like a lover's caress, only the lover herself missing.

Finished with his clam roll, he deposited the paper boat and napkins in the trash bin, then went over to the fence that discouraged dimwits from attempting to climb down the cliffs. Peering over the rim, he was immediately overcome by vertigo, the white surf below impossibly far away. What jellied his knees, though, had less to do with height or distance than the swift collapse of time.

MONDAY MORNING OF Memorial Day weekend had found all of them hungover and out of sorts. In truth, Jacy hadn't seemed quite herself since the moment she stepped off the ferry, though she insisted nothing was wrong. They'd assumed it must have something to do with the wedding, now mere weeks away. Maybe she and her asshole fiancé had been quarreling. As the weekend progressed, her mood had improved a little, though to Teddy her mind still appeared to be elsewhere.

Mickey's own sour mood that morning had been predictable. As usual he'd drunk more than the others the night before, so he had the worst hangover, but there'd also been an incident the previous afternoon. A guy named Mason Troyer, whose parents owned the house down the hill, had showed up uninvited with his townie girlfriend. They knew him from previous visits and didn't much like him. He was invariably boorish and unpleasant to be around, but Mickey hated to dismiss out of hand anyone who could be relied on to procure quality weed. At some point Troyer had gone inside to use "the head," as he called it, and when he didn't return, Mickey, suspicious, had followed him indoors. Good thing, too, because Troyer had cornered Jacy in the kitchen, where he had one hand on her ass and the other on her braless right breast.

"Come over here a minute," Mickey told him, as if he meant to whisper a secret in Troyer's ear.

"Why?" said Troyer, irked. In order to do so he'd have to unhand the girl he'd gone to so much trouble to corral.

"Because I just said to," Mickey explained.

When Troyer reluctantly unhanded her, Jacy scooted away. "Everything's cool, Mick," she said, though clearly she was relieved to get rescued. "Just let it go."

"She's with you?" Troyer said, raising both hands in surrender, as if Mickey were holding a gun on him. "Sorry, man. How the fuck was I supposed to know?"

To Teddy and Lincoln, who were still out on the deck with Troyer's girlfriend, the first indication that something might be amiss indoors was a thunderous crash that rattled the glass in the deck's sliding door. When Troyer had finally come out from behind the kitchen island, hands still in the air, he'd been met with an uppercut from Mickey that according to Jacy had lifted him clean off his feet. Overnight Mickey's right hand had swollen to twice its normal size.

Lincoln, too, had been in a crappy mood, but that happened from time to time. Even at their raucous Friday afternoon hasher parties, with some of the prettiest girls at Minerva crowded into the front room of their apartment, the music on so loud the walls vibrated, Lincoln would disappear and Teddy would find him stretched out in his bedroom reading, with the door shut, as if he'd just remembered that he had a religious vocation and had promised to avoid temptations of the flesh. Teddy hadn't known what to make of all this until he met Lincoln's father, a deeply strange man, who also, for reasons both religious and philosophical, distrusted the pleasure principle. His only unalloyed enjoyment seemed to be golf, though he claimed to derive no enjoyment from that, either. According to Wolfgang Amadeus Moser, anybody with half a brain could see that golf had nothing to do with fun. It was about the value of repetition and discipline, which, when learned, could be used to master other disorderly impulses that derived from Man's fallen condition. Lincoln seemed to realize how odd his father was, even as he appeared blind to the possibility that any of this peculiarity had rubbed off on himself.

Anyway, after waking up that morning, they'd gone into town for pancakes, and when they returned to Chilmark, Mickey immediately sacked out on the couch and fell asleep. Lincoln retreated to his bedroom, so he could call Anita, who from what they could gather wasn't thrilled that he was spending the holiday weekend with them instead of her. Despite her intelligence and beauty, Teddy suspected that deep down Anita, too, was pretty conventional. What she seemed to offer Lincoln was help in mastering any disorderly impulses that golf and W. A. Moser hadn't already brought under control.

Coming out onto the deck where Teddy was reading, Jacy, clearly frustrated with all three of them, said, "Here's the deal. We *could* stick around and listen to Mickey snore, or the two of us could drive out to Gay Head and you could show me those cliffs I keep hearing about. We'll be back before they even know we left."

After she purchased her postcard, they bought ice-cream cones from a nearby stand and brought them over to this exact scenic overlook. Mounted along the fence were several coin-operated binoculars that brought the more distant sections of the cliffs up close, the shutter clacking down abruptly when your time was up. They'd happily fed coins into the slot until they both ran out. "Question," she said, and Teddy was surprised to see that her eyes were moist.

"Yeah?"

Staring out to sea, she said, "How come everything has to be so fucked up?"

He shrugged. "You mean, like the war?"

"Yeah, that. And everything else. After this weekend who knows if we'll ever see each other again."

"Of course we will," Teddy said, though the same thought had crossed his mind.

She looked like she had more to say, but decided not to. "Don't mind me," she said, forcing a smile. Turning to face him, she noticed a small drip of sun-melted ice cream on his shirtfront and dabbed at it with her napkin, a gesture so intimate that his heart started pounding. "How do you get down to the beach?"

Teddy told her there was a trail. "It's clothing optional down there, though."

"Yeah?" she said, brightening. "Cool!"

The dirt path that ran between the road and the cliff edge was bordered on both sides by tall grass and beach-plum bushes. Teddy surrendered himself to the warm sun that was now almost directly overhead, the pounding of the nearby surf and a heady mix of excitement and sheer terror that intensified the closer they got to the beach. Was it possible the question that had haunted his young life—never far from his mind, no matter how desperately he tried to banish it—was about to get answered?

Where the path merged with the beach was crowded with families, everyone clad in swimsuits. Jacy, slipping off her sandals, was clearly disappointed. "I thought you said—"

"Over that way," he pointed.

They moved down the beach, the clay cliffs rising on their right. Though the air was almost hot, the late-May water was still icy, and just a few brave souls ventured in, most of them only to their knees. As they progressed, more people had opted out of swimwear. Most, in Teddy's view, probably shouldn't have, but he decided that if being grossly overweight and out of shape didn't embarrass them, why should it trouble him? Others, despite signs strictly prohibiting this, had coated their naked bodies with moist clay from the cliffs to ghoulish effect. Finally, rounding the point, where the cliffs angled off toward Menemsha, he and Jacy found themselves alone, and it took her about two breathtaking seconds to shuck her clothes and dart, whooping, into the frigid water, calling, "Come *on*, Teddy!" over her shoulder.

Disobeying the commands of beautiful naked girls was something Teddy had zero experience of, so he disrobed clumsily, dropping his clothes in a pile next to hers. Pausing at the water's edge to gauge the temperature, he heard Jacy, already thirty yards out into the surf, yell, "No, you coward! You have to get in all at once!"

So again he did as instructed, dashing straight into the water, stumbling and nearly falling when the drop-off he was expecting didn't materialize. As the first of a series of waves bore down on him, he almost lost his nerve, but then at the last second, instead of turning his back and going up on his tiptoes, he dove into it headfirst, as he'd seen Jacy do. Never before had he felt such cold, the chill of a thousand stinging needles. Regaining his feet on the other side of the wave, he discovered he was still only thigh deep, the undertow so fierce that he immediately lost his balance and toppled over. Before he could get to his feet again, the next wave was on him, knocking him back toward the shore. He expected to hear Jacy's laughter at his comic incompetence but saw that she was heading straight out to sea, as if she meant to swim to Spain. "Wait up!" he called, diving under the next wave and the one after that. By the time he caught sight of her again, she'd made it out beyond where the waves were breaking. There the water swelled more gently, and he watched her rise on each crest and then lower gracefully into its trough. Feeling himself begin to harden, he feared he might weep for pure joy.

When he, too, finally made it out beyond the waves, he wondered if she might allow him to take her in his arms; and if so, what sort of betrayal would that be? Of her fiancé? Of the two friends they'd left back at the house in Chilmark? Of God, for anyone considering divinity school? But he found he was simply too happy to care, and before he could resolve the initial question, Jacy drew him to her, her body somehow warm against his icy skin. How was this possible? Two people, nearly frozen solid, yet conveying warmth to each other?

"Have you ever been so cold in your life?!" Jacy squealed, delighted, as if freezing were a grand thing that no sensible person could ever get enough of.

"No!" he said, his teeth actually clacking. He'd heard about people being so cold their teeth chattered but assumed it must be a figure of speech. "*G-G-God*, no!"

Her teeth were chattering, too.

"Jacy?" he said. His happiness, complete a moment before, was now assailed by a terrible doubt.

"What's the matter?"

Nothing. Everything. "It's just . . . I don't know what this means," he said, his teeth rattling so badly that he marveled when she seemed to understand.

"What *what* means?"

"*This!*" That she'd wanted to come here with him in the first place, just the two of them. That she was naked and joyous and nestled comfortably in his arms. That she seemed to be about to kiss him. No, that she *was* kissing him, kisses even more deliriously thrilling than the one she'd given him the night they'd returned from the dog track. But *that* night she'd kissed Lincoln and Mickey, too. Since then each of them had been wondering the same thing: which one she'd choose in the unlikely event it ever came to that. Was *that* what this moment, this embrace, this sweetly salty kiss meant? Could she actually have chosen *him*?

"This right here?" she said, pulling him to her even tighter as they rose and then descended on every new swell. "I think this means I might not be getting married after all."

Lincoln

And there she was. Beyond beautiful, even on grainy black-and-white microfilm. Lincoln had forgotten the slight asymmetry of her face, her right eye slightly lower than the left, the smile just a tad lopsided. So different from what passed for beauty nowadays. That Britney Spears girl, the left side of her face identical to the right, as if beauty were about perfection and symmetry. And right on top of this, another jolt. Her name. *Justine Calloway.* To Lincoln she'd always been just "Jacy." She had no more need of a surname than Madonna or Cher. Two names identified a person as a mere mortal.

The story in the *Gazette* had run in mid-June, two full weeks after Jacy's disappearance, and it included the same appeal her parents had placed in the Cape Cod and coastal Connecticut newspapers: HAVE YOU SEEN THIS GIRL? *No*, Lincoln thought, *not in forty-four years.*

Aware that neither her parents nor her fiancé would approve of her going off to Martha's Vineyard with Lincoln and Teddy and Mickey, she'd told them all she was spending the weekend in New York with her maid of honor and some other Thetas. There was no such thing as bachelorette parties back then, but something along those lines must've been her pitch: one last girls' night out before the wedding. She'd be back in Connecticut in plenty of time to meet her fiancé when he returned from North Carolina, where law school was letting out for the summer. When she didn't return as planned, her parents had telephoned the maid of honor, who informed them that, no, Jacy hadn't come to the city and, no, she had no idea where she might be. Next they called Minerva on the off chance that she'd gone there, but of course the Theta house was closed up tight and the campus was mostly deserted. Now alarmed, they called the maid of honor again to see if Jacy'd been in touch, and this time the girl, whom Jacy had sworn to secrecy, caved, telling them she'd spent the Memorial Day weekend on Martha's Vineyard. She'd been having second thoughts about the wedding, the girl claimed, and just wanted to get away and think. She was staying at a house in Chilmark with some boys who worked as hashers at the Theta house. The weather had been unseasonably warm and they'd probably just decided to stay a couple extra days. Did the maid of honor know the exact address of the Chilmark house? She did not. Had Jacy left her the phone number there? No. Reluctantly, however, she surrendered the names of the boys she'd been staying with, though of course by then Lincoln and Teddy and Mickey had all returned to the mainland.

When the end of the week came and there was still no sign of her, the Calloways went to the police, who at first were not terribly helpful. The girl hadn't been gone that long, for one thing, and for another, if the maid of honor was correct and Jacy was getting cold feet about the wedding, well, a runaway bride was hardly of concern to the cops. She'd turn up when she was ready. They did, however, contact Minerva and were given the address of the off-campus apartment Lincoln, Teddy and Mickey had shared. Their landlord let the local police in to search the place, but there was no evidence of anyone having been there since the boys turned in their keys. What kind of tenants had they been? Well, they were college boys. They drank beer and played their music too loud, but other than that they'd been okay. Paid their rent on time and left the place in better condition than you'd expect, given their youth and gender.

Though Lincoln wouldn't hear about Jacy's disappearance until he and Anita arrived in Arizona, the Greenwich police called

Dunbar—Minerva had provided the home phone numbers for all three boys—and spoke to his mother, who informed them her son was driving back to Arizona with the girl he planned to marry (no, her name wasn't Jacy) and was for the time being unreachable. Yes, she'd known that her son and his friends were at the Chilmark house over the holiday weekend. Yes, they had permission. No, she hadn't been aware that there was a girl with them, but it didn't surprise her. They'd all been best friends at college. Jacy, she understood, was marrying another boy entirely. Yes, she would have her son phone them as soon as he arrived in Dunbar.

Teddy's parents had been even less helpful. Their son had a summer internship at one of the Boston newspapers, they seemed to remember, and after that he'd be attending divinity school, to what end they couldn't imagine, since they hadn't raised him to be superstitious. Nor could they locate the new phone number he'd recently given them. And no, they couldn't drop everything and go look for it. *College* classes might be over, but *they* were high-school teachers who had two more weeks of instruction and stacks of exams to grade.

The home number the cops had for Mickey turned out to be an old one listed in his deceased father's name; the current one, which the college didn't have, was in his mother's. By the time they finally cleared up this confusion, Mickey had lit out for Canada. (Years later, when he finally returned to the States after the amnesty, Mickey would explain that when the cops called, his mother had assumed they wanted to know why he hadn't shown up for his induction into the army. And when they said they were calling about a missing girl, she hadn't believed them.)

Somewhere on this time line the Massachusetts State Police had interviewed several Steamship Authority employees, both in Woods Hole on the mainland and in Vineyard Haven and Oak Bluffs on the island, to ask if anybody remembered seeing Jacy on the ferry that Tuesday morning. A woman working in the ferry's snack bar thought she recognized her from the photograph she was shown, but she'd been busy and couldn't be certain. In all likelihood Jacy had paid cash for a round-trip ticket in Woods Hole, and there was no way of determining if she'd actually used the return. Woods Hole and nearby Falmouth were serviced by several bus lines, but there was no record of Jacy having purchased a ticket back to Connecticut, and no one at the bus station recognized her from her photograph.

In retrospect, Lincoln wondered why the police hadn't pursued him and his friends more tenaciously. After all, they were the last people to see Jacy, and if there'd been any hint of foul play, they logically would've been the first people to interview. Instead, when he'd called the Greenwich police from Dunbar, the conversation couldn't have been more pro forma. Basically, he told them that Jacy had been anxious to get on the road that Tuesday morning and left them a note saying she meant to catch an early ferry. No, nothing out of the ordinary had happened on the island. (He'd seen no reason to mention the incident with Troyer.) If Jacy seemed upset about anything, it was the fact that Mickey was headed to Vietnam soon. He told them they could probably reach Teddy at the *Globe*, but they'd never followed up.

One reason the authorities weren't terribly interested in them was that they seemed to be focused on Jacy's fiancé, whom they interviewed shortly after he returned home from Durham. Had he spoken with Jacy at all that weekend? No, he hadn't. Was that unusual? Not really. Had she recently changed her mind about marrying him? Of course not. Because they'd heard from her maid of honor that maybe she had. Only when thus confronted had the man reluctantly produced the Gay Head postcard that had arrived the day after he returned home. Postmarked Vineyard Haven, Massachusetts, it said, simply, *I'm sorry. I thought maybe I could, but I can't. Try and be happy.* How had that made him feel? He hadn't felt anything, because he didn't believe it was true. Brides sometimes got the jitters. He and Jacy loved each other, he was certain of that. In due course she would come to her senses. Why hadn't he told them about the postcard up front? Same reason. It didn't mean anything. Could he prove he was in North Carolina all weekend? He could, definitely.

Lincoln, his eyes suddenly full, reached forward and touched Jacy's face on the microfilm machine. *Hey, Jace. Guess what? We're all here. Teddy. Mick. Me. On the island. Remember the Chilmark house? Our last night together on the deck? How we all linked arms and sang? You'd laugh if you could see us now. Old men, the three of us. Old men haunted by you.*

Feeling like an idiot, he wiped his eyes on the back of his sleeve and switched off the machine and just that quickly she was gone. Again.

"FIND WHAT YOU WERE looking for?" the woman asked when he emerged from the microfilm room. *Beverly.* Lincoln suddenly recalled—with a small measure of pride—the name she'd told him earlier. He'd always been bad with names and was getting worse, which made traveling without Anita perilous. Aware that he sometimes forgot the names of people he'd just been introduced to, Anita would work those names into the conversation, and by the third or fourth mention he'd be up to speed. She claimed that he was better at remembering men's names than women's, and better at attractive women's names than plain ones'. Lincoln would've objected to this unflattering assessment had it not been so accurate.

"No luck, Beverly," he admitted. (Okay, she *was* an attractive woman.) He was surprised to hear in his own voice something akin to relief. After switching the microfilm machine off and sitting in the dark for a few moments to compose himself, he'd turned it back on again and scanned another two months' worth of *Gazette*s on the off chance there'd been some kind of response to the original story, but didn't find a single item. Clearly the police had concluded that Jacy left the island that morning as planned, and why not? Hadn't the snack-bar woman seen a girl who looked like her on the ferry? If there was no record of her buying a bus ticket in Woods Hole, that meant only that she'd paid cash. Back then you didn't have to show your ID for most travel. Or maybe she'd met somebody on the ferry who was headed to New York City and didn't mind dropping her off in Greenwich. It was even possible she'd decided to hitchhike.

The important thing was that if she had left the island, then her disappearance didn't involve Mason Troyer. Which, admit it, was where his mind had gone—or rather leaped, the narrative already fully formed. Still chafing over the humiliation of having Mickey coldcock him the day before, Troyer had been watching the house that morning, just as he would years later, when he "dropped in" on Anita, giving *her* the creeps. Seeing Jacy leave by herself, he'd followed and offered her a lift to the ferry. And once he had her alone, he'd . . .

Okay, the narrative wasn't *fully* formed, and right here, Lincoln had to admit, was where it broke down. Yes, Troyer was a lout who according to Google had a history of harassing women, but that didn't make him a murderer, which was what Lincoln's half-baked narrative needed him to be. No matter how hard he squinted, however, the story refused to track. In the first place, Jacy never would've gotten into a car with him, not after he'd groped her. And even supposing she *had* done such a foolish thing, and supposing Troyer actually meant to harm her, exactly how would his intention have played out? Sure, a young woman hitchhiking alone was always vulnerable, but Troyer couldn't have been sure that she'd be either alone or hitchhiking. In fact, he naturally would've assumed she and Lincoln and Teddy and Mickey would all be leaving the island together. Which meant that if he'd somehow managed to abduct her, he'd acted on impulse. Which in turn made no sense. State Road, where Jacy would've been hitching, was, if not exactly busy that early in the season, at least well traveled, and you could never be certain another driver or walker or jogger wouldn't appear at exactly the wrong moment. And even if Troyer, fueled by rage, had been willing to roll the dice, to what logical end? He was a big guy, so sure, if he somehow got Jacy into the car, he could overpower her, but then what? If he meant to rape her, he'd have to take her someplace where there wouldn't be any witnesses, but again, then what? How would he keep her from going to the cops afterward? Well, he could threaten her. That often worked on terrified young women who felt not just fear but shame. But *often* wasn't *always*, so how could he count on it? And what if, instead of going to the cops, she returned to Chilmark and told her friends? Mickey had already laid the asshole out cold for—compared to rape, at least—a relatively minor transgression. What sort of punishment would he mete out for the greater offense? No, to keep his victim quiet, he'd have to kill her, but kill her how? Dispose of her body how? And later, when she was reported missing, the cops would question Lincoln and Teddy and Mickey, who'd be quick to tell them about the incident in the kitchen, after which he'd be the prime suspect.

No, it was a fever dream. Loathing Troyer, he'd turned a lout into a monster so as to explain the inexplicable.

"Turns out I was looking for a ghost," he reluctantly admitted to Beverly.

"Oooh, tell me," she said, motioning for him to take a seat. "I love ghost stories."

No, he told himself. *Just leave.*

"Unfortunately, this one lacks an ending," he said, taking the offered chair.

"That's okay, I'm excellent at endings."

And so, keeping Troyer out of the narrative, he gave Beverly the short version of that long-ago holiday weekend and Jacy's disappearance. As he spoke, she made notes on her blotter, as if there might be a quiz later. When at last he finished talking, she said, without hesitation, "She's here on the island."

Lincoln swallowed hard, feeling his face go white. For a moment he was unable to locate his voice.

"In a story, I mean. You and your friends look for her all over the world, only to discover that she's been right here the whole time. That's how I'd write it." Then, having apparently registered his expression, she winced. "Ouch. I forgot we were talking about an actual person. Somebody you—"

"It's okay," Lincoln assured her, though what she'd said had given him the bends, as if she'd recognized Jacy today from his description of her in 1971 and knew right where she lived on the island. As if her name and phone number were waiting there on Beverly's Rolodex. As if they could all meet for lunch. "It was a long time ago. Who was it who said to let the dead bury the dead?"

"That would be Jesus, I believe."

"Right," said Lincoln, glad that Dub-Yay wasn't here to witness this lapse. Except that of course he was. Like many fathers, Lincoln's now had two permanent residences—one in Dunbar, Arizona, the other in his only son's head. *This right here is what comes of attending college in New England and marrying a Roman Catholic,* he heard the old man say in his whine. *I'm glad your poor mother didn't live to see this day.* "I'm not sure what he meant, though, Beverly. Are you?"

"Maybe that we should focus on what we can change and not what's beyond our sphere of influence?"

"Not bad advice," Lincoln said, getting stiffly to his feet. Too much sitting in front of that damn microfilm machine.

Beverly's handshake was warm and firm. "Why don't you leave me your cell number," she suggested. "I've got a couple reporter friends on the Cape. Maybe a follow-up ran in one of the papers there."

At the door, he paused. "While I'm here," he said, trying to sound nonchalant, "I wonder if you know a neighbor of mine out in Chilmark. Mason Troyer?"

Immediately her expression darkened with suspicion and, unless he was mistaken, fear. "Is he a friend of yours?"

"Barely know the man. He wants to buy my house."

"He's fifty different kinds of trouble," she said. "If you tell him I said that, I'll deny it."

"I wouldn't dream of it."

He was halfway out the door when he heard her gasp, and when he turned around, Beverly's hand was covering her mouth.

"Oh my God!" she said. "Are you thinking—"

"No, Beverly," he was quick to tell her. "No, I'm not."

Teddy

S o long ago, that euphoria, and so short-lived. And, like life itself, over before it could be fully comprehended. A cheat, really.

Returning to the picnic table where he'd made small talk with the Christians, Teddy took out the postcard he'd purchased earlier and studied its painted cliffs, themselves a cheat, their colors brighter than the real ones. When Jacy'd bought this same card back in '71, he had no idea what she meant to do with it, though he remembered thinking it odd, given how cheap they were, that she'd bought just one. Only later would he learn who she'd sent it to.

Later that summer her fiancé—Vance? Lance? Chance?—had somehow learned that Tom Ford had helped Teddy land an internship at the *Globe* and called him there, wondering if he'd heard from Jacy. When Teddy told him no, he seemed satisfied but went on to say he'd be in Boston the following week and suggested they meet for coffee. Teddy, surprised by the invitation, hadn't been able to come up with an excuse on the spot, so they'd met at a Greek diner not far from the *Globe* offices, where Lance/Chance/Vance, with his short hair and preppy attire, couldn't have looked more out of place. Who, Teddy remembered wondering, did this guy remind him of?

They'd taken a booth in the back, "away from prying ears," as Vance hilariously put it, as if their conversation would naturally be of interest to others, maybe the entire readership of the *Globe*.

When Teddy ordered only coffee, Lance said, "You sure you don't want some pie? I'm buying." Teddy said no, just coffee, to which the would-be lawyer replied, "Suit yourself," and ordered a slice of Boston cream to go with his coffee. For someone left a few scant blocks from the altar, Chance seemed to be in excellent spirits. "So," he said when his pie arrived, fixing Teddy with his pale blue eyes, "there's news."

At this Teddy's heart leaped. It was August by then and she'd been gone for a solid two months. "About Jacy?"

Vance shook his head. The news was actually about her parents, and get this: *they were divorcing.* Nobody'd seen *that* coming, Lance said, including his own parents, and the two couples had been best friends for as long as he could remember. Teddy started to ask how any of this was relevant, but Chance cut him off—because *there was more.* Jacy's dad had apparently been caught up in the latest insider-trading Wall Street scandal. Did Teddy know? It was in all the papers. Word was he'd be lucky to escape jail. Jacy's mother, originally from California, planned to sell the Greenwich house as soon as it was legally hers and move back. Which meant that if Jacy didn't show up soon, she'd have neither a home nor married parents to return to.

To Teddy, none of this was as surprising as the fact that Vance seemed to have adjusted to the fact that if Jacy ever did come home, it wouldn't be to him. "I guess some things just aren't meant to be," he said, causing Teddy to wonder if he'd begun to see the writing on the wall prior to his fiancée's disappearance. Had they been quarreling in the run-up to the wedding? Teddy knew they argued about the war, and gathered there were other serious disagreements as well, such as where they'd live after they married. Jacy wanted out of Greenwich, whereas Chance was in favor of finding a place near their parents. Why not? Free babysitting once they started having kids, which Lance apparently thought would happen right away, despite Jacy's stated disinclination to ever have any. So, when he said that some things just weren't meant to be, was he acknowledging that they were fundamentally mismatched? Or had he, in Jacy's continued absence, begun recalling the hundreds of minor irritants that inevitably cropped up between any two people, stuff that in the moment didn't rise to the level of genuine discord?

"For a while, it felt like the end of the world," Chance was saying, "but you know what, Teddy?" (He didn't, but was surprised to hear his name, in direct address, from the mouth of a man he'd only just met.) "Turns out that only the end of the world"—here he paused so Teddy could savor the profundity of what was coming next—"is the end of the world." In *fact*, Lance went on, his knuckles drumming on the table, did Teddy know why he was *really* in Boston? (No, how could he?) *Well*, Vance was visiting a *girl*. They'd only lately been introduced, so it was too soon to know if it was serious, but jeez, you know what, Teddy? Stranger things happened all the time. When he offered congratulations, Lance said, "Thanks, pal. Really, that . . . means a lot."

Was it the *pal* that made the penny drop? Whatever the reason, Teddy was suddenly sure that Vance, with all this phony camaraderie, was setting a trap. Had, in fact, already set it.

"But, you know what, Teddy? There's one other thing you could do for me that would mean even more."

"What's that, Lance?"

"*Vance*," he said, his friendly façade falling completely away.

"Right." Well, now he knew.

"You could tell me what really happened on that island over Memorial Day. The four of you all alone in that house. Three guys. One girl. Make me understand."

"Nothing happened," Teddy told him, a lie that put Jacy in his arms all over again, their bodies rising and lowering, weightless in the swell. "We were all just good friends."

"*That's* what I want you to make me understand. How that works. Because I have some questions."

He wasn't kidding, either, and once they started, the questions came fast and furious. He barely gave him the opportunity to answer one before asking the next, as if Teddy were hooked up to a lie detector and the answers to the initial questions—name, address, age, occupation—were already known to the questioner, worthwhile only to establish a baseline for what followed. Had Jacy said anything about not wanting to go through with the wedding? Anything about Vance himself that would indicate why she would want to break off their engagement? Was she nursing a grievance of some sort? Did she seem unhappy? Was she worried about anything? Was she acting strangely? Because otherwise—you know what, Teddy? It didn't really add up, did it? In fact, the whole thing was troubling. *Deeply* troubling.

And did Teddy know what troubled Vance most of all? It was this whole just-good-friends deal: was he actually supposed to *believe* that? Because if they *were* just good friends, why had Jacy been so secretive about where she was going that weekend? Okay, sure, he could understand her not leveling with her parents, who definitely *would fucking not* have approved. But why not tell *him*, her fiancé, unless of course she was feeling guilty about something? What did Teddy think? Did Jacy have some reason to feel guilty? What were the sleeping arrangements like that weekend? Did Jacy have her own room, or was it like one big pajama party? Did they *wear* pajamas, Teddy? Had they smoked a lot of marijuana? (That was the actual word he'd used, not *pot* or *weed* or even *grass*.) How much did they drink, these three guys and one girl? Did they get her drunk? Who tucked her in at night? "Explain these things to me, Teddy. Explain what *good friends* means to somebody like you."

Teddy chose his words carefully, partly because precision was called for, but also because with each new loaded, sarcastic question it became evident that the young man sitting across the booth from him was seething with rage. "Well, it's true we were good friends," Teddy said, "but as you know, *Vance*, it's impossible to be around Jacy without being in love with her, at least a little."

"You, too, Teddy? Were you in love with her?"

"I guess."

"You *guess*," he said, sneering now. "Did you fuck her? That's a question you should be able to answer without guesswork."

"No," Teddy told him, wondering if he actually *had* been connected to a lie detector right then what the needle would be doing. "I did not."

"How about your two pals? Did they get any luckier?"

"She had her own room. Us guys took turns sleeping on the couch."

"Did the doors have locks?"

"They didn't need to. Look, Lincoln's in love with someone else, a girl named Anita. They're practically engaged. The two of them headed to Arizona later that same week."

"And the big guy? What's his name again?"

"Mickey."

"Bingo. He's the one she liked the best, right?"

Teddy felt a powerful urge to deny this, but held his tongue. "Nothing happened between them, okay?"

"Yeah, but how would you *know* that?"

Because, Teddy thought, Mickey wouldn't have been able to contain his joy. "Because we're friends."

"That word again," Vance said. "Okay, let's go back to you. Tell me again that there was nothing going on between you and my fiancée." Teddy, noting the accusation was phrased differently this time, said nothing. For his part, Vance didn't seem to care whether he answered or not. "I mean, you would've, right? If you had the chance? Sure, she was *fucking engaged*. But you were in *love* with her, right? So, what was the problem? Didn't she like you?"

"She did, actually." Chose him, in fact. Over Mickey and Lincoln. Also over this aggrieved rich kid sitting across the table from him now. And the rapture of that simple fact was every bit as powerful now as it had been in the surf off Gay Head, so powerful, indeed, that Teddy was seriously tempted to tell Vance everything. Paint him a picture he'd never forget.

"Why not, then?" Vance continued. "Are you a queer, Teddy? I heard you might be."

"You heard wrong."

Vance ignored this. "Girls like fags, right? Tell 'em things they wouldn't even confide to their best girlfriends. Did Jacy confide in you, Teddy? Like which one of your asshole friends she preferred to me?"

Somehow Teddy managed to keep his voice under control. "Judging by how things turned out," he said, "she preferred *all* of us to you."

Vance had eaten only a few bites of his pie, his professed appetite another part of an elaborate ruse that he couldn't quite pull off. Picking up his fork, he pointed it at Teddy. "You know what I ought to do?"

This whole time Teddy had been racking his brain, trying to remember who Vance reminded him of, and now, threatened with serious bodily harm, it came to him: it was Nelson, the high-school kid that Coach instructed to bang Teddy around, to "toughen the pansy up."

"Yeah," Teddy said, feeling strangely calm. Usually when violence was imminent he felt physically ill. "I *do* know. You ought to believe everything I'm telling you, because except for the fact that you want me to be lying, there's no reason not to. Because my friends and I have no more idea than you do where Jacy went or why. When she comes back, you can ask *her*, and then you'll know."

Vance, still clutching his fork, leaned toward him across the table. "Except she's not *coming* back, is she, Teddy?"

And just that quickly Teddy's righteous anger leaked away. Looking down at his barely touched coffee, he was suddenly unable to meet his companion's eye. All summer long he'd waited for the phone to ring with the news that Jacy had returned, safe and sound. Lincoln, also expecting such news, had called from Arizona twice to see if he'd heard anything. At some point, though, and Teddy didn't know exactly when, a switch had flipped in his brain: if Jacy was coming back, by now she would've.

When he finally forced himself to look up from his coffee, Teddy saw that tears were streaming down his companion's face. A moment earlier he'd expected him to come flying across the table and stab him with his fork, but now he realized that Vance had also been on an emotional roller coaster these last two months, hope giving way to despair, despair to grief, grief to rage, and all of it over again. "Did you kill her, Teddy? You and your pals? Did you kill my girl? Did you get her drunk and force yourselves on her? Did you bury her on that island? Or take her out on a boat and toss her over the side? Did you guys do that?"

"No, Vance," Teddy told him, feeling his own eyes fill now. "Of course we didn't."

"Ah . . . fuck," he said, dropping his fork and pounding his broad forehead violently with the heels of both hands. "I thought if I talked to you, I'd be able to tell if you were lying, but I can't."

"Look," Teddy told him, "I *did* lie before. I wasn't *half* in love with Jacy. I was head over heels. We all were. We never would've hurt her."

"Yeah, well, I lied, too," Vance admitted, pulling a napkin out of the dispenser to dry his eyes. "There's no girl here in Boston. There's just Jacy and she's fucking gone."

"I'm sorry, Vance," he said, surprised to discover it was true.

"Well, fuck you anyway," he said, tossing the wadded napkin onto the table and sliding out of the booth. "Somebody said you got a high draft number."

Teddy nodded.

"Just so you know, dipshit, *I'll* be serving my country," he said. "JAG Corps. The minute I finish law school. And you know what? I hope they send me to Vietnam. I hope I get killed."

Teddy, who'd been feeling sorry for him a moment earlier, was incredulous in the face of such obviously bogus emotion. "You actually believe *lawyers* are dying in Vietnam?"

Vance didn't seem to hear this, which was probably just as well. "Tell me something," he said, standing at faux military attention, chin jutting out, in full-sneer mode. "Guys like you and your friends? What right would you even have to fall in love with a girl like Jacy?" Planting both hands onto the table, he leaned forward aggressively, right in Teddy's face. "You were fucking *hashers*."

And then he was gone, the tinkling bell above the front door signaling his departure. A moment later, their waitress arrived with the check.

A FEW DAYS AFTER MEETING Jacy's fiancé, Teddy had another of his chronic spells, this one a paralyzing panic attack. Unable to sleep, his tortured mind on a loop, he checked himself into Mass General, cutting short by a couple weeks his *Globe* internship. Had this been brought on by the meeting with Vance, or by the mental switch that got tripped earlier, his brain finally acknowledging that Jacy might be gone for good? All summer he'd been haunted by the same questions that were clearly tormenting Jacy's fiancé. What could have happened to her after she left the island? Instead of taking the bus back home, *had* she decided to hitchhike? Had she been picked up by some predator? Teddy didn't want to believe that she'd met with such a fate, but if she was alive, where was she? Why couldn't the police find her? Why hadn't she contacted her parents or any of her Theta friends? Or, for that matter, himself at the *Globe*?

In the hospital he received the usual antianxiety medications, which allowed him to sleep, though whenever he woke up he had the impression that his dreams had been struggling to address the same unanswerable questions. Worse, he could feel himself slipping into a kind of narcotics-induced solipsism. As if Jacy's fate wasn't really so much about her as about himself. It had been a summer of losses. Lincoln had gone back West, which probably meant the end of their friendship. Mickey was also gone, though not to Vietnam as they'd feared. A few days before he was to report for duty, he'd apparently changed his mind and fled to Canada, just as he and Jacy had been begging him to do for so long. Yet another loss, though this one was an ongoing feature of his life, was the unrelenting aloofness of his parents. Teddy had let them know when he checked himself into the hospital, and his mother had come to visit him there. She'd stayed only a couple days, however, claiming that the fall semester was bearing down and she had classes to prepare.

Though he vowed to refuse, he'd expected her to invite him to come stay with them in Madison until he managed to get back on his feet, but the invitation never came, and that had wounded him more deeply than he would've predicted. Maybe the time had come to stop expecting things to change. He was clearly destined to live a solitary life. Wasn't this what his infatuation with Merton had been signaling? Hadn't Tom Ford, who also lived alone, intimated as much at Minerva? What had happened with Jacy at Gay Head, coupled with her subsequent disappearance, now made a kind of bitter sense. Because her continued existence was at odds with his own solitary destiny, Jacy *had* to disappear. In a sense, he'd killed her.

Something else occurred to him, too. What if he was going about everything all wrong? In the past, whenever he went down this now-familiar rabbit hole, his first order of business had been to somehow gather himself and climb back up into the light, gradually restore his mental health, get his routine back to normal, or anyway what was normal for him. But was normal—*his* normal—a state worth preserving? Was he, *normally*, a person worth much effort? Replaying his encounter with Jacy's fiancé, he was surprised by how little real empathy he'd shown. Okay, sure, Vance was an asshole, but that was hardly the point. The guy had obviously been suffering, and it had been within Teddy's power to set his mind at ease. Not completely, of course. He couldn't very well tell Vance about Gay Head, but other than that the weekend had been innocent, hadn't it? Why hadn't he taken the trouble to paint Vance a narrative picture of how they all had spent their time together? He'd assured Jacy's fiancé that none of them would have ever harmed her, but why hadn't it occurred to him to tell Vance how they—or at least Mickey—had actually protected her from harm that afternoon when Troyer came by and tried to grope her in the kitchen?

But on second thought, no. This wasn't a comforting story to share with Vance. In order to tell it honestly, he'd have had to explain how they'd all been sitting out on the deck, Creedence on the stereo, drinking beer, lazily passing a joint around. Okay, sure, the story would illustrate that, far from harming her, they'd served as her protectors. But it certainly wouldn't have put straight-arrow Vance's mind at ease to picture his fiancée out on that deck, drinking beer and listening to protest music and smoking weed with a pack of fucking hippies. Plus, if she hadn't gone with them to the island in the first place, she wouldn't have *needed* them to defend her against the ghastly neighbor.

Probably better to have explained why Jacy had decided to join them for the weekend. She wasn't looking to party before the wedding, far from it. Teddy had talked her into coming along in hopes of tag-teaming Mickey over those three long days, convincing him to head to Canada instead of reporting for duty. She'd been pleading with him pretty much nonstop since the night they all got their draft numbers. *(You wouldn't actually go, though, right? Tell me you wouldn't be that stupid.)* In the months leading up to graduation, Teddy had also been pressuring Mickey to rethink his options, for all the good that had done. How could you argue with somebody who conceded the validity of every single point you made? *Yes*, Mickey agreed, the war was both stupid and immoral. *No*, he had no desire to either kill or be killed, certainly not in a steaming jungle on the far side of the world in a cause no one had bothered to really articulate. *Yes*, heading to Canada *would* be the smart move. *No*, he didn't worry about people calling him a coward.

"Then *why*, Mick?" Teddy had implored him. "Explain why you'd do the wrong, dumb thing when you could do the right, smart one?"

"Because I said I would."

That's what it came down to. His father, Michael Sr., a veteran of the Second World War, had hated every minute he'd spent in the service, but was proud, as he put it to Mickey, to have done his bit. *When they call, you answer. You don't get to ask why. That's not how it works. Not how it's ever worked. Your country calls, you answer.* A pipefitter by trade, he was by all accounts a squared-away, no-bullshit kind of guy. Gruff and uneducated to be sure, but salt of the earth, too. He worked his forty-hour-a-week union job and then, most weekends, worked off the books to make his large family's ends meet. Growing up, Mickey had been raised as much by his older sisters as their worn-out parents, so it was only later, after he went off to Minerva, that he and his old man had become close, which was strange, if you thought about it. At a time when so many fathers and sons were increasingly at odds, the two of them had forged a bond so deep and durable that it took them both by surprise.

Which was why his father's sudden death the summer of Mickey's junior year had hit him like a sledgehammer to the base of the skull. A big guy like his son, Michael Sr. had been eating with his crew at a local lunch counter, and when it came time to go back to work, the other guys all rose from their stools and he didn't, his heart having detonated five seconds earlier. Turned out he'd known for some time that something like this would likely happen, but never said a word. Not to his wife, not to his grown daughters, not to his son. No, the last thing he'd said to Mickey was *Your country calls, you answer.*

But again, nope. None of this would've impressed gung-ho, love-it-or-leave-it Vance. He couldn't imagine, much less approve of, his fiancée going to the island to turn Mickey into a draft dodger. Nor would Teddy's portrait of Michael Sr. have moved Vance to admiration. If anything, it would've provided further evidence, were any needed, that this working stiff's son had no business falling in love with a girl like Jacy.

At the diner, when Vance came unglued and asked if Teddy and his friends had murdered his fiancée, he'd been shocked that anybody could dream up such a ludicrous possibility. And that he might've done so simply because they were *hashers* made the suggestion even more offensive. Yet as Teddy lay in his hospital bed pondering how little he'd done to alleviate the suffering of a fellow human being, he had to admit that some of Vance's other suspicions hit closer to home. Because when it came right down to it—when the opportunity presented itself—Teddy *hadn't* cared that Jacy was engaged, that she was somebody else's girl. The fact that she'd chosen him, that she conceivably might end up *his* girl, had readily vanquished all ethical considerations. Had Mickey been given the same opportunity, would *he* have acted any differently? Or Lincoln? Even more disconcerting than his own moral failings was that his justification, had he been asked for one, wouldn't have been dissimilar from Vance's own. At Gay Head, when Jacy said that being there with him meant that maybe she wouldn't be marrying her fiancé after all, what Teddy had felt was not just joy but also— why not admit it?—triumph. By choosing *him*, Jacy was rejecting not just Vance but others of his ilk. Teddy wasn't so much stealing another guy's girl as saving her from somebody who didn't deserve her. It was actually a *noble* thing he was doing, because Vance was a privileged, prep-school, Greenwich Connecticut asshole, who, on account of all that, *deserved* to suffer.

So, yes, a summer of losses. Minerva. Lincoln. Mickey. Jacy. His ever-more-aloof parents. And had those losses ended there, Teddy might've still felt the urge to claw his way back out of the dark rabbit hole. But it came to him that he'd suffered another loss as well, this one even more profound. The Teddy Novak who'd followed Jacy out into the freezing waves had been an innocent, propelled not only by love and almost unbearable desire but also by a desperate *need* to know. That person had been a boy, really, a boy Teddy couldn't find it in his heart to blame too much. How quickly everything had pivoted, though, innocence morphing into pride, and pride into crushing disappointment, into despair, into bitterness and finally into resignation and self-loathing. If he, like Vance, was suffering, it was because they *both* deserved to be.

Lincoln

Lincoln was halfway back to Chilmark when his cell buzzed, probably Teddy or Mickey wondering what had become of him. Except the number was local, and when he answered, it was a woman's voice on the line.

"Mr. Moser? It's Beverly. Listen, after you left, I got to thinking. You should talk to Joe Coffin."

"Who's he?"

"My father-in-law, actually, but also the former chief of police in Oak Bluffs. Back in the seventies, though, he worked up island. Anyway, I phoned him, and he said he'd be willing to speak to you."

"He remembers Jacy going missing?"

"I don't know, but after he retired, he kept a lot of old files. I've been after him to put them in order. They could be the basis for a pretty interesting memoir. You know, the silly things people who live here do? Or maybe a cozy detective series? Like Alexander McCall Smith?"

She seemed to be waiting for him to weigh in on this idea. Apparently this McCall Smith guy was somebody he was supposed to recognize. What on earth was a cozy detective series?

"Anyway, if nothing else, he might be able to provide some insight. He's been a policeman here his whole life. He's got some great stories."

Lincoln couldn't help smiling. Perhaps because she worked for a paper, the woman couldn't seem to get it out of her head that it was a *story* he'd told her: *beautiful young woman disappears without a trace and is never heard from again.*

"He lives in a senior-housing complex in Vineyard Haven, if you'd like to drop by."

"Maybe I will tomorrow," he said, though he had no such intention. Despite arriving at the *Vineyard Gazette* as a man on a mission, he'd left feeling unexpectedly relieved not to have found anything. Telling Beverly about Jacy actually made him feel a bit silly, like at age sixty-six he was still carrying a torch for a girl he'd never even dated. Him. Lincoln Moser. A happily married man with six children and a growing passel of grandkids. Also chronic lower-back pain. He needed to stick to the original plan. Figure out what needed to be done to the Chilmark house and get the place listed. Enjoy his friends. Return home.

"That's the thing," Beverly said. "He's going off island tomorrow for major surgery in Boston. You're only here for a few days, right?"

"You really think he might have some information?"

"It's possible?"

Hanging up, Lincoln wondered why so many women did that—turned statements into questions. He'd have to remember to ask Anita. She, like their daughters, always enjoyed explaining how what was wrong with women was really men's fault.

LIKE MOST OTHER BUILDINGS on the island, the ones that constituted Tisbury Village were gray shingled. Set back from the road and nestled among some scrub pines, the complex looked nicer and better maintained than most low-income, government-subsidized housing Lincoln had run across, but there was no disguising the function of such places. You didn't end up here if things had gone like you'd hoped.

Joe Coffin's apartment was on the second floor, and he must've seen him pull into the lot below, because he answered the door before Lincoln could complete his three-rap knock. A big barrel-chested man, he had a full head of gunmetal-gray hair that he kept extremely short on the sides. *White sidewalls*, Lincoln thought, recalling an old Dunbar expression. But did those tires even exist anymore? He and Coffin had to be roughly the same age, but the old cop's face was an unhealthy gray and deeply lined from what Lincoln suspected was a lifetime of smoking and drinking, so he looked easily a decade older. Despite the season, he was dressed in a long-sleeved flannel shirt. "You must be Mr. Moser," he said, stepping aside so Lincoln could come in. His obvious ill health notwithstanding, he looked like a man who could still hold his own in a bar fight, provided it didn't go more than one round.

His apartment—a small, generic one-bedroom—wasn't what Lincoln had been expecting. When it came time to downsize, most elderly people had a difficult time surrendering their hard-won possessions. They shoehorned everything from their larger, former home into a new much-smaller crib, making it impossible to navigate without banging into stuff. Whereas Coffin's apartment was more like a monk's cell, as if he'd taken a vow of poverty early in life and stuck to it. An off-brand flat-screen TV sat in the far corner of the room on a cheap fiberboard stand that also contained a DVD player, but no cable box for movie channels or on-demand. Nor were any other electronic gizmos in evidence. A rickety four-shelf bookcase contained a couple dozen volumes, most of which looked like he checked them out of the library. Forming an L in front of the TV was a sofa, end table and recliner. The walls were decorated with black-and-white photos of island wildlife: plovers on the beach, a gull roosting atop a wood piling, a gaggle of wild turkeys crossing the bike path, an elongated V of black geese against a gray sky.

"My daughter-in-law Beverly's the photographer," he said when he saw Lincoln studying them.

"She's good."

"That fella there's out in Katama," he said, pointing to a picture of a hawk perched majestically on a telephone line that drooped visibly under its weight. "I've seen as many as two hundred birds crowd onto that same telephone line, sitting there wing to wing like birds do. But when *he's* there? Not another bird as far as the eye can see."

"You're an animal lover?"

He nodded. "Like most cops, I prefer them to people. I've never known one to lie to me. Please, have a seat while I look for that file."

Sit where, exactly? Clearly the recliner was Coffin's usual spot, so not there. On the other hand, the couch—a sleeper sofa, by the look of it—bore the shape of a heavy man, and a pillow, not a decorative one, resting on one arm. Unable to resolve the conundrum, Lincoln perched on the sofa's other arm, from which he had an unobstructed view of the bedroom, which his host had converted into an office. Against the far wall was a metal desk, on top of which sat an ancient computer that had, unless Lincoln was mistaken, an external disk drive. Did they even make floppy disks anymore? Along another wall stood a row of filing cabinets, beneath framed photographs of uniformed policemen. Not a single civilian.

"Nineteen seventy-one, you said?" Coffin called over his shoulder.

"Right," Lincoln told him, though of course he hadn't ever *said* anything to him.

"May of nineteen and seventy-one," he heard the man mutter. "Here we go." Leaving the file drawer open, he returned to the front room and tossed a manila folder onto the coffee table. Its tab read MISSING GIRL. No other information, not even Jacy's name, which struck Lincoln as odd until he thought about it. In big cities, girls went missing every week. For all he knew, Jacy might be one of only a handful to disappear from here in the last century.

"Beverly says you're retired?"

"Two years ago yesterday, not that I'm keeping track."

"You're allowed to take files home?"

"No original documents. Just photocopies. Your own notes."

"Well, I appreciate your taking the time to see me," Lincoln said.

"Time's my long suit," he replied, seemingly aware of the statement's irony. The guy's days might be numbered, but that didn't make the hours of those same days any easier to fill. It occurred to

Lincoln that Beverly might've urged him to visit in hopes it would take the man's mind off tomorrow's operation, maybe even give him a sense of purpose. If so, it meant that he was probably wasting his time. "If it wasn't for my daughter-in-law," he said, as if he were a mind reader, "I'd probably never leave the apartment. She takes me grocery shopping. We go for coffee every now and then. To church on Sunday. You a religious man, Mr. Moser?"

"Lincoln, please. And no, not really." He was glad Dub-Yay wasn't hearing him say this.

"Me neither. I like going to church, though. The feel of it, I guess."

"You don't drive?"

"Not often these days. I still have a vehicle, but my blood pressure's all over the place. Mostly high, but every now and then it falls off the cliff and I black out. I'd hate like hell to be behind the wheel when that happens. Run over some kid, with my luck. You want a cup of coffee?"

"No, I'm good."

"It's no trouble. Beverly bought me one of those Keurigs."

Lincoln nodded. "We got my father one last year."

"How old is *he*?"

"Early nineties."

"Good for him. And what'd he do?"

"He was part owner of a small copper mine in Arizona."

"You sure you don't want a cup?" he said. "I think better when I'm fully caffeinated."

"Okay, why not?" Lincoln said.

"I like the one cup at a time," Coffin said from the kitchen. "I just wish there was something you could do with the pods besides toss 'em in the trash. Must be millions of these things in the dump."

"I'm not sure I even know where the landfill is."

"That's because there isn't one," Coffin said. "There used to be, years ago. Now all our trash gets hauled off to the mainland. Somebody else's problem. The older I get, the more I think about things like that. People who don't even know us have to deal with our shit."

"I doubt they do it for free," Lincoln said, for the sake of argument. Listening to the Keurig hiss and gurgle in the kitchen, he was tempted to sneak a peek at what was in the suspiciously thin folder, but he resisted.

"No, I'm sure they don't, but still. I read somewhere that out in the middle of the Pacific there's this vortex of trash. Ocean currents bring it all right there. You toss one of these plastic pods overboard off the coast of Oregon and another into the Sea of Japan and they both end up in the same spot. A hundred miles of Keurig pods and plastic bags and all manner of crap bobbing there in the waves, and not a human in sight. Nothing to connect you and me to the crime. Your old man ever worry about stuff like that—the world we're leaving behind for our children to deal with?"

Lincoln had to smile at this. "I'm not sure my father fully believes the world will continue to exist after he leaves it." Then once Coffin returned to the living room with two steaming coffee mugs, Lincoln said, "I hear you're having an operation tomorrow."

"That's the plan. They're gonna Roto-Rooter a couple clogged arteries. Put in a stent. I'm told the whole deal should come in at under a million dollars. I'd tell 'em to go fuck themselves if it was me."

"Ummm," Lincoln said. "It *is* you."

"Yeah, but not *just* me. It's never just about us, Lincoln."

This was, unless he was mistaken, another reference to his daughter-in-law, who seemed to play an outsize role in his life. He clearly lived here alone, so no wife. Had she died or were they divorced? And where was the son who'd married Beverly? Why was there no loving photographic evidence of any of them?

Donning a pair of drugstore reading glasses, Coffin picked up and opened the folder, which Lincoln now saw contained only two items—the article from the *Vineyard Gazette* he'd just read and some handwritten notes that were stapled together. Was it his imagination or was *Troyer* scrawled there? "Okay, give me a minute to refresh my memory," Coffin said. He shifted slightly, so Lincoln couldn't see what was on the pages.

Lincoln sipped his coffee while the man read, his expression darkening as he did. When he finally closed the folder, he tapped its edge against his knee and said, "Justine Calloway. That the girl we're talkin' about?"

"Jacy. Yes."

Coffin turned his gimlet gaze on Lincoln, holding him with it uncomfortably. "So you're telling me this Jacy never turned up?"

Lincoln nodded.

"Never called her folks?"

"Not that I'm aware of."

When the other man said nothing, Lincoln felt compelled to continue. "They divorced not long after she went missing. Her father had some legal difficulties about then."

"What sort of difficulties?"

"White-collar crime of some kind. I want to say insider trading. I think he might've ended up in jail."

Coffin stared out the window now, apparently deep in thought. "Says here there was a fiancé. She never got back in touch with him, either?"

"Not to my knowledge."

Coffin rubbed his stubbled chin thoughtfully, and Lincoln saw a thought scroll across his gray brow, plain as day: *Dead, then.* "Well, you being here begs a fairly obvious question, Lincoln. What's your interest after all these years?"

"She and my pals Teddy and Mick, we were all best friends in college."

"Where was that?"

"Minerva College. In Connecticut."

"Oh, I know where Minerva's at, Lincoln. What I'm asking is, why now?"

"I guess we never forgot her, how she just . . . disappeared. I mean, we were all going our separate ways now that college was over. It wasn't like we expected to see each other anytime soon. But I think we imagined we'd always be part of each other's lives."

"Have you been?"

"Us guys? Yeah. Maybe not as much as we planned on. I moved out West. Mick's the only one who stayed in New England." Or returned here after the amnesty, but there was no reason to bring that up. "We'll lose touch for a while—a year or two at a stretch—but then one of us will call out of the blue. And now there's e-mail."

"She come up in conversation, does she? This Jacy?"

"Sometimes," he said. "Not often. Being here on the island brings it all back, I guess."

Coffin seemed to consider all this as you would a math problem involving both numbers and letters. His expression had become less friendly. "You married, Lincoln?"

"Yes."

"Happily?"

"I'm sorry?"

"Do you love your wife? Simple question."

"Yes," Lincoln told him, not that it was any of his business.

"You rich?"

"In what respect?"

"Money, Lincoln. What most people mean by *rich*."

Lincoln squirmed, surprised by how easily the old cop had put him on the defensive. "We had more before 2008," he said, hoping to elicit at least a smile, and failing utterly. "Why do you ask?"

"I had a friend went to Minerva. Not a cheap ticket."

"I was there on scholarship. So were my friends."

"Not the girl?"

"Nope, she was from Greenwich." He almost added *Connecticut*, but didn't want to raise the man's class hackles again.

"You got kids?"

"Yes."

"Grandkids?"

"Uh-huh."

"So. Things have worked out, wouldn't you say? Minerva College paid some dividends, did it?"

"I guess you could say that." Though probably not in the sense that Coffin meant. They hadn't learned any secret handshakes there, or joined any secret societies. For the most part their classes had been good. Their teachers were mostly knowledgeable and pretty friendly. A few, like Professor Ford, whom he'd just been talking about with Teddy, had really challenged them, altering their trajectory by teaching them how to think more critically. Indeed, it could be argued that those were the true dividends of a liberal arts education, though he doubted that's what Coffin was getting at. He was still dwelling on money, what most people thought of when they heard the word *rich*.

"Okay if I ask you something?" Lincoln said.

"Go ahead."

"Did I manage to piss you off somehow, Mr. Coffin?"

"Not you, Lincoln. *This*." He was still tapping the edge of the folder against his knee. "This right here really *does* piss me off. Girl goes missing? Never turns up? Seems to me somebody dropped the damn ball. Which makes me wonder if that somebody was me. What? I say something funny?"

It was true. Lincoln *was* grinning. "No, it's just . . . you really were a cop, weren't you."

"That's right, Lincoln, I really was." But he was grinning now, too, if a little sheepishly. "Damn doctors don't let me smoke anymore. I'm not supposed to drink or eat red meat, either. And now that I'm retired I go three, four weeks at a time without anybody to interrogate. Then you come along, reminding me of my failures."

"That was hardly my intention."

"I know it," he conceded. "All those files in there?" he said, waving his thumb back at the wall of metal cabinets. "Beverly wants me to sit down with her and go through them. Annotate the more interesting cases. 'Put flesh on the bones' is how she puts it. But what she doesn't understand, Lincoln, is that most of what's in those folders is bruised flesh on broken bones."

"Yeah?"

"And here's the thing. If you *could* get to the bottom of this, find the truth about what happened forty-four years ago, that's what you'd likely find. Bruised flesh. Broken bones."

"What are you trying to tell me, Mr. Coffin?"

"I'm telling you to go home, Lincoln. Bounce those grandkids on your knee. Things worked out. Be happy."

Lincoln nodded at the folder that Coffin had put on the coffee table. "There's really nothing you can tell me? Besides what was in the paper?"

Coffin reluctantly took up the folder again. "Okay, here's what I remember. I went out there to your place. State guys asked me to check it out. Course by then you'd all left. The place was locked up tight."

"We usually didn't have renters much before the Fourth of July."

Coffin was studying him intently now. "No neighbors close by."

"Just the Troyers down the hill. They were away at the time, but their son was there. Mason."

"Yeah, I spoke to him."

So Lincoln had been right. He *had* glimpsed the name Troyer in the file. "You did?"

Coffin took off his glasses and set them and the folder on the table. "I gather there was some trouble that weekend?"

"He dropped by, uninvited."

"And what happened?"

"We drank some beer on the deck."

"That's all? Just beer?"

Lincoln shrugged. "It was 1971. There might've been some weed passed around."

"No coke?"

"Of course not. Anyhow, at some point Troyer and Jacy were alone in the kitchen and he tried to get too friendly with her. My friend Mickey walked in on them. Took exception to what he saw."

Coffin nodded. "Took one hell of an exception, I'd say. When I talked to him he still had two black eyes and his jaw was wired shut. He said your friend sucker punched him."

"I was out on the deck with the others when it happened, but knowing Mickey, there probably wasn't much of a conversation."

"Got a temper, then, this friend of yours? Zero to sixty in three point two seconds? That kind of guy?"

"Actually, he's pretty gentle most of the time."

"Most of the time."

"He never would've hurt Jacy, if that's what you're getting at."

Coffin shrugged. "You're the one that knows him."

"Anyway," Lincoln said, "all that happened on Sunday. I don't see the relevance, given that we all left the island on Tuesday."

Putting his glasses back on, he picked up the folder again. "Says here you didn't all leave at the same time, though. How come?"

"Jacy woke up early and snuck out when we were still asleep. Left us a note saying she hated goodbyes. Anyway, the point is she left the island, right? Somebody who worked for the Steamship Authority identified her?"

"I wouldn't call it a positive ID. More like *Yeah, maybe*. When I spoke to the lady, she didn't seem any too sure."

"Are you suggesting Jacy never left here?"

"No, I'm saying it can't be completely ruled out."

"What's your best guess?"

"Well, for what it's worth, the staties were pretty convinced she was on one of those morning ferries. I don't know how they could be, based on that one witness, but they could've had some additional information they didn't share with us locals."

"So it's *possible* something could have happened to her here?"

"It's also possible she was abducted by aliens," Coffin said. "Look at it this way, Lincoln. Either she's alive or she's dead. If she's dead, if somebody *killed* her, what happened to the body? Because for me that's a problem."

Also for the dead girl, Lincoln thought.

"Okay, here's a scenario. You're the killer."

"Me?" Because Lincoln's distinct impression was that his host didn't consider this proposition to be completely outlandish.

"Hypothetical, Lincoln. We're using our imaginations here. You're on the ferry and you spot this good-looking hippie chick. It's the early seventies, so she's going braless. You watch her the whole time, till the ferry docks in Woods Hole. She goes ashore with the other foot passengers, while you go down into the boat to retrieve your vehicle, telling yourself to forget about her. She's just a girl. Except when you drive off the boat, there she is on the Falmouth road with her thumb out. You pull over. Offer her a ride. She gets in. You talk. Maybe you ask her what hippie chicks have got against bras. What's all *that* about? You think you're being witty, but she takes your question seriously. Tells you it's all about freedom, and that pisses you off. *Freedom.* Maybe you're just back from 'Nam. You got married young. Had a couple kids before you could turn around. Who the fuck's *free*? Not you. You work on the island, landscaping or maybe cleaning rich people's pools. Anyway, you work there, but you sure as hell can't afford to live there. No, you live in New Bedford, because that's where people like you live. Summers you make pretty decent money, but it's not cheap bringing your pickup over on the ferry. You work eight, ten days in a row, flop on somebody's couch when you can. You go home for two or three days to look in on the wife and kids, so they can tell you about all the shit they want that you can't afford. If somebody asked you to describe your life, the first word that popped into your head sure as hell wouldn't be *free*. Only a privileged, burn-your-bra hippie chick would use such a stupid word."

Lincoln thought about telling the man he was *way* off base, that he had no idea who Jacy was. He was just making her up as he went, his scenario probably born of all the hippie chicks he himself never got to have sex with. And yet there was something compelling about the tale he was weaving, its gritty specificity. And some of the details were spot-on. Jacy definitely wouldn't have been wearing a bra.

"For a while," Coffin continued, "you behave yourself. You got no choice. Traffic's bumper to bumper till you get over the damn bridge. It's the end of the long holiday weekend, so everybody's trying to get off the Cape at once. Eventually, though, the traffic thins out. You say something, suggest something. Or maybe you reach over and touch her. Anyhow, she spooks. Tells you to pull over, let her the hell out. Like suddenly you smell bad, or she got a better look at you and decided she doesn't like what she sees. Maybe she uses that word again, *freedom,* and now she's demanding her own. Like she's the one in charge. Like she can just choose and you have to do what she says. After you were nice enough to offer her a lift and didn't even ask her for gas money, like you could've done, gas not being *free,* either. Anyway, if she thinks she's the one giving the orders here, you got news for her. That ain't how it works. When you explain this to her, things go bad, then worse. It all happens real quick. Maybe she tries to get out of the truck. Back then, she's probably not wearing a seat belt, so when you jam on the brakes she goes headfirst into the dash or the windshield. Or maybe you hit her with something. Doesn't matter. All of a sudden you've got a dead girl in your cab. Now you've really done it. You've gone and done it. Your mind's on fire, but you put your thoughts in order, or try to. First thing is to get off the busy highway. Find some old country road, then a dirt one you can pull off onto. Find a secluded spot. Drag her into the trees."

"That's one dark imagination you've got, Mr. Coffin," Lincoln said, though in fact his narrative bore some remarkable similarities to the one he himself had entertained earlier in the offices of the *Vineyard Gazette,* with Mason Troyer in the villain's role.

"Yeah, maybe I do, but here's my point, Lincoln. That girl's body gets discovered. If she's just laying there in the trees, some hiker comes across her. You had a shovel in the back of your pickup? You buried her in the soft ground? Doesn't matter, same result. Animals find her after the first heavy rain. Either way, it takes about two minutes for the cops to connect that body to the girl who went missing over Memorial Day weekend."

"So what you're actually saying is that we *can* rule your scenario out?" After all that grim, granular realism? Really?

"No, but it's got problems. Close to insurmountable, seems to me."

"So . . . she's alive?"

Coffin shook his head sadly. "Problems there, too, Lincoln. If she's alive, you have to wonder why in all these years she never once called her folks or her fiancé or any of her friends. If she's out there in the world, didn't she ever run into anybody she knew? How come she never applied for credit cards or a passport or a home loan? How come she didn't fall in love and get married, have some kids, or get divorced. Enter the public record like living people do."

Lincoln sighed deeply. "First you say she can't be dead, now you say she can't be alive."

"I'm not saying she *can't* be either one. I'm saying that no matter what, something doesn't add up. I don't know what happened to her, Lincoln. But I do know this: you guys lucked out."

"*We* lucked out?"

"Motive. Means. Opportunity. Except for when that neighbor stopped by, she was alone with you and your friends that whole weekend. Back then? If *I'm* leading the investigation, I'm thinking it's one of you. One of you did it, and the other two are helping cover it up. Or all three of you did it. If it's me, I'm thinking you spent the weekend trying to talk her out of marrying her fiancé—and getting nowhere. Could be she explains the facts of life, the stuff they didn't teach you at Minerva College in Connecticut. This guy she's gonna marry has money and prospects. You don't. Which isn't what you want to hear. It's not at all how you figured things would go, which was more along the lines of any girl who goes off for a long weekend with three guys must be looking to have a little fun before she gets hitched. Or maybe your friend Mickey decides he deserves a reward for rescuing her in the kitchen. Or it could be he plays the pity card, reminding her he's going off to war and could come home dead. She should at least send him off happy, right? What kind of girl says no to such a request? But no is what she says, and there's that quick temper of his."

"Except that's not what happened," Lincoln said.

Coffin ignored this as if Lincoln hadn't spoken. "At first you panic, because . . . *dead girl*. But gradually you calm down and start thinking straight. You all decide to stick together. You wait till dark to bury her. You talk through what you'll tell the cops. You've got some time before she's reported missing. You? You head west like you planned to with some other girl. Your friends—"

Lincoln had to stop him. "Mr. Coffin," he said. "Please, listen. None of that happened."

"I'm not saying it did, Lincoln. I'm saying that's what I would've been thinking in 1971. And I'll tell you something else. I'd've rented a backhoe and dug up every square inch of that place of yours out in Chilmark. I'd've dug until I knew for a fact that it was the one place on the planet that girl wasn't at."

He finally tossed the folder back on the coffee table, as if he'd been using it as a prop this whole time, and for a minute they both sat there staring at it. Finally Lincoln ventured, "You sound like maybe you still believe that's what happened."

"No, Lincoln, I don't."

Though relieved to hear this, he said, "How come?"

"Because if you *did* have something to do with that girl's disappearance forty-four years ago, you wouldn't be snooping around the *Gazette* this afternoon. You wouldn't have told Beverly that story. And you sure wouldn't have come out here asking a retired cop questions you already knew the answers to. No, I'd say you're mostly in the clear."

Mostly. Lincoln took a deep breath and got stiffly to his feet, feeling like he'd been interrogated with a rubber hose. No wonder people confessed to crimes they didn't commit.

At the door, when they shook hands, it occurred to Lincoln to ask one final thing. "So, did Troyer say anything else when you interviewed him?"

"In fact, he suggested I arrest your friend Mickey for assault. At least that's what I think he was trying to say. With his jaw wired shut, he was kind of hard to understand."

"That was the first time you met him? I ask because I know he's had some run-ins with the law over the years."

"No, Mason and I go way back. We won the Island Cup together, actually."

"The Island Cup?"

"Football. The Vineyard versus Nantucket."

"You were teammates?"

He nodded.

"But . . . the Troyers were summer people."

"True. They lived in Wellesley, I think. Mason got into some kind of trouble junior year. Got a girl pregnant was the rumor. Anyhow, senior year his parents sent him to live with a family here on the island." Now Coffin was the one who looked uncomfortable. "Mason's what kids these days call a real douchebag. But he's no murderer, if that's what you're thinking."

"Sorry, Mr. Coffin, but you sound a little like the woman who worked the snack bar on the ferry. None too sure."

The other man's face darkened again. "Oh, I'm pretty sure, Lincoln. I'm pretty damn sure."

Lincoln had a thought. "You wouldn't happen to remember the name of that island family he lived with that year, would you?"

"I'm not likely to forget," he said. "Their name was Coffin."

Teddy

Theresa answered on the first ring. "Teddy Novak," she said. "As I live and breathe. Hold on while I go outside. The movers are here."

When she came back on the line, he admitted, "I wasn't sure you'd pick up."

"Are you disappointed?" Could it be mirth he detected in her voice? Bitterness? "Were you hoping to just leave a message?"

Bitterness, then. When he didn't immediately respond, she said, "I'm sorry. That wasn't very nice. It's possible I've been nursing a grievance or two."

"That's why I called, as it happens. To apologize."

"Okay, but what for?" More challenge than curiosity in the question.

He chuckled. "Now that *is* sort of unkind."

"Explain."

"Well, how long have we known each other? I've probably messed up any number of times. If I guess wrong about why you're mad at me, I get to keep apologizing."

"Then you better think hard. This is Double Jeopardy, where the questions are harder, the dollar values are doubled and scores can really change."

This was why he'd called her, actually. Not to apologize, though he knew he'd have to. They'd always communicated obliquely, their statements wry codes, and rich with cultural references. She was fun, in other words. "I'll take relationships for two hundred, Alex."

"Art."

"Nah, I know very little about art."

"Art *Fleming*," she clarified. "The original host of *Jeopardy!* Nobody remembers him anymore." She sounded genuinely rueful about this, as if to concede that being forgotten was a destiny shared by most human beings. "What's that sound?"

"The wind." It had picked up enough to blow an empty plastic cup left behind by the Christians off the picnic table and up against the chain-link fence. His shirt, drenched with sweat earlier, was now dry as a bone. He angled himself differently, against the breeze. "Is this any better?"

"A little. Are you still on Nantucket?"

"Martha's Vineyard," he corrected. "Bad idea, as it turns out. This trip."

"How so?"

"Memory lane is vastly overrated. I should've stayed in Syracuse. I could've given you a hand with your move."

She made a loud, rasping noise. "That was Beulah the Buzzer signaling an incorrect response. The movers are doing everything. I'm not lifting a finger. So if *that's* what you called to apologize for, I'll have to dock you."

"Objection, Your Honor. The fact that you don't need me doesn't mean I shouldn't have offered."

"Point taken, but objection overruled. How are your friends? Washington? Mackey?"

"Lincoln and Mickey." He smiled. Clearly she was making these mistakes on purpose; small acts of retribution. "Different. The same."

"Well . . ."

"I wish you weren't leaving," he told her, expecting to hear Beulah the Buzzer again, but instead there was only silence. "I guess what I really called to say is that you deserved more than I was able to give."

"Why, I wonder. I've *been* wondering, actually."

"I can't really explain, except to say that it had nothing to do with you."

"You mean that I'm black?"

"No!" Teddy told her. "Of course not."

"Oh, please. A simple *no* I could accept, but spare me the *of course not*."

"You really think that of me?"

"Well, in the absence of data, imagination has to work overtime," she said. "So if it wasn't me, then what? I mean, I heard the rumors, so—"

"I'm not gay, Theresa."

"I kind of hoped you were, to tell you the truth, because then it really *wouldn't* have been about me."

"No, it was more . . . I don't know . . . call it the habit of a lifetime. I guess I'm risk averse."

"Okay, fine. But when did that start? And where? And why?"

"When? Nineteen seventy-one. Where? Right here. This island." This exact spot, though he wasn't about to go into *that*.

"Which leaves only why."

"You could probably guess."

"Yeah, but I've worn myself out guessing. How about you just tell me?"

He took a deep breath. *This*, of course, was why he'd really called her.

AFTER HE AND JACY RETURNED to Chilmark, Teddy turned off the ignition and they just sat for a minute, listening to the ticking engine cool. When he closed his eyes, he could still feel the strong undertow of the waves, their come-hither pull coaxing him out to sea. Why hadn't he just let them?

Finally Jacy said, "Do the guys know?"

Teddy shook his head. He thought she'd cried herself out on the beach, but he saw now that her eyes were full again.

"Well," she said, "they won't hear it from me."

"No?"

She took his hand. "Of course not."

"I'm not sure I can go in there," he admitted.

"But you can't very well stay out here."

That much was true. "What should I say about . . ."

"About what?"

About us, he wanted to say, but of course that would be wrong. There was no *us* and there never would be. "They'll want to know where we've been."

She wiped her eyes on her sleeve and put on a game face. "How about I do the talking?"

They found Mickey out on the deck, drinking a beer left-handed and flexing the fingers of his swollen right hand.

"Where've you two been?" he said.

"Gay Head," Jacy informed him.

"You went without us?" It was the first time all weekend that they weren't a foursome.

"You were asleep," she reminded him. "Lincoln was on the phone."

"What'd you do there?"

Could he tell they'd been swimming? Teddy wondered. They'd driven back to Chilmark with the windows down. Jacy's hair had been windblown dry. After dressing they'd brushed the sand off their legs and ankles.

"I bought a postcard," she said, taking it out of the back pocket of her cutoffs and showing him. As if it were proof of something. "We had ice cream."

"Did you bring us any?"

"Cones," she explained. "They would've melted."

As Jacy responded to Mickey's questions, Teddy found himself regarding her with new eyes. She wasn't lying, exactly, but her poise was unsettling. Where had she learned to dissemble so convincingly? Had she ever used this talent on *him*? Back at Minerva, had she slipped off with Mickey at some point? Or Lincoln? Was Teddy not first but last to feel her naked body against his? That he should entertain such a possibility, even in passing, filled him with shame and disgust. These, then, were the so-called wages of sin. Having betrayed his friends' trust, he now suspected them of having already betrayed him, the people he knew and loved best suddenly strangers, the old familiar world grown strange, uncertain. He'd written a paper on the effects of sin in one of Tom Ford's classes. At the time it hadn't occurred to him that one day he would know firsthand whereof he spoke.

"Where's Lincoln?" Jacy was saying.

Mickey made a *you have to ask?* face.

Jacy sighed. "Again?"

Mickey shrugged. "Yeah, but seriously. Show of hands. Who here really expects him to end up anything except pussy-whipped?"

Jacy glanced at her watch. "Assuming we're still going to Menemsha, we need to get a move on." For their last evening, they'd planned a cookout. Burgers and brats on the grill, cold potato salad, even some deli-bought cheesecake for after. Schlep it all down to west-facing Menemsha Beach, where they could watch the sun go down.

"I think there's been a change of plan," Mickey told her. "We've only got the one vehicle, and there's no way we get the four of us plus the grill and the charcoal and the beer and the food in that little piece-of-shit Nova."

"We could make two trips," offered Teddy, whose piece of shit the Nova was.

Mickey shrugged again. "Talk to Lincoln."

"I thought the whole idea was to watch the sunset," Jacy said.

"Watch it from here," Mickey said.

"Right," Jacy said, gesturing toward the horizon. "The sun might set in the south tonight. It doesn't usually, but who knows?"

"If you're going inside," Mickey said, when Teddy took a step in that direction, "grab me another cold one. And put some music on."

Inside, Teddy could hear Lincoln's voice, muted, through his closed bedroom door, but otherwise it was quiet. It came to him then that he could just walk out the front door, get into his piece-of-shit Nova and drive away. Onto the ferry in Vineyard Haven and off the island. After this weekend, what was the likelihood that he'd ever see any of these people again?

Instead, he put on some Crosby, Stills & Nash, something that under normal circumstances Mickey would never permit. If you went near the stereo, he'd say, "Get away from there before you hurt yourself."

Grabbing three beers from the fridge, he returned to the deck, where Jacy was trying to get Mickey to let her look at his hand. "Git," he told her, hiding it under his armpit. "Away. From me."

"It's broken, Mickey."

"It's fine."

"It's not fine," she said. "Let's go to the hospital and get an x-ray."

"Jace," he said. "It's fine. Leave it alone, okay?"

"All right, be like that," she told him. "I'm gonna go inside and write my postcard. Let me know when you *men* have decided how everything's going to happen."

When the door slid closed behind her, Mickey raised a questioning eyebrow. "What's the matter with her?"

"*Us* is my impression," Teddy said, recalling what she'd said earlier about everything being fucked up. "Men. We ignore women when they're right and we start wars and generally screw things up."

"We are as God made us," Mickey replied, draining the last of his beer. "I'll take one of those, unless you plan to drink all three."

Teddy, who'd forgotten he was holding them, handed one over.

"Mind twisting off the cap?"

Teddy did, and Mickey took it. "You okay?"

"Yeah, why?"

"You look funny. You're *acting* funny."

"She's right, you know," Teddy said, anxious to change the subject. "You should get that x-rayed."

"I will," he said, flexing his fingers again and wincing, "*but . . .*"

"But what?"

Here he met and held Teddy's eye. "But it's *my* decision. Not hers. Not yours."

"Are we still talking about your hand?"

"No, I guess we're not," he admitted. When they'd met his ferry on Friday evening, the first words out of his mouth had been, "We're not going to talk about it, hear me? The fucking war isn't going to ruin our last weekend together."

They'd reluctantly agreed, but the war had put a damper on things anyway, or so it seemed to Teddy. Sure, they'd enjoyed one another's company—gone to the beach and into Edgartown for lunch and strolled through the Camp Meeting Ground in Oak Bluffs, imagining a day when they might all invest in one of its gingerbread cottages. They'd studiously avoided the evening news and kept their conversations light, but Vietnam seemed to hover in every silence. Unless Teddy was mistaken, it had added velocity and torque to the blow that had lifted Mason Troyer off his feet. And if that was true, then what was Mickey's grotesquely swollen hand but another manifestation of that misbegotten conflict? The injury, sustained in a minor hostility, in idyllic Chilmark, no less, brought into focus the specter of far greater, perhaps even fatal, injury in a genuine war zone. Though he hated to admit it, even to himself, it might also have been the war that drove Jacy out of the arms of her hawkish boyfriend and into Teddy's that afternoon.

They sat quietly for a while, until Mickey said, "You and Jacy?"

Teddy immediately felt faint. But, *If he asks*, he thought, *why not tell him?* What difference could it possibly make now?

But no, Mickey's mind was apparently elsewhere. "You both need to be more like Lincoln," he said. "Whatever I decide, and whatever happens as a result of that decision, is on me, not you. He's figured that out. You two haven't."

"Whatever happened to all for one and one for all?" The question, of course, was one Teddy might well have asked himself. At Gay Head, when it seemed that Jacy might be his and his alone, he'd forsworn *all for one* without blinking.

Mickey sighed. "There is no all. Just millions of ones."

WORRIED THAT the crushing disappointment of Gay Head might trigger one of his spells, Teddy had decided on a brisk walk before dinner. The exercise wouldn't prevent an episode, but it might delay its arrival and thereby allow him to get through the evening. If he woke up in the middle of the night in a flop sweat, he could curl up into the fetal position and ride it out. No one would have to know, and by morning the worst would be over. And it would explain what Mickey had seen as his "funny" behavior after returning from Gay Head. As he hiked among Chilmark's rolling hills, however, his spirits, already at low ebb, plummeted even deeper. It came to him that the whole weekend had been a mistake, a misguided attempt to preserve something already lost. Clearly the friendship that had served them all so well had played itself out. When they graduated from Minerva, they'd somehow, without meaning to, graduated from one another. Maybe, he told himself, it was just as well. At least the evening wouldn't become maudlin. Thank God for Mickey in this respect. He would never permit straightforward testimonials or unironic declarations of affection. For him, simply that they'd come together for one last weekend spoke volumes. Perhaps because Teddy was born of parents who made their living talking, he'd never really understood the peculiarly male conviction that silence conveyed one's feelings better than anything else, but maybe tonight it would. *Get through the evening*, he commanded himself. That was what mattered. Tomorrow they would all board the ferry and go their separate ways and that would be that. They all, he felt certain, were feeling the same way.

But evidently not. Returning from his walk, Teddy was surprised to discover that his friends' spirits had markedly improved. Lincoln had finally emerged from his room and confessed to what they'd suspected was true: Anita hadn't wanted him to spend the weekend with them on the island. Now that it was nearly over, though, she'd relented, not only forgiving him but even telling him to enjoy himself on their last night together. After an hour alone in her room,

Jacy also seemed to be in a better mood. She apologized to Mickey for being so pissy earlier, an apology he accepted by giving her a hug and promising to have his hand checked out as soon as he got home. Then, their fellowship restored, he ordered "Tedioski" to "Please, for the love of God, put some real fucking music on." By which he meant Creedence. All weekend long they'd been listening to "Suzie Q" on a seemingly endless loop, Fogerty's distorted guitar solo overstaying its welcome, but Teddy put it on again and they all got to work. While Lincoln fired up the grill, Mickey stocked the Igloo full of cold beer and dragged it out onto the deck with his good hand so they wouldn't have to keep running back and forth to the fridge. Jacy set the picnic table and Teddy opened a bag of potato chips and some onion dip to tide them over until the real food came. At one point, when Mickey went inside to pee and Lincoln was busy flipping burgers, Jacy came over and gave Teddy's shoulder a squeeze. "Try to have a good time, okay? Our last night?" she said, and something about her tone suggested that would be heavy lifting for her as well.

Then after they ate and ferried the dirty dishes inside, everyone seemed content to sit on the deck as darkness descended, the music on low, talking quietly about things that didn't matter—those that did being off-limits, as they had been all weekend. Teddy, who'd eaten little, could feel the salutary effects of his long walk begin to dissipate. Whatever this part of their lives had been about, it was all but over. There would be no debriefing, no attempts to articulate what they'd meant to one another these last four years. He kept hoping that Jacy would let Lincoln and Mickey in on her change of heart regarding the wedding, because *that* would've been worth celebrating. But she said nothing, causing Teddy to wonder if she'd changed her mind back again. And if he himself, or rather her disappointment in him, was why.

At some point in the evening the wind shifted, and though the beach was a good half mile away, they could hear the surf pounding, and when the moon rose out of the waves, it was suddenly, for Teddy at least, all too much. Going inside, he closed the bathroom door and studied his face in the mirror to see if the desolation and hopelessness he was feeling might be written there. Was it obvious to his friends that after tonight he had little real interest in what lay ahead? Probably Lincoln and Mickey were questioning Jacy right now, wanting to know if something "funny" had happened out at Gay Head. She'd probably tell them that he was just down in the dumps, that of the four of them he was the only one at loose ends. Lincoln was heading west with Anita. Mickey would be reporting for boot camp. She herself was getting married. Yes, Teddy was thinking about divinity school after his internship at the *Globe*, but only because he couldn't think of what else to do. Ever the general-ist, his major, weeks *after* graduation, remained undecided.

There was also the possibility that, despite promising not to, she was telling them everything. She wouldn't do it to hurt him, he knew, but rather because they were all friends who, if they knew, maybe could help. They couldn't, of course. Nobody could.

By the time he returned to the deck—how long had he been gone?—the temperature had dropped and Lincoln had ducked inside for sweaters and sweatshirts. They paid Teddy no special attention, which he assumed meant Jacy had kept her promise. The music had stopped playing, but she and Mickey were slow dancing in the middle of the deck. "Chances are," Mickey crooned, " 'cause I wear a silly grin, the moment you come into view. Chances are you think that I'm in love with you."

"Fine," Lincoln chuckled good-naturedly. "Have fun at my expense."

Jacy evidently took this as permission to join in. "Just because," she warbled drunkenly, "my composure sort of slips the moment that your lips meet mine. Chances are you think my heart's your valentine."

As Teddy passed by, Jacy grabbed him by the elbow, determined, despite his protests that he didn't know the words, that he would sing along with them, leaving Lincoln with little choice but to join in as well. How many verses did they sing? Teddy lost track, but at some point it occurred to him that Mickey no longer was making fun of Johnny Mathis. Indeed, he was singing the song as if he'd penned the schmaltzy lyrics himself and couldn't be prouder of them. As they all grew more confident of the lyrics, they turned, arm in arm, and serenaded the night itself, the moonlight rippling on the distant ocean. They sang as if they were still all for one and one for all and would be so forever. To his astonishment, Teddy felt his own heavy burden begin to lift, at least a little. Maybe, he thought, if they just sang loud enough, everything would be okay after all. Mickey would somehow return from Vietnam unharmed. Lincoln's service would not be required. Jacy would marry her fiancé or she wouldn't, but she would remain always their fourth Musketeer. And Teddy himself? For no good reason, he suddenly felt hopeful. Because there *was* magic in the world. Just that afternoon a girl he'd been in love with throughout college had chosen him. *Him.* And what was that if not magic? Why abandon hope in the face of possibility?

There on the deck, pleasantly drunk, they seemed to have found something they each could agree on: that *chances were their chances were . . . awfully good.* Whether the sentiment was true or—like the world they were taking possession of—a bright, shining lie seemed, right then, beside the point.

THE NEXT MORNING the sun was barely up when Teddy, lying awake on the living room couch, heard Jacy stirring in her bedroom. When her door squeaked open and she emerged on tiptoe, fully dressed, her pack slung over her shoulder, he realized that she meant to slip away without saying goodbye. This was confirmed when she placed a note in the center of the dining room table where they couldn't fail to see it.

Only when the front door closed behind her did he stand and go over to the window to watch her make her way up the gravel drive. How brave she looked under her backpack. How beautiful.

Poor girl. She'd cried her heart out yesterday when he talked about the afternoon in the gym when he'd gone up for that rebound and Nelson, his burly teammate, had undercut him. How his tail-bone had been the first thing to hit the hardwood court, the impact paralyzing him so completely that at first he'd felt no pain, only shock. How he'd been taken to the emergency room in an ambulance, unable to feel his legs, though by the time they arrived there some sensation had returned and he could wiggle his toes. According to the ER doctors, this was a good sign, as was the nauseating pain, which led to vomiting and later, long after his stomach was empty, dry heaves. He'd been kept overnight for observation but sent home the next morning in a brace, told that he was young and strong and all he needed was rest for the hairline fracture to heal. In no time he'd be good as new. Though there was one thing to keep an eye out for, a doctor had warned, almost as an afterthought. While it was unlikely, spinal injuries could be tricky. Teddy, at sixteen, hadn't really known what *erectile dysfunction* meant, but he'd instinctively grasped what he was "to keep an eye out for," and that this oh-by-the-way afterthought was anything but.

Yesterday, with Jacy sobbing in his arms, he'd wanted more than anything to comfort her, to convince her that even though his chances weren't awfully good, neither were his circumstances hopeless. Normal function, he told her, was sometimes restored even years after the injury. No need to mention that with each passing year that possibility became less likely, not more. Nor did he tell her that right from the start he'd somehow known that he wouldn't be one of the lucky ones, that how he was at present—able to ejaculate but not to engage in intercourse, able to fall deeply in love but not to express it—was how he would remain.

"I've gotten used to it, actually," he assured her. "It was a mistake to get my hopes up. I just thought that, with you, maybe . . ."

Which made her cry even harder. "Anyway, it could be worse, right?" he continued, knowing full well that he was about to say something truly horrible, something that would haunt him forever. "I could be headed for Vietnam."

Forty-four years later, high above the beach where he'd spoken those words, sharing the whole sad story with Theresa, he still couldn't fully fathom what had possessed him, or even what he'd meant to say. There were days when he could almost absolve himself for uttering the words. Surely he'd meant only that, on the night of the lottery, he'd been fortunate to draw a number that would spare him from that danger. And really, that was about all the good fortune boys of his generation had any right to expect. Yet it sometimes felt as if he'd made an unwitting bargain with God: Give me a high number tonight and I'll never ask you for anything else. Because *that* would explain the trade-off he was now being asked to accept—his happiness for his life. Things could always be worse. He could be headed to Vietnam.

But by asserting that things could've been worse for himself, wasn't he also saying that they definitely *were* worse for his friends? For Mickey and, yes, possibly for Lincoln? Had Jacy heard in the statement some bitter satisfaction? That if *he* couldn't be a man, there was comfort to be taken from knowing that his friends—men who could not only love but also express love—might have to pay an even-bigger price? That if he couldn't have Jacy, then at least they wouldn't, either? Was *that* what she'd heard? Was that what he'd *meant*?

As he watched her make her way up the drive, he couldn't help feeling that it wasn't so much Jacy departing as life itself, and that he had it coming.

He was still staring out the window when Lincoln appeared in his bedroom doorway, wearing gym shorts and an old Minerva College T-shirt, scratching his chin thoughtfully. "She's gone?" he said.

Teddy nodded. "There's a note."

Lincoln read it, first to himself, then out loud: *No goodbyes. I couldn't bear it.* "Well," he said. "That's that, then."

Why had they let her go like that? he wondered after saying goodbye to Theresa, another woman he'd managed to disappoint profoundly. Why hadn't they rousted Mickey and gone after her. There was a breakfast place near the ferry terminal where they could've dispatched their hangovers with scrambled eggs and home fries and coffee, then put her on the ferry and waved goodbye as the boat departed. Wasn't that what good friends would do?

Except that, as her fiancé would later allege, they *weren't* good friends, or weren't *just* good friends. Her note made clear that she was leaving them collectively, three young men on the cusp of adulthood. The reason they hadn't gone after her was that they saw it differently. They'd *begun* seeing things differently back in 1969, in the Theta house's hasher room, where on a small TV they'd learned just how alone they really were in the world. They'd entered that room all in the same loud, raucous boat only to drift away silent and solitary, envy and fear making it impossible for them to look one another in the eye. No, the love they bore Jacy was not communal but individual. She wasn't leaving her Musketeers collectively, but rather individually—Athos, Porthos, Aramis.

Forever, as it turned out.

Lincoln

There was a Wi-Fi router at the house, but Lincoln wouldn't be able to discover the password until Monday morning, when the management company opened. Out in Chilmark he'd have one bar of reception at best, so he decided to check his e-mail in the Tisbury Village parking lot before heading back. In addition to the usual crap—relentless appeals for funds from organizations he'd already unsubscribed from multiple times, inducements to travel *(Secret prices, Lincoln, just for you!)*, the usual clickbait *(You Won't Believe What Happens Next)*—a couple agents in his office were looking for advice on transactions. Nothing that Andrea, his office manager, couldn't have dealt with, except that the agents in question, both men, had coveted her position and were now showing their displeasure by doing end runs around her. While he was tapping out curt responses, a text message from Anita came in: *Arrived Dunbar. Guess who's still full of beans? You owe me, buster.* He texted back: *I know. I know. The guys say hey.* When he pressed SEND, the phone vibrated in his hand, an incoming call this time, another local number.

"Lincoln? It's Marty calling." Ah, his realtor. "Look, I was doing some research on your place and came across something interesting. Are you in Chilmark?"

"Vineyard Haven. Just about to drive out there, though."

"Want to swing by before you do?"

"Why not?"

Before he turned his key in the ignition, Joe Coffin emerged from his apartment, went down the stairs and made his way across the parking lot to a battered old gray pickup, the vehicular equivalent of its apparent owner. "You don't drive anymore, Joe," Lincoln said out loud to himself as the other man unlocked the door and climbed in. "You told me so yourself." Which suggested that he was either going someplace urgently or to a place he didn't want Beverly, his usual chauffeur, to take him. Lincoln watched as the truck shuddered to life and backed out of its space. When Coffin hung a left onto the Edgartown–Vineyard Haven Road, Lincoln started up his rental car and put it in gear. Leaving the lot, he also turned left, telling himself that he was just heading into Edgartown as promised, not *following* anybody, though he took care to remain several car lengths back. Up ahead was a convenience market and Lincoln half expected the pickup to turn in. Having offered his unexpected guest coffee, maybe Coffin had run out of milk or something. Maybe he didn't consider running a quick errand as *driving*. But no, the pickup sailed right on by. Katama, then? To see if his favorite hawk in that photo was perched on its accustomed telephone wire? Had he somehow gotten it into his head that he might not make it off the operating table, and wanted to see the bird one last time before his surname proved prophetic? Coffin hadn't seemed all that concerned about his upcoming surgery, but neither did he come across as the sort of man to let on if he was.

As they approached the Barnes Road rotary, Lincoln slowed, grateful for the two cars between him and Coffin. The last thing he wanted was to get spotted in the guy's rearview. What would his suspicious cop's brain make of that? Lincoln figured the man would go halfway around the circle and stay on the Edgartown Road, or else take the next turn into Oak Bluffs. But again Coffin surprised him by taking the first exit off the rotary, the route you'd take to the airport.

Or to Chilmark. Lincoln suppressed a shiver. Was he headed up island to warn Troyer that someone was sniffing around about Jacy's disappearance? Strange, now that he thought about it, that Coffin hadn't come clean about their relationship—that they'd nearly grown up together—until Lincoln pressed him.

There was another reason he might be going to Chilmark, though, and it was even more unsettling. Did Coffin, like his imaginary rapist, have a shovel in the back of the truck? Was he headed not to Troyer's place but to Lincoln's, intent on excavating the yard? *Don't be ridiculous,* he told himself. An old man with a shovel and no idea where on Lincoln's *two acres* to dig? But the more important question was why Lincoln's thoughts were racing toward such bizarre conclusions. After all, it was a big island with plenty of places Coffin could be heading. Still, entering the rotary himself, it was all Lincoln could do not to blow off his meeting with Marty, follow the old cop and *know* where he was going.

Because admit it, ever since setting foot on the Vineyard, guilt or something akin to it had been his more or less constant companion. He'd assumed its source was the decision to put his mother's house on the market, but what if it was something else? Earlier, in the dark microfilm room at the *Vineyard Gazette,* when Jacy's face appeared on the screen this ambient sense of guilt had morphed into something more like dread; and later, after he'd explained the disappearance and Beverly concluded that Jacy was still on the island, his stomach had done a somersault. Whatever this was about, it was more than real estate. He'd gone to Coffin's apartment hoping he might alleviate his growing apprehensions, and in a way the old cop's vivid scenario of Jacy being stalked, raped, killed and buried somewhere on the mainland had been strangely comforting, because if she'd died after leaving the island, then he and his friends were off the hook. Whereas if something happened to her here, they were, in a sense, complicit. Okay, sure, it was *beyond* ridiculous to imagine that Jacy lay buried in the backyard of the house he was now, over forty years later, putting up for sale. Why, then, was its symmetry so compelling?

Halfway to Edgartown, he pulled off to the side of the road.

He was able to hold off until several other vehicles were safely past before vomiting his Bloody Mary into the ditch.

"MINT?" Lincoln offered.

Instead of going directly to Marty's office, he'd stopped to buy a large roll of them and a package of Wet Wipes, having managed to splash his loafers. Had Anita been along, this errand would've been unnecessary. Being a woman, she always carried both mints and wipes in her purse. *Not* being a woman, he had no idea why they would imagine that at some point during the day you just might, for example, vomit onto your shoes and need them.

"You okay?" Marty said, studying him thoughtfully as he crunched his mint. "You look a little pale."

"I'm fine," Lincoln said to him. "What's up?"

"Come around the desk and take a gander at this tax map. This is you here," he explained, running his finger over Lincoln's property. "And this is our friend Troyer. These other two lots"—he penciled *X*s onto them—"also belong to him. Probably to keep anybody from ruining his water view. And at some point either his parents or the previous owners also owned *this* lot." He marked another *X* there as well. "But they sold it."

"So he owns all this now?"

"Correct."

"Lucky him."

"Except for one thing." Here Marty indicated the dirt road that led to Lincoln's house, then snaked down the hill to Troyer's, where it dead-ended. "This is the only way for him to get home from the main road."

"Does he need another?"

"He wouldn't if he had an easement, but guess what? He doesn't."

Lincoln shook his head. "How can that be?"

"I don't know, but I just came from the Dukes County Registry and there's no mention of one on either your deed or his."

"Again, how could that happen?"

Marty leaned back in his chair, hands laced behind his head. "Hard to say. Possibly an unspoken neighborly agreement going back as far as anybody can remember, and the issue's never come up because neither property ever went on the market. It happens. You say your place was in your mother's family for some time?"

"I don't know exactly how long, but yeah."

"The other possibility is that the lot they sold off was where the easement used to be, and at the time of the sale nobody caught it. Whatever the reason, he certainly doesn't have one now."

"And you think he knows this?"

"It could explain why he's been so keen to buy your property."

Lincoln nodded. "But not why he keeps coming at us with low-ball offers."

"Maybe he doesn't want to tip his hand?"

"I don't know, Marty. Are you positive about all this?"

"Nope, but I can go back down to the registry of deeds and poke around some more. Though there's a chance he may get wind of it if I do."

"Are you saying we shouldn't?"

"On the contrary, I think we have to. Due diligence and all that. I only mention it because I gather you're not terribly fond of each other."

"I'll only be on island another four or five days."

"How about I hold off until you're safely back in Vegas?"

"That might be best," Lincoln said, although now that his curiosity was roused, he wanted clarity.

"But you catch my drift?" Marty asked, rolling up the map. "Whether you like him or not, Mason Troyer's your ideal buyer. He doesn't just *want* to buy your place. He *needs* to."

Teddy

eddy returned from Gay Head both physically exhausted from the long bike ride and emotionally spent from his conversation with Theresa. Unburdening himself to her was painful, though not as devastating as it had been with Jacy a lifetime ago, perhaps because he wasn't that kid anymore, but also because Theresa hadn't reacted as he'd anticipated. With kindness, yes, because that was her nature, but he'd also expected intrusive curiosity *(When was the last time you saw a specialist? Have you tried Viagra?)* and maybe even pushback *(But there were things we could've . . .)*. Instead she'd waited patiently until he was finished and then said only that she wished he'd somehow found it in himself to trust her. By behaving as if the only way for souls to touch was through muscle and tissue and blood, he'd denied them both the intimacy of sharing, honesty and understanding. When he began explaining that he'd been trying to protect her from profound disappointment, she said, "Sorry. Too late."

When Teddy climbed off the bike and put it back in the shed, Mickey's Harley was lying right where it tipped over that morning. He half expected to find him still snoring on the sofa, but instead he was outside on the deck talking on his cell. The sliding glass door was shut, but not completely. "I haven't forgotten," Teddy heard him say. "I know you need the money." Catching sight of him inside, Mickey waved, then turned his back and continued, his voice lowered.

Not wanting to eavesdrop, Teddy sat down at the kitchen table and took out his own phone. He'd noticed a Trump sign in Troyer's front yard when he rode by and wondered if Lincoln had seen it. Probably not, since it wasn't visible from the deck. *Care to guess*, he texted, *which (need I say) Republican candidate your friendly neighbor supports?*

Mickey's voice, louder now, was audible again. "I don't know what to tell you, Delia, except I'll be back on Monday and we can talk about it then. Okay?"

Delia? Teddy thought. They hadn't heard about any Delia, had they? Was it possible Mickey had married again and never told them? Well, it'd be just like him. He'd gotten married twice before in spur-of-the-moment civil ceremonies, though Teddy and Lincoln hadn't heard about either union until the divorces were final. "I need to stop meeting girls in bars" was the only explanation he'd offered. To which Lincoln replied, "Where else do you go?"

Mickey'd conceded, "See, that's the thing."

When Teddy joined him out on the deck, Mickey was glaring at his phone as if he was considering giving it a good, long toss, then said, "Do you have any reception out here?"

"One bar."

Disgusted, Mickey stuffed the cell in his pocket. "That's what I had until I lost it."

"Everything okay?"

"More or less," he said. "You know, I figured by the time I was sixty-six I'd have my own dedicated barstool somewhere and be paying for my beer with social security."

"You're not on social security?"

"I am, but it's a funny thing. If you don't put much of anything in, you can't take much of anything out. Who knew?"

"Everybody?"

Mickey shrugged, looked around. "Where's Lincoln? I woke up and everybody was gone."

"He drove into town for some reason. I took a bike ride."

"I was thinking about running into town myself. Some guy in Oak Bluffs has a Beatles-era Rickenbacker for sale. Cherry condition. Thought I'd check it out. Want to come along?"

"Nah, I need a shower, and after that I've got some stuff to do."

"You guys both work way too hard," Mickey said. "It's unnatural. Unhealthy. Un-American."

"In fact," Teddy said, "studies have shown Americans put in longer hours than anybody and take fewer vacations."

"I don't see how that can be true," Mickey replied. "Half the people I know are on disability and don't work at all. The other half are musicians. Anyway, no work this evening, either one of you. Tonight we eat barbecue, drink beer and listen to rock and roll played at a very high volume."

After he left, Teddy had a long shower, then put on fresh jeans and a T-shirt and took his manuscript back out onto the deck. He realized after marking up a few pages that they'd actually captured his interest, and rereading the ones he'd edited on the ferry yesterday he found that they, too, were better than he remembered. Which maybe shouldn't have come as a surprise. He knew from experience that in the run-up to his spells, his judgment was dubious. Food he normally enjoyed tasted off. Movies seemed vacuous, music grating. Was it possible that confiding in Theresa had somehow forestalled the attack he'd assumed was right around the corner? Had the truth set him free? Could a truism really be true?

His phone vibrated, Lincoln texting back: *Make America White Again? See you soon.* Teddy smiled. Though Lincoln was a lifelong Republican, their politics probably aligned more closely now than ever before, though in the voting booth they'd likely tick their preferred boxes.

At some point, working on the manuscript with renewed interest, he became aware of loud voices down at Troyer's place. An argument between him and the perpetually naked girlfriend was his first thought, but no, unless he was mistaken, both voices were male. An old gray pickup truck that hadn't been there before now sat in the drive.

THROUGHOUT THE WOOLLY, disjointed narrative there was a flapping sound, like wings, that Teddy couldn't account for. Identifying its source seemed urgent, though he couldn't imagine why it should be. Hearing heavy, actual footfalls on the stairs, he swam toward consciousness, grateful it was only a dream and he could stop trying to figure out what was flapping. Rotating in his deck chair, he started to apologize to Lincoln for napping in the middle of the afternoon when he saw that the man lumbering up the steps was instead a beefy, red-faced guy wearing cargo shorts, flip-flops and no shirt. From the top step, Troyer cocked his head and squinted at him for a long, insolent beat and then, pleased with himself, said, "*I* remember you," as if by doing so he'd qualified for a prize.

The gentle breeze that had sprung up before Teddy drifted off had apparently strengthened while he dozed, and a sheet of manuscript magically leaped out of its cardboard box and took flight—the sound of it identical to the one in his dream. Troyer, who could've snatched the page floating by, watched it sail past, unconcerned. And Teddy, rising from his chair, saw to his horror that the deck was littered with sheets of manuscript. So, less densely, was the sloping lawn below. The box, nearly full when he'd fallen asleep, was now half empty.

"I'd help you chase those all over Chilmark," Troyer told him, "if I wanted to look like an idiot."

Because he had another copy of the manuscript back home, Teddy himself was momentarily inclined to let those pages go. Chasing them around the yard, as Troyer looked on, would be humiliating. Unfortunately, many of them had been edited, and to do it all over again would take more hours than Teddy wanted to count up, so off he raced. On the lawn below he found himself in a Charlie Chaplin movie. Every time he bent over to pick up a page, it danced away on a fresh gust. "This is wonderful!" Troyer called from the deck. He was, Teddy saw, filming the whole thing with his phone.

Give the man this much credit, though. By the time Teddy returned to the deck, having recaptured maybe seventy-five pages of text, Troyer had picked up the ones lying on the floor and put them back in the cardboard box and secured them with a stone. He was now stretched out on the chaise lounge, reading a page Teddy had just edited and chortling nastily. "You *wrote* this?"

"No," Teddy said, holding out his hand for it.

"Thank Christ," Troyer said, passing him the page. "I mean, how bored would a man have to be to commit thoughts like this to paper?"

Teddy put the page on top of the others in the box. Later, he'd have to put them all back in order, see how many were missing and re-edit those. "It's a book I'm going to publish later this year, actually."

Troyer studied him for a long beat, his brow knit. "Why?"

Since this was a question Teddy had been asking himself, he couldn't help smiling.

"Okay," Troyer said, scratching his hairy, sunburned chest, "then answer me this. Because I'm having a hard time wrapping my mind around it. You're the same three guys from before, right? You and Moser and the big guy?"

"If by *before* you mean 1971, then yeah."

"What, you've been, like, *roommates* this whole fucking time?"

"Hardly," Teddy said.

"Because *that* would be truly pathetic."

Indeed, the notion, even after Teddy had disabused him of it, seemed to fill him with profound disgust, as if enduring friendship were both unnatural and vile. What unsettled Teddy even more was that this man, though he bore little resemblance to the person Teddy remembered from '71, inspired the same visceral loathing. "Lincoln's not here," he said. "I assume he's the one you're looking for."

Troyer leaned back on the chaise and locked his fingers behind his head, as if settling in for what remained of the afternoon. *"Lincoln,"* he repeated. "Why would a white man name his kid Lincoln?"

Teddy resisted the impulse to tell him that the white man who'd done it was himself named Wolfgang Amadeus. "Maybe because he hoped his son was destined for greatness? That he might even grow up to be president?"

Troyer snorted. "And get shot in the head?"

"This being America, there's a decent chance he'll get shot no matter what he's called."

Troyer groaned, looking skyward. "It must be summer," he said. "The libs are returning. And speaking of liberals, remind me. What's the name of that college all you guys went to?"

"Minerva."

"That's right, *Minerva.* Jesus."

Evidently, for him Minerva College ranked right up there with enduring friendship.

"Is there something I can *do* for you?" Teddy said.

The man scowled. "Yeah. You can tell President Lincoln that he can take this place of his"—he threw his arms out wide open—"and shove it right the fuck up his ass. Tell him I don't need him or it. Can you remember all that?"

Teddy nodded. "Got it. You're no longer interested in purchasing his property. You wish him luck finding another buyer."

Troyer, sitting up now, ignored this. "This next part is even more important. Tell him I had nothing to do with that hippie chick going missing."

Teddy felt his head jerk back, as if from a good, stiff jab, and he swallowed hard. "Are you talking about Jacy?"

"Whatever the fuck her name was. The last time I saw her was the day the big galoot sucker punched me. You know I had to go to Boston to get my fucking jaw wired shut?"

"Gee," Teddy said, "that must've been unpleasant."

"Yeah, you could say that. For a month I ate my meals through a straw."

"Well, you had it coming," Teddy reminded him. "Also, it happened over forty years ago."

"Okay, but here's the thing. You know where I've been that whole time? Right here. See, I don't *visit* this island, I fucking *live* here. And I don't need some Vegas dickweed spreading rumors about me."

"What rumors?"

"The fucking guy *Googles* me? Digs up some twenty-year-old court appearance? Finds out that some Beacon Hill twat took out a restraining order against me after I slapped her big fat mouth for her outside the Edgartown Yacht Club? And decides he *knows* me? Like that gives him the right to wonder out loud if this Jacy girl from the fucking seventies maybe's buried somewhere out here?"

"Question," Teddy said. "Is Lincoln going to have *any* idea what you're talking about?"

If Troyer heard this question, he gave no sign. "Okay, so I copped a feel that day. She had great tits, that I do remember. But we were all what? Twenty? Twenty-one? And you come here in *twenty fucking fifteen* and accuse me?"

"I'm not accusing you of anything," Teddy said. "And I doubt Lincoln is, either."

Troyer got to his feet now and came over to where Teddy sat, looming over him. "Then why the fuck is Joey Coffin knocking on my door and asking me a bunch of bullshit questions?"

"Who's Joey Coffin?"

"You know what?" Troyer said, his face flushing now. "Fuck you. Fuck all three of you."

"Troyer. Who is Joey Coffin?"

"A *cop's* who he is. A retired ex-cop with time on his hands that thanks to your pal is now trying to decide if I'm his new hobby."

"I don't think—"

"I don't give even a tiny little shit what you think," Troyer snapped. "Or *Lincoln*, either. Just tell him the next time he opens his mouth, my name better not come out of it. He doesn't fuckin' know me. *Google* doesn't know me. *Chilmark* doesn't know me. The summer people think I'm an asshole? Good. I *love* that. I'm not politically correct and that rubs them the wrong way? I fucking *live* for that. With enemies like them, who needs friends? But tell your pal Lincoln I *do* have friends. In fact, tell him Joey Coffin and I go back even farther than you three assholes."

"Are we done here?" Teddy said.

Troyer had moved over to the stairs and was about to leave, but now spun back around.

"No, come to think of it, there's one more fucking thing. Tell your friend if he *really* wants to know what happened to that girl, he should be asking the big guy, not me."

Teddy blinked. "You mean Mickey? You're out of your mind. He was in love with her." He was about to add *We all were* when Troyer again broke into his nasty chortle.

"Right," he said. "Like nobody in the history of the fucking world ever killed a girl he was in love with."

Then he lumbered noisily down the steps and across the sloping lawn, his stiff, awkward gait that of a man approaching old age at a gallop, his body breaking down all at once. Stepping over the low stone wall that marked his boundary, he spotted something and bent over to pick it up—a manuscript page that had escaped Teddy's notice. "Minerva College?" he called up to him, wadding the paper into a ball. "What a fucking joke."

Lincoln

S o," said Lincoln, trying hard to process what Teddy had just finished telling him, the gist being that (1) Mason Troyer was no longer interested in purchasing his house and (2) he'd had nothing to do with Jacy's disappearance. Lincoln couldn't decide which of these pronouncements was more unexpected. After all, twenty minutes ago Marty had informed him that the man *needed* to buy the property. Was it possible he was wrong and Troyer knew nothing of the easement issue? Even more mind-boggling was that he'd denied involvement in a crime Lincoln hadn't actually accused him of. "He just appeared on the deck? No warning?"

"He might've thought I was you," Teddy said.

Lincoln shook his head. "He knows me on sight."

"Yeah, but my back was to him as he came up the lawn. You should've seen the look on his face when he recognized me from 1971."

"And he just started in on you?"

"Yep. He seemed to think I'd know what he was talking about."

Lincoln went over to the sliding screen door but didn't go outside. If Troyer saw he'd returned, he might come charging back up the hill. "Did he threaten you?"

"Not really," Teddy said. "He was seriously pissed off, but more than anything he seemed to be blowing off steam. For some reason, the fact that we all went to Minerva really set him off. Like he applied there and didn't get in, so we were looking down on him."

Lincoln nodded, recalling that Coffin had exhibited a similar class resentment.

"He strikes me as one of those people who's always ginned up about something," Teddy continued. "He's also got it in for the summer people who apparently shun him for not sharing their lordly liberalism."

The late-model Mercedes that usually sat in the driveway— Troyer's, Lincoln assumed—was now the only vehicle there. "This visitor? You say he was driving an old pickup?"

"There was some sort of argument, I think. Too far away for me to make out what they were saying."

So, Lincoln thought, his earlier intuition at the rotary had been right. "And Troyer actually brought up Jacy? By name?"

Teddy shook his head. "No, he called her 'that hippie chick,' but it was definitely Jacy he was talking about. Where in the world did he get the idea you thought *he* was involved?"

Lincoln collapsed onto the sofa, stared up at the ceiling and said, "Shit." Feeling he had little choice, he gave Teddy a condensed version of how Marty had gotten the ball rolling by suggesting that Troyer might be trouble. How yesterday evening, Google had revealed that he had a history of harassing women. How all that had sent him to the *Vineyard Gazette* to look for details about the investigation in '71. And finally how Beverly, at the mention of Troyer's name, had recommended he talk with this retired cop named Joe Coffin.

"Oh, that's the other thing Troyer wanted me to tell you," Teddy recalled. "That he and this 'Joey' Coffin were pals."

Which wasn't, Lincoln thought, how Coffin himself had described it. Yes, after Troyer got in trouble in Wellesley, the Coffins had taken him in for his senior year—information that Lincoln had to pull out of him—but he didn't have the impression that the boys had become friends, despite living under the same roof. "They were apparently teammates back in the day," he told Teddy. "Won something called the Island Cup that I'm told is a big deal locally."

"So you think this guy Coffin came out here to warn Troyer that you were nosing around?"

"Either that," Lincoln said, trying to think it through, "or after our conversation he got to thinking."

"About Troyer's history with women."

Lincoln nodded. "That, but also about the three of us. Coffin said that if he'd been in charge of the investigation back in seventy-one, we would've been his chief suspects. As he put it, we had motive, means and opportunity."

"*What* motive?"

"He figured maybe we lured her here thinking she'd put out for us and were disappointed when she refused."

Teddy looked ill. "Does he still believe that?"

"He claims not to. If we'd done something to Jacy back then, why would I be snooping around now? And what kind of sense would it make for all three of us to return to the scene of the crime forty-four years later? No, here's what I think happened. Our conversation triggered something. It can't be a coincidence that a few minutes after we said goodbye, Coffin drove right out here and started interrogating the guy, can it?"

"So," Teddy said, "you *do* think Troyer was involved?"

Lincoln massaged his temples. "I did yesterday, after learning about his issues with women. I mean, a lot of people here seem to think he's dangerous. It felt like all of the pieces of the puzzle were coming together. And it explained some things."

"Like?"

"Well, one reason that investigation didn't yield any results is that it took so long to get going. Once the cops heard Jacy was getting married, they figured she'd gotten cold feet and run off. We did, too, that first month or so, right? All along we'd taken it for granted that she and Vance were getting married. They were engaged, after all. But after she disappeared, all that changed. Suddenly her marrying Vance didn't compute. She never talked about the guy or seemed to miss him when they were apart. They disagreed about everything—where they'd live, whether to have kids or not, you name it."

"The war, too."

"Right. But if Troyer's involved, that's all irrelevant."

"Except there's a problem. Troyer claims Mickey broke his jaw with that punch and he had to go to Boston to get it wired shut."

Lincoln nodded. "Coffin interviewed him a week or so after we all left the island, and it was wired shut then."

"Which means he might not've even been *on* the island that Tuesday."

"I know. Today, the whole thing feels like a fever dream. Basically I wanted him to be a murderer because he's an asshole, and it doesn't work that way."

"No, it doesn't."

"Tell me something," Lincoln said, his mind zigzagging. "Anita says our coming out here was my idea. Is that how you remember it?"

"More or less. You and I talked about it first, and Mickey wasn't hard to convince. We didn't think Jacy would come, not with the wedding just a few weeks off."

"I don't even remember inviting her."

"That's because I did."

"Really? You're sure?"

Teddy winced, as if the memory were painful. "Yeah, I have a pretty clear recollection, actually. She answered the phone there at her parents' place, and her voice sounded strange, like I'd woken her up. Then she asked me to repeat my name, as if she'd already forgotten who I was. But when I said again who it was, she was *really* happy, like I was the answer to a prayer. Neither response felt right, somehow. Anyway, my plan was to pitch the weekend as one last attempt to convince Mickey not to report for duty, but she said she'd come even before I got the chance."

"I guess I was thinking along those same lines. Maybe her agreeing to come didn't have anything to do with us. What if she was just looking for an excuse to escape Greenwich for a few days?"

"Why?"

"Maybe the cops were right about her having second thoughts about getting married. Still, I just can't help feeling we're missing something."

Teddy started to speak, then changed his mind.

"What?"

"Well, actually, the day she and I went out to Gay Head? She *did* hint about having misgivings."

His eyes, Lincoln noticed, were brimming. "You never told us that."

Teddy shrugged. "I guess it felt like she'd spoken in confidence. She didn't say she wasn't going to get married. Just that she wasn't sure anymore."

Getting to his feet again, Lincoln went back over to the screen door and stared outside. In the late-afternoon shadows the elongated outline of his mother's house stretched all the way down to Troyer's place. Weakening sunlight still sparkled on the ocean in the distance.

"Anyway," Teddy said, "now it makes sense. Why you were talking earlier about that history class we took with Tom Ford. He was forever harping on remote and proximate causes. How attractive the proximate ones can be, even though the real truth's usually buried deeper."

"I have to say," Lincoln admitted, "that if Troyer wasn't involved, it would be a relief."

"How so?"

"That's another thing Coffin said. That if *he'd* been in charge, he'd have had a backhoe dig up every inch of this property." Lincoln shook his head now. "The one thing I don't think I could bear would be to find out she's been lying dead out here all these years. Under this very ground."

They were silent, then, until Teddy finally voiced what they both were thinking. "We never should've let her slip away that morning.

We could've rousted Mick and gone after her. Given her a lift to the ferry instead of letting her hitch. Why didn't we do *that*?"

"I wouldn't say this to anybody except you," Lincoln said, "but the truth is, I was relieved she was gone."

If this surprised Teddy, he didn't show it. "I remember what you said that morning."

Lincoln didn't, and wasn't sure he wanted Teddy to remind him. "You said, 'That's that, then.'"

It was true, too. That's exactly what he'd said, Lincoln recalled now. Almost as if he'd known even back then that they'd never see Jacy again.

Down the hill, a screen door banged. Troyer had come out onto his deck and was now standing there, shirtless, with both hands on the railing, gazing up in their direction.

"DO YOU EVER WONDER about Mickey?" Teddy said.

They were on their way to a club in Oak Bluffs where they'd meet up with Mickey, who'd e-mailed Lincoln earlier: *Face Man. Be at Rockers at 7. Bring Tedioski. Don't let him weasel out, either.* Predictably, the message had lifted Lincoln's spirits. From their freshman year at Minerva, Mickey's ability to put things in perspective had always been his greatest gift. Lincoln and Teddy were both prone to taking life too seriously, so Mickey provided a natural antidote to their brooding. And how bad could the world be if he was in it? Nor had he lost this knack over time. His insistence that Lincoln was still Face Man and Teddy still Tedioski demonstrated his conviction that four decades had neither damaged nor corrupted them. Somehow, in Mickey's presence everything seemed less threatening, as if life had taken his measure and decided not to fuck with him. It didn't really matter whether Troyer was the villain of Lincoln's earlier fever dream or just a garden-variety dickhead. Mickey had made short work of him before and would do so again should the need arise.

Teddy, for some reason, looked like he was on a different wavelength. Their earlier conversation seemed to have plunged him into a reverie, and Lincoln now regretted sharing Coffin's dark speculations about what might've happened to Jacy. He hadn't had much choice though, not after Troyer's visit.

"Wonder about him how?" Lincoln said, the question coming at him out of left field.

Teddy shrugged. "What his life's like? I mean, you and I know a lot more about each other than we do about him."

"Yeah, but with him there's less to know."

Teddy raised an eyebrow at this.

"Okay, that didn't come out right," Lincoln admitted. "What I mean is, Mickey's always been a what-you-see-is-what-you-get kind of guy."

Teddy didn't disagree, but something was clearly troubling him. "Why do you think he punched that pledge at the SAE house?"

"He was drunk."

"Even drunks have reasons."

"True, but most of the time they make sense only to them." He couldn't help chuckling at this memory. "He claimed at the time those stone lions out front pissed him off, remember?"

"Okay, but why?"

"I'm supposed to explain why statuary would piss off a drunk?"

Teddy shrugged again. "Okay, so how about this. Why do you think he stayed in the kitchen scrubbing pots when he could've been out front with us?"

"I just assumed he was being Mickey."

"That's a tautology, not an explanation."

"I'd look up the word, but I'm driving."

"Well, the door-prize question is why he changed his mind and went to Canada."

At least this one made sense to Lincoln. "I've always wondered. In the end I suppose I thought you and Jacy convinced him. You'd both been riding him since December. Maybe when the time came to actually report, he saw the light. Like Paul on the road to Damascus? Anyway, where are you going with all this?"

"I don't know," Teddy confessed, "but back in college I used to think you could change people's minds. You'd reason with them, and if you knew more and you were clever and persistent, you'd eventually win them over."

Now Lincoln couldn't help smiling. "In addition to yourself, you're describing our current president." Of the many bones he had to pick with Obama, this one topped the list; the man seemed to believe the world was a rational place in which everyone proceeded from goodwill.

"Isn't that the whole idea of serious debate? We forget that even under Nixon, most people supported the war. Eventually, though, there was just too much evidence."

"There's your answer, then. Mickey was like the rest of the country. He reached a tipping point."

"Except in his case, it was never about the evidence, and reason never came into it. He promised his father he'd go. Nothing else mattered."

Lincoln nodded, beginning to understand. "So what you're saying is—"

"If *we* didn't change his mind, what did?"

"Okay, I guess that's fair enough, but why is this suddenly so important?"

"I guess what I'm getting at is there's a lot we don't know about people, even the ones we love best. There are things I've never told you about myself, and there are probably things that are none of my business that you haven't told me. But the things we keep secret tend to be right at the center of who we are. Tom Ford never let on that he was gay, for instance."

"True," Lincoln said, "but we knew."

"I didn't."

"Really?" Though now that he thought about it, Lincoln wasn't sure he did, either, not when they were at Minerva. A decade later, though, when he read of Ford's death in the alumni magazine he hadn't been surprised; at some point, subconsciously, he must've put two and two together.

"What's interesting," Teddy was saying, "is that people aren't more curious about each other."

"Don't we all have a right to privacy?"

"Absolutely. But that's not what I'm talking about. We let people keep their secrets but then convince ourselves we know them anyway. Take Jacy. We all were in love with her, but what did we really *know* about her? I'd never *met* anybody like her before, so I had no frame of reference. And if you think about it, she was in the same boat. We must've been as mysterious to her as she was to us."

"Except there's nothing very mysterious about us." But as soon as Lincoln said this, he realized it was bogus. Because there *had* been times when she seemed to be studying them and puzzling over their entire non-Greenwich existence. Public schools. Split-levels with Ford Galaxies in the driveways. Mortgages. Neighborhoods full of first- and second-generation immigrants. Two-week summer vacations someplace nearby. People for whom *summer* wasn't a verb. She appeared to be drinking it all in. Had she been wondering if maybe it was as good as or maybe even better than what she knew? "Did I ever tell you my mother's take on her?"

"Your mother *met* her?"

"No, but I talked about her. How wild she was. I even gave her a slightly sanitized version of the night at the dog track in Bridgeport and our barhopping back to the Theta house. Then about Jacy giving us big wet kisses in front of the house president. When I finished, my mother had this strange look on her face, like she couldn't figure out how a son of hers could be so dim-witted. She wanted to know if it hadn't occurred to me that Jacy might be waiting for one of us—okay, I guess *me*—to work up the courage to declare his true feelings."

"She really said that?"

"It gets better," Lincoln told him. "When I explained how unlikely this was, that Jacy was engaged to a law student from a rich family, Mom said that maybe she wanted to be *un*engaged both to him and them."

Teddy was smiling broadly. "Kind of makes you wonder what your mom was like as a girl."

"My exact thought at the time. When I asked about that, she just gave this rueful laugh and said she'd had this friend that Jacy reminded her of. Then she told me the world wasn't always kind to fiery girls who didn't have strong men to protect them. I think she was hinting that I might've been that man for Jacy, and that her biggest fear was that I'd end up being somebody who played things safe."

Nobody said anything until Teddy broke the silence. "I'm envious, actually. Your parents both cared about you enough to give you bad advice."

Lincoln chuckled yet again. "What's that poem you're always quoting? About parents?"

Teddy nodded. "Larkin. 'They fuck you up, your mum and dad. They may not mean to, but they do . . .'"

"The original proximate causes."

They were coming into Oak Bluffs now, the Atlantic on their right, Teddy staring out across its expanse as if he could see whatever lay on the far side.

"Hey," Lincoln said. "You gonna be okay?"

"Yep," his friend replied. "I'm ready. Put me in, Coach."

When they turned onto Circuit Avenue, Mickey's Harley was parked right in front of the neon ROCKERS sign.

Teddy took a deep breath, his hand already on the door handle. "Here we go," he said. "Rock and roll, played at a very high volume."

Teddy

They selected one of the tables farthest from the stage. Though their first set wasn't until nine, over an hour away, the band Mickey had dragged them into Oak Bluffs to hear had already set up, and their sound system, given the size of the room, was truly terrifying to behold. In addition to several enormous guitar amps, there were four column speakers on adjustable stands that almost reached the acoustic-tiled ceiling, as well as several smaller stage-mounted amps pointing back where the musicians would stand, presumably so they, too, could hear the deafness-inducing sound. Even more disconcerting were the three microphones arranged on the floor around the drum kit. In a room this small, why would drums need further amplification?

At Mickey's insistence they'd all ordered ribs, the best on the island, he claimed, no point in even glancing at the menu. Each order came with coleslaw, baked beans, cornbread, pickles, a mountain of fries and, incredibly, two deviled eggs. Teddy, who hadn't had anything to eat since that clam roll at Gay Head, should've been hungry but wasn't, a possible sign that the episode he'd hoped had been forestalled might still be lurking. If so, he'd just have to deal with it, like always. Meanwhile, his goal would be to get through the threatened evening of beer drinking and very loud music. When they arrived, Mickey made them promise to stay for at least one full set, after which they were free to head back to Chilmark and be fucking dweebs if they wanted to. Copy that. And in the morning, if Teddy was still feeling iffy, he'd catch an early ferry off the island, then decide whether to visit Brother John or just head back to Syracuse. A Marx Brothers marathon and some long walks in the Vermont woods would be a pleasant distraction but little more unless he took his old friend up on his standing offer to move in. The idea of a cloistered religious setting wasn't wholly without appeal. Possibly this was what had attracted him to Merton so long ago. Nor would not having any attractive women around be a bad idea, either. Now that Theresa was all but gone, he could admit to being more than a little in love with her. Why risk that happening again? Unfortunately, present company excepted, he generally liked women better than men and was happier in their less competitive proximity. Maybe there was a convent somewhere that would take him in.

At the moment Lincoln was watching with undisguised amazement as Mickey devoured a full rack of ribs; Lincoln and Teddy ordered the half. "Tell me you don't eat like this all the time," he said.

"Like what?" Mickey replied, a tiny spot of barbecue sauce on the tip of his nose.

"Like *this*," Lincoln said, gesturing widely at what was an astonishing amount of food, even for three grown men.

Mickey pointed a gnawed rib bone at him, and he leaned back away from it. "This is *food*. So yeah, I do eat like this all the time. What do you eat, tofu?"

"Occasionally," Lincoln confessed. "Pasta. Vegetables."

"Hey, *I* eat vegetables. Just this morning I ate a stalk of celery with my Bloody Mary. You want my coleslaw? Because that I probably *won't* eat."

"Of course not. It's the one mostly healthy thing on the plate."

Mickey considered this, his eyes narrowing. "Why *mostly*?"

"Well, I assume it's dressed with mayonnaise."

"I should fucking *hope* so," an indignant Mickey said before turning his attention to Teddy. "How about you, Teduski? What are you ingesting these days?"

Having anticipated this question, Teddy was prepared. "Lately, I'm really into crudo," he said.

"Crudo," Mickey repeated, glancing at Lincoln for enlightenment. When Lincoln shrugged, he fixed Teddy suspiciously. "The fuck is crudo."

"Raw fish," Teddy explained. "Tuna. Salmon. Scallops."

The look of outrage on his friend's face was deeply satisfying. "That's bait."

Teddy nodded. "Yum."

"See?" Mickey said, this time pointing the rib bone at him. "This is what comes of listening to fucking Belle and Sebastian. You're not going to finish those?"

Teddy handed over what remained of his half rack. At least a quarter.

Ever since they'd arrived at Rockers, he'd been studying his friend, trying to imagine whatever could've possessed Troyer to suggest it was Mickey they should be talking to if they wanted to find out what happened to Jacy. Probably he'd meant only to divert attention from himself. When Teddy pointed out that Mickey had been in love with her, Troyer had scoffed, but why? Was he just projecting his own hatred of women onto someone against whom he already held a grudge, or did he actually have a reason to believe Mickey might be one of those men capable of harming a woman he loved? That afternoon they all spent drinking beer on the deck, had Mickey said or done anything Troyer could have misinterpreted? Teddy racked his brain but came up empty.

"Also," Mickey was saying, "I'm guessing you guys eat three meals a day, right? While I have one."

"Seriously?" Lincoln frowned.

"Hey, musicians are nocturnal. When I was younger I'd still be up at dawn, which meant I could eat breakfast before heading home. Double stack of pancakes, side of greasy sausage, pile of home fries, toast. Kill the hangover before it starts. These days I'm home by three at the latest, which means I'm down to a single meal."

"Well"—Lincoln shook his head—"this one's a doozy."

"Tedmarek," Mickey said, shifting gears. "Why the hell are you rushing back to the Rust Belt tomorrow? Come hang out with me on the Cape for a few days. I've got a pullout sofa."

Okay, Teddy thought, *so who is Delia?* The conversation he'd overheard part of earlier had sounded intimate, but whoever she was, this Delia person must not be living with Mickey, or he wouldn't have extended the invitation so cavalierly.

"My dog won't like you sleeping on it," Mickey conceded, "but his affection and forgiveness can usually be bought with chocolate."

"You have a dog?" Lincoln said, surprised.

Mickey nodded. "Clapton."

"Clapton?"

Mickey turned to Teddy. "Again," he said, "can you tell when he's joking?" When Teddy shrugged, he continued, "He wandered in one day. He's old now. Blind. Arthritic. Occasionally incontinent."

"You make staying with you sound really attractive," Teddy told him.

"Hey, don't turn your nose up. By the end of the week I'll have you eating real food again. I bet I could cure you of that Mumford and Sons disorder, too."

"Hey, what was the upshot with that guitar?" Teddy asked.

Mickey blinked at him. "What guitar?"

"You said some guy had a Rickenbacker for sale."

"Oh, right," Mickey said, pushing his plate toward the center of the table and stifling a well-earned belch. "He wants too much, so I'm letting him sweat a bit. I may call him again before heading home."

It was still fifteen minutes until the first set, but Rockers, nearly empty when they got there, was starting to fill up. Having drunk two pints of beer, Teddy was, too. On his way to the men's room, he passed the stage and marveled again at how crammed it was with sound equipment. Back at Minerva all Mickey's band had required was a couple amps and a small, portable PA system. How much did all this extra stuff cost? he wondered. There were two bass drums, their facings covered with drop cloths for some reason (had the drummer recently quit a band with another name to join this one?) as well as two snares and four cymbals of varying sizes. Did a local rock band really require a keyboard *and* a synthesizer? What was with all the foot pedals? The musicians had apparently done their sound check earlier because the amps were humming with static electricity, the mics picking up an ambient buzz of conversation from nearby tables. At one of these, off to the side, lounged four wraithlike guys who had to be the band. Only four, Teddy thought, counting the instruments again. In addition to the keyboards and drums, an electric bass and two six-string guitars were propped on their stands. One of them, he now noticed, was an old Rickenbacker that looked to be in cherry condition, as Mickey had put it.

Teddy was still chuckling to himself when the door opened and Mickey appeared in the men's room mirror, unzipping at an adjacent urinal. "Asshole," he said. "You figured it out, didn't you?"

"Yep."

"Don't you dare tell Lincoln."

"I won't."

They peed side by side, two men with prostates that, like the rest of their organs, had seen better days. "All kidding aside," Mickey said when Teddy zipped up and moved to the sink. "You should come hang out on the Cape for a few days."

Had he and Lincoln been talking? Not that it mattered. Nothing he'd told Lincoln about his spells had been in confidence. Of course it was also possible that Lincoln hadn't said a thing. Mickey might've looked him over and concluded he was in a bad way. "I wish I could."

"Why can't you? You're done teaching, right?"

"Yeah, but I need to get back."

Mickey made a don't-shit-a-shitter face. "BS," he said. Friendly enough, but a challenge nevertheless.

Teddy decided to be forthright. "You can't help me, Mick. I appreciate the concern, but I'll just have to soldier through it, like always."

Mickey zipped up and joined him at the sink. "Maybe it's time to try something different," he offered, "though for the record, the invitation wasn't about you. There's somebody I'd like you to meet."

"Yeah? Who?" Because if there *was* somebody new in Mickey's life, Teddy was happy for him, even if that happiness was tinged with envy.

"No dice," Mickey said. "It's a surprise." He grabbed a fistful of paper towels from the dispenser. "Anyway, think about it."

When their eyes met in the mirror, it occurred to Teddy that his friend might actually be asking for a favor. If so, it would be his first ever. "Okay," he promised, "I will."

When they returned to the table, their plates had been cleared away, and the musicians were casually mounting the stage. "You're gonna like these guys," Mickey said, draining the last of his beer.

The waitress came by to see if they wanted another round, and both Lincoln and Teddy nodded. Mickey shook his head almost imperceptibly, a gesture Lincoln didn't catch, though he did notice when Mickey and Teddy grinned at each other. "What?" he said, immediately suspicious.

"Nothing, Your Honor," Mickey assured him.

"Nothing," Teddy agreed.

When the drummer hit the rim of his snare, it sounded like a gunshot played through a bullhorn, and the bassist thumped a note that Teddy didn't so much hear as feel in the pit of his stomach. The keyboard player adjusted his dials so that the instrument sounded like a honky-tonk piano. One of the bartenders, a muscle-bound, goateed, midthirties guy in a white T-shirt, both arms sleeved with tattoos, yelled, "Rock and roll!" The drummer, arms raised above his head, clicked his sticks—one, two, three—and the rhythm guitarist and keyboard man came in on the downbeat, which started the crowd clapping. The Rickenbacker guitar sat unclaimed in the middle of the stage. "Well," Mickey said, grinning over at Lincoln. "I guess I'll see you boys later."

The audience was no longer looking at the stage but instead had pivoted in their direction, and suddenly a spotlight blinded them. The look on Lincoln's face, Teddy had to admit, was priceless. "I don't—" he began, bewildered and blinking, until the spotlight left them to follow Mickey as he strode to the stage, which he bounded onto with one leap. The drummer had removed the drop cloths that had covered his two bass drums, one of which now read BIG MICK and the other ON POTS, the name of Mickey's old band. The drummer also joined in literally with both feet. Slinging the Rickenbacker over his shoulder, Mickey stepped to the mic, his voice filling the room with thunder. "Church house, gin house!"

To which the other singers and the crowd responded, "School house, out house!"

Mickey: "Highway number nineteen!"

Crowd: "People keep the city clean!"

Teddy recognized the song, "Nutbush City Limits," the old Ike and Tina Turner hit, and of course he thought again of Jacy, because this was exactly the kind of song she would've belted out back in the day. Only there was no Jacy anymore, so it was the Bob Seger version they were playing, Mickey's voice all rasp and grind.

"Nutbush!" he called.

"Nutbush City!" the crowd roared back.

"Nutbush City Limits!"

Everyone in the room agreed. "Nutbush City Limits!"

Teddy glanced over at Lincoln, who was shaking his head but also grinning ear to ear, having finally realized that he was the only one not in the know. "Tell me something," he shouted, so as to be heard over the roar of the guitars and the pounding drums and the frenzied crowd. "How did I get such dicks for friends?" But he had his phone out and Teddy watched him switch it from photo mode to video. With everybody in the joint on their feet, his only chance of getting a clear shot of the band was to climb up on a chair, so

Lincoln did. Teddy followed suit, sorry all over again that Theresa was no longer in his life. If he, too, made a recording, he'd have no one to share it with.

Maybe, he thought, Mickey was right. Maybe it wasn't too late to try a new tack. Maybe give the monastery a chance. What he couldn't quite decide was whether that would constitute a bold new direction or just a timid recycling of the old divinity school idea. At twenty-one, having given up on love, cloistered life had seemed a sensible option. Like so many serious young men back then, he'd been genuinely taken with the idea (Merton's, actually) of a simple, consecrated life, far outside the madness of the secular world. But now? Who was he kidding? At some point, probably not long after starting Seven Storey Books, it'd dawned on him that he in fact hated Merton and despised how he'd turned his back on the world in favor of religious devotion. Ego-driven, self-deceived little shit that he was, old Tom had been every bit as competitive about piety as he'd been in the pursuit of carnal pleasure. Perhaps because so many people had concluded wrongly that Teddy was gay, he'd always rejected any suggestion that Merton might be, but now he wasn't so sure. Why had he been so vague and coy about his sexual adventures in *Seven Storey Mountain*? Why did he seem to hang out only with men? Even Aramis, Dumas's middle Musketeer, a serial adulterer even as he prepared for the priesthood, had been less dishonest.

"Nutbush!" Mickey howled, the song's refrain having come back around again, and the emotion on his friend's face was one Teddy hadn't felt in such a long time that he at first couldn't identify it. Joy. Pure, unadulterated joy. What Mickey loved now—rock and roll played at a very high volume—was what he'd loved as a boy. Recognizing what filled his soul to bursting, he'd cleaved to it, and across the decades they had remained the most faithful of lovers. It also occurred to Teddy that his not letting him and Lincoln in on whose band was playing tonight was exactly the kind of secret Mickey loved to keep and then reveal at the precise right moment, as if to prove that the world truly was a magical place full of wondrous surprises. Otherwise, just as Lincoln said earlier, he really was a what-you-see-is-what-you-get kind of guy. He'd stayed in the steamy sorority-house kitchen washing pots because he preferred doing that to flirting with pretty girls in the front room. There was only one Theta he ever cared about, and he never pretended otherwise. He'd punched that SAE pledge because those stone lions out front, whatever they represented to him in that drunken moment, *had* in fact pissed him off. Why, at the last possible moment, had he changed his mind and gone to Canada instead of reporting for duty in Vietnam? Well, okay, Teddy didn't have a clue, but he was confident that the answer, if revealed, wouldn't be complicated, because Mickey himself wasn't complicated. No general studies major, he knew who and what he loved; in other words he knew who he was. If Troyer had arrived at a different conclusion, he was full of shit.

"Nutbush City!" the crowd roared, their fists pumping in the air.

"Nutbush City Limits!" cried Mickey.

Cried the crowd.

Cried Lincoln.

Cried Teddy himself, his own fist pumping with the rest.

"Nutbush City Limits!"

Lincoln

Mickey, surrounded by fans, came over to the edge of the stage when Lincoln called to him. "Jesus, Face Man. Don't tell me you're leaving?"

"No," Lincoln assured him. "I just need to return a call." He waved his phone, which had vibrated during the set—no doubt Anita responding to the video he'd sent.

"So what'd you think?"

"You're good. Great, actually."

Mickey shrugged. "After four decades, you're supposed to be, right?" But Lincoln could see that the compliment pleased him.

"What I don't understand is why you aren't deaf."

"What?"

"I *said* . . ." Lincoln began, then got it. "Oh, right. So . . . how come you told Teddy what was up and not me?"

"I didn't. He figured it out. Seriously, is he going to be okay? He doesn't look so hot."

"I wish I knew."

"I'm trying to get him to hang out on the Cape for a couple days, but he won't."

"I know." He consulted his watch. "How long's your break?"

"Half an hour. Give Anita my love."

Since he hadn't told Mickey who he was phoning, he said, "I could be calling someone else, you know."

"Yeah, but you're not."

Outside, night had fallen, and the chill in the air was autumnal. Half of Rockers' audience was now smoking on the narrow sidewalk, so Lincoln headed into the Camp Meeting Grounds, which, this late in the season, felt abandoned. The silence, after the pounding music, felt preternatural.

Anita answered on the first ring. "Lincoln."

"Pretty crazy, huh?" he said. "The band's actually called Big Mick on Pots, just like back in Minerva."

"Lincoln."

This time he heard the urgency in her voice. "Wait, didn't you get the video I sent?"

"Something came through, but I haven't looked at it. Your father's in the hospital. It looks like he's going to be okay, but it was scary."

"What happened?"

"We were having dinner and all of a sudden he went rigid, like he'd stuck his finger in an electric socket. Then he slumped over and started speaking gibberish. Anyway, we got him to the hospital—"

"We?"

"Angela and I."

"Angela."

"His lady friend. At least that's what I'm assuming she is. She doesn't speak much English."

"What language does she speak?"

"Spanish, of course."

"But Dad doesn't speak Spanish."

"I know that. What's important here? Your father's health or his living arrangements?"

Lincoln opened his mouth to respond, but his phone vibrated again. He half expected the caller to be Dub-Yay himself, determined to take over the narrative as always, but this was a local number.

"Lincoln? Are you still there?"

"Sorry. I had an incoming call."

"This one is more important."

"I know that. I'm sorry. I'm just feeling a bit blindsided."

"Should I continue?"

"I'm listening."

"So the doctors are still running tests, but the initial diagnosis is a TIA, what they call a ministroke. Apparently he's been having them for a while."

"You got this from a woman who doesn't speak English?"

"No, from your father. The language impairment from strokes like these doesn't last long. By the time the ambulance arrived, he was making sense again. He might say *bike* when he means *rake*, but you can kind of figure it out."

"Put him on, then."

"He's resting. The doctors say he'll probably sleep through till morning. The strokes are exhausting, even the baby ones. But here's the thing. Each one is like a valve that relieves pressure, but then the pressure builds back up again. There's apparently a bigger one coming."

"When?"

"Unknown."

Lincoln sighed. "I'm really sorry, babe. This should not have happened on your watch."

"I'm just glad I was here. Meanwhile, he's comfortable and in no immediate danger. Angela and I are heading back to the house now."

"You and Angela." His phone vibrated again. Whoever called earlier had apparently left a message. "The old bastard."

"Lincoln."

"I'm just saying."

"I *know* what you're saying, but you're awfully hard on him. The only thing he's ever really wanted is to be important."

"What he wants is his own way."

"Yeah, and there's a lot of that going around." When he didn't respond to that, she said, "Sorry, that sounded like I meant you, and I didn't."

"You sure?"

"*Pretty* sure."

He was silent for a moment. "Have I mentioned recently that I love you?"

"I know you do. I never doubt that."

"I really wish you were here."

"Right this minute, so do I."

"That's good. You prefer me to Angela, at least?"

"I do, yes. Wait, you sent a video?"

"Watch it. It'll cheer you up." He knew he should let her go, but he didn't want to. "You should see Mickey on that stage. He's like a kid."

"Yeah?"

"Of all of us, he's the one who seems to be living the life he was meant to."

"Are you saying you've lived the wrong life?"

"No, only that I don't feel about commercial real estate like Mick feels about rock and roll."

"He isn't married. He doesn't have kids. Kids whose educations *your* hard work paid for."

"*Our* hard work."

"We did what needed doing. Both of us."

"I know. Okay, I'll shut up now."

"Finish your business on the island and come home. You *are* coming back, right?"

"Of course I'm coming back."

"Good. I miss you. So does your father."

"You think?"

"He loves you."

"Because he thinks I'm his clone. Loving me is just another form of self-love. And this Angela woman—"

"What does it matter, if she makes him happy?"

"Why should *he* be happy? Did my mother get to be happy?"

"Do you know that she wasn't?"

"Not for a fact, no."

"Look, I know she's on your mind. It's natural. Just finish up and come home."

Rockers was even more jammed when he returned. It took him forever to elbow through to their table in the back of the room. For some reason Teddy was peering intently at the stage, as if it posed a riddle. "Everything okay?" he asked, before looking Lincoln in the face.

"Dub-Yay's in the hospital. He's been having these ministrokes?"

But Teddy was still only half listening. "Can you see what's going on up there?"

Lincoln couldn't, at least not very well. The musicians had been joined onstage by a woman who looked too old to have spiky purple hair. She was holding a mic, and when Mickey reached for it she backed away, holding it out of reach. "There's someone who seems to think it's open-mic night."

Teddy shook his head. "I'm *not* believing this," he said. Though Lincoln couldn't imagine why, he seemed genuinely alarmed. Mickey and the woman with spiked hair did seem to be having some sort of disagreement, but the look on Teddy's face suggested he was witnessing something far more serious. What was it he'd told Lincoln that morning? That sometimes his spells took the form of premonitions? Was he having one of those?

Only when his phone vibrated in his pocket did Lincoln remember the other call that had come in while he was talking to Anita. Was there time to check his voice messages before the band roared back to life? The audience had already begun to clap in anticipation. Punching PLAY, Lincoln covered his right ear so he could hear the message playing in his left. It was Joe Coffin's voice. "Lincoln. Call me when you get this message. I've been doing some snooping."

Teddy grabbed his shoulder. "You have to see this!"

Expecting the argument between Mickey and the spiky-haired woman to have escalated, Lincoln was surprised to see that things had actually calmed down on the stage. Her back to the audience, the purple-haired woman was talking with the other band members.

Apparently they were going to let her sing. Even more inexplicably the crowd seemed thrilled by this development. The clapping was even louder now.

"Hang on a minute," he told Teddy.

Obviously, the thing to do was to go back outside and make the call from the street, but the place was heaving. It'd take him forever to make his way to the door, so he hit CALL BACK.

Coffin must've been sitting with his hand on the phone because he answered immediately. "Where are you, Lincoln?"

"Place called Rockers."

"That explains the noise. Let's meet. Not there, though."

"Tomorrow?"

"Tonight would be better."

"Lincoln!" Teddy's eyes were still on the stage, his grip on Lincoln's shoulder viselike.

"Why?"

"So I can explain about your friend Mickey," he said.

"What about him?"

"Did you know he beat a guy half to death back in the eighties?"

"What are you talking about?"

"Wanna guess the man's name?"

Feeling a chill, he turned to face Teddy, who was now regarding him with an expression that Lincoln could only interpret as sorrow, as if he too had somehow been privy to the conversation and already knew what Coffin was about to reveal. "I have no idea," Lincoln admitted.

And yet he must have, or he would've been surprised when Coffin said it. If the name he spoke hadn't already been in the back of his mind, he wouldn't have thought to himself, *Of course.*

Three clicks of the drummer's sticks and the entire band came in on the fourth, a wall of sound. Lincoln recognized the singer's voice immediately, evidence as undeniable as a fingerprint. "WHEN THE TRUTH IS FOUND," it boomed. Though he hadn't been willing to admit it, he'd sensed her presence the moment he stepped off the ferry and again, more powerfully, at the *Vineyard Gazette.*

And now here she was. Of all the female singers Jacy had covered with Mickey's band, it was Grace Slick she'd loved best, and this particular song—"Somebody to Love"—had been her signature. She'd sung it with complete conviction, as if she'd written the lyrics herself and knew their backstory, so Lincoln anticipated the next line before she sang it, "TO BEEEEEEEE . . . LIES."

The crash that accompanied the word *lies* sounded like a cymbal, except that it didn't come from the stage but closer to hand—Teddy, losing consciousness and pitching sideways onto an adjacent table and then to the floor, where he lay twitching in a puddle of beer threaded with blood.

Teddy

Instead of heeding the anesthesiologist's instructions to count backward from one hundred, Teddy decided his more urgent need was to make an inventory of what he knew to be true. It would be succinct, he suspected, the events of the weekend having turned the solid ground beneath his feet to sand. Best to be quick about it, too, because the drugs he'd been given by the EMTs were *very* good. They'd not only made short work of the breathtaking pain *(Hooray!)*, but also routed his anxiety so completely that he could no longer say with certainty what he'd been so anxious about *(Hooray again!)*. He doubted, however, that those same narcotics were bolstering his analytical faculties.

So . . . what did he know for sure? Well, he was reasonably certain he'd passed out back at Rockers. He remembered feeling woozy when he rose to his feet, but then everything went dark, and there'd been a loud bang, the sound, he now speculated, of his own head ricocheting off a nearby table. He was also pretty sure—because he'd overheard the EMTs discussing the possibility—that he might lose his right eye, or maybe just the vision in it. Evidently he'd fallen on and shattered a wineglass, shards of which had burrowed deep into his cheekbone, one coming to rest dangerously close to his optic nerve. He should ask Lincoln, who was around somewhere. While being wheeled to the operating room he'd heard his friend telling him not to worry, that everything would be fine. Had Lincoln been acquainted with his history of falling, he wouldn't have been so sanguine. *Oh, by the way,* that other long-ago doctor had told him after he'd landed on his tailbone, *with spinal injuries there was one thing to keep an eye out for.* (*Whoa!* Teddy thought. *Keep an eye out!* Now *here* was an expression poised to take on a whole new meaning.) Back then, at sixteen, the odds of a full recovery had been very much in his favor. (*Chances* were *his chances* were *awfully good.*) Whereas the results had been . . . well, awfully *bad.*

And yet, to be fair, he *had* been lucky, right? *Un*lucky would've meant a wheelchair for the rest of his life. Like causality, luck could be further parsed into proximate and remote. Yes, he'd been lucky that day in the gym, but it would've been luckier still not to have fallen in the first place, and if you were talking about *real* luck, he might've begun life with a different father, one more like Mickey's, who would've recognized his parental duty to teach his son that bullies and louts had to be met head-on, sometimes even with violence. At some point, surely, Michael Sr. must've sat Mick down and explained such things to him, even showed him how to deliver the kind of punch that had knocked Troyer clean off his feet.

If Teddy himself had been blessed with such a parent, things couldn't have helped turning out differently. The first time that vicious little shit Nelson had intentionally tripped him when he knifed through the lane, Teddy would've picked himself up off the hardwood floor, recognized the situation's imperative and broken the kid's nose for him. Then, later, when Teddy went up for that destiny-forging rebound, Nelson would've thought twice about undercutting him, and instead of coming down on his tailbone Teddy would've landed right on his feet and gone through life with a working dick. At Gay Head, when Jacy chose him, she would've been choosing the man she imagined him to be, instead of the one he was. They would've arrived back at the Chilmark house as a *couple.* And in the fullness of time they, like Lincoln and Anita, would've married and had a passel of kids and grandkids.

Pretty though all this alternative reality was to contemplate, Teddy suspected it wouldn't bear close scrutiny. For one thing, a kid fathered by a man like Michael Sr. wouldn't have been Teddy at all, but rather a kid like *Mickey.* Moreover, would this new, improved Teddy have been guaranteed a better outcome? Not necessarily. If he'd been the kind of boy who could break another kid's nose for tripping him, then mightn't he also have discovered that he enjoyed doing so? Indeed, over time he himself might've evolved into an ignorant brute (Brom Bones!) not unlike Nelson. And later still, having developed a taste for risk and physical confrontation, he might've ignored his high draft number, enlisted, gone to Vietnam and gotten himself killed there. Or, had he survived, he might've become a Republican, a supporter of other dim-witted foreign adventures that got other young men killed. Squinted at in this fashion—when he awoke from surgery with only one eye, would *squint* still be an operable verb?—human destiny was both complex (it had a lot of working parts) and simple (in the end, you were who you were).

Because was it not for this very reason—that Teddy was who he was and not some other hypothetical human—that he'd fallen again? *Falling* was apparently written in caps somewhere in his genetic code, and *this* time the chances of a good outcome were apparently not *awfully good.* Earlier, when he overheard one of the doctors say, "Okay, let's see if we can save that eye," he'd taken it to mean, *We might as well give it a whirl—maybe we'll get lucky.* An hour or two from now, when he regained consciousness and was again instructed by his doctors to be on the lookout for this or that, he could have just the one eye with which to look. If he had any kingly aspirations, he'd have to locate and travel to the Land of the Blind. This would be his new normal.

So, was that it? The sum total of what could be said for sure? Well, he was pretty darn sure that in addition to an eye, he was also losing his mind. Indeed, his reason had been under siege from the moment he arrived on Martha's Vineyard, perhaps even earlier. The first sign of his unraveling had been on the deck of the ferry, when he'd identified the young woman standing next to Lincoln on the pier as Jacy. The question was, why? What was going on in his head that he'd conjured her up like that? It wasn't as if he'd been obsessing over her nonstop for the last four decades. Okay, sure, dark-haired young women of a particular type had invariably reminded him of her, and whenever there was a story in the newspaper or on TV or the Internet about a young woman going missing, he always felt compelled to read, watch or click. But such triggers were normal, weren't they? Even if Jacy *had* been haunting him all these years, would that have been so strange? She was the first girl he'd ever fallen deeply in love with, and who *ever* forgets first love? Granted, he remembered her with profound sadness, but it wasn't as if losing her had been the end of his life.

Here on the island, though, every emotion he felt when he thought of her was somehow amplified, as if playing through Big Mick on Pots' lethal sound system. This morning, riding out to Gay Head, he'd sensed the volume being turned up past HIGH all the way to STUN. Why had he kept pedaling toward its source? Had he been *trying* to conjure her, or was *she* demanding to be conjured? If she was a ghost, what was she born of? Even ghosts had motives. Did she blame him (or Lincoln or Mickey) for whatever horrible thing had befallen her all those years ago? Or did she want him to know that she still loved him (and Lincoln and Mickey)? Even more puzzling was her timing—why now, on this particular morning? Could it be that her ghostly power derived from the island itself? Had she, like Prospero, been waiting all these years for him/them to return? Could she really be buried here, as the old cop Lincoln had spoken to seemed to believe? In a ghost story that would explain why she was so much more present now than she'd been at any time in the last forty-four years, when her signal had been lost in the noise of the larger world. According to the eerie logic of such tales, she, a restless ghost, had contacted him as soon as he came within range. Had he sensed her reaching out to him there on the ferry? Was that why, instead of going out onto the deck, he'd remained inside? Had he sensed the danger even before it manifested?

What Teddy found reassuring about this occult possibility was that it meant he had company. Maybe he was losing his mind, but wasn't Lincoln as well? A happily married man, his friend probably thought about Jacy less often than Teddy did, and when he did think of her it probably caused less distress. Yet he'd no sooner arrived on the island than he'd become obsessed with the mystery of her disappearance. Like Teddy, when he got close enough to receive her signal, he, too, had fallen under her spell. Why? Because he, too, had loved her. Love, timeless love, had opened a new frequency that allowed her to communicate even with someone as settled, squared away and unimaginative as Lincoln.

And Mickey? You only had to take one look to know that he, too, was haunted, maybe even more than Lincoln or Teddy himself. And didn't it make perfect sense that he should be, given his geographical proximity. On the Cape, when the psychic wind was right, he was able to hear her siren call, whereas Teddy and Lincoln were too far away. Hadn't the two women Mickey had married, then quickly divorced, both resembled Jacy? Had they at some point realized that they were mere stand-ins for the woman he was really in love with? Was that why the marriages had failed?

Damn, Teddy thought. What was *in* those drugs he'd been given? There had to be some psychedelic, mind-altering component, because he was suddenly seeing things that until now had been shrouded. He was having what amounted to a genuine Carlos Castaneda moment. What worried him was that any second now the anesthesia would kick in and that would be the end of it. Maybe he'd be able to convince his doctors to prescribe another dose for later. If not, he'd have to find a shaman who could return him to this place of magical clarity, because he felt close, *really* close, to understanding, well, in a word, *everything*.

Alas, the only thing he was unable to bring into meaningful focus was at the very center of it all: the singer with the purple hair back at Rockers. Even though he couldn't get a good look at her from the other side of the crowded room, he'd been certain it was Jacy. Yeah, okay, he'd also thought that girl on the pier was Jacy, but this was different. The one on the pier had been dark haired and about Jacy's size and in her early twenties, as Jacy had been when she disappeared. But he'd quickly recognized her for what she was: a wish. Or, as Lincoln had put it, a fever dream. Teddy had wanted her to be Jacy, wanted for Jacy to be alive, and so, for a second or two, she was. By contrast, the purple-haired singer hadn't *looked* like Jacy, she'd *been* Jacy. Teddy would've known her anywhere. There hadn't been a doubt in his mind. Except she also *wasn't* Jacy for the simple reason that she *couldn't* be. His reason might be under assault—sure, he might be having visions—but he wasn't completely untethered from reality, and the facts were all wrong. The singer had been late thirties? Early forties? Jacy, if she were alive, would be a woman on the cusp of old age, just as he and Lincoln and Mickey were. *So what* if her voice was Jacy's? *So what* if she was channeling Grace Slick, as Jacy had so often done back at Minerva? *What difference* did it make that she'd chosen to open her set with "Somebody to Love," Jacy's favorite, a song that asks what happens *when the truth is found to be lies*? None of that mattered. He recalled an essay he'd once written for Tom Ford, where he'd cleverly marshaled a mountain of evidence in support of a truly ingenious thesis. There'd been just one small, troublesome fact that unfortunately invalidated the whole thing. He'd tried his best to explain it away, but to no avail. *What can't be true, isn't,* Ford had written in his endnote, *no matter how much you want it to be.*

"Teddy?" said a voice.

"I'm sorry," he said, or tried to say, assuming it was the anesthesiologist, reprimanding him for not counting backward from a hundred as instructed and drifting off into blissful, untroubled sleep, so they could get on with botching his surgery and shepherding him into the final stage of his life as a pathetic, general studies, limp-dicked, one-eyed man.

Except it was a nurse and she was wheeling him somewhere

else on a gurney. "You're going to be fine," she assured him. "The operation was a success."

When they got to where they were going and she came around to the foot of the contraption, he got a good look at her, a dark-haired woman his own age. "Jacy," he said. "I love you."

The old nurse grinned down at him. "Hey, I love you, too."

Lincoln

I t was nearly one o'clock by the time Lincoln got back to
Rockers, which had emptied out, and not a single musician
was in sight. At the far end of the long bar, a few stragglers
were watching a West Coast baseball game. When the goateed, tat-
tooed bartender who'd shouted "Rock and roll!" several hours earlier
noticed Lincoln frowning at the stage, which was still crammed
with sound equipment, he came down and told him that Big Mick
on Pots was done for the night.

"I figured they'd play to closing," Lincoln said, extending his
hand across the bar. "I'm Lincoln, by the way."

"Kevin," the guy said as they shook. "Normally they do. How's
your friend?"

"Looks like he's going to be okay."

"Man, that was a lot of blood," Kevin said, eyeing Lincoln's polo
shirt, patches of which were now rust colored, as were his chinos.
He'd cleaned up as best he could at the hospital, but he was still a
sight to behold.

"You know Mickey?"

Crossing his massive arms in front of his chest, the bartender
snorted. "Everybody knows Big Mick." *Big guys,* his body language seemed to say, *all know one another.* Guys Lincoln's size
wouldn't necessarily be cognizant of that. "He's a legend in these
parts."

That fact, Lincoln thought, could be added to all the other things he apparently didn't know about his friend. In the hospital's waiting room he'd revisited the questions Teddy had posed when they were driving here, questions that loomed larger now. Why *had* Mickey punched that SAE pledge all those years ago? Had this been the first real evidence of rage simmering just below his usually good-natured surface? And why *had* he continued to scrub pots in the steamy kitchen of the Theta House, his shirt drenched with sweat by the end of every shift, when he might have worked the cool, dry dining room serving some of the prettiest girls on campus? It couldn't have been social awkwardness. Having grown up with all those sisters, he was pretty much at ease around even the sexiest Thetas, most of whom treated him like a big brother. And, finally, why *had* he gone to Canada instead of reporting for duty? A spur of the moment decision, or an intention he'd had from the start but hadn't trusted his friends enough to confide in them?

If Lincoln was unable to answer such questions after four decades of friendship, how could he hope to fathom what Joe Coffin had told him on the phone just before Teddy fainted—that Mickey, for reasons Lincoln couldn't begin to imagine, had beaten Jacy's father, a man they'd all met for the first time at graduation, into a coma with his bare fists? What possible explanation could there be for that? Surely their meeting couldn't have been coincidental. Had Mickey gone looking for him, and to what end? Did he have some reason to believe that Donald Calloway might know of his daughter's whereabouts? If her father knew where she was, wouldn't everybody? Unless it was the other way around and Calloway, hearing that Mickey was back in the States, had come looking for *him*. But again, to what possible purpose? Did he believe that Mickey was somehow involved in his daughter's disappearance? That he'd gone to Canada not to dodge the draft but to escape interrogation and possible arrest? But that made no sense, either. If the man had been suspicious of Mickey, wouldn't he, like Coffin, have suspected Lincoln and Teddy as well? Jacy had spent the weekend with all three of them. Why single Mickey out?

"Any idea where he might be?" Lincoln asked. "I was really hoping to talk to him."

Kevin shrugged. "He's staying someplace here on the island is my understanding. But he's dealing with Delia now, so who knows? He might've hired a water taxi to take her back to the Cape."

"Delia?"

"The singer? Purple hair?"

"What's her story?"

The bartender made a syringe with his thumb and forefinger and injected himself in the arm. "She was supposed to be in rehab, but apparently checked herself out."

"She usually sings with the band?"

"When she's clean. Great set of pipes."

"Are she and Mickey together?"

"That I wouldn't know." For some reason Lincoln suspected otherwise, but the man's tone made it clear that he was through answering questions. "Can I get you something?"

Not wanting to head back to Chilmark until he had a better sense of where things stood, he ordered a beer and checked his phone for messages. If Kevin was right and Mickey had taken this Delia person back to the mainland by water taxi, he'd probably call or text when he got there and return to the island by ferry in the morning. He had tried to reach Lincoln earlier, but the hospital had a strict no-cell-phone policy, so Lincoln's had been switched off, and he didn't see that Mickey had called until he went outside later and turned it back on. The background noise at Rockers had been so loud that he'd had to listen to his voicemail three times: *Text me when there's word on Teddy. Got a little problem here myself. I'll explain later. Sorry about all this, Lincoln.* Something about this message had felt off, so he listened to it again now. Was it the word *all*? If he was reading between the lines correctly, it wasn't just what had happened to Teddy that Mick was feeling bad about, but also whatever had led up to it. In hindsight, he probably wished he hadn't dragged them to Rockers to hear his band play in the first place. Since now the whole weekend was a clusterfuck. But maybe the regret was more specific—the purple-haired singer who'd shown up unexpectedly. Had Mickey known she'd be there, he maybe would've warned them that her voice was a dead ringer for Jacy's—possibly why he had hired her—and that she'd be covering many of the same songs Jacy used to sing. Whatever. If Mickey had regrets, he could join the club, because Lincoln did, too. He never should've returned Coffin's call. If he hadn't been distracted by what the man was telling him, he might've truly registered Teddy's distress and caught him before he passed out. Come to that, he wished he'd never gone to see Coffin in the first place. Really, had he done a single thing right since stepping off the ferry?

"Jesus," said a familiar voice at his elbow. "What kind of shape is the other guy in?"

Lincoln had been so deep in thought that Joe Coffin, speak of the devil, had managed to slide unnoticed onto an adjacent barstool.

"He's in the hospital, in fact," Lincoln told him. "It's my friend Teddy. He fell on a wineglass."

Coffin studied him, blinking, his eyes red. He'd clearly been drinking, with purpose, unless Lincoln was mistaken. "Trouble does seem to follow you three guys," he said, and then, before Lincoln could respond, he rotated on his stool and called down the bar, "Kevin! I hope you're not pretending you didn't see me come in, because we both know you did."

The bartender regarded Coffin over his shoulder for a long, weary beat before heading in their direction.

"Tell me something, Lincoln," Coffin said when Kevin arrived and assumed the iconic stance, both hands flat on the bar. "Do you have an opinion about guys with goatees and tats who wear their baseball caps backward? Is that a thing where you live?"

Kevin shook his head. "You gonna cause trouble, Joey?"

"No, I'm not," Coffin replied matter-of-factly, which Lincoln was relieved to hear, the same possibility having occurred to him. "How about you, Lincoln?" Coffin nudged him with his elbow. "You gonna cause any trouble?"

Lincoln assured both men that he wasn't.

"There you go," Coffin said. "No trouble at all." He eyed Lincoln's beer, saw that he'd barely touched it, and ordered one for himself.

Kevin held a fresh glass under the tap. "One's your limit tonight, Joey."

"And why's that?"

"Because you're already shit-faced. Did you drive here?"

"I didn't walk."

"So, one beer. You get in an accident on the way home, your old friends will send me to jail for serving you."

"Ah, but you could go to jail for any number of reasons, Kevin."

"One beer," he repeated, setting the draft down on a coaster.

"You can leave us alone now," Coffin told him. "I doubt this conversation will turn to sports, but if it does we'll let you know."

When he was gone, Coffin clinked Lincoln's glass. "The thing is," he began, as if resuming an ongoing conversation, "we don't do right by girls."

"Who doesn't?"

"Us. You and me. Men in general. We close ranks, every one of us. Cops especially. We shouldn't, but that's what we do."

"Are we talking about Jacy, Mr. Coffin?"

As if Lincoln hadn't spoken, he said, "There isn't much real crime here. You know why?"

Lincoln allowed that he didn't.

"Stands to reason, when you think about it. Say you do some shitty thing. You shoot somebody. You rob a bank."

Lincoln couldn't help smiling. This morning Coffin had imagined him as a rapist and murderer; tonight he'd been demoted to a mere bank robber.

"So, what happens next?"

"I wouldn't know," Lincoln said. "I'm not a criminal. You run away?"

"Close. You *drive* away. At a high rate of speed. At least that's what you do other places. Here you wait for the ferry. Islands just aren't conducive to crime, Lincoln. That's a fact. Especially ones that require flight. Or premeditation. Impulse crime, where you know better, but just can't help yourself? Like domestic assault? Our strong suit, especially in the winter, after all the tourists leave and times are lean. No rich people around. Nobody hiring you to mow their lawn or clean their pool. Columbus Day to Memorial Day. Hell, you do your best. You budget for this and that—kid needs braces, vehicle needs a new transmission, all the shit that's gonna happen. Waves of it, believe me. But every year? It's the thing you don't see coming that fucks you up. Somebody slips on the ice and breaks a hip. All of a sudden you got medical bills. You're behind on your rent, payments on that snowmobile you never should've bought in the first place. You start getting calls from bill collectors. Are you familiar with these problems, Lincoln?"

"Not firsthand, no."

"I'm glad to hear it," Coffin said unconvincingly. "But a lot of people who live here year round are. Anyhow, come January, a friend of yours somehow scores tickets to a Patriots playoff game, say, in Denver. Wants to know if you're in. You're not in, Lincoln. You wouldn't be in if the game was in Foxborough and you could fly there using your own arms for wings. But man, you'd *love* to go to that game. You try to think of somebody who might loan you the money, who might think you're good for it, but you're kidding yourself. It's an island, Lincoln, and everybody you know knows you right back. You look around for somebody else to blame. Your wife's handy, so you explain the whole thing to her. How she's a piece of shit. How it's all her fault."

Lincoln sighed and settled in. Like their conversation that morning, this one was clearly headed down a rabbit hole, and this time he was drunk to boot. "Why are you telling me all this, Mr. Coffin?"

His face immediately clouded over. "Shut up, Lincoln."

"I'm sorry?" Because it was stunning. He tried to recall the last time someone had told him to shut up, and couldn't.

"I'm explaining something here, so do me the courtesy. Besides, you heard me tell Kevin there wasn't going to be any trouble. Don't make a liar out of me."

This, it occurred to Lincoln, was the sort of thing Anita had been worried about earlier—that left to his own devices he'd end up sitting next to a belligerent drunk at one in the morning. There were men who saw things coming and others who didn't, and he belonged in the latter category. Wet Wipes weren't the only thing he failed to anticipate the need for. He seriously considered just getting down off his stool and heading for the door, but he was pretty sure that if he did Coffin would lay a heavy paw on his shoulder and command him to sit. Seeing this, Kevin might come down the bar and intervene, but that wouldn't be good, either. In the end, though, what kept Lincoln seated was that, in addition to menace, there was something almost plaintive in the man's request that he not be made a liar of.

"Thank you," he said once it was clear that Lincoln had settled in. "Where was I?"

"I was explaining to my wife how everything's her fault," Lincoln reminded him.

"Right. Which she already knew because you and she have had this conversation before and it's *always* her fault. She also knows better than to give you any lip, because that never ends well. So instead she just stands there between you and the refrigerator, not giving you lip and waiting for what comes next. Someday, Lincoln, somebody's gonna do a study and what they're going to discover is the one place you absolutely do *not* want to be, if you're a woman living with an abusive drunk, is between him and the fridge. Anyhow, you shove her the fuck out of the way, harder than you meant to, and down she goes. Lays there whimpering on the floor until you order her to get up. No fool, she does as she's told. Stands there looking at you, blubbering, all *what did* I *do?* And do you know what you think, Lincoln?"

Having been warned against speech, Lincoln just shook his head.

"You think, *Not the girl I fell for.* Sloppy fat now, hair all straggly. You never forgot how slim and sexy she used to be and it makes you want to punch her right in her fat, ugly face. Which you'll eventually do, Lincoln. Not tonight, but no question, that's where you're headed. You know it and she knows it and finally it happens and this time when you tell her to get up off the floor, she doesn't because she can't. She just lays there, blinking, dazed. And even though you've known for a while this was inevitable, it still surprises you that you actually hit her, how quick it happened, and what surprises you even more is that you feel bad about it, because you can't remember the last time you had any tender feelings for this fucking bitch. But there it is: shame. Shame . . . on . . . you. So you think, *No more.* Tell yourself it's a one-and-done deal and you got it all out of your system. But in your heart of hearts you know better, Lincoln. You know you've got a *lot* more where this came from. She knows it, too, which is why the next time she sees it coming, sees that look in your eye and your hand balling into a fist, she doesn't wait around. She locks herself in the bathroom with her cell phone and calls 911. That's when we show up."

Lincoln decided to risk asking the obvious question. "What happens then?" Because now that he was down the rabbit hole, he had to admit he was interested. Also, thanks to all this *you*-ing, he felt personally vested. What *would* happen to him?

"These days? I don't know. I'm talking about how it used to be." A subtle change had come over the man, with his earlier menace mostly dissipated and leaving him almost forlorn. "There's more female officers now. Everybody gets more training. Back in the day, though, you and your partner would just take the guy outside." *Thank God,* Lincoln thought. Coffin was still *you*-ing him, but at least now he was a cop, not a perp. "Not out on the front porch, where the neighbors can see. Out back, Lincoln, where it's dark and private. You tell the guy: *If you keep this up you're going to hurt her bad. Whole thing'll be in the newspaper. You don't want that, do you? Everybody knowin' you beat the shit out of your wife?* By this time the guy's drifted into a fugue state, so you can't really be sure how much is getting through. He's just standing there looking at you, like he's waiting for this to be over, for you to stop talking and go away, which he knows you will, eventually. If you were going to arrest him, you'd have done it already. You tell him, *Next time, maybe you kill her. That happens, you go to prison. You don't think your life can get any worse, but it sure the fuck can. That* gets through, because even this dumb son of a bitch knows that much. Life's always getting worse. You can see how conflicted he is, Lincoln. Part of him would like to explain how this all came to be, but he resents having to. I mean, we're all guys, right? The three of us? Why should he have to explain about women to another guy? It's just that sometimes . . . he just gets so fucking angry. You gotta know what that's like, right? How women make you feel? Fucking cunts, all of 'em."

Coffin paused here, studying Lincoln and looking perplexed. "What I fear, Lincoln, is that you're not really following me here."

"I am, though."

"Then tell me. What's my point?"

"That we don't do right by girls?"

The other man cocked his head, his eyes narrowing dangerously, and Lincoln could read his mind: *Are you making fun of me, Lincoln?* And he did his best, wordlessly, to convey that nothing could be further from the truth.

"No, Lincoln, that would be my . . . my overarching theme. My *point* is that when we take this jerk-off outside, it's really *him* we're trying to protect, not her. If he keeps this up, something bad is going to happen to *him*, and we don't want that. We don't want him to lose his job, if he's got one, or his kids, if he's got any."

"Right," Lincoln said. "I'm with you."

"I'm glad to hear it, Lincoln, but ask me why we even care about this asshole. You gotta be at least a little curious."

"Why do you care about him, Mr. Coffin?" Lincoln said, because, yeah, he did want to know.

"Well, probably back in high school we knew him, or somebody like him. If we're the same age, maybe we were teammates."

"Like you and Troyer, playing for the Island Cup?"

He ignored this. "Or if we were younger, maybe we watched him play and wanted to be like him when it was our turn. Okay, sure, *now* he's this pathetic fuckwad, but we knew him when. In our opinion what he needs to do is remember who he used to be and become that guy again. It's *that* guy, the one we used to know, that we're really trying to get through to out there in the dark. What we're hoping is that he's still in there somewhere. That's where we're not too bright, Lincoln, because he's long gone."

Gone as in long, Lincoln thought, the phrase Mickey had used that morning to describe Jacy. "Mr. Coffin—"

"Who*ever* the fuck we're talking to, we need him to say he understands what we're telling him, because those are the magic words that'll make us disappear: *I understand.* As soon as he says that, poof, we're outta there."

"Mr. Coffin—"

Now he held up a cautionary index finger. "You've been a good boy, Lincoln, and we're almost done. This is the home stretch we're in."

Lincoln nodded, took a swig of shitty warm beer.

"Here's something else you've got to be wondering, Lincoln. After he says those magic words, do we go back inside and check on the woman before leaving?"

"I'm going to guess no."

"And you'd be right. We do not. Why? Well, to be honest, we don't want to see her sitting at the kitchen table holding a sock full of ice cubes on her eye or lip. What would we say to her then? *You know this guy's not going to stop, right?* She knows that already, or part of her does. *You'd be better off leaving him?* Maybe she would and maybe she wouldn't. The next guy could be even worse. Damned if she knows how, but she always seems to attract the bad ones. *There's a safe place you can go?* Yeah, we could *say* that. And maybe there *is* someplace safer than where she's at right now. But eventually, unless she goes off island, he's gonna find her. That's a given. In fact she'll probably call him herself, tell him right where she is. So no, Lincoln, we don't want to talk to her. We're a couple of big, husky guys, but you know what? We're scared of her. Afraid that if we go back in that house, she might actually *thank* us. Thank us for coming out and calming him down. Because that's all he really needed to do. Sitting there bleeding into a paper towel, *that's* what she wants *us* to understand—that deep down he's a good man. Give her half a chance and that's the lie she'll tell you."

At this point Coffin unexpectedly exploded into laughter, causing Kevin and the men at the other end of the bar to glance over. "See, Lincoln, if I was to write that book my daughter-in-law wants me to, about my experiences as an island cop? What I've been telling you would *be* that book."

Lincoln decided to try one more time. "But again, why tell *me* all this, Mr. Coffin? What am I supposed to take from it? That if something bad happened to Jacy back in seventy-one, the cops might've known who did it and closed ranks? Engaged in a cover-up?"

"No, Lincoln, that's not remotely what I'm saying."

"This hypothetical guy of yours who beats up women? Are we talking about Troyer?"

Now Coffin started massaging his temples with his thumbs. "Jeez, Lincoln, I have to say this is really discouraging. No, we're talking about men in general. As a species. Was I unclear about that? Troyer's a man, so sure we're talking about him, but also about you and me and your pal Mickey."

"Yeah, okay, but—"

"And there's one other person we're talking about."

Here we go, Lincoln thought, *back down the rabbit hole*. "Who would that be?"

"My own son, Lincoln. We're also talking about him."

Lincoln wasn't sure what he'd been expecting, but this wasn't it. Suddenly the man looked ill, his pallor dark gray, and his breathing had become ragged. Then it finally occurred to Lincoln that this was where they'd been headed all along. "Beverly's husband?"

"Ex-husband. Tell me something, Lincoln. Can you imagine raising your hand to a woman like her?"

"Mr. Coffin?" Lincoln said. "I know it's none of my business, but you don't look well. How about I give you a lift home? You're having surgery tomorrow, right?"

"That surgery's elective, Lincoln. I'm electing not to have it. I just decided."

"Is that a good idea?"

"Search me," he said. He was regarding Lincoln with increased interest now, apparently puzzled about something. "You said earlier that your life has pretty much worked out?"

"Yes," Lincoln told him, feeling in this admission both its truth and something akin to shame. Like most blessed people, he probably didn't count his blessings nearly often enough, but he was keenly aware of them and aware, too, that good fortune in general and his own in particular had little to do with virtue. In this he was different from Wolfgang Amadeus, and it might well have been the main difference between them. Dub-Yay was a Calvinist. Wherever he looked he saw signs not just of his own election but also of Lincoln's. Other people, not so much. He'd taken one look at Teddy and seen no evidence of godly favor. Was he wrong? Earlier tonight, as he'd followed the gurney that wheeled Teddy into surgery, Lincoln couldn't help wondering if what had happened back at Rockers was best viewed as an isolated incident or as part of a long-established pattern, one that could be summed up as Teddy's life not, to borrow Coffin's term, *working out*. Even back at Minerva, Teddy had seemed resigned to the likelihood that it wouldn't. Which begged a question: was such resignation a cause or an effect? Had Teddy meekly accepted what he saw as the inevitable trajectory of his life, or had he courageously accepted what he couldn't possibly change?

And what of Mickey? Had life worked out for him? Earlier, watching him play his beloved rock and roll at very high volume, Lincoln would've said yes. Wasn't that what he'd told Anita? That of the three of them Mickey seemed to be the one who was living the life he was supposed to? Now, a few short hours later, he wasn't so sure. Thanks in large part to the philosophical ramblings of a world-weary drunk, doubts about his old friend, however hard Lincoln was trying to resist them, were emerging, and he again recalled the expression on Mickey's face this morning as he sat astride his Harley and stared off into the distance, his face a mask of . . . what? Disillusionment? Sorrow? Regret? Was music his life, or his escape from it?

"Well, I'm glad it did," Coffin said, without apparent irony or bitterness. "Maybe you'll stay lucky. In my experience lucky people usually do."

More Calvinism. The elect stayed elected, the damned, damned. Having once made up his mind, God never wavered in his judgment, which was just fine with Wolfgang Amadeus Mosher, convinced as he was that he'd somehow merited his election and that others had somehow failed a crucial test, possibly in utero. By contrast, Coffin seemed exhausted by a lifetime of attempting to alter a foregone conclusion.

"Mr. Coffin?" Lincoln said.

"Yes, Lincoln?"

"I really have to pee."

"You don't need my permission."

"Somehow I was under the impression I did."

In the men's room Lincoln took out his phone and scrolled through his RECENTS log until he found the number Beverly had called from that morning. When a groggy female voice answered, he said, "Beverly? It's Lincoln Moser. Remember me?"

"*Ummm.* Yes?"

"I'm sorry to call so late. It's about your father-in-law."

"Is he all right? I've been trying to reach him."

"He's at a club called Rockers in Oak Bluffs."

"Has he been drinking?"

"Quite a lot, I'd say."

"He's supposed to have surgery tomorrow."

"He told me he's decided against it."

When she didn't respond immediately, it took him a moment to realize it was because she was crying. Finally she said, "It'll take me fifteen minutes to get there. Can you keep him talking?"

"I don't think that'll be a problem."

When Lincoln slid back onto his barstool, Coffin said, "Okay, here's what's going to happen, Lincoln. The chief of police in Edgartown is a friend of mine. Tomorrow, I'm going to go see him. Tell him what I suspect."

"Which is?"

"That girl never left this island."

"You've changed your mind, then."

"Yes."

"Okay, but again, why tell me?"

His chuckle was entirely devoid of mirth. "Because, Lincoln, I'm offering you an opportunity to join the We Don't Do Right by Girls Club. As a charter member, I can do that. You want to warn your friend Mickey? Let him make a run for it? Be my guest."

"Look, Mr. Coffin, I respect your professional instincts, but Mickey didn't have anything to do with Jacy's disappearance."

The other man just shook his head at this. "But you don't *know* that. You *believe* it. Take it from me, knowledge and belief are two completely different animals."

"Have it your way."

"*No*, Lincoln. It's not about me having it my way or you having it yours. It's about facing facts. Like the fact that your friend Mickey has a criminal record in the state of Connecticut, where he was arrested for beating a man into a coma with his bare hands. Two hours ago you didn't know that. Now you do."

"Except I don't *know* any such thing, because, no disrespect intended, I don't really know *you*. We only met today—well, yesterday—and you just spent the last half hour telling me about all the wife beaters you tried to protect when you were a cop. You and Troyer are old friends. Why wouldn't I believe you're protecting *him*?"

"Well, reason it out. You're a Minerva College graduate. Why would I tell you something about your friend that you could easily disprove if I'm lying."

"Because I might just believe you."

"But you don't."

"No, it doesn't track. If Mickey's got a criminal record . . . if he assaulted Jacy's father like you say, how come he never went to jail?"

"Ah, Lincoln, I feel sorry for you. I really do. He *did* go to jail. It's all part of the public record. He spent a full week in the county lockup. Where he *didn't* go was prison. Because when the guy he beat the shit out of finally came to, he refused to press charges."

"Why?"

"Well, if Mickey was *my* friend, I'd ask *him*."

"Is that why you drove out to Chilmark today? To ask *your* friend if he was involved in Jacy's disappearance?"

"That was the reason."

"And he denied it?"

"Correct."

"And you believed him."

"I'll put it this way, Lincoln. I didn't *dis*believe him."

"Okay, so how did he convince you?"

"Well, that day your friend punched him? Mason's got a different version of what went down. The version *you* tell, when your gentle, good-natured pal came upon the two of them in the kitchen, Troyer had the girl backed into a corner and was groping her. So it's Mickey to the rescue."

"That's what happened."

"Not the way Mason tells it. According to him, the girl didn't exactly mind getting groped."

"That's bullshit."

Coffin ignored this. "The way *he* tells it, he stepped in front of the girl because he thought your friend meant to hit *her*, not him."

"That's—"

"Were you there in the room?" When Lincoln hesitated, Coffin continued, "No, I didn't think so. Which means you don't *know*, Lincoln. You *believe*. And like all true believers, you reject out of hand anything that undermines your belief."

"Okay, but doesn't that same logic apply to you? Neither of us wants to disbelieve a friend."

"Our circumstances are similar, Lincoln, but not identical. Mason and I do go back a long time. He's needed my help now and then, it's true, and in the spirit of full disclosure I'll admit there was a time when I bottomed out and it was Mason who pulled me back from the brink. So, yeah, I *do* want to believe he's telling the truth.

But I'm under no illusions. He's always been ten different kinds of jerk, especially where women are concerned. So yeah, I've considered the possibility that he's gaslighting me. Can you honestly say the same when it comes to your pal Mickey?"

Just then a cheer went up at the other end of the bar. "Jesus," somebody said, "I gotta see that again."

"I get it, Lincoln," Coffin went on. "Loyalty. Faith. You think I didn't want to believe my son when he told me how his wife kept getting those bruises? And her always backing him up? Explaining how she'd been born a klutz?"

"I'm sorry—"

"There's no reason for *you* to be sorry, Lincoln. Like I said, I'm glad your life has worked out. I'm glad you never staked out your own kid's house because deep down you suspected he was a lying sack of shit. Suspected it because you'd seen how *other* women came by injuries like hers, and I'm *really* glad you weren't peering in the window the night a son of yours grabbed his wife by the throat and flung her clear across the room. Because that's where I was, Lincoln. Outside their house, looking in the window. I could've prevented the concussion she got when the back of her head hit the wall, because I saw what was coming plain as day, but until he actually did it I didn't *know*. Until that moment? Until I fucking cuffed him? I could still *believe*."

If Lincoln hadn't been expecting her, he wouldn't have recognized the woman who entered Rockers then as Beverly. At the *Vineyard Gazette*, nicely dressed and made-up, she'd been attractive enough to make Lincoln feel guilty for noticing. Now, sans makeup and wearing baggy shorts and a threadbare sweatshirt, she looked every one of her years and then some. Given what he'd just been told, it was hard not to see her as a woman who'd once been thrown across the room by an abusive husband. Only when she placed a hand on Coffin's shoulder did he look up from the dregs of his beer and locate his daughter-in-law in the backbar's mirror, his expression inexpressibly sad, as if their speaking of her had conjured the woman up in her current, diminished state. Then, all too quickly, his expression darkened. "Kevin," he called, the dark malice that Lincoln had glimpsed earlier back in force.

Lincoln took a deep breath. If things were going to go really, really bad, it would happen right now. "I was the one who called her, Mr. Coffin, not him."

If Coffin heard this, he gave no sign. Having put a twenty on the bar earlier, he now pushed it toward the approaching bartender. Kevin nodded hello at Beverly, then pushed it back. "On me, Joey. Be real good, though, if you didn't come in here anymore."

Coffin, leaving the bill right where it was, turned to Lincoln. "You know what happens to bodybuilders who eat steroids?" he said. "And don't say they get stupid, because they're already that or they wouldn't be bodybuilders."

"Joe," Beverly implored him. He still hadn't acknowledged her presence. "Come on, let's get you home."

"They get this bright red rash up their spine. Looks like a strawberry patch."

"Mr. Coffin—" Lincoln began.

"Am I right, Kevin? You got a rash like that up your back? This twenty says you do."

Kevin shook his head. "You really want me to come around this bar, Joey?"

"No, I just want you to show my new friend Lincoln your rash. He's never seen one, and he's the kind of guy who doesn't believe what you tell him unless he sees it with his own two eyes."

"Because if I do come around there, Joey, I'm not going to be gentle with you. I know you used to be a tough guy, but you're old now and those days are gone."

"Please?" Beverly pleaded. "Joe?"

"This isn't necessary, Mr. Coffin," Lincoln assured him. "I believe you, okay?" He was trying to diffuse the situation, of course, but when he said the words they didn't feel like a lie.

"You're not just blowin' smoke, Lincoln? I wouldn't want you to say that just to save Kevin a beating."

"That's hilarious," Kevin told him.

"No. I believe you," Lincoln repeated, and it didn't feel like a lie this time, either.

Coffin studied him drunkenly, deciding. Finally, he said, "All righty then. I guess we can all go home." Again he pushed the twenty toward the bartender. "Put this in your tip jar. Use it to buy some medicated cream for that rash."

Sliding off his stool, Coffin lost his balance and probably would've fallen if Beverly hadn't been there to steady him. Something about how she managed this suggested it wasn't the first occasion she'd had to. For his part, Coffin seemed emptied out, not just of energy but even of a pulse, as if talking to Lincoln had drained him completely. Lincoln hoped that wasn't the case, because there was something he needed to ask. "Before you go?" he said.

"Yes, Lincoln?"

"That incident you told me about earlier? Involving my friend Mickey? You wouldn't happen to remember when that took place?"

Coffin stared into the middle distance. "I want to say 1974, but like I said, you can look it up."

"Okay, thanks. Can I give you a hand outside?"

It was really Beverly he was asking, but Coffin answered, "No, I think the evening has been humiliating enough without that."

Nineteen seventy-four, Lincoln thought when the door finally swung shut behind them. If memory served, that fall was when Gerald Ford declared amnesty for draft resisters, and when Mickey, like so many others, returned home. While he was in Canada, except for a single postcard, they hadn't been in touch. The card had arrived care of his parents in Dunbar in October of '71, by which time Mickey had been gone several months. It pictured the magnificent Château Frontenac in Quebec City, and on the back Mickey had scrawled: *Thought you might like to see my new digs.* He'd signed it *Big Mick on Pots.* Excited, Lincoln had called Teddy, only to learn that *his* parents had received the identical card and message. "I guess he must not have heard about Jacy," Teddy speculated, "or he would have asked if she'd been in touch." Only later did it occur to Lincoln that his friend's logic was flawed. If Mickey'd wanted to know about that, he would've needed to provide a return address, which of course he wouldn't have, lest the information fall into the wrong hands.

It wasn't until early '75, after the amnesty, that Lincoln heard from him again, this in the form of a belated Christmas card letting him know that he was back and would contact them all again once he was settled. For now he was in West Haven, living with his mother while he looked for work and an apartment. He knew a couple guys who were looking to form a band, so he might do that. This time he did mention her: *I guess nobody's heard from Jacy?* A month or two after that they spoke on the phone and he explained that his mother, with whom he'd been in touch while he was in Canada, had told him Jacy had evidently run off rather than get married, which Mickey accepted as the most likely reason for her disappearance. When Lincoln expressed his own doubts on this score, Mickey waved them away. "Mark my words," he said. "She'll turn up one of these days with a European husband and brag about being a foreign correspondent based in Singapore or some fucking place." When asked how *he* was doing, he claimed things were coming together, but Lincoln heard something in his voice that made him wonder if he might be struggling more than he was admitting. Now that he was back home, did he regret having gone to Canada? Was he being treated like a pariah? *You should come see us in Arizona,* Lincoln told him, and Mickey said he definitely would, once he got settled, but that visit never happened.

So if what Coffin was telling him now was true, most of this had been at best an evasion and at worst outright deception. His friend's first order of business hadn't been to find a job or an apartment or to form a new band. Nor had he really been sanguine about Jacy's disappearance. No, Job One had apparently been to locate her father. But why? Did he think Donald Calloway would know his daughter's whereabouts? Most of the time Mickey was in Canada the man had been in jail. The person more likely to have heard from Jacy during this period was her mother. Wouldn't it have made more sense to track *her* down? Lincoln tried to understand all this, but it was like coming across an old jigsaw puzzle in the back of a closet, with half its pieces missing.

Taking out his cell, he considered trying Mickey again. If he'd hauled this Delia person home by water taxi, he'd surely have arrived on the mainland by now and would have reception. But if he answered, Lincoln would need to decide whether he was calling as friend or inquisitor, as a member of the We Don't Do Right by Girls Club, urging him to flee while he had the chance, or as Jacy's avenger, determined to know the truth regardless of the cost. He hated to admit it, but Coffin was right. Belief and knowledge *were* different animals. It was the latter he'd been after when he first Googled Troyer and again when he visited the *Vineyard Gazette*. When he went to see Coffin in Vineyard Haven, it was still information, answers, he'd been looking for. Why hadn't it occurred to him that asking questions about the past might disturb the present, that in the end he might want to unlearn what he'd found out?

Son? came the hitch-pitched voice of Wolfgang Amadeus, piping up all the way from Dunbar, Arizona, no trace of a stroke in his voice. *I fear you've forgotten your Genesis. Yes, it was the Tree of Knowledge in the Garden. But Adam's sin was pride.*

Put a sock in it, Dad, Lincoln told him. *I'm trying to* think, *here.*

The old buzzard did have a point, though. He *had* been prideful. Perhaps even vainglorious, another of his father's favorite words. Solving the mystery of Jacy's disappearance was a task he'd let himself believe he was equal to. But his quest for knowledge, for understanding, hadn't really been about her. Or about truth, or justice. It'd been about himself. How ridiculous was that? Sixty-six years old and still trying to prove to a girl four decades dead that he was the one she should've chosen.

So you admit it, his father said. *I'm right.*

Mind your own damn business, Dad, Lincoln told him. *Go talk Spanglish to your new girlfriend.*

Now, Son, replied Dub-Yay, *that right there was a low blow.*

LINCOLN EXPECTED COFFIN and his daughter-in-law to be gone, as in long, when he emerged from Rockers, but there they were, just up the dark, deserted street, Beverly trying her best to wedge his carcass into her VW's passenger seat. Had he fallen crossing the street? Was that why they'd made so little progress? Or did she have to argue him out of driving himself back to Vineyard Haven? Since neither seemed to notice him, Lincoln slipped quietly behind the wheel of his rental car and scrunched down so he could surveil the tableau playing out. When Beverly tried to belt him in, Coffin swatted her hand away, and she rested her forehead on the door's frame. Then, giving up, she closed the door and moved around to the driver's side.

There's your serpent right there, Dub-Yay chimed in.

No, Dad. That's just a sick old man. Like you.

Though again, he did have a point. The serpent in Genesis *had* been a cunning, insidious whisperer of half-truths and innuendo, his pitch to Adam not unlike Coffin's rabbit-hole soliloquy about men not doing right by girls, which—why not admit it?—had entered Lincoln's bloodstream like venom. The narrative's myriad details had been vivid and had the ring of truth, but could the same be said for the whole? Lincoln wasn't sure. Its main thrust seemed to be that male misbehavior existed on a spectrum, like autism. Sure, some men were better behaved than others, but in the end they were all complicit because they closed ranks, as he'd put it, whenever it became truly necessary. As if to prove his point he'd offered Lincoln the opportunity to join that club himself. What made Lincoln suspicious was the man's most plausible intention—to convince him that his belief in his lifelong friend was divorced from real, cop-worthy knowledge. Coffin's circuitous monologue also trailed an unmistakable warning: that the knowledge Lincoln had been chasing earlier might now be chasing *him.* Resistance was futile. Ultimately, his faith in his friend would crumble before the relentless assault of *fact*, like those who had tried so hard to believe that the Vietnam War was just and necessary.

But hadn't Coffin also overplayed his hand? Not content to cheapen Lincoln's faith in Mickey, he'd also slandered Jacy. Even if you granted his assertion that men didn't do right by girls, what was his assault on Jacy's character besides another instance of victim blaming? Yes, Jacy had been as wild as the times they were then living through, but she'd also possessed an innocence that Coffin, who'd never met her, had utterly no knowledge of. She'd been both loyal and true. Their all-for-one and one-for-all friendship at Minerva had never once been contaminated by irony. *I couldn't bear it* was what she had written to them on that final morning about the prospect of having to say goodbye. It was that loyalty, that innocence, that Coffin's narrative sought to undermine by painting Jacy as a tramp, who'd maybe been disappointed when Mickey arrived on the scene and spoiled her fun, the kind she never got to have with the three of them because they were such cowards and prudes. It was a cynical, insidious argument that Lincoln would've rejected out of hand if it hadn't semi-aligned with his mother's own assessment of the situation—that Jacy might've been waiting in vain for one of them to find the courage to declare himself. They'd all been perfect gentlemen with her. What if it wasn't a gentleman she'd been looking for?

All of which made Lincoln yearn for the one thing he clearly couldn't have: he wanted his friends back, all three of them, and not just back but back as they'd been at Minerva, with their whole lives ahead of them.

What you really want, Son, Dub-Yay assured him, *is your own lost youth.*

But no, Lincoln was pretty sure that wasn't it. He and his friends weren't entitled to a second youth any more than they deserved a second chance to do everything right. Nor was it really about lost innocence, because by '71 that had already been shaken by what they were learning about life in their classes, as well as at the Theta house, not to mention the war and a draft lottery that could alter their individual trajectories.

Then what? Dub-Yay wanted to know. *If not youth or innocence, then what is it?*

At first Lincoln didn't know, but then he did. What he really longed for, he realized, was his generation's naïve conviction that if the world turned out to be irredeemably corrupt, they could just opt out. Embarrassing, when you put it like that, but hadn't that been the central article of their faith? They'd believed that being right about the war their parents were so stubbornly wrong about meant that they were somehow special, maybe even exceptional. They would change the world. Or at least they'd give its crass inducements, its various bribes and dishonest incentives, a miss. Wolfgang Amadeus might be wrong about a lot of things, but neither he nor Lincoln's mother, nor anyone else in their generation, had been fool enough to imagine you could bail out of the world that made you.

Up the street, Beverly's VW was backing away from the curb. Lincoln watched it drive up Circuit Avenue until the taillights disappeared. *Joe,* she'd called her father-in-law, not *Dad,* as Anita occasionally referred to Wolfgang Amadeus. And just like that Lincoln was certain that the two were, or had been at some point, more than friends. Yet more venomous, unwanted knowledge.

When his phone vibrated in his pocket, Lincoln thought about letting the call go to voicemail, but Wolfgang Amadeus wouldn't hear of it. *God hates a coward, Son.*

"Lincoln," Mickey said. Not Face Man, Lincoln noted.

"Mick. Where are you?"

"Your place. Chilmark. You need to go fetch Ted." Not Teddy. Not Tedioski, not Teduski, not Tedwicki, not Tedmarek. *Ted.*

"He's still in recovery."

"No, he isn't. I just talked to him."

"They won't release him until morning, Mickey. At the earliest."

"Just pull up in front. He'll be waiting."

"Mick—"

"Do it, Lincoln."

An order, and in or under it something in his friend's voice that he'd never heard before.

Okay, Dad, he thought. *What now?*

But of course the connection had gone dead. The purpose of such imaginary conversations, he knew, was to practice for the day in the not-too-distant future when Dub-Yay, like Lincoln's mother, would exist only in Lincoln's mind. Bad timing, too. The world he and his friends had imagined they could either reinvent or opt out of had at last come calling. In fact it was banging at the door, demanding to be let in so it could present its past-due bill for payment.

"Tell me why," Lincoln said, making a demand of his own, though to his ears it sounded both petulant and pleading. "Give me one good reason."

"Because you *both* need to be here" came Mickey's reply. "Because I'm only telling this fucking story once."

Mickey

Though the season was different—the end of summer, not the beginning—the moon rose over the distant waves just like it did back in 1971. That night, too, there'd been a chill in the air, one that eventually drove them inside. Down the slope Mason Troyer's house was dark, just as it had been then. Yesterday Mickey had even considered strolling down there and offering a much-belated apology for punching him. Had the man's jaw completely healed? Mickey's own right hand, which he'd never seen a doctor about, still ached on rainy days and was prone to swelling. His own damn fault, of course. His father, who'd been a brawler in his youth, had warned him about physical violence, both its dangers and, especially, its pleasures. When you threw a punch, whatever was coiled in you got released, and release, well, what was better than that? Starting and finishing a fight with a single punch, as Mickey'd done with Troyer? That was the absolute best. Proving that any job, no matter how dubious, could be done well. Indeed, it was his father that Mickey had been thinking about that afternoon outside the SAE house. Bert. That's what the guys in his father's crew all called Michael Sr., due to his resemblance to Bert Lahr, the Cowardly Lion in *The Wizard of Oz*. "Hey, Bert," they'd say. "What makes the muskrat guard his musk?" And his old man, playing along, would reply, *"Kuh-ridge."* And damned if those stone lions hadn't looked just like him, too.

By contrast, the beating Mickey'd given Jacy's father had felt like a distasteful duty, not even remotely pleasurable. Maybe it was the office setting, and that there'd been so many people around, the majority of them women, all of them horrified. Mickey's first punch had reduced the man's nose to ruined cartilage, and yeah, okay, that *had* felt pretty good. So had saying, "Your daughter says hello," as the man lay there on the snazzy carpet. Maybe if that first punch had landed flush and he was out for the count, Mickey would feel better about it. Instead, Calloway had struggled to his feet not once but three more times, as if he didn't want Mickey to stint on the beating they both knew he had coming. So Mickey had obliged, though with each subsequent punch he'd applied less force and torque. When the cops arrived and cuffed him, he was glad. He wouldn't have to hit the man anymore. The experience had so soured him on violence that he hadn't punched anyone since, except occasionally in his dreams.

Though the moon on the waves and the chill in the air were reminiscent of 1971, tonight was different, too, and not just because Jacy was gone. This night there would be no singing. They were sixty-six now, far too old to convince themselves that their chances were awfully good, that the world gave the tiniest little fuck about their hopes and dreams, assuming they had any left. Even so, before coming out onto the deck, he put some music on low. Delia, still pissed at him for blaming her for how things had turned out, finally did drift off, and she slept more soundly when there was music playing. Most nights she went to bed wearing headphones, claiming music muted the voices in her head that always reminded her that she was a piece of shit. Tonight, to mute his own dark thoughts, Mickey had rooted around in the kitchen cabinets until he found the bottle of good scotch Lincoln had mentioned buying in town. He hardly ever drank hard liquor anymore, not since going to the doctor with shortness of breath and being told about his defective heart valve. Of *course* it was defective. Was he not his father's son? The pitcher of Bloody Marys he'd mixed that morning was the first booze he'd tasted in over a year. He'd promised Delia he was done with the hard stuff, and until today he'd kept his word in the vain hope that it might help her keep hers. Fat fucking chance. Mickey disliked standing in judgment, but he did wish people wouldn't lie about being clean when they weren't. Was that so much to ask?

Yet what was his own life but a web of lies, most of them unnecessary. That he should want his friends to believe he was still a serious boozer when all he ever had anymore was beer—which his doctors told him would kill him less quickly—mystified him. The mountain of ribs he'd eaten tonight had also been for show. Hell, if there'd been any coke around, he probably would've done that, too, all to convince Lincoln and Teddy that he was who he'd always been, that his life was proceeding according to plan, that he regretted nothing because there was nothing to regret. He wouldn't even have admitted to the motorcycle accident if the evidence weren't so gruesomely visible, the livid white scar at his hairline. If it had been just Lincoln, he might've taken his chances. One day back at Minerva, Lincoln had noticed his government professor limping and asked why. Because, the man informed him, his left leg was a prosthesis right up to the hip. He'd been clomping around like Captain Ahab all term, but Lincoln had only just noticed. In some ways his friend's habit of not really taking things in made him the perfect college student, more interested in what things meant than that they existed in the first place, as if you could determine the significance of something without actually observing it. Teddy, however, had an eagle eye, especially for anything involving bodily injury. It was as if he expected whatever he came in contact with to maim him. No hope whatsoever he wasn't going to notice the scar.

Had his father lived, things would've been different, Mickey thought, but maybe this was another lie. Strange, and yet somehow fitting, to be back here where the life of deception he hadn't planned on had begun. This island. This house.

BY THE TIME the guys returned, Mickey had dozed off out on the deck. The crunch of tires on gravel woke him, and then he heard car doors open and close, his friends' voices muted in the soft night. He was relieved. He'd told Lincoln that Teddy would be ready and waiting for him when he arrived at the hospital, but he hadn't been at all sure that would happen. Teddy hadn't been officially discharged, so it was possible the graveyard nurse might try to stop him. Or maybe when he tried to get out of bed and dress himself, Teddy would find he couldn't. But no, here they were. A light came on inside and a moment later Lincoln appeared behind the glass door, his face a thundercloud. Sliding it open, he stepped aside for Teddy, who paused in the doorway, wobbling and woozy. A thick white bandage the size of a tennis ball was affixed over his right eye.

Mickey stood up. "Can I help?"

"I got him," Lincoln said, his fury barely contained as he guided Teddy outside. When he was settled, Lincoln started to take a seat himself but noticed the whiskey bottle and went back into the kitchen.

"Well," Mickey said, looking Teddy over, "you look better than you did at the club. How do you feel?"

"Weak. Not much pain at the moment."

"What'd they give you?"

"I forget. Some next-gen pain pills. They're working, is the main thing."

"I hear the trick is to stop taking them when the pain goes away. You up to this?"

"Wake me up if I nod off. I think I've already figured out most of it."

"Yeah?" Mickey didn't see how that could conceivably be true.

"Not figured out, exactly," Teddy said. "It's more like . . . I just woke up knowing."

Mickey chuckled. "Good, then *you* can tell it."

When Teddy offered up the weakest of smiles, Mickey felt a wave of guilt wash over him. What he was doing—demanding that his friends listen to his story this very night—was both selfish and cruel, though the alternative would've been to sneak off the island with Delia and let them imagine the worst, which Lincoln, quite possibly, was already doing.

When the door slid open again, Lincoln reappeared with two glasses holding a few cubes of ice and set them in the middle of the table. "You probably shouldn't," he told Teddy, who took a glass anyway. Lincoln poured himself two fingers, gave Teddy a splash, then set the bottle down within Mickey's reach. The message was clear: he could pour his own, which he did. "Okay," he began. "I'm not sure where to start, but—"

"It was an accident," Lincoln blurted. "Begin there."

"I'm sorry?"

"How she died. Explain how it was an accident."

"Lincoln," Teddy said, his voice almost a whisper. "Let him tell his own story."

"Yeah, Mick," Lincoln agreed. "Tell us how Jacy died."

"She died in my arms," Mickey said. He could feel her there still, almost forty years later.

"An accident."

"Yes," he confessed, though he had no idea how Lincoln could've intuited this.

Lincoln swallowed hard. "Is she buried here?"

Stunned, Mickey shook his head. If the idea weren't completely lunatic, he'd have sworn that by *here* his friend meant under this very sloping lawn. "I'm lost, man," he said. "Why would she be buried here?"

"Don't lie," Lincoln said. "Don't you fucking lie, Mick. The cops will be here tomorrow and they'll dig up every inch of this place. If she's here, they'll find her."

Laughing was exactly the wrong thing to do, of course, but really, he couldn't help himself. Lie your ass off for forty years and everybody believes you, but when you finally decide to tell the truth . . . "Lincoln," he said, "I don't have the first clue what you're—"

But this was as far as he got, because Lincoln, showing no signs of back stiffness now, came flying out of his chair. Grabbing Mickey by the throat with his left hand, his right was balled into a fist and cocked. He would've thrown the punch, too, Mickey was certain, if the door to the deck hadn't slid open just then. Seeing Delia in the doorway, blinking and groggy, Lincoln let go of Mickey's neck, straightened up and turned to face her. When Mickey rose to his feet, Teddy did, too.

"It's okay," Mickey told her, his voice raspy. "Come on out and meet my friends."

For a tortuous moment nobody moved. But then Teddy went over to where Delia stood in the doorway and put his arms around her. Startled, she glanced at Mickey over his shoulder, but allowed the embrace. After another long moment Teddy stepped back so he could study her at arm's length. "You look like your mom," he said, smiling.

The smile she returned was Jacy's, to a T.

THEY'D AGREED TO MEET at the restaurant adjacent to the ferry landing in Woods Hole, but he wasn't sure she'd show up. Their hasty plan was hatched yesterday afternoon when Lincoln was on the phone with Anita, and Teddy, in one of his periodic funks, had gone for a walk.

But a lot had happened since then, and Mickey wouldn't have blamed her for having second thoughts. "Since when have we started keeping secrets from each other?" he'd asked her, the question not entirely rhetorical. She and Teddy had snuck off to Gay Head earlier in the day, and to judge by his demeanor when they returned, something must've happened there. Poor Teddy. They were all hopelessly in love with her, but he seemed the furthest gone. Had he lost his composure and confessed his feelings, begged her not to marry Vance? Had she then clipped his wings? She would've done so gently, of course, because Mickey suspected Teddy was her favorite. On the other hand, if he'd violated their unspoken pact, well, didn't he kind of have it coming?

Thinking this, he immediately felt guilty. After all, if their pact was unspoken, who could say they even *had* one? He'd always assumed that that's what *all for one and one for all* amounted to—a coded agreement that they'd never go behind one another's backs in pursuit of Jacy's affections, which was all the more convenient since she was engaged to someone else entirely. If it existed at all, their understanding amounted to little more than a noncompete clause that there would be no need to ever enforce. Yet in a sense they *had* been competing, even when they were together, and if Jacy was going to marry someone not named Mickey, he preferred it wouldn't be to someone named Lincoln or Teddy. A shameful admission, but there it was, and unless he was mistaken his friends felt the same way. Vance probably *was* a complete asshole, and Jacy certainly deserved better, but Mickey had accepted the idea that they would get married as one of the many things in life he was powerless to alter, like his father's death or his own lottery number. But if Jacy were to end up with either Teddy or Lincoln, well, he wasn't sure he'd ever get used to that.

Anyway, it was possible that after last night's all-for-one singing and boozing she'd thought better of their planned assignation and hopped on a bus to New York City, as she'd originally intended. In fact, looking around the restaurant and not seeing her, he felt both crushing disappointment and—hey, relief. But then a young woman in a big floppy hat and dark glasses, sitting by herself on the deck, waved to him.

Going outside, he pulled up a chair opposite her. "Is that supposed to be a disguise?" She looked like a hippie version of Audrey Hepburn in *Charade*.

Jacy narrowed her eyes theatrically. "Were they suspicious?"

Mickey shook his head. Lincoln and Teddy had dropped him off at the entrance to the Steamship Authority lot in Falmouth, where they said their awkward guy-goodbyes.

"I wish you'd listen to reason," Teddy told him. "Hell, *I'd* go to Canada with you if it'd keep you out of Vietnam."

Mickey, moved by the offer, had deflected it with humor, assuring both friends that he was really more worried about them than himself, especially Lincoln, given how pussy-whipped he already was and not even engaged yet. With Mickey gone, he'd be without a male role model.

To which Teddy said, "Thanks a lot."

In the end, Lincoln had refused to allow either a joke farewell or the offer of a handshake, saying only "Come here" and pulling Mickey into a tight embrace, whispering, "Good luck, man," which meant that Teddy had to hug him, too.

Once they drove off, Mickey, feeling like a heel for deceiving them, retrieved his car and drove back to Woods Hole.

"So," he told Jacy. "Explain what we're doing here, because I don't understand."

"All in good time," she said. "Let me see your hand."

He flexed his fingers for her, trying not to wince. "It's better today. Not so swollen."

She just shook her head and gave him her why-are-men-so-full-of-shit smile, one of his favorites, though he loved them all.

Her Bloody Mary looked like just the thing, so when the waitress came by he ordered one, too. "I'm assuming we have time?" he said.

Jacy nodded. "I got nowhere to be."

"I thought you were spending a day or two with Kelsey in New York."

"So I lied."

When the truth is found, Mickey thought. "Next you'll be telling me you aren't getting married."

"An *excellent* prediction!"

He tried not to beam at this news, but he could feel he was. "Does Vance know this?"

"Not yet, but he won't be surprised."

"How about your parents?"

"They'll be shocked." Now *she* was beaming.

"So what happened?"

Jacy sighed. "We couldn't decide where to live. I was thinking Haight-Ashbury. His idea was Greenwich, midway between our parents' houses."

"You could've compromised. I keep hearing that's what marriage is all about."

She shook her head. "Vance laid down the law. Which, if you're a woman, *is* what marriage is about."

The ferry, loaded up again, sounded its horn and pulled away from the slip, island-bound people waving from the upper deck. When the waitress brought Mickey's Bloody Mary, he swilled a third of it and felt his hangover instantly recede. "Teddy said he'd go with me to Canada, if it'd keep me out of the war."

"Poor Teddy," she said, looking away now, her eyes glistening.

"Did something weird happen at Gay Head yesterday?"

"We went skinny-dipping."

"Yeah? Whose idea was that?"

"Mine," she said, meeting his eyes now, and there was a challenge in this admission. Was it some sort of a test? *Don't ask*, he thought, but of course he had to. "Did anything else happen?"

She was still looking directly at him. "That was it."

Well, he thought, that would explain Teddy's funk. He'd looked guilty, but he was really just broken-hearted. No wonder they'd had to coax him into singing "Chances Are" with them on the deck. His own slim chances had just been rendered null and void, whereas Mickey's own were now magically revived.

"Anyway," Jacy said. "You can't go to Canada with him."

"No?"

"It's out of the question."

"Why?"

"Because you're going there with me."

"have you ever been to Bar Harbor?" she wanted to know two days later. She'd lapsed into silence an hour earlier, and Mickey sensed she didn't want him to fill it in with chatter. It was possible, he thought, that the gravity of what they were doing—running off to Canada without money or even a real plan for what they'd do when they got there—might finally be dawning on her. He'd been expecting the next words out of her mouth to be *Okay, turn the car around. This was a dumb idea.*

Since leaving Woods Hole, they'd made it halfway up the coast of Maine, with the Atlantic always on their right, sometimes only a hundred yards off, then disappearing completely for an hour or more. When he'd pointed out that there were more direct routes into Canada, she said, "Your days of going anywhere directly are over," a statement he took to be metaphorical, though its meaning still eluded him. She'd promised to answer the question he'd posed back in Woods Hole *(What are we doing?)*, as well as a host of others that had occurred to him since *(Shouldn't you call your parents so they don't worry? Shouldn't you let Vance know the wedding's off? What about Lincoln and Teddy? Why all the secrecy?)*. But every single one had gone unanswered. Something seemed to be troubling her, but all he could get out of her was that he'd understand everything in the fullness of time.

"When would I have visited Bar Harbor?" he snorted.

She shrugged. "I don't know. Where'd your parents take you on vacation when you were a kid?"

"We went to the lake."

"Which lake?"

"See, that's the thing, poor little rich girl. When I was a kid I thought there was just the one. We'd go for a week in August. Sometimes two, if we were flush. Everybody from the neighborhood vacationed there."

She squinted at him. "So . . . when you went on vacation, you saw the same people you saw the rest of the year? On the street where you lived?"

"People stop and stare," Mickey warbled, "they don't bother me . . . 'cause there's nowhere on this earth that I would rather be . . ."

How long would it be before she understood, he wondered—this *thing*, his life before Minerva, that he was forever trying and failing to explain. Even Teddy and Lincoln—neither of whom came from money, though Lincoln's family was pretty comfortable—seemed to have a hard time grasping why he clung to certain ideas so stubbornly. They'd been incredulous, for instance, when he chose to remain in the kitchen scrubbing pots when he could've been a face man swanning around in the dining room. How did one explain the Acropolis, a West Haven diner and his real first job—yeah, scrubbing pots—where Nestor, the owner, paid him under the table? Just a few hours after school and a few more on weekends. Each day an abundance of pots and pans awaited him on the long drainboard where they'd been sitting, crusting up, since lunch. Over the next two hours he'd slowly plow through them, imagining what that Fender Stratocaster he'd had his eye on for a while would feel like slung over his shoulder, the frets along its sleek neck smooth beneath his callused fingers. Aware that his parents wouldn't approve of a job after school when he was supposedly getting his grades up, he told them he'd joined a Catholic Youth study group, not the kind of lie that he judged would keep him out of heaven. But back then his old man was suspicious of everything that came out of Mickey's mouth, and one day when he finished up in back, he found Michael Sr. seated at the counter, eating a piece of cheesecake. When he indicated the vacant stool next to him, Mickey slid onto it. "You want a soda?" his father said. "You look all sweaty." When the Coke arrived, his father said, "So what's this all about?"

"A guitar," Mickey confessed.

"You already got a guitar."

"This is a better one."

His father's eyes narrowed. Dangerous territory, this. "The one we got you last Christmas isn't good enough?" An off-brand Nu-Tone, with a bowed neck and raised frets that buzzed and barked.

"Think of it . . . as a tool," Mickey explained, pleased to locate an analogy his old man might accept. *A man's no better than his tools* was one of his favorite sayings.

"Okay," his father said, willing, for the moment, to concede the point, "but there's this other thing."

"What other thing?"

"You lied to your mother."

This was his father in a nutshell. Whenever Mickey got caught doing something he shouldn't, it was always his mother he was disappointing, not both of them. As if his father had long ago written him off as a lost cause.

"You told her you were in study hall or some horseshit. Sorry," he added, because the waitress had appeared just then to warm up his coffee.

"You gonna tell Mom about that cheesecake?" Mickey said. Because his father's last visit to the doctor had revealed both high blood pressure and elevated blood-sugar levels. Since he'd been instructed to lose weight, sweets were no longer on his diet, except for Sunday mornings when they made a special trip to Wooster Street for Italian pastries.

His father appealed to the waitress, who looked like she might be a diabetes candidate herself. "Do you believe the mouth on this kid?"

"These days, they all got 'em," she replied, winking at Mickey.

"His is gonna be the death of him," his father said, slapping a twenty on the counter.

Outside in the car, Mickey said, "So I can keep the job?"

"For now," his father said, "granted your mother agrees. Is Nestor treating you right?"

"Yeah, he's okay."

"He'd better be. I got a piece of broken PVC pipe in the trunk that'd fit in his ear just perfect. You like the work? The only reason I ask is I've never known you to wash a dish at home."

Mickey started to say no, that washing pots was just a means to an end, but then realized that wasn't quite true. Yeah, that pile of pots was always dispiriting to contemplate when he first walked in, but he actually kind of liked working through them at his own pace, and he liked the feeling of being finished even more, of having accomplished a task, even if that task was mindless and left you smelling like a dishcloth that had been marinating in bacon grease. "It's okay, I guess."

"Good," his father said. "I don't ever want to hear about you doing a half-assed job. That PVC pipe would fit in your ear, too, *capisce?*"

This was what Lincoln and Teddy—never mind Jacy—couldn't seem to wrap their minds around. They suspected he stayed in the kitchen because he had something against rich girls, didn't like the idea of having to be nice to them. But he really just liked it in the back of the house. The cooks reminded him of his mother's friends in West Haven, and he even liked the long stainless-steel drainboard, the industrial-strength sprayer above the sink and the always-humid air, all of which took him back to the Acropolis and the thrill of that first Stratocaster he'd bought with the money he earned there. To Mickey, the Theta house's kitchen felt a little like a church, or rather how he imagined church was supposed to feel but never did, at least not to him. He'd enjoyed Minerva, but unlike Lincoln and Teddy he'd never truly believed he belonged there. Sure it was *better* than West Haven, but that didn't mean he had to love it. He also was slowly coming to understand that his father's greatness, what made the man worth emulating, was his ability to love what he'd been given, what had been thrust upon him, what he had little choice but to accept.

He would've liked to explain all this to Jacy now. The questions she asked him about his earlier life always suggested genuine interest, though he could also tell that, for her, it was like studying a foreign language. She was able to recognize cognates and build a small, pragmatic vocabulary, but to become really fluent she'd have to immerse herself. And what Greenwich, Connecticut, girl would want to immerse herself in West Haven, with its construction workers and overweight cops and preening bodybuilders? While he liked that she was curious, his answers didn't seem to lead to real understanding, just more questions. (*Why* hadn't *his parents taken him to Bar Harbor? Okay, maybe they couldn't afford to stay for very long or at the nicer places, but couldn't they at least* go?) Even with him as a guidebook, she remained a tourist. Not that he blamed her. What did it matter if she really didn't speak his language fluently? At Minerva he'd learned to speak a dialect closer to hers than his own, right? It wasn't like they couldn't communicate. If a gap remained, over time they would bridge it.

"So, Bar Harbor was your family's regular summer spot?"

"Not every year. Sometimes we went to the Berkshires. Or the Cape. Or Nantucket."

"Just the three of you?"

"Occasionally we'd go with another couple. Usually somebody from Donald's firm."

Mickey was about to ask who Donald was when he remembered Jacy always referred to her parents by their given names. Donald and Vivian. Don and Viv.

August on Nantucket versus a week at the lake. *That* was the gap they needed to bridge for this to work. Not a gap, a chasm. Still, he supposed it might've been wider. He might've been poorer, she even richer. He might've been black. Yet the gap was real and not nothing. Love might help, assuming that's what they were feeling. In fact, wasn't love the so-called answer?

And there was another gap. Running off to Canada instead of reporting for duty, after the solemn promise he'd made his father. "I'm not sure I can do it," he'd told her back in Woods Hole.

"But it's the right thing," she insisted. "You must see that. This war is crazy. Not to mention immoral."

True enough, and it was also true that his father *would* understand, at least in part. "Marrying your mother was the smartest thing I ever did," he was fond of saying when she wasn't around to hear it. He would surely recognize the power of his own feelings for Jacy. But although the man was dead, Mickey could also picture the two of them perched on stools at the Acropolis, his father scarfing down forbidden cheesecake. *So what's all this about?* he would ask. *Not another fucking guitar, I hope.*

A girl, Mickey would reply.

Okay, sure, his father would agree. *That's fine, but there's this other thing.*

What other thing?

This war.

It's stupid, Dad.

They're all stupid. That's not the point.

What is?

The point is, if you don't go, somebody goes in your place, capisce? *Look around right here, this diner. Half a dozen guys your age in here. A couple right over there in that booth. Which one should go in your place? Point him out to me, because I can't tell.*

The point is nobody should go.

Yeah, but somebody will. Some poor bastard is *going.*

And you think it should be me.

No. In fact, I'd go in your place, if they had any fucking use for a middle-aged pipefitter with a bum ticker.

And he would've, too. Mickey was sure of it. More than anything else, he wished that his father was alive for Jacy to meet. Because *then* she'd have understood what she was asking him to do.

I'm sorry, Pop. I'll try to make it up to you.

Except it's not between me and you. It's between you *and you.*

"So," Mickey said, "do you want to spend tonight in Bar Harbor?"

"God, no," Jacy told him. "I hate the fucking place."

THEY SPENT THAT NIGHT in a run-down motel on a hill overlooking the Atlantic, not far from the Canadian border. Jacy, still in her Audrey Hepburn disguise, waited in the car while Mickey went inside to register, just as she had the night before. "They couldn't care less," he assured her, "it's 1971." Free spirit that she was, it seemed out of character for her to worry about what strangers might think. Was it possible he'd misjudged her? He'd always assumed she and Vance were having sex, but he didn't know it for a fact. Was it possible Jacy was secretly chaste? There were plenty of girls like that in West Haven—especially the Italian ones from the neighborhood, girls who talked a good game and let on that there'd be sex galore, maybe even tomorrow, except tomorrow never came. It was hard to imagine that Jacy was one of these, but there was no telling. Nor, he reminded himself, did it necessarily follow that her decision not to marry Vance meant that she'd leap right into bed with him.

She certainly hadn't the night before. Of course, they'd both been exhausted after a long day on the road, and their room had two single beds. But Mickey suspected it wouldn't have mattered if there'd been a king. She'd gone into the bathroom, where he'd heard the shower running, but when she emerged she was wearing a long nightshirt and she'd immediately climbed into one of the twins, saying, "It's all yours." Meaning what? The bathroom? The shower? That he *needed* a shower? He took one, just in case. But when he came out, wearing a towel around his waist, the room was dark except for the reading lamp next to the empty bed, a signal that even he could interpret. That she didn't want to have sex was disappointing, though this troubled him less than the fact that she seemed not to want any affection at all. No cuddle. No kiss goodnight. Was she afraid she'd get his motor running and then there'd be no way to turn it off? Or was she having second thoughts, great big ones? Maybe changing her mind about getting married had opened the floodgates of self-doubt and she wasn't sure about anything anymore. Beyond exhausted himself, he'd fallen asleep before reaching any conclusions. Tonight, though, he had to wonder if it'd be more of the same. And the night after, too.

The room was cheap enough, but when Mickey checked in and pulled out his wallet to pay he was a few dollars short. So far she'd let him pay for everything—lodging, food, gas. He knew he was getting low on funds and meant to stop at some bank to see if he could cash a check, but it had slipped his mind. Back at the car, humiliated, he said, "Sorry, but I need to borrow five bucks."

"Oh, right," she said, but when he opened the trunk so she could get her backpack, she held it so he couldn't see anything. Then, after zipping it back up, she handed him a bill that he pocketed without a glance. Only when he was in the office did he notice it was a hundred. He hadn't seen one of those since his father died. Michael Sr., like many workingmen, always carried his money in a roll in his front pocket, no doubt comforted by its weight, the illusion of control you couldn't get from a flimsy credit card. *What am I doing here, Pop?* he wondered as the woman at the front desk counted out his change, though he knew what his response would've been: *Find out, Son.*

For dinner they went to a family restaurant just up the road, where he ordered a chicken-fried steak, Jacy the baked haddock. For some reason, maybe because they'd be safe in Canada tomorrow, her mood had brightened. "What exactly *is* chicken-fried steak?" she said when the food was served. "I've always wondered."

That gap again, Mickey thought, forking over a piece.

She chewed it thoughtfully. "It tastes like beef-flavored breading."

He shrugged.

She grinned at him. "Cracker fare, according to Don and Viv."

Mickey nodded. "The food of my people."

"Oh, come on. Your people are Italian."

Which made him chuckle. "What do you think's in a meatball?"

"Meat?"

"Maybe a little, but mostly bread crumbs. Some other stuff that's cheaper than meat."

"When the truth is found," she sang, "to *beeeeeeee* . . . lies."

THEY APPEARED TO BE the only guests at the motel, which made sense this far north, still weeks before high summer. Each room had a small concrete patio in the rear with two plastic deck chairs. Mickey still had a smidgen of the weed he'd scored from Troyer before punching his lights out, and he figured they'd smoke that and watch the distant ocean as night fell. Also, driving back from the restaurant, they'd stopped at a convenience store and he bought a six-pack of beer. He'd also paid for dinner out of the hundred she'd given him. There was still some cash left, but he had to wonder: was this how life was going to be now? Him turning to her for money when he ran out? So halfway through the first beer, he decided to bring it up at an angle. "Once we get to wherever we're going," he ventured, "how do you see this working?"

"What do you mean, 'working'?"

"We'll need jobs."

"I'll wait tables. You'll tend bar." She said this as if it pained her to state the obvious. After all, they weren't likely to find work as nuclear physicists. "At some point you'll start a band."

"In that case," he said, "we should've gone home first and picked up my guitar." He had some money in his checking account, assuming he could find somebody in Canada to cash a check, but not enough to replace his Stratocaster. Since graduation he hadn't given much thought to money, figuring Uncle Sam would soon start picking up the tab. Now, suddenly, it was an issue again. "Anyway," he continued, "that sounds like what we'd be doing if we hadn't gone to college."

She took a swig of beer. "You got a better plan?"

"No, that *was* my plan. I was hoping you'd have a better one."

"Nope."

"How do you see *us* working? You and me."

She reached over and took his hand. "Things will be different once we're in Canada."

"Yeah?" he said, pleasantly surprised. It hadn't occurred to him that sexual intimacy might have a geographical component. If it did, she might've mentioned it earlier. They were only twenty miles from the border, and he'd have happily driven the extra half hour had he known such a reward was awaiting him on the other side. Hell, he'd have sung "O Canada!" the whole way. Which naturally made him think of the evening when he'd gotten the draft number that set this particular journey in motion.

When he finished his beer, he said, "I noticed a pay phone in the lobby. I really should call my mother."

"Why?"

"Because I was supposed to get home yesterday. She'll be worried. Also, before long she's going to start getting phone calls from the draft board wondering where the fuck I am."

"Okay," she agreed, reluctantly, it seemed to him. "But you can't mention that I'm with you."

"No?"

"No. Promise me. Nobody can know."

"What're you so worried about?" he said. "It's me they'll be after, not you."

"That's what you think."

Which gave him genuine pause. Did she mean Vance? Her parents? The sorority sisters who'd so faithfully guarded her virtue at Minerva? All of Greenwich, Connecticut? He knew what they were doing would have serious consequences for him, but until now it hadn't fully registered that Jacy was turning her back on her entire world.

"I need your word, Mick."

"You have it."

When he rose from his chair, she said, "Can it wait until morning?"

"Sure," he said, sitting back down. "I guess."

"Good. Because tonight I need to tell you about my father." When he remained silent, she said, "Nobody knows about this. You'll be the first to hear it."

"I don't understand. You mean Donald? Of Don and Viv?"

She blew a raspberry. "Who said anything about him?"

IT PROBABLY SHOULDN'T HAVE come as a surprise. After all, she didn't look anything like tall, sandy-haired Donald Calloway, who'd always referred to her as "our little Gypsy" because of her dark, curly hair and olive complexion. She was a kid, though, and what kid doubts what her parents tell her? But then eighth grade happened, with all its casual cruelty, its constant, roiling fluctuations of social capital. And boys. There was this one, Todd, that she'd liked because he was funny, always clowning around. She had to warn him not to when she introduced him to her parents, especially her father, who was aggressively humorless and thought she was too young to go out on dates. The kid managed to behave himself in their home, but once they were out the door he said, "Wow! How old were you?" When she asked what he was talking about, he said, "You know, when you were adopted?"

She told herself it was just one of his jokes, but she remembered feeling sick to her stomach and wasn't able to laugh it off. They'd gone to play miniature golf, and Todd paid, which he seemed to think gave him the right to continue teasing her even after she begged him to cut it out. Had she been adopted from an agency, or did she just get left on her parents' doorstep? Or was she found floating down the Connecticut River in a basket?

The most difficult hole was the Volcano, where you had to putt up a steep slope at the top of which was a tiny, shallow crater. If you misjudged your speed or didn't hit the center of the cup, the ball would rim out and roll all the way back down the mountainside, then you'd have to start all over again. Rattled by Todd's teasing, Jacy couldn't seem to get the hang of it, rimming out one shot after another. By rule, ten was the maximum score for any one hole, but Todd refused to move on until she sank the putt. When she finally did, she burst into tears and refused to continue, demanding he take her home. There, she crawled straight into bed, but it was impossible, even with the covers pulled over her head, to compose herself. The boy had opened a door into the part of her brain where riddles were stored. Things that had long puzzled her now began to make sense. How many times had she entered a room full of her mother's friends, only to have them all stop talking at once and regard her guiltily? And what about her father's cryptic remarks when he and her mother discussed some disagreeable habit of Jacy's ("Well, Viv, she certainly doesn't get that from *me*").

The following morning Todd called to apologize, claiming he hadn't meant anything. Lots of kids didn't look like their parents until later in life. He'd even asked her out the following weekend to make it up to her, but she said no. Her father, suspecting that something must've happened, insisted that she tell him what the boy had done, because he'd fucking kill the little prick, but Jacy said only that he'd made fun of her when she couldn't sink her putt on the Volcano hole. She could tell he didn't believe her.

It took Jacy a month to work up the courage to broach the subject with her mother. She expected her to go ballistic, but instead she went into the master bedroom and came back with the metal box where important documents were kept. It contained Jacy's birth certificate, and of course there she was: a baby girl, Justine, six pounds, eleven ounces, born to Vivian Calloway. Seeing this, thirteen-year-old Jacy once again began to sob, this time tears of relief. She was who she'd always been, not some other person from some other place full of dark-skinned, curly-haired people. Later, though, when she replayed the scene in her head, the banished doubts returned. When she'd asked point-blank if she was adopted, why hadn't her mother been surprised? It was as if she'd been expecting this day and was prepared. Documents, Jacy recalled thinking, could be forged.

TWO YEARS PASSED. She was in high school now and not the same girl at all. She was vigilant, questioned everything. She watched both her parents like a hawk. Made a study of them. Why did they argue so much? Why did her father get so many calls after working hours and always take them in the den with the door closed? Why did her mother become so annoyed when Jacy dragged out old photo albums and pored over them intently? "What are you looking for?" she wanted to know. *Evidence* was the short answer Jacy couldn't give. Evidence that she was who she was supposed to be. There were almost no photos of her father as a young man—because he was the youngest of eight siblings, he claimed—whereas her mother's life had been well documented. The photos that meant the most to Jacy were of her mother as a girl, because there she thought she could see a resemblance. Okay, sure, different color hair and lighter skin, but the same posture, the same delicate nose and round eyes. Which meant the birth certificate wasn't forged. She was who she was. Why, then, was she unable to shake the feeling that something was being kept from her? Why did everything feel like a lie?

One day when she got home from school, a taxi was sitting at their curb, completely out of place in their upscale Greenwich neighborhood. She was trying to figure out what it was doing there when their front door opened and a middle-aged man in a dark, ill-fitting suit lurched out. Jacy instinctively ducked behind the privet hedge. Her mother appeared behind him and called, "Wait! Wait! Let me help you!" He said something in response, but his voice had a strange, braying quality, and she couldn't make out what. Clearly, something was the matter with this man. As he came down the steps, his gait was spastic and his elbows jerked wildly, as if pulled at by invisible strings. She expected him to regain his balance on level ground, but instead he reeled around even more uncontrollably, and when her mother, catching up, reached out to steady him, he keeled over onto the lawn, where he lay on his side while his legs kept churning as if he were still upright. "Andy!" her mother cried. "You have to let me help you!" Eventually, she managed to get him on his feet and back onto the sidewalk, and it was then they both noticed Jacy, who'd stepped out from behind the hedge. "Mom?" she said. "What's going on?"

Her mother stiffened with surprise but quickly gathered herself. "Inside!" she ordered. "Now! This instant!"

Jacy would've liked nothing better than to do as she was told, but she couldn't take her eyes off the man in the dark suit. Though she was sure she'd never laid eyes on him before, he looked somehow familiar. His gaze was now fixed on her as well. Was that a smile on his face, or a grimace? When he reached out to her, his hand jerking, she quickly backed away from him.

"Inside!" her mother hissed.

"*Aaaace!*" the man bleated, trying once again to touch her.

This time she ran up the brick walkway and the front steps, stopping in the open doorway. A car, invisible behind the long privet hedge, was roaring up the street in their direction, and she knew who it would be before her father's Mercedes came to a rocking halt behind the taxi.

Her mother stepped in front of the stranger as her father came trotting toward them. "Don!" she said, holding up both hands. "Everything's okay. Andy was just leaving."

But her father was having none of this. Elbowing his wife aside, he planted both hands on the stranger's chest and shoved. The man took two quick, awkward steps backward, arms windmilling, and fell flat on his back. "What the fuck are you *doing* here, Andy?"

"Don!" her mother was yelling now. "Don't hurt him! He's leaving!"

"You're goddamn right he is," her father said, standing over the man now, both hands clenched into fists.

"How can he go away if you won't let him up?"

Apparently the taxi driver had seen enough. Putting the vehicle in gear, he pulled away from the curb. "Hey!" her father yelled, chasing it down the street. "Come back here! Do you hear? Come back!" The driver stuck his arm out the window and flipped her father off.

By the time he returned to the lawn, her mother had the man they'd called Andy back on his feet again. He just stood there, docile, his head hung low, as if to concede that all this was his fault.

"Now what?" her mother wanted to know, seemingly of both men.

"Now we go for a ride," her father said, grabbing the man by the elbow.

"Don't you *dare* hurt him," she called after them as Jacy's father dragged the man to the Mercedes and shoved him roughly inside. As he went around to the driver's side, the stranger's face was framed in the passenger window. At first Jacy thought he was looking at her mother, but then saw that, no, he was looking straight at her.

When the Mercedes raced up the street and out of sight, her mother didn't immediately turn around. When she finally did, she just stood there staring at the house, as if seeing it for the first time.

To Jacy, still frozen in the doorway, she looked like a woman casting around for nonexistent options.

Q&A. THE KITCHEN. Twenty minutes have passed since the scene on the lawn. A pot of coffee has been brewed. Jacy's mother has wrapped some ice cubes in a dishcloth and applied it to the fat lip she somehow got in the struggle. Mother and daughter are seated on opposite sides of the kitchen island.

Her mother's first words are predictable. "Thank God there's never anybody around this time of the afternoon. I don't think anyone saw."

"Who is he?"

"A drunk."

"Who is he?"

"A drunk," she repeats. "A falling-down drunk. Couldn't you see?"

"Who *is* he?"

Finally her mother meets her gaze with a pleading expression of her own. "Someone I knew a long time ago."

"Tell me."

"He has nothing to do with you. Forget about him."

"He said my name. He *tried* to say my name."

"No, he didn't."

"I heard him."

"You heard something."

"He reached out. To touch me."

"He's never going to get his hands on you. Ever."

She says it. Just fucking *says* it. "He's my father, isn't he."

Her mother looks away.

"*Isn't* he."

When her mother turns back, her eyes have gone icy hard. It's a look she's seen before, but it's always been directed at her father, never at her. "You've got a choice to make, little girl, and you're going to have to make it now, before your father gets home."

"My father's not coming home."

Her mother actually laughs. "Hey, you're lucky. You get to choose. Who do you want in your life? The man you've always known as your father, who treats you like his daughter, who pays for the food you eat and the clothes on your back and the roof over your head. Or that . . . *thing*"—here mimicking the man's spastic arm motions—"you saw on the lawn."

"He has a name. Andy. I heard you say it."

"Yes, his name is Andy, and we've said it for the last time in this house."

"Andy," she repeats.

Lightning quick, her mother reaches across the island and slaps her face. "You ungrateful little bitch. Do you have any idea what I saved you from?"

She doesn't. She has no idea about anything, except that it's all a lie, that it's never been anything *but* a lie.

Outside, her father's Mercedes pulls into the driveway. No, not her father. It's Donald. That's who he'll be from now on. And her mother will be Vivian. Don and Viv. And one day soon—though not soon enough—she'll be free of them.

LIKE ON THAT LONG-AGO evening, their last together on the island, the temperature tonight had continued to drop, and despite their windbreakers and the whiskey bottle, all three friends were now shivering in the chill. When Lincoln went inside to search for blankets they could drape around their shoulders, Teddy said, "Look, Mick, you don't have to do this."

"I do, though," he said. "I should've come clean a long time ago."

"Why didn't you?"

"She made me swear." Which was true, though not, he had to admit, the whole truth and nothing but. "Also, I was ashamed. When we left the island that morning and you guys dropped me off at the Falmouth parking lot? I convinced myself that not telling you how Jacy and I were planning to meet up back in Woods

Hole wasn't really a lie, or at least not the kind that keeps you out of heaven. But that's the thing about lies, right? Individually they don't amount to much, but you never know how many others you'll need to tell in order to protect that first one, and damned if they don't add up. Over time they get all tangled up until one day you realize it isn't even the lies themselves that matter. It's that somehow lying has become your default mode. And the person you lie to most is yourself."

The deck's sliding door rumbled open, Lincoln returning with blankets and the flashlight Mickey'd requested. Was it his imagination or had Lincoln, just in the last hour, segued into old age? It seemed impossible this was the same man who'd so recently come flying out of his chair, his face burning with fury. Now that same face was a collapsed wreck, and despite his gruesome injury, Teddy appeared to be in better shape. Mickey's own fault, all of this.

"Okay," Lincoln said, sitting back down, "what did I miss?"

"Nothing much," Mickey assured him. "Ted was just asking, in the nicest way possible, how I could've been a big-enough asshole to keep all this from you until now. Here's your answer, or part of it." Taking out the photo he'd brought with him to the island on the off chance he'd somehow locate the courage (*Kuh-ridge!*) to fess up, he slid it down the table. "I've never shown this to anybody."

When Lincoln switched the flashlight on, Mickey, not wanting to witness their reactions, purposely looked out at the dark Atlantic. That didn't keep him from hearing Lincoln's sharp intake of breath, though. He studied the photo for a good minute before passing it and the flashlight to Teddy, who examined it for at least that long before saying, "Dear God." Switching the flashlight off, he said, "That afternoon when Andy came by? He wasn't drunk, was he."

SHE LOOKED FOR HIM everywhere, Mickey told them. Especially on holidays and birthdays. Also at sporting events (tennis, field hockey) where she was a participant. It had come to her gradually that it wasn't her mother that Andy had come to see that afternoon but herself. That he wanted to be part of his daughter's life was the only explanation that made any sense. But didn't that mean he would keep trying? Mostly she dreaded the possibility, because she always imagined him lurching toward her, bleating at her, unable even to say her name. Why, then, at other times, did she long to see him again? Because when he looked at her, there'd been love in his eyes; surely she hadn't imagined that. And the fact that he'd been drunk that afternoon didn't mean he always was, did it? That she could both dread and yearn for something confused and frightened her. Was she losing her mind? *Andy*, she kept thinking, his name just there in her head. *Andy*. The more she tried to banish it, the more insistent the voice became. At least that's how it was in the beginning. Gradually, though, as she came to understand that he was probably gone for good, the voice receded, disappearing entirely for long stretches, until suddenly it would be there again, a whisper now: *Andy*. And when this happened, all she wanted to do was to crawl into bed and pull the covers up over her head as she'd done when that boy Todd brought all this into question.

She thought about trying to find him, but how? All she knew was his first name. She couldn't very well ask her mother or fucking Donald. Looking for clues, she once again returned to the family photo albums, searching them for some younger version of the man she'd seen on the front lawn. There were a few pages where photos had been removed, and she stared at these absences as if she could conjure up the missing images by sheer force of will. The summer between her high-school graduation and her freshman year at Minerva, when her mother and father had attended a weeklong conference in Hawaii, she used the time alone to toss the house. It took her all of two minutes to locate the metal box that contained her birth certificate, but its other contents—passports, mortgage documents, her parents' marriage license, various insurance policies, the titles to their two cars—were of no interest. The box yielded neither letters nor additional photos. Frustrated but determined, she went through every room and closet in the house, examining the contents of every shoebox and plastic bin. The desk in Donald's office was always locked, which suggested it might contain the treasure she was seeking, so she jimmied the lock with a letter opener, scarring both. She went through each drawer methodically, including the large one that contained Donald's clients' file folders, though none of these bore the name Andy or Andrew. But of course that made sense. Why would her real father hire Donald, the man who'd stolen his daughter, to manage his portfolio? Would a drunk even *have* a portfolio?

On the opposite wall, behind the Renoir, she discovered a small safe that she never suspected was there. She tried various numerical sequences related to Donald's and her mother's birthdays, their anniversary, even her own birthday, but no luck. Thinking the combination might be written down somewhere, she went through the desk again, this time looking for numbers in three sequences of two, and again came up empty. She was about to give up when she noticed that the desk's center drawer was slightly cockeyed, as if it had been removed and returned to its runners inexpertly. Pulling the drawer completely out, she used a flashlight to peer into the cavity, thinking the combination might be scratched onto one of the interior walls. She was about to slide the drawer back onto its runners when she noticed a yellowed piece of masking tape affixed to its back panel. The numbers written on it were badly faded but legible. The first two digits were preceded by the letter *L*, the next two by an *R*, the third by another *L*. She dialed these carefully, but the safe didn't open. She tried twice more, even more carefully, with the same result. She was about to concede defeat when she remembered the padlock on her school locker. You couldn't go directly from the first number to the second. You had to pass the first number in the opposite direction. Only then could you proceed to the second and third. This time, bingo! The tumblers clicked into place and the door thunked open. Inside were stacks of bills, mostly twenties and fifties, totaling at least a hundred thousand dollars. Maybe twice that. But there were no documents, no letters or postcards, no photos. No Andy.

Face it, she told herself, he was gone. Donald's volcanic anger had driven him away, and he was too frightened to return. And, really, she asked herself, why should that be such a big deal? For most of her life Andy hadn't existed, then for a very few minutes he had. Why should she feel more bereft and alone now than she had when his existence was undreamed of? If he could live without her, she could live without him. And, for the most part, this strategy had worked, right? Minerva—being out of Don and Viv's orbit nine months out of the year—had helped. So had her burgeoning friendship with Mickey and Teddy and Lincoln. Gradually Andy's ambient presence faded, like a Polaroid left out in the sun.

Why, then, as graduation approached—not to mention her June wedding—did she find herself backsliding, once again imagining that for these events her father would materialize? Sometimes she pictured him in the auditorium's front row, beaming up at her with fatherly pride. More often, genuflecting before reason (because, really, how would Andy score a front-row seat?), she located him in the back of the hall where distant relatives, family friends and college staff congregated. The problem with this scenario (speaking of realism) was: how could she recognize him at such a distance? She'd only seen the man once, six years earlier, and then only briefly. Would she even be able to pick him out of a police lineup? Would she know who he was if she passed him on the street? If he wasn't drunk and bleating, how *would* she recognize him? If he was sober, a model father, wouldn't that amount to a disguise? *Somehow*, she told herself. She would know him *somehow*. Her logic? She would know him because otherwise his presence there would serve no purpose.

The rational part of her brain identified all this as magical thinking, so she gave herself a stern talking-to. After all, who graduates from college still believing that wishing will make anything come true? Six years without so much as a Christmas card, and her father would turn up now? How would he even know where she'd *gone* to college? For all she knew he lived in California. Or Switzerland. Or Australia. Worse, inherent in her magical thinking was an implied pact, an unenforceable *if-then* contract. *If* her father showed up for her graduation, *then* it would be a sign that she was meant to jettison the central falsehood of her life—that she was Jacy Calloway, daughter of Donald Calloway, of Greenwich, Connecticut. *If* Andy came to her graduation, *then* she would somehow (always *somehow*) find the strength to disavow not only Don and Viv but their entire universe, which of course included her fiancé, who not only wanted them to live in Greenwich but actually saw their parents' lives as a template. ("Our folks didn't get where they are by luck," he liked to say, and invariably got pissed off when she asked what being born into wealth and privilege was if not *pure* fucking luck.) Anyway, screw Vance. The way Jacy saw it, if Andy came to her graduation, he wouldn't just be claiming her as his daughter but also giving her permission to break off her engagement to a man who had little beyond material comfort to offer. *If* Andy, not Donald, was her father, *then* she got to be a whole new person. Armed with her new identity she would (again, *somehow*) become a girl (no, a *woman*) capable of charting her own course. Okay, she didn't really need Andy's permission for any of this. She was twenty-one and could do as she pleased, but there was comfort to be taken from genetic validation, wasn't there?

Even so, as bargains went, she had to admit this one was piss-poor. *If* Andy's showing up meant that she could be a whole new person, *then* his failure to show up, which was far more likely, must mean that she *was* Jacy Calloway after all and was therefore meant to do what was expected of her. Worse, it would mean that she'd just spent the last four years at Minerva playing at rebellion—drinking beer from kegs and smoking weed and burning (metaphorically) her bra and protesting the stupid war, when at the end of the day, because she lacked the courage to fight for a truer life, she'd meekly marry Vance and breed little Republicans.

Over graduation weekend Jacy learned something about loneliness that she hadn't suspected before: that its most terrifying and virulent form could only be experienced in a crowd. Naturally, the campus was a mob scene of parents and siblings and alums, every single minute accounted for. In addition to a wide array of scheduled events, there were her sorority sisters and favorite professors to bid farewell to, all of which had to be done with Don and Viv, as well as Vance and his parents, in tow. Had she been able to hang out with Mickey and Teddy and Lincoln, she might've gotten through it unscathed, maybe even enjoyed some of it, but of course they had their own bizarre families to deal with (What a squirrelly little man Lincoln's father was!) and they had no idea she was in crisis. Her own fault, of course. How many times had she considered confiding in one of them that Donald Calloway wasn't really her father? But which one? Teddy would've been easiest because he was such a good, sympathetic listener, and of the three he was also the most obviously smitten with her. But so was Mickey, who would also have listened. The problem here was that he'd lost his own father the year before, and she wasn't sure she wanted to share with him a tale of woe that involved her having a pair of them. Lincoln? Lately he'd seemed determined to tamp down any feelings he had for her, pivoting toward Anita, her sorority sister, a girl Jacy admired and was secretly jealous of, without knowing exactly why. More to the point, all three were best friends. If she confided in one, she would in effect be confiding in all three—*all for one and one for all*—and she wasn't sure she could bear to have three people knowing this terrible truth. And of course there was that even-darker shame that she'd made up her mind never to tell anyone. What if she got started telling the truth and was unable to stop? So she'd let their final semester together slip away, and the window of opportunity to share her burden had shut. Face it, she told herself. She was alone.

Graduation itself was a blur. The whole weekend felt like a ride on a merry-go-round, where all her jubilant classmates straddled colorful horses that went up and down, while she alone was consigned to a stationary bench that resembled a church pew—on the same ride as everybody else but somehow not sharing the same experience. Would the circular motion, the hideous calliope music, never stop? Halfway through the commencement speaker's address, the girl seated next to Jacy asked if she was okay, and only then did she realize she was crying. What a fool she'd been to hold out hope. Four years of college classes, some of them taught by feminist professors, yet here she was on graduation day waiting to be rescued by a man. Preposterous. Ridiculous. Time to pull herself together, to see things as they were. And not tomorrow, right fucking now. Wiping her eyes on the sleeve of her gown, she resolved that when it was her turn to cross the stage and receive her diploma, she would make a point of *not* scanning the audience for Andy, the father who had so clearly abandoned her.

Yet here, too, she was thwarted. An hour earlier, when they'd all paraded down the hill from the chapel, across the quad and into the auditorium, it'd been cloudy, gray and humid, but by the time the commencement speaker finally took his seat, the clouds were breaking up and a fresh breeze was blowing in through the hall's wide-open doors. And wouldn't you know it? Right when her row lined up at the foot of the stage, the sun broke through, shooting bright shafts of light down through the hall's high windows, spot-lighting the people standing along the back wall, exactly where, in her mind's eye, Jacy had so often pictured her father. It was as if God was telling her right where to look. In that moment all her fears of not recognizing her father were dispelled. Of *course* she'd be able to pick him out! How could she fail to recognize her own father? He would be smiling, for one thing, and looking straight at her. And he would wave. Not wildly, mind you, nothing that would attract the attention of bellicose Donald. Just a subtle gesture to reveal who he was, what they were to each other, that he was there for her and always would be.

Later, when it was all over and they were making their way toward Donald's Mercedes, she was still looking for Andy, scanning the crowd as it dispersed, panicked now, her fears redoubling just that quickly. *Had* he been there? Had she *missed* him? Until her mother grabbed her by the elbow and whispered, "Stop it. This instant. He's *gone*."

"I hate him," Jacy whispered back, not sure if it was Andy she was referring to or Donald, who the night of the incident with Andy on the front lawn had come into her room. He was dressed, as always when he visited her, in his bathrobe, fresh from the shower, his hair glistening wet. "You see?" he said, sitting at the edge of her bed and taking her hand. "It's like I've been telling you." What he wanted her to understand was that what they'd done wasn't so bad. It wasn't like he was her *real* father. It wasn't as if he was Andy.

THOUGH SHE'D TRIED to prepare herself for it, Andy's non-appearance at graduation left Jacy empty of everything but the desire to drown Viv and Don, and, yes, Vance too, in a sea of sarcasm. She would become, she decided, a perfect bitch, a goal that struck her as both reasonable and attainable. The only thing slowing her progress was that something strange, something she wasn't privy to, was going on at home. Donald, claiming to be working on a special project, hadn't gone into the New York office all week. A new, dedicated phone line had been set up to his home office and it rang all hours of the day and night. Twice, men from the New York headquarters had driven out to see him, and earlier in the week Jacy had come upon her mother listening outside his office door. ("Wipe that smirk off your face, young lady.") Then yesterday Viv announced that she and Don were going to an important meeting in Hartford that afternoon and that Jacy should wish them luck. "Why?" she said. "When have you ever been *un*lucky?"

At this, her mother closed her eyes and just stood there, refusing to open them for so long that Jacy wondered if she'd had a stroke. She really hoped not, because that would mean she'd have to stop tormenting her, at least until she recovered. Finally, eyes still shut, her mother said, "Okay, be like that."

"I will. I am."

"Maybe Vance will be able to do something with you." They were flying him up from Durham for the weekend in the hopes of cheering her up. "Something your father and I can't seem to."

"By my *father* do you mean Donald?"

At last she opened her eyes. "You know what I'd like to do right now?" she said. "I'd like to slap you silly. You stupid, stupid, *stupid* girl."

When they left for Hartford, Jacy took the opportunity to break into Donald's office. When she opened the door to the safe, it was so full of money that several stacks of banded, large-denomination bills tumbled out onto the floor. Try as she might, she was unable to cram them all back in again. No matter. There was plenty of room under her mattress for the ones that didn't fit and a few extras as well.

THAT SUNDAY, she and Vance and both sets of parents were meeting for brunch at the club, which was celebrating its centennial. The walls of the long entryway were hung with photographs of the clubhouse itself and its members over the years. *Time Machine*, it was called, and the photos were displayed in chronological order so that as you proceeded down the corridor you dove deeper into the past. Vance loved it. "So fascinating," he enthused, stopping every few feet to examine another picture or newspaper article about renovations to the dining room or the construction of the Olympic-sized swimming pool. "So much history!"

"Right!" Jacy mocked back. "Find the Negro and win a prize!"

Brunch was a disaster. Jacy, monosyllabic throughout, drank two Bloody Marys, barely touched her eggs Florentine and insisted they leave before dessert, Vance's favorite part of any lunch or dinner. Since their return from Hartford, Don and Viv had both been out of sorts, so it had fallen to Vance and his parents to carry the conversation for the entire table.

"Will you please tell me what's wrong?" Vance begged, when the ordeal was finally over. There was a bottleneck in the corridor, people oohing and aahing over the *Time Machine* photos.

"*Nothing* is wrong," she assured him, though *everything* would have been closer to the truth.

"Well, you obviously haven't been yourself all weekend."

Actually, she thought, *I have been. This is the new me.*

"You were disrespectful to our parents in there and, frankly, rude to me. In fact, you act as if you don't love me at all."

It's not an act, Vance. I don't love you. Not even a little.

"If you're worried about the wedding, that's understandable. The future's always scary. I get it."

The future with you *is scary. And you* don't *get it.*

"But we're going to be happy, Jace. We are. I promise."

No, we're going to be miserable. I'm going to see to it. You have no idea how completely devoted I am to our misery, now and till the end of time.

"We're going to be just like those guys right there."

He was pointing at one of the *Time Machine* pictures, of Don and Viv, together with Vance's parents, all four in their twenties, raising champagne flutes, Vance's mother clearly pregnant. The caption read: *A Toast to the Future!*

And there he was, behind them, the grinning tuxedoed bartender, champagne bottle raised, as if to top them all off. Young, dark skinned, curly haired, handsome. The only person in the picture not looking at the camera was Viv, whose head was turned so she could regard the bartender, and the expression on her young face was one Jacy had never seen before. The names of those in the photo were listed beneath. The bartender's was Andres Demopoulos.

Andy.

THE NEXT DAY Jacy heard the phone ring in her father's office. Her mother must've heard it, too, because when Don emerged she was waiting for him. From the top of the stairs Jacy was able to eavesdrop, though they kept their voices low.

"I just got a tip," Donald said. "They're on their way."

"What's going to happen?"

"Nothing. They're fishing."

"Fish get caught."

"I'm not the fish they're after. The worst that happens to me is a slap on the wrist."

"Why not give them the fish they want?"

"How about you leave this to me."

Ten minutes later a dark sedan pulled into their drive and two nondescript men wearing dark suits got out. Donald met them at the door and invited them in. When his office door closed behind them, Jacy joined her mother in the kitchen, where Viv sat staring into a cup of tea as if she were trying to read the leaves in the bottom. Jacy had considered confronting her yesterday when they returned from brunch, but decided that a *perfect* bitch would let her new discovery marinate. She would wait for the precise right moment, which had now arrived. With Don occupied behind his closed office door, her mother was alone and vulnerable, a sickly wildebeest culled from the herd. Sitting down across from her, Jacy said, "Andres Demopoulos." When her mother blinked but said nothing, she repeated the name.

"Your father is being investigated for insider trading and money laundering," her mother replied. *A plea for sympathy? Good luck with that, lady.* "He claims it's not going to happen, but there's a chance he might go to jail."

"Your *husband* may go to jail. My father is Andres Demopoulos."

Her mother lit a cigarette, inhaled deeply. "Exactly what is it that you want from me, little girl?"

"To start, it would be nice if you didn't call me 'little girl.'"

"It would be *nice* if you didn't call me Viv. It would be nice if you didn't call your father Donald."

"I call my father Andy. And what I want is for you to tell me about him."

Her mother appeared to ponder how to best respond, or maybe just whether to. Finally she said, "He's just a man I once knew. He was handsome. Charming."

"You loved him?"

"No." But she looked away.

"He loved you?"

A pause. Then, "Yes."

"This was before Donald?" And when Viv didn't respond, "During?" When she didn't respond to this either, "Okay, *during*. And for how long?"

"Not very."

"How long?"

"What difference does it make?"

"Did Don know?"

"Of course not. Your father's a narcissist. That I'd be interested in another man would never occur to him."

"My father is Andy—"

"I know. You don't have to keep saying his name."

"I like the sound of it."

Now her mother looked at her. "You can't be serious."

Jacy ignored this. "But eventually Don found out."

"Well, you were born a month early, with olive skin and dark, curly hair."

"And what was his reaction?"

She stubbed the half-smoked cigarette out in the ashtray, which contained several other butts. "It was a rough couple of weeks."

"That's all?"

"If your father understands anything it's the importance of appearances. Divorcing me wouldn't have looked good."

"Okay," Jacy said, "but you were lying before."

"When?"

"When you said you didn't love him. There's a photo of you and Don and Vance's parents at the club. And my father. Everybody is looking at the camera but you. You're looking at Andy. You loved him."

Her mother was studying the half-smoked cigarette in the ash-tray with what appeared to be genuine regret. It'd been a mistake to stub it out. "Like I said, he was charming."

"Why can't you admit you loved him?"

"What good would it do?"

"Do you still love him?"

"Don't be ridiculous."

"What happened? If he loved you and you loved him—"

"He went away." She picked up her coffee spoon and she used it to push the half-smoked cigarette around.

"Why?"

She shrugged. "He got fired. For drinking on the job."

"Did he know you were pregnant?"

That got a nasty laugh. "*I* didn't even know I was pregnant, little girl."

"So he went away. Just like that. He loved you, but left anyway."

"I told him to go."

"Why?"

Her mother continued fooling around with the cigarette. "Because there was no future for us. He was an immigrant. He didn't even have papers. He could barely speak English. I was engaged to your father. How many reasons do you need?"

"So, you just told him to go away and off he went?"

She looked up now, and Jacy saw that her cheeks were wet. "I had to be very, *very* cruel to him."

"Tell me what you said."

"The truth."

"That he was an immigrant? That he could barely speak English?"

"That I could never introduce him to my parents. That if we married, we'd be poor. That I had no intention of being poor."

"So instead you married a man you didn't love," Jacy said.

Her mother stood up and took the ashtray over to the sink, where she held her last cigarette under the running faucet until she was sure it was out, then dumped all of them into the trash.

When she sat down again, Jacy said, "So when did Andy find out about me?"

"When you won that junior tennis tournament. Your picture was in the paper."

"You're lying again. If he went away, how could he have seen my picture?"

"He subscribed to *Greenwich Time*."

"Why would he do that?"

"Think about it."

She did. "He was still in love with you. Even after the horrible things you said to him."

She shrugged. "I guess."

"Even though you'd married my . . . married Don."

"So it would seem."

"He knew you had a child?"

Another shrug.

"But not that I was his?"

"Not until he saw your picture."

"God, you're so fucked up."

"You're not to use that word in this house."

"Oh, right. You get to fuck my father and toss him out with the trash, but I don't get to say a dirty word?"

"I didn't . . . ," Viv began, then stopped. Wiping her eyes on a napkin, she said, "I made a choice."

"And now the man you chose is going to jail. Well done."

"We don't know that for sure. It's only a possibility."

"It would serve you right."

"Also a possibility." She rose again, this time setting her cup and saucer next to the sink before returning.

"Who knows that Donald's under investigation?"

"Nobody."

"Vance's parents?"

"No."

"How long before they do? How long before everybody knows?"

"Feds don't talk. Besides, it's his boss they're after. And his boss's boss."

"Tell me something, Viv. Do you even know about the safe behind the Renoir?"

At this her mother started. "You vicious little snoop."

"*Mmmm*," she agreed, then, "How do I get in touch with my father?"

"He's down the hall. Just knock on the door."

"How do I get in touch with Andy?"

"You don't. He's gone. How many times do I have to say it?"

That made it twice that she'd used the word *gone* to describe him. Jacy swallowed hard. "I want to see him."

"You can't."

"Why not?"

"He died."

"Stop . . . fucking . . . lying."

"Keep your voice down."

They stared at each other for a long moment. Finally her mother said, "How about we make a deal? I give you what you want. You give me what I want." And when Jacy hesitated, "What's the matter, little girl? You don't like being the one who has to choose?" Her mother wore a different expression now, and when Jacy recognized it as triumph, she realized she'd somehow misplayed her hand. Her mother knew what Jacy wanted, but she had no idea what Viv wanted in return. "Your call, little girl. Do we have a deal?"

THE OBITUARY PAGE from the *Danbury News-Times*, which her mother produced as her part of the bargain, contained half a dozen death notices, some running to several columns. Her father's was by far the shortest. It stated that Andres Demopoulos had passed away at the age of forty-five at Holloway House, a nursing facility in nearby Bethel. He'd originally come to America via Canada with his older brother Dimitri. They'd grown up in New York City, but after his brother's untimely death he'd moved to Connecticut, where he'd worked in the food-service industry before falling ill. He had—his daughter read—no surviving relatives. Which meant that somehow the grinning young man from the *Time Machine* photo was gone again. What little Jacy had of her father—a few terrifying minutes on the front lawn of their home, a glimpse of an old photograph and the few thin facts of the obituary—was all she'd ever have.

Finally, after Jacy'd read the obit several times, her mother spoke. "I'm sorry."

Which sent Jacy into a warp-drive fury, though she kept her voice down. "Really, Viv? You're sorry? About what? Are you sorry he died? That he loved you? That you loved him? That he loved *me*? That you kept him from me and me from him?"

"That he had such a hard life."

"You're the one that made it hard. You and Donald."

"For your sake."

"Don't . . . you *dare* say that. You *chose*. You said so yourself. You didn't even know you were pregnant when you made that choice."

"You don't know the whole story."

"I don't know *any* of the story. You weren't even going to tell me that he existed."

"That's right, and I'm sorry you found out. Look what knowing has done to you. Your ignorance was bliss. Don't you remember how happy you used to be?"

Was this true? *Had* she been happy? If so, that happiness was so long ago that it now felt like someone else's. "How do we even know that any of this is true? How would a newspaper in Danbury know that my father had a brother named Dimitri? It says he had no living relatives, so who would've told them?" Her mother just looked at her, waiting for her to understand. Finally, she did. "You."

"There was no one else."

"*You* wrote my father's obituary."

"I answered their questions. They wrote it."

"You told them he fell ill?"

"He did."

"Alcoholics don't 'fall ill.'"

"He wasn't an alcoholic."

"Stop lying, Viv. You can't even keep your story straight. That day on the lawn you told me yourself he was a falling-down drunk. Just now you said he got fired from the club for drinking on the job."

"That's what he was fired for, yes."

Jacy rubbed her temples, trying to force the few facts she knew into alignment. Clearly, her mother was choosing her words carefully. Rhetorical hairs were being split. But to what end? "Did he or did he not drink himself to death?"

The smile her mother offered then—an odd mix of wonder and shame—was one Jacy knew would stay with her for a long, long time. "Strange you should put it that way," she said, "because in a sense that's exactly what happened. He choked to death drinking a glass of water."

"You are so full of—"

"Cerebellar ataxia is what it's called. A degenerative disease of the nervous system, like MS. Over time you lose motor function. Your speech slurs. Your limbs flail. You look and sound drunk. That's what you were seeing on the lawn that afternoon."

"But you *told* me—"

"I know what I told you. It seemed best."

"For you."

"For me, for everyone. He didn't want you to see him like that."

"That's a lie. I'm the one he came here to see, not you."

"He wanted you to know he existed, that's all. Okay, it's true he wanted to see you, to . . . take you in. But when he saw how terrified you were, he knew the whole thing was a mistake. I knew where he was living, so I went to see him there, and he made me promise never to tell you the truth. He said it would be easiest for you if you believed he was a drunk. In time you'd forget he ever existed."

"Except I didn't."

"No, you certainly didn't."

"You stole him from me."

"For your own good."

"I could've helped him."

"No. No one could help him."

"I could've been with him. Comforted him."

"Don't lie to yourself, little girl. It's a bad habit. Take it from one who knows."

Jacy ignored this. "How did you even learn that he died? Am I supposed to believe you read the *Danbury News-Times*?"

"Of course not. We hired someone to keep tabs on him, your father and I. Don and I. We didn't want a repetition of that day on the lawn."

"Right. God forbid that I should ever see my father again."

"Also, he had expenses. His condition . . . deteriorated. He was unable to work. By the end he needed . . . well, almost everything."

"You're saying *you* paid?"

"We paid. Your father . . . Don and I. We paid."

"Why would Don pay? He hated Andy. I could see the hatred in his eyes that afternoon."

"He didn't want to. I made him."

"How?"

"Simple. I told him I knew."

Suddenly there was no air in the room. "Knew what?"

Her mother just looked at her.

Jacy felt her stomach rise. "How long have you known?"

"I can't answer that. One day I didn't and then I did. That day on the lawn, maybe. I saw the hope in your eyes. The hope that Andy would come and take you away. From me, was my first thought, because I knew you despised me. Then I thought again."

"But you did nothing."

"Well, I didn't really *know*, did I."

"You just said you did."

"I told myself it couldn't be true. Made myself believe it wasn't."

"Ignorance is bliss."

"That it is, little girl, and don't ever let anybody tell you different. The truth will set you free? Don't make me laugh."

Down the hall there was a rustling, the sound of chairs sliding back, men getting to their feet.

Jacy felt hot tears welling up, but she refused to cry. Instead, she said, "You know what, Viv? I never thought I'd hear myself say this, but I want to be just like you. I want to be selfish. I want to not give the tiniest little shit about anyone but myself. I want to be able to do the kinds of things you do and never suffer the consequences."

"You think I don't suffer?"

"Not enough."

They heard the office door open and men emerge into the hall.

"Your turn, little girl." She was smiling now.

Suddenly Jacy knew something that until now had managed to elude her, though she'd been staring right at it for years. "My God," she said. "You hate him, too, don't you."

"You'll never know how much."

"Do you want to get a pen and paper?"

"That won't be necessary."

In the hallway the front door opened, then shut again, and now Donald's footsteps were coming in their direction. She told her mother the combination to the safe.

THAT SAME NIGHT she awoke in the darkness of her childhood bedroom to the knowledge that she'd decided something in her sleep: she would end her life. The decision felt both momentous and oddly anticlimactic. Her mother's medicine cabinet was full of sleeping pills, and she couldn't think of any reason not to take them. That evening she'd watched the news and seen the jungles of Vietnam and Cambodia burst into flame, and she knew boys her age were being incinerated there. Against all reason Mickey would be heading toward that conflagration in a matter of weeks, and by next year Lincoln might well follow. They would both die there; she was certain of it. Death was everywhere, universal, a joke in bad taste. If you could die drinking a glass of water, as her father had, what was the point of living? In fact, Jacy thought sleepily, there was no reason to not do the deed right now. Nothing to prevent her from just climbing out of bed, walking across the hall and grabbing a bottle of pills. Easy. Fill a large glass with water and just start swallowing, the very thing her father hadn't been able to do, and thereby achieve the identical, symmetrical result. There'd be both beauty and justice in that, wouldn't there? Her poor father. Brokenhearted, he'd given her the gift of his absence. Now that he was gone and beyond further injury, she would absent herself. That was her last thought before drifting into a heavy, black sleep.

The next thing she knew it was morning, the sun streaming in her window, the phone on her bedside table jangling. Since there was no one she wanted to talk to, she waited for Viv to pick up down in the kitchen, answering only when the ringing continued. Groggy, she didn't immediately recognize Teddy's voice. It seemed so long ago that they'd all been friends. If she understood him correctly, he was suggesting they all spend one last weekend together before going their separate ways. He and Lincoln had already talked Mickey into joining them on Martha's Vineyard, he said, so how about it? All for one? One for all?

Only after hearing herself agree to join them and hanging up did she remember her dark-of-the-night resolution to end her life. How could she have forgotten something so profound? The clock on her bedside table said it was nearly ten-thirty. Was that possible? After deciding to commit suicide, she'd fucking *slept in*? And then agreed to celebrate the beginning of summer with friends on the Vineyard, as if nothing of significance had changed since graduation? Was this any way to repay poor Andres Demopoulos, who in order to ensure his daughter a normal life had exiled himself from it and died alone? No. Fuck no. Living would mean that Don and Viv had won, that the whole shit-eating world, with its innumerable falsehoods and treacheries, had won. So, no. This simply wouldn't stand. Don and Viv were apparently off somewhere. She had the house to herself. The time was now.

Still muzzy from too much sleep, she went into her mother's bathroom and found, as expected, an unopened bottle of sleeping pills. Not wanting to die in Viv's bathroom, she returned with the pills and a large glass of cold water to her own room. The bottle had one of those newfangled caps, so she set the glass down on top of Andres Demopoulos's obituary so she could line up the tiny arrows and push up on the cap with both thumbs. When it finally popped off, she poured a handful of pills into her palm and sat down on the edge of the bed. It felt lumpy. Feeling between the box spring and mattress, she found the stacks of bills she'd stashed there earlier. What had she meant to do with the money? She couldn't imagine. For money to be of use you had to want something money could buy, and she didn't. Not anymore. She had a single need: to not exist. When she put the whole handful of pills in her mouth at once, her gag reflex kicked in, but she got herself under control and picked up the glass of water. As she went to drink, though, she saw that her father's obituary had stuck to the bottom of the glass. The date of his death—May 2, 1971—was magnified, like the key words you're intended to pick out of a printed text on a movie screen. She gagged again, this time spitting the pills back into her hand.

May 2nd. How many times had she read the obituary without noticing the date, its significance? She'd graduated from Minerva on May 9th. On the drive back to Greenwich with Don and Viv she'd given herself another good talking-to. *Let him go.* If her father didn't come to her graduation, if he didn't care even that much, if he could live without her, then she was done with him as well. Except that by the time she'd climbed onto that stage to receive her diploma, Andres Demopoulos was already dead. It was as if he was now trying to communicate with her from beyond the grave, like he'd somehow directed her to set the glass of water down on the obituary so that the date of his death would be highlighted. As if he was begging her not to do it. *Nonsense,* she told herself. *More magical thinking.* But maybe not. What if Andy was trying to tell her that living, not dying, was the best revenge on Don and Viv and the whole shit-eating world? She remembered the haunted, pleading look in her father's eyes that terrible afternoon, remembered how desperately he'd tried to say her name, that he'd tried to reach out and touch her. It was as if, years earlier, he'd foreseen this day, this exact moment.

In the bathroom, she flushed the pills down the toilet. And even before the last one disappeared, a new plan began taking shape.

AND LESS THAN a month later, sitting in the dark out behind the crappy motel a few short miles from the Canadian border, that plan was about to bear fruit. She would live, and so would Mickey. *That* would be Andres Demopoulos's legacy. That it also happened to be a giant *fuck you* to Don and Viv was the icing on the cake. Taking the stacks of bills from her backpack, she handed them to Mickey, who counted the money in the light of a waning moon that had just that moment come out from behind the scudding clouds. When he finished—there was enough there for twenty Stratocasters, maybe a hundred—he said, "Okay. Tomorrow we'll find someplace to rent on the Canadian side, but then I need to head back to Connecticut."

"What for?"

"Because I'm going to find your old man and beat him bloody."

"Don, you mean?"

"Yes, Don. After I've done that, I'll rejoin you."

"What if you get arrested?"

"I don't care."

"I do," she said, getting to her feet. "And your life is mine now."

"How do you figure?"

"I'm saving it. Therefore."

"Yeah?"

She pulled her shirt over her head then and stood still in the darkness while Mickey, stubborn, pretended he had some choice in the matter. Was this how her mother had seduced Andres Demopoulos? she wondered. Had the poor guy even known what hit him? She found herself wondering if Viv had cleaned out the safe yet. Probably not. She would wait to see how things played out. If they took her husband away in handcuffs, she'd do it then. There would be no record of the freshly laundered bills. With Donald safely behind bars, she'd sell the house and go somewhere else, maybe back to California. She'd have plenty of money to live on until she could find herself a new Donald. You *almost* had to admire her, Jacy thought, waiting for Mickey, who still believed that his mind was his own, to make it up.

"Well?" she said finally.

"Yeah," he said, getting to his feet, and they both heard the surrender in his voice. "Yeah. Okay."

Teddy

I n the bathroom Teddy, who'd asked for a short break so he
could take another painkiller, did so, then stood staring
at the wreck of the man in the mirror and marveling, as
he always did in the aftermath of his spells, just how much they
resembled tropical storms. As they approached, he often could sense
the change in barometric pressure, as he had done on the ferry, even
though the storm was still far out at sea, churning away, gathering
force, bearing down. When it finally came ashore there wasn't much
to do but ride it out, just let it howl and rage and do its worst. At
some point his buffeted, terrified psyche simply gave way to a profound sense of calm, there in the storm's gentle eye. It wasn't unlike
what people coming down from acid trips often described—the self
simply dissipating. To Teddy, a breathtaking moment of splendid,
weightless drifting away. In another second or two the world and
its cares would cease to matter. In their place, blessed oblivion.
But then the winds returned, the shard pierced flesh, and he would
know the truth—that escape was yet another false narrative. Later,
bloodied and chastened and exhausted, he would do what he always
did—claw up into the light, blinking, and survey the damage. Make
an inventory of what was irretrievably lost, what was merely damaged and in need of mending, and then, most vitally, somehow locate
and reestablish that charmless but necessary even keel that allowed
for smooth, if unadventurous, sailing. What he called his life.

Making matters even worse was the fact that the world he returned to was, of course, unaffected by the storm. Given the blows he himself had sustained, he half expected to see trees uprooted, roofs blown off of houses and corrugated metal in the streets, whereas, naturally, the physical world was unscathed. In this one respect, however, tonight seemed different. Returning to the deck, Teddy couldn't help feeling that his personal tempest had somehow broken containment, wreaking its havoc on not just himself but also his friends.

Lincoln had gone over to the railing, where he leaned staring out into the distance, perhaps at the dark outline of Troyer's house, but more likely beyond that, to where moonlight was glittering on the waves. A blanket draped over his shoulders, he reminded Teddy of the forlorn Syrian refugees who for months now had been washing up on Greek islands. Earlier, looking out across this same expanse of lawn, he'd confided his fear that Jacy lay buried beneath it, as well as his own sense of culpability should that prove true: whatever befell her wouldn't have if he hadn't invited her to the island. Whereas now they knew the opposite to be true. Their invitation had actually saved her life, at least in the sense that it postponed her death. Instead of swallowing that handful of sleeping pills in Greenwich, Jacy had lived a few years longer, much of that as the girl in the photo Mickey'd showed them: wheelchair-bound, emaciated, unable to control her gnarled, flailing limbs. Thanks to her friends, she was able to fulfill her destiny of genetic misfortune. Was that what Lincoln was thinking now as he peered out into the darkness: be careful what you wish for?

Mickey, too, appeared gutted. Leaning back in his chair, he stared straight up at the night sky. To Teddy he looked emptied out, a hollow shell of the man who'd performed at Rockers just a few short hours earlier, as if for him the music had perhaps stopped playing permanently. He was determined to finish, though, and when Teddy was seated again, his blanket once more draped around his shoulders, Mickey said, "Home stretch. You think you can make it?"

Teddy assured him he would.

"Lincoln?"

"Coming," Lincoln said, straightening up, or trying to.

When all three were settled, Teddy asked the question that was foremost in his mind. "How long was it before her own symptoms began to manifest?"

Mickey ran his hands through his hair. "Not long. A month or two? We'd be walking along and she'd suddenly wobble, like she'd felt a tremor in the earth, and when she got tired she developed this hitch in her gait. Other times she'd reach for something on the table—the saltshaker, a juice glass—and send it flying. Problem was, in addition to smoking weed, we were also drinking a fair amount, so she wasn't the only one stumbling around, knocking things over. Still, I was pretty sure something wasn't right. One day I snuck off to the library and did a little research. Even back then they were pretty sure ataxia was genetic. Sometimes it skipped a generation, though, and I remember holding on to that hope."

"Do you think she knew anything was wrong when we were here on the island?" Teddy wondered, recalling what she'd said—*How come everything has to be so fucked up?*—when they were out at Gay Head. Captive to his own desolation, he hadn't questioned what that *everything* might mean.

"That occurred to me, too," Mickey admitted. "Probably not, though, or she wouldn't have let herself get pregnant. But it's true she was in flight mode. Desperate to escape her dickhead fiancé. Greenwich. Don and Viv. Her father's horrible death. So, yeah, she might have imagined the disease was one more thing she could run away from."

"You didn't talk about it?"

He shook his head. "That was the worst part. Every time I showed concern, she'd fly into a rage. And I mean a *real* rage. We all saw her get angry at Minerva, but this was different. She'd scream at me that if she wanted a fucking mother she'd have stayed in fucking Greenwich. That I should mind my own fucking business.

Which would piss me off, but then the symptoms would disappear for weeks at a stretch and I'd think maybe she was right and I was acting paranoid.

"Also, there was the band. Man, you wouldn't believe how good we were. Like, ten times better than what you heard tonight. Tight? Jesus, we could read each other's minds." Despite himself, he was smiling. *Joy,* Teddy thought. The one thing his own even keel did not permit. For him such bliss led to euphoria, which inevitably pivoted, plunging headlong into depression and despair. Was this, like Jacy's ataxia, also genetic? Had his parents ever experienced real joy? Or had they, too, had to guard themselves against emotional extremes? They seemed to want nothing more than they had. Each other. The Sunday *New York Times.* Each autumn, a fresh batch of high-school students to mold. Their own version of that even keel of his.

"We were a hot ticket all over Montreal," Mickey was saying. "Throughout Quebec, really. We also made some serious dough, which was good because I never could reconcile myself to living off the money Jacy took from her old man's safe. We blew a good chunk of it on amps and mics and a sound system. Plus an old hearse we repurposed to schlep all the equipment around in. I told myself I'd pay back every cent once we were famous, which it actually looked like we might be for a while. When Jacy sang, man, people just lost it. Her evolution was amazing. When we started out, she was doing maybe one song per set, but before long she was singing lead on, like, every other song and backup harmonies on most of the others. In the beginning we had to coax her up onstage. By the end, you couldn't get her off it. And with every performance she got more bold, more free. It was the part of our lives she loved the most. Like I said, she was in escape mode, and performing, for her, was the best escape of all."

His expression darkened now. "At gigs she liked to wear these miniskirts and she had this deal where she'd leap, microphone in hand, from the stage onto a table in the front row. As you can imagine, that gave anybody sitting there a pretty good view. She always wore black panties, so when the assholes looked up her skirt, for that split second, they wouldn't be sure what they were seeing."

Lincoln shifted uncomfortably in his chair. "She admitted this?"

Mickey sighed. "Okay, look, I wasn't going to go into this, but if I don't, you're never going to understand. Jacy's relationship to sex was complicated. She loved it, but it had to be on her terms, and it always, *always* had to be her idea."

Which was certainly how it had been at Gay Head, Teddy remembered. Jacy, merrily shucking her clothes as he looked on, paralyzed, in wonder and fear and gratitude. Shouting "Come *on*, Teddy!" when he didn't follow her into the icy waves quickly enough. Then pulling him into her embrace, her surprising strength overruling his moral qualms. Had her power over him been what excited her most?

"You always got the impression that sex itself was somehow secondary, as if she was driven by something even more powerful than desire, or maybe *apart* from desire. Like that night at the Theta house. I'm not saying she didn't enjoy kissing us, but those kisses weren't really *about* us."

Of course they weren't, Teddy thought. Given what had been going on in her home for so long, how could she be anything but confused by sex? Why *wouldn't* she be tempted to weaponize it?

"Anyway," Mickey continued, "it was like that with music, too. She loved to sing, don't get me wrong. But it wasn't really *about* singing. Audiences? They couldn't get enough. People weren't coming to *hear* us, they were coming to *see* her. She wanted us to start writing and performing our own material, so after we caught our big break, we wouldn't just be doing covers. She couldn't wait for the war to be over, not because it was stupid and immoral anymore—that was the old Jacy—but because when it ended we could go back home and show Vance and Don and Viv and all of Greenwich what she'd become. She made me promise we'd change the name of the band from Big Mick on Pots to Andy's Revenge."

Lincoln still looked uncomfortable. "It must've worried you, how *she* was changing."

"I guess I should've been," Mickey acknowledged. "I mean, her need to drive men nuts? The guys in the band were all talking about it. But it was the early seventies, you know? Janice Joplin was drinking a quart of Southern Comfort at every show. The Who were smashing their guitars onstage. Jim Morrison was whipping it out in front of live audiences. It was all about freedom, remember? Richie Havens at Woodstock?"

Teddy couldn't help smiling. The decade Mickey was trying so hard to explain through its iconic cultural moments was one Lincoln had basically opted out of. Richie Havens?

"Anyway," he continued, "one night she missed the table and that was that."

"What happened?"

"Too much weed? Too much mescal? The ataxia? Maybe she just got tangled up in the mic cord. But when she landed . . ."

He paused, remembering. Vividly, Teddy could tell.

"Anyway, end result? Concussion, broken elbow, busted kneecap and two cracked ribs. She was in the hospital for a week, which was where most of her remaining money went. Not being Canadian citizens, we didn't qualify for the public health care. Anyhow, we paid the bill, or most of it, and we were sent home with two different prescriptions, one for a painkiller, the other for depression, because it was clear from the beginning that it wasn't just bones she'd broken. Overnight, she became a whole different person. Bitter. Morose. For her, it was all over. She'd never return to the States in triumph. We'd never play that gig in Greenwich. Andy would never have his revenge and neither would she.

"I tried my best to cheer her up. Told her she'd be back with the band in no time, but she'd just look at me like I was somebody she'd known a long time ago and couldn't quite place. Her right leg was in a cast from calf to midthigh. She'd raise it up off the sofa and say, 'That's what you think, Mick? You *really* believe I'll be back leaping on tables anytime soon?' When I pointed out that some people did manage to sing without jumping onto tables, she told me to go fuck myself. Because for her, that's what singing was *about*.

"Anyhow, it all unraveled. I kept hoping that once the cast came off and she was mobile again, her spirits would improve. Most nights we had gigs, which meant leaving her alone in the apartment because she wouldn't dream of letting anybody see her in a wheelchair. We weren't nearly as good without her, of course. We had to go back to playing smaller, crappier venues. It was just music again, no show at all. I told myself we needed the money, but I was just glad, really, to get away for a few hours, to lose myself in the music. Mostly I went home as soon as we finished the gig, but this one night I went out with the guys instead. Got pretty hammered. Did some coke. By the time I got back to the apartment, the sun was coming up. I figured she'd be asleep. Her meds made her sleepy, and most days she was out till noon, but no, that morning she was wide awake, watching an old movie. 'It occurs to me now what I should've done,' she said when I came in, not taking her eyes off the TV. 'I should've fucking let you go to Vietnam.' I remember standing there looking at her, thinking that eventually she'd say she was sorry, but that was the thing about Jacy. You couldn't shame her. She wouldn't say she was sorry until she *was* fucking sorry.

"Anyhow, that afternoon the cast came off, so heading home from the hospital I suggested we go get a beer to celebrate, kind of a no-hard-feelings gesture. 'Do you realize,' she said, in the same voice she'd used that morning, 'there isn't a single fucking thing in the whole apartment to eat?' So instead of having that beer, I dropped her off and went to get us something for dinner." After a heavy pause. "By the time I got back she was gone. I didn't see her again for over a year. Didn't get so much as a postcard that whole time."

Lincoln shook his head. "Where did she go?"

"No clue. After a few weeks, I figured she must've gone back to the States. Someplace I couldn't follow her. For all I knew she'd patched things up with Vance and got married. Mostly I tried not to think about it. In fact, that whole year's a blur. Every single way a man can be messed up, I was. When the band fell apart, I moved to Vancouver and formed another one there, but we never really clicked, and my heart wasn't in it. I got a couple part-time gigs as a sound engineer. Made ends meet, somehow. I was living in this tiny second-floor walk-up, above a nice elderly couple. I have no idea how Jacy found me, but one evening I came home and there she was, outside my door, with a backpack in her lap, fast asleep in her wheelchair. Somebody must've helped her up there, because the stairs were really steep and there obviously wasn't a ramp.

"I'll tell you the truth. I didn't recognize her at first. She was skin and bones and you know what? I was scared to wake her up, afraid she'd start in yelling at me again. But then she twitched awake and smiled at me, and I saw she was the old Jacy. She said, 'Did you hear the news?' and it took me a moment to understand what she was asking because her speech was slurred and the effort to speak caused the elbow she'd broken to spasm. But I finally said, 'What news is that?' since I'd been in a sound booth all day. 'The amnesty. Gerald Ford says all's forgiven.' I said, 'You came to tell me that?' She said, 'No, I came to give you . . .' The rest was so garbled I couldn't make it out, so she tried again, and I finally understood that she'd come to give me my life back. I was holding a bag of groceries, so I said, 'In that case, stay for dinner' and wheeled her inside."

Teddy thought he heard Lincoln let out a low moan, but he purposely didn't look over at him.

"I offered to sleep on the couch, because the bath was off the bedroom, but she said no, it was okay. Her balance was for shit and she didn't have much strength in her legs, but she could walk short distances when she needed to. Which apparently was true, because when I woke up in the middle of the night she was sitting on the edge of the bed. 'I just want you to know I never hated you,' she said. 'I left because I didn't want you looking at me the way I looked at my father that day on the lawn.' Just like I *was* looking at her right then, she didn't have to say it. Anyhow, I told her I didn't care about the damn ataxia or anything else, so long as she was back. She started to cry then, so I scooted over so she could lie down next to me. When she stopped crying, I asked, 'What about the baby,' because not long after she left something came in the mail for her. The hospital reminding her of her first prenatal-care appointment. She told me not to worry, that she'd taken care of it.

"The next morning I had to go to work, but I told her when I got back we'd talk about the future. I said whatever she wanted was fine with me. We'd get married if she wanted—or not, if she didn't. We could go back home to the States, or find a bigger apartment right there in Vancouver. Whatever suited her. She said okay, we'd talk about all that when I got back. Something about how she said it made me wonder if maybe I'd pushed too hard, but really, I was too happy to be worried. During that year she was gone and I was so messed up, I'd gotten it into my head that she and I were meant to live our lives together, and now here she was, which proved I was right.

"Except I wasn't. I'd barely walked in when the station manager came into the recording booth and told me I needed to get home right away. I think her plan must've been to make her way down the stairs by hanging on to the banister, then ask that old couple to call her a taxi. They heard her fall—a terrible crash, they said—and found her crumpled at the bottom of the stairs. Naturally they wanted to call an ambulance, but she was alert and coherent, and somehow she convinced them she wasn't badly hurt. All she needed was for them to fetch her wheelchair, which was still up there on the landing, and call her a cab. That if they could just do those two things, she'd be fine. It's also possible her speech was slurred and they thought she was drunk. Anyway, while her husband wrestled the chair down the steep staircase—no easy task for a man his age—the wife went inside and called the taxi. Hanging up, though, she had second thoughts. She knew where I worked and decided to call me, too. By the time I got there Jacy had lost consciousness and they'd called the ambulance they should've called earlier, but by then she'd stopped breathing. The EMTs tried to revive her, but she was gone. Our Jacy."

———

AT SOME POINT during the evening the breeze had shifted, and the waves could now be heard pounding the beach below, seemingly proximate but in reality remote.

Mickey put his hands flat on the table. "I should let you guys go to bed," he said, "but before you do there's one more thing you need to understand. Not about her. About me. A couple years ago I finally broke down and went to the Vietnam Veterans Memorial, which I'd been putting off. Anyway, I'm standing there scanning down the rows of names, section after section, and I realize I'm looking for the guy who died in my place. And just like that I'm back in the Acropolis Diner with my old man, and he's pointing out all the guys my age and wanting to know which one of them should go if I didn't. See, it's no use arguing whether going would've been the right thing. The point is I'd promised my father I would, and instead of keeping my word, I went with Jacy up to Maine and then I did what the guy you used to know never would've done. I hid in the trunk of the car while Jacy drove us across the border. That's what you need to understand. The guy you remember is gone, just like Jacy."

Teddy glanced over at Lincoln, who was shaking his head. "Sorry, but that's bullshit," he said. "When you pulled in yesterday, my first thought was *There's Mick*. You were older, sure, and a bit more banged up. But I recognized you. That you were still the same."

"Also tonight," Teddy added, "when you sang."

But he could tell Mickey was having none of it. "Don't get me wrong," he said, drumming his fingers on the table. "I'm glad you feel that way. And part of what you say is true. Sometimes, when I'm on the Harley, I do feel like the guy I used to be, and yeah, I can channel him through certain songs." He turned to Teddy now. "It's the reason I hate most of today's music. I know it's good, a lot of it. But I can't find myself in it. And it's the guy I used to be, before Canada, that I'm always looking for and not finding."

"You're being too damn hard on yourself," Lincoln said.

"Sweet of you to say, but—"

"You just happened to be the one she chose," Teddy said, surprising himself in the process. In the end, how easy it was to surrender the thing you cherished most. All these years, Jacy's choosing him over Mickey or Lincoln had been a source of pride. He'd clutched that knowledge to his heart. "I would've climbed into that trunk, too."

"So would I," Lincoln said, an admission that couldn't have been easy to make, Teddy knew. A life as blessed as Lincoln's would be painful to forswear, even as an imaginative, nonbinding exercise.

"Well, you're good friends to say so," Mickey said. "And *you*," he told Lincoln, "are a particularly fine man."

Lincoln, who just then clearly had his doubts on that score, arched an eyebrow. "How so?"

"I've been waiting patiently for you to point out the moral of my story, but you're too decent to do it."

"There was a moral?"

"More of an irony, I guess. After all the grief I used to give you about being pussy-whipped, I ended up even worse."

Obviously an attempt at humor, but if Mickey was still Mickey, then Lincoln was still Lincoln, and so, true to form, he took it seriously. "I guess my own irony would be that all three of us were head over heels in love with a girl we didn't know."

"Aw, hell, Face Man," Mickey said. "We didn't even know ourselves." Then he kicked Teddy gently under the table. "What do *you* think, Tedwicki?"

What Teddy thought was that maybe knowledge was overrated. Sure, after hearing Mickey's story, they all knew Jacy better than they had when they were young, but the added information made no difference, at least not to him. He'd loved her then and loved her still . . . regardless . . . in spite of everything. Mickey and Lincoln, the friends of his youth? He loved them, too. *Still. Anyway. In spite of.* Exactly how he himself had always hoped to be loved. The way everyone hopes to be.

Lincoln

Groggy after getting only four hours' sleep, Lincoln was rinsing glasses in the sink when Mickey emerged from the bath, freshly showered, wearing gym shorts and a faded Bob Seger tour T-shirt. "Who's Bob Seger?" Lincoln asked.

Mickey just shook his head. "You'd think by now I could tell when you're pullin' my chain."

"I know who Bob Seger is," Lincoln assured him, though the irony of the assertion wasn't lost on him. If you couldn't fully know your best friends, how in the world could you claim to know Bob Seger?

Mickey took one of the glasses Lincoln had just rinsed, filled it from the tap and drained half of it standing there at the sink. From where they stood, through the kitchen window, Teddy and Delia could be seen strolling along the stone wall that marked the boundary between Lincoln's property and Troyer's. In the last half hour they'd made several laps around the perimeter of the yard. "You gotta wonder what *that's* about," Mickey said.

"He's probably telling her stories about her mom."

"He does seem to be doing most of the talking."

"None of my business," Lincoln said, "but has Delia exhibited any symptoms?"

"Nope," Mickey said, "and she probably would've by now if she was going to. There don't seem to be any hard-and-fast rules, though. Andres's symptoms showed up early but progressed slowly. Jacy became a cripple in a matter of months. All that pot smoking probably contributed, or so they're saying now."

"Yeah, but nobody could've known that at the time."

Mickey shrugged, apparently disinterested in his weak attempt at absolution.

"Mind my asking how you found each other? When Jacy said she'd taken care of the baby, you must've concluded that she'd had an abortion, right?"

Mickey set the empty glass back on the drainboard. "Delia found *me*. Not that long ago, actually. Couple years? The band had a gig out in Truro. We're doing our sound check, and this woman comes up behind me and says, 'How you doin', Pop?'" He massaged his forehead at the memory.

"How did she locate you?"

"How do you find anybody these days? Google. When Jacy put her up for adoption, she listed me as the father. Under nationality, she put *American;* under occupation, *musician*. Delia did the math and assumed I went back to the States after the amnesty. My name got her to the Big Mick on Pots website. I guess I looked enough like her to *maybe* be her father, and of course I was the right age . . ."

Lincoln tried to fathom it—having a child and not knowing about her for forty years. "And you recognized her as your daughter?"

"No, but I sure as hell recognized her as Jacy's. In fact, I just about keeled over."

"What'd you say to her?"

He chortled. "I said I hope you're not here for money, because I don't have a lot of that."

"And she said?"

He grinned. "You'll love this. She said, 'I don't want your damn money. I'm here to try out for your band.' I said, 'Can you do Tina Turner?' and she said, 'What the fuck use would I be otherwise?' I'm guessing your own daughters don't talk like that to you?"

"They speak their minds pretty freely," Lincoln allowed, "but no."

They lapsed into silence then, just stood there at the window watching Teddy and Delia slowly circumnavigate the sloping lawn that Lincoln had only yesterday feared her mother lay buried beneath.

"I'm ashamed, Mick," he said finally, feeling his throat constrict with these three words.

Mickey waved this away as you would a dangling thread of spiderweb. "Forget it."

"I wish I could," Lincoln told him.

"You really thought I might've hurt her?"

Lincoln nodded. "I made the mistake of going to see this retired ex-cop, thinking he might have some information about Jacy's disappearance that never made it into the papers. Like, if anybody had been questioned or suspected. If you can believe it, I'd gotten it into my head that Troyer might've been involved. Except it turned out he and this cop are old friends, and rather than being suspicious of him, he got suspicious about you. When he started digging, he found out about you and Jacy's father."

"I always dreaded the day you or Ted would find out about that," Mickey said. "No way to explain it without fessing up to everything."

"It knocked me pretty much sideways," Lincoln admitted. "Made me wonder"—here he had to pause and swallow hard before continuing—"if I really knew you."

"Well, there's no hard feelings, if that's what you're worrying about."

"No, I know that. I'm just disappointed in myself, I guess." This was an understatement, actually. For reasons he didn't fully comprehend even now, he'd allowed himself to be seduced by Coffin's narrative, its trash-vortex worldview. Instead of using the lens of his own experience, he'd genuflected before Coffin's. The other man's brutal, ugly stories of bad men and bad marriages had somehow undermined the validity of his own good one. Instead of seeing the idea of Jacy being buried beneath the sloping lawn of the Chilmark house as too horrible to be true, he'd accepted it as too horrible *not* to be. But why would he do that? Had something about the possibility appealed to him for some reason? Maybe awakened dormant vestiges of the unforgiving, oppressive religion he'd been raised in? Or was there some other darkness he was unaware of, something far more primitive than religious doctrine? Had he first glimpsed it the night of the draft lottery when Mickey's number was drawn ahead of his own? Hadn't something whispered to him then that *all for one and one for all* was just a lie they'd convinced themselves to believe in? Was this how wars happened, the seeds of conflict, large and small, growing in the gap between what people wanted to believe and what they feared must be true?

"Well," Mickey said, "if it's yourself you're disappointed in, I can show you where the line forms. Last night, I told you I kept what happened to Jacy a secret because I'd promised her I would. And that's true, as far as it goes. But it was also an easy promise to keep, because, deep down, I didn't want to share her. Not the girl we were all in love with back in college. Not even the one you saw in the photo. *Especially* not her." As he spoke, he rubbed his sternum, as if all the food he'd consumed last night at Rockers was having its belated revenge. "Delia changed all that. When I made Jacy that promise, I didn't know I had a daughter. And as messed up as she is, I wanted you and Teddy to know about her. She had the drug problem before we met, but I blame myself for the shape she's in. She needs better treatment than I can afford."

"I'll speak to Anita—"

He shot Lincoln a warning glance. "No, you won't. I mean it."

After a moment, Lincoln said, "I will have to tell her about all this, you know."

"What?" Mickey said, his mock outrage momentarily convincing. "Just because you've been married to the woman for four decades, you have to tell her stuff?"

"I know. Pussy-whipped to the bitter end."

"Yeah, but you'd have ended up pussy-whipped no matter who you married. At least Anita's a class act."

"I'll tell her you said so," Lincoln smiled. Somehow their conversation, painful though it was, had cleared the air, and for that he was profoundly grateful. Maybe they weren't all for one and one for all. Maybe they never had been. But they'd been friends, really good ones, and apparently they still were. "How about a cup of coffee?"

"Nah, I'll gather my shit and then we'll be off. It's not going to be easy talking Delia back into her program. The longer she's AWOL, the tougher it'll be."

She and Teddy were heading up the center of the lawn now, their conversation, whatever it had been about, apparently concluded. "Tedlowski better not be telling her about Jacy jumping on tables when she sang, because *that* would definitely appeal to her." He looked around now. "You're really gonna sell this place?"

"You think I shouldn't?"

Mickey shrugged. "How would I know?"

"Most people have opinions."

"Not me," Mickey said.

It had always been one of the most endearing things about him, Lincoln thought—this ability to say perfectly ridiculous things and make them sound absolutely true.

"LOOKED LIKE YOU and Delia had quite the conversation this morning," Lincoln ventured. He was driving Teddy to the hospital, where he'd have his eye checked and the bandage replaced. The damaged side of his face seemed even more swollen than it had that morning, the bruising more vivid, but the nap he'd taken after Mickey and his daughter left seemed to have done him good, and Lincoln marveled at his recuperative powers. "What do you make of her?"

"I'm not sure," Teddy replied, as if this were the very question he'd just been pondering. "It's like one minute Jacy's in there, looking out through those eyes, and the next she's completely gone and there's just this stranger."

Lincoln nodded. Though he himself had barely spoken to the woman, he'd come away with the same impression.

"She's definitely a coarser version of her mother," Teddy continued, "but I guess that's to be expected. Take away Greenwich, Connecticut, and good private schools, and replace those with shitty public ones, and Delia's what you get. But I found myself liking her. Quite a lot, actually. She's defensive and stubborn, like anyone would be after bouncing around foster homes. She can't quite figure Mickey out, but she seems to like him well enough."

"*Like* him?"

Teddy shrugged. "I read somewhere that babies in Russian orphanages stop crying after they learn it doesn't do them any good. Which of course ruins them emotionally for the rest of their lives. I think something like that might be happening with Delia. If she let herself really love her father, she'd be vulnerable. She'd rather be tough, even if that means being resigned to bad outcomes. On the other hand, she wouldn't have come looking for him if she hadn't been hoping for *something*. Having found him, though, she doesn't seem to know what comes next. Could be she just needs a friend who isn't her father."

"Yeah?"

Teddy must've heard the skepticism in his voice, because he gave him a one-eyed look of disapproval. "You don't feel any obligation? She's Jacy's daughter."

In truth Lincoln wasn't sure. Earlier he'd offered to help pay for a better treatment facility than Mickey could afford, but the obligation he'd felt then was to him, not her. Anita factored into it, too. What would she think if he allowed himself an emotional attachment to the daughter of a girl they both knew he'd once been in love with? Didn't she deserve to be shut of her rival at last? He'd hoped that finding out what happened to Jacy would at long last settle his own mind, but now, thanks to Delia, that might never happen. Although she was a couple thousand miles away and still knew nothing of Delia's existence, Anita nevertheless seemed to sense her presence when she'd phoned earlier. "What's wrong?" she wanted to know as soon as she heard his voice. Instead of giving her a complete accounting, he'd told her only about Teddy, how he'd passed out, fallen on a shattered wineglass and nearly lost an eye as a result. "Actually, there's more," he admitted, "but I can't really talk now. I'll tell you all about it as soon as the guys are gone, I promise." When she didn't say anything to that, he took the opportunity to change the subject. "How's everything where you are?"

"Your father says hello."

"Yeah? How is the old reprobate?"

"Okay, except he keeps calling this new woman Trudy. When she reminds him that she's not your mother, he says"—and here she mimicked his high, squeaky voice—"'I can tell that just by looking at you.'"

Lincoln laughed out loud, as he always did when his wife allowed herself to mimic his father. She'd had Dub-Yay down about ten minutes after meeting the man, but she was usually too kind to mock him.

"And here's the part you'll love," she continued. "She's Catholic."

"*Roman* Catholic?"

"She took him to Mass last Sunday."

Lincoln felt the earth wobble. "Wolfgang Amadeus Moser went to Mass?"

"Yep."

"The end times approach."

"I don't know, Lincoln," she said, sounding exhausted, as if this were an ongoing argument she'd given up winning long ago. "People change."

Why, he wondered, was he so resistant to that possibility? Just last night Mickey had tried to convince them he was no longer the same person they'd known back in the seventies, but wasn't he really just talking about disillusionment? Okay, sure, the night he and Jacy became lovers, he'd discovered something about himself that surprised and frightened him. He'd always thought of himself as a chip off the old block, the sort of man who, like his father, always knew what was right and did it. Certainly not someone who hid in the trunk of a car to avoid military service. And after following Jacy into that motel room, he no doubt *felt* changed, and from that point forward everything he did—from using money Jacy had stolen from her father to buy instruments and sound equipment, to drinking too much and smoking too much weed—had strengthened his conviction that he was no longer the same person. But wasn't that the point? If he was feeling shame, it was *himself* he was ashamed of, not some new person born of moral weakness. Adam didn't become a different man after eating the apple. He was who he'd always been, except miserable.

And yet. W. A. Moser attending *Mass*? That *did* feel like a sea change. Was it possible the old man was actually admitting, albeit obliquely, to being wrong about something? Not Catholicism, of course. That wouldn't happen in a hundred lifetimes. But wasn't his attending Mass with this new woman tantamount to confessing he'd been wrong to insist on his wife's conversion? And therefore wrong to oppose his son's marrying a Catholic? Wrong to taunt him for the better part of four decades for a betrayal that existed only in his own imagination?

"Tell him I'll come visit as soon as I get back," Lincoln said.

"Is that wise?" she replied. Because he'd made similar promises many times and broken as many as he'd kept, and the latter had been more out of duty than love. *Why keep making halfhearted promises?* was his wife's point. *Because*, he wanted to say, maybe it was time to stop pretending, even to himself, he didn't love the old bugger. After all, paternal love *was* permitted, even if your father could be summed up in a single word and the word was *impossible*. Even if he was Wolfgang Amadeus Moser.

THE HOSPITAL'S WAITING ROOM was mobbed. Lincoln offered to stick around, but Teddy said there was no reason to if he had better things to do. He'd shoot Lincoln a text when they were finished with him. Ten minutes later, when Lincoln knocked on Coffin's apartment door, it was Beverly who answered. She was wearing the same loose shorts and sweatshirt (the latter probably Coffin's, since she was swimming in it) she'd had on last night at Rockers. They both said "Oh!" at the same instant, and then, in the next, "I wasn't expecting . . ."

When she recovered enough poise to invite him in, Lincoln said no thanks, perhaps a little more emphatically than necessary. Yesterday, at the *Vineyard Gazette*, he'd allowed himself to be attracted to the woman and enjoyed that she seemed attracted to him as well. At the time it had seemed harmless enough. Today, though, nothing felt harmless. "I just stopped by to see how Mr. Coffin was doing," he told her. Not the whole truth, but still.

"That's nice of you," she said, "but he went out a couple hours ago and didn't say where he was going. Anywhere I'm *not* was my impression."

"I'm sorry to—"

"I'm a scold, it seems." She made a face that signaled a mixture of resignation and exhaustion. No doubt they'd spent the morning arguing about the surgery he'd vowed to skip last night at Rockers. "Nothing I say seems to get through."

"Maybe he's hearing more than you think," Lincoln told her, though he had no idea whether or not this was true. "I know he cares for you."

"He told you this?"

"Not in so many words," Lincoln admitted weakly, "but he can't seem to go more than two or three sentences without alluding to you. It's none of my business, but is his son still in the picture?"

"He told you about Eric?"

Lincoln nodded.

"No, he took him to the ferry the night he . . . hurt me. Told him to never come back or he'd . . ." No need to finish this sentence. "We have no idea where he went. I still have all his things. I think Joe regrets driving him away, but he'd never admit it. We don't talk about him."

"I'm sorry," Lincoln told her, which was true. He'd never seen a man so at war with himself as Joe Coffin.

"He's hard on people," she continued, as if reading his mind. "Especially himself. Did you know he went to Dartmouth?"

"No," Lincoln said, though he wasn't that surprised, given how offended he'd been when Lincoln mentioned where Minerva was located.

"One semester. But his mother got sick and he came home to help out. He never went back. What money there was went to her doctors instead."

"That's a tough break, all right," Lincoln said, trying to imagine what it would've been like for him if he'd had to go back to Dunbar after a semester at Minerva. "Would you let him know I dropped by? I have some news that might interest him."

"I'm so embarrassed," she said when he turned to leave. "I've forgotten your name."

"Lincoln," he reminded her, feeling some of the wind go out of his sails. Which no doubt served him right.

On a hunch he drove out to Katama, and there, a couple hundred yards from the beach, was the old pickup, parked on the strip of grass between the road and the bike path. Coffin registered his presence in the rearview mirror when Lincoln pulled in behind him.

"Even if I believed in coincidences, I wouldn't buy into this one," he said, having rolled down his window as Lincoln walked up.

Lincoln nodded. "I had an idea you might want to see your hawk again."

"Turns out that not everything you want to see feels like seeing you."

It occurred to Lincoln that he might not be talking about the bird. "I won't bother you for long."

"I apologize for last night," Coffin said. "Did I frighten you?"

"A little," Lincoln admitted.

"That wasn't my intention. It was Kevin I was hoping to scare. He pushes steroids to local kids dumb enough to think they could be pro athletes if they could just bulk up. Did he look scared to you?"

"Not particularly."

"Yeah, he definitely took my attempts at menace in stride. Anyway, you're too late. I've already talked to my friend the police chief. I expect he'll pay you a visit soon."

"He'll be wasting his time," Lincoln said. "I found out last night that Jacy died back in the seventies."

"You *know* this?"

Lincoln couldn't help smiling. "No, but I *believe* it. Turns out she was on that ferry after all. She and Mickey secretly met up in Woods Hole. She convinced him to go to Canada with her instead of reporting for induction."

He was prepared for Coffin to find fault with this narrative, but he just nodded thoughtfully. "A girl that good-looking? He's lucky she didn't want him to rob banks. Doesn't explain why she never told her parents, though."

"Long story, there."

"You say she died?"

"Of the same neurological disease that killed her biological father."

Lincoln could see the man's mind working. "In other words, not the same guy your friend Mickey beat the shit out of?"

"Nope."

"I guess I can fill in the blank there."

"See, Mr. Coffin, that's the reason I'm telling you all this. Because filling in the blanks, as you put it, is exactly what you and your friend Troyer have been doing, except you've been filling them in wrong."

Here, too, he expected pushback that didn't come. Coffin only shrugged, as if he'd been shown an arithmetic error in his checkbook. "It happens, Lincoln."

"Yeah, but when it does, aren't you supposed to rethink things? Pause to consider all the other things you might be wrong about?"

"Like what?"

"Well, in your shoes what I'd rethink is my decision not to have that operation. You get that right and maybe you've bought yourself some time to consider all the other stuff."

"More time to contemplate everything I've done wrong and all the people I've misjudged? You don't make it sound all that attractive, Lincoln, especially when the alternative is dying peacefully in my sleep while believing I did my best."

"You sleep peacefully?"

He sighed mightily. "Well, you got me there, Lincoln. No, I do not sleep peacefully."

"Mr. Coffin?"

"Yeah?"

"Beverly really does care about you."

His expression darkened. "I'm aware of that. You have a point?"

"Well, you're always saying we ought to do better by girls? Why not do better by her? For your own good, let her win this one."

Coffin studied him for a long beat, then said, "Shit, Lincoln. I just lost an argument, didn't I."

"I believe you did, yes."

"And now you're all proud of yourself."

Lincoln shrugged. "Maybe a little."

"I don't know, my friend. It's a slippery slope giving women what they want. First thing this one's going to do when I come out from under the anesthesia is start ragging me about writing that cozy mystery book. Make me the laughingstock of this entire island. The whole thing'll be your fault and you'll be gone and I'll have to find some innocent person to take it out on."

"You see the future very clearly."

He nodded, rolling his window back up. "It's a gift."

ONE FINAL DUTY, Lincoln thought, saved for last because it was the most distasteful.

Troyer answered his knock wearing nothing but a Speedo—a relief, actually, though Lincoln did wonder, and not for the first time, why men with prodigious beer guts were so often proud of their physiques. For Troyer's part, when he saw who was on his doorstep, he laughed out loud and called over his shoulder, "Roxy! Put some damn clothes on. We got company."

Even with Troyer standing in the doorway, Lincoln had a direct line of sight out onto the deck, where the woman in question rose from the chaise lounge, came over to the screen door and peered inside through cupped hands and said, "What?"

"Nothing!" Troyer barked back. Then muttered, more to Lincoln than to her, "Show the whole damn world your pussy. See if I care."

When he stepped aside so his visitor could enter, Lincoln shook his head. "I only have a minute."

"Okay, I'll come out," Troyer said, letting the screen door clap shut behind him, to gunshot effect. Lincoln suppressed a smile. Earlier, when he'd announced his intention to pay Troyer a visit, Teddy offered to come along. Lincoln told him that wouldn't be necessary, just to call the cops if he heard gunfire. In his mind's eye he could see Teddy dialing 911.

"What's the deal?" Troyer wanted to know. "Your friend didn't give you my message?"

"No, I got it. I just wanted to let you know I won't be putting my place on the market after all."

"You don't want to sell it. I don't want to buy it. So why tell me?"

"Well, my realtor noticed something when he was looking at the survey of my lot."

The other man stiffened visibly.

"Apparently you don't have an easement through my property. Were you aware of that?"

"Oh, *now* I get it," he said, his eyes narrowing. "You don't want to sell me your house, you want to sell me an easement for the *price* of your house."

"No, I was thinking one dollar would do it. Of course if there are legal costs, you'd pay for those."

Troyer cocked his head. "You're saying you'd sell me an easement for a dollar?"

"Correct."

"Why?"

There was a long answer that involved an apology Lincoln didn't feel like making, so he opted for a shorter one that didn't. "Why not?" he said. "We're neighbors, right?"

"Not really. You're never here."

"Actually, my wife and I are thinking about spending a couple weeks here next summer," Lincoln told him, though he hadn't broached the subject with Anita yet. "Maybe bring my father along, if he's well enough." Who knew? If Dub-Yay was going to Mass, maybe he'd be game for this, as well.

"Avoid August," Troyer advised, relaxing a bit now, but still suspicious. "That's when Obama comes. Him and all the other libs."

Lincoln indicated the man's Trump sign. "You wouldn't actually vote for him, would you?"

Troyer snorted. "Nah. That's just there to piss off the rest of Chilmark." But then he shrugged. "On the other hand, if he gets the nomination, I just might."

Lincoln felt a chill, but shrugged it off. "The price of your easement just doubled," he said.

He was halfway back up the hill, when he heard his name shouted. Turning, he saw Troyer loping uphill toward him, his gut jiggling over his Speedo. He arrived winded and clutching a swatch of papers. Lincoln didn't recognize them as pages from Teddy's manuscript until the other man handed them over. "Roxy found these in the yard."

Unless Lincoln was mistaken, they'd been crumpled up and tossed in the trash and, just now, retrieved and hastily smoothed out. "Thanks. Teddy will be pleased."

"So . . . this whole easement thing? Does this mean we're good? No more bad blood?"

Lincoln nodded. "That's what it means."

"All right, then," he said, offering his hand. "Good deal."

Lincoln swallowed hard and shook it.

Teddy

You're sure Anita's okay with this?" Teddy said.

It was late Tuesday morning and they were leaning against Lincoln's rental car in the Oak Bluffs ferry terminal's vehicle reservation line. The boat pulling into the slip was half empty, but it would be full going back, more people leaving the island this time of year than coming to it. Yesterday, Teddy had taken the same ferry on foot, retrieved his car from the Falmouth lot and brought it over to the island. Tomorrow he'd call the college and resign from his position there, letting people know that unless they could find a new editor-in-chief he'd be shutting down Seven Storey Books. Later in the week he'd have the English department send a work-study student over to his apartment to gather up whatever he'd need for the autumn—warmer clothes, work boots, his laptop—and ship it here to the island. The apartment itself he'd hold on to until the first of the year, just in case things didn't work out on the Vineyard. And they might not. He knew that. In the aftermath of a spell, a manic stage often ensued, with bright possibilities everywhere that would fizzle out after a week or two. Something about this new plan felt right, though, and anyway it had been a long time since he'd been really excited about anything.

"Actually, Anita likes the idea a lot," Lincoln assured him. The Mosers had been on the phone half a dozen times yesterday making a long list of things that needed doing in the Chilmark house before they listed it in the spring. Teddy thought he could handle most of it on his own. He couldn't do electrical work, and a couple other tasks would likely require two people, but he'd be one of them, and if things went as he hoped he knew who the other would be. "You'll be saving us money."

Teddy supposed that might be true, but he also worried that his proposal had caught Lincoln off guard and he'd been unable to come up with a good-enough reason to say no to an old friend. On the other hand, he seemed genuinely of two minds about selling the place, so maybe putting off the decision until spring made sense for them, too. "Well," Teddy said, "if you change your minds, just let me know, and I'll clear out."

"We won't," Lincoln assured him. "I just hope . . ." But then his voice trailed off.

"I know," Teddy said. What probably worried Lincoln, who'd always been a thorough planner and averse to risk, was that Teddy was acting impulsively, committing to such an important life change without really having thought things through. "You hope I'm not setting myself up for a major disappointment." He hoped the same thing himself. Exhausted as he'd been the night Mickey told his story, he was unable to fall asleep afterward, partly because his eye was pulsing to the beat of his breathing. When the sky finally started to lighten in the east, he'd dressed quietly and gone out into the kitchen to make himself a cup of Keurig coffee. He was doctoring it when Delia appeared in the doorway. She started to say something, but Teddy put an index finger to his lips and indicated the front room, where her father lay snoring on the sofa. When she joined him at the counter, Teddy handed her his coffee, made himself another and whispered, "Take a walk with me?"

She looked dubious but followed him out onto the deck and then down to the lawn below. When they were out of earshot, he extended his hand. "I don't think we've been formally introduced. I'm Teddy."

When she took it, he noticed her fingernails were chewed down to the quick. "I recognized you from your photo in the Minerva yearbook."

Teddy was surprised Mickey still had one of those. Did he dig it out to show her, or had she found it herself in a closet or on some dusty bookshelf?

"Plus he talks about you and Lincoln all the time. I know the two of you a hell of a lot better than I know him, actually. Is it true all three of you were in love with my mother?"

"Yes, it is."

"So what the fuck was she thinking when she chose him?"

Teddy couldn't tell whether this was supposed to be a joke or a sincere if rudely put question. "Hey," he said, "the other two scenarios don't result in you."

"Big loss for the world, right?"

"Lose the sarcasm, and I'd agree with you."

"Nice of you to say, except you don't know me."

"I feel like I kind of do."

"Feel however you like, dude, but trust me, you don't."

Teddy couldn't help chuckling. "You sounded *just* like your mother right then." They were quiet for a while until Teddy tried a different tack. "So your father doesn't talk about himself that much?"

She made a yeah-right face. "He says that what I see is what I'm getting."

"What would you like to know?"

She took a deep breath. "Why he's like he is? What he was like when he was young? How he can be so laid-back most of the time, and then be, like, a total dick?"

So, he'd just started in. Told her about Mickey's family in West Haven, Connecticut. How as a boy he'd been spoiled by his sisters and by the time he was sixteen was sneaking out to play in bars with older musicians. How his father always called Fender guitars Fensons. (This elicited a smile.) How Mickey'd stunned everyone by acing his SATs. How one day Michael Sr. and his crew had lunch at their local diner, and when it was time to go back to work, everybody but Mickey's dad stood up, and he'd just sat there, his heart having quit on him. How the three of them had met at Jacy's sorority, where they all slung hash, and how Mickey had opted to scrub pots in the kitchen. ("So *that's* where *Big Mick on Pots* came from!") How the three of them and her mother, who was engaged at the time, had returned to the Theta house late one night, and Jacy, after being called a slut by a sorority sister, had given all three of them big, wet kisses right in front of her. How another time, after one of their Friday afternoon keg parties, Mickey and some of the other hashers had gone over to the SAE house and her father, pissed off by the stone lions out front, had coldcocked the pledge who'd opened the door to welcome them to the party. ("Okay, that *does* sound like him.") And, most important, how he and Lincoln and Mickey had all watched the first Vietnam draft lottery together in the sorority's back room, when her father's number had been nine out of three hundred and sixty-six, and how Jacy had been waiting for them out in the parking lot afterward and had cried when she heard. And finally how their motto had been All for One and One for All. By now, Delia had gone completely silent, and her eyes were liquid. It only took a moment, though, for her to return to what Teddy recognized as her default mode. "So basically what you're saying is I'm an asshole for not appreciating what a great guy he is."

"No, I'm saying that if he doesn't open up to you, it's because he's his father's son and guys like them just don't. They come at everything on a slant, especially emotions. If he hasn't told you he loves you, it doesn't mean he doesn't."

"Yeah, but it also doesn't mean he does."

Again he noticed her mangled fingernails. "Okay if I ask you a personal question?"

"I guess."

"What's hardest for you right now?"

"You know I'm a junkie, right?"

"I know you have a problem with opioids."

"Like I said, a junkie. He wants me to quit. *I* want to quit. But the thing is, there are just too many fucking hours in the day."

"I understand that, actually." She looked as if she might want to ask what he meant, but decided not to.

"Also, no matter what anybody tells you, junkies are junkies because drugs turn bad times into good times, and who the fuck doesn't want to have those? Anyhow, I think he's going to give up on me soon, and then it won't matter."

Teddy snorted at this. "If you think he's *ever* going to give up on you, then you really don't know him."

"I guess we'll see."

Her tone of voice was infuriating, but instead of letting on that she was pissing him off, Teddy said, "So, tell me what you're good at."

"I'm good at something?"

"You're a fine singer."

"I'm an *okay* singer."

"Is that what you'd like to do for the rest of your life?"

She shrugged. "Why do you ask?"

"Just wondering if you might not be selling yourself short. A lot of people do."

"Kinda feels like we might be talking about you now."

Ah, he thought. Mickey was right. She *was* smart.

"Okay," she said, "so what're *you* good at?"

He thought about it. "I guess I'd have to say repairing what's broken."

"Like what?"

"Lots of stuff. As a kid I fixed things at home. Toasters. Radios. Whatever went on the fritz."

"That must've pleased your parents."

"Not really. They were high-school English teachers. They looked down at people who knew practical things."

"What do you fix now?"

"Other people's books."

"Why don't you write one of your own if you're so good at it?"

"See? You've gone right to the heart of the matter. My favorite teacher in college advised me not to write a book until it was impossible *not* to. I appear to have taken his advice."

At this she offered a sly smile. "I wouldn't wait much longer. You don't look so hot."

"That's true, but I don't always look as bad as I do right now."

"I'll take your word for it."

"I don't suppose you know how to swing a hammer?"

She looked at him as if he'd said something in Swahili. "Like, at a nail?"

"Yes, exactly like that."

"Not really."

"Would you like to learn?"

"Not really." But he could tell she was intrigued. "Why?"

"I was just thinking about what you said earlier. All those hours you have trouble filling. I read somewhere that physical labor is a good distraction for a troubled mind."

"This would be a paying gig?"

"Absolutely."

"Oh, I get it. You think if I'm here, away from my regular dealers, I won't be able to score?"

"No." Though, yes, that thought had crossed his mind.

"Because I could score on this island in about two seconds flat."

"You'll be too busy."

"Also, just so you know? If we work together, you're more likely to end up a junkie than I am to get straight."

"I'll take my chances."

"Also, *I'm* not something you can repair, if that's what you're thinking."

Which of course he had been. "I suppose you're right. Still, all those empty hours, and I've got a ton more stories."

"You're actually serious?"

"Why not?"

"Because it's fucking crazy, is why not."

"You don't have to say anything now. Just think about it. I'll give you my cell number and you can call me later if you're interested." But he knew he was going to find out right then. If she *was* interested, she'd give him her number; if not, she'd say she could get his from her father.

She took out her phone. "Go."

She was a two-thumbed, smart-phone typist, a trick Teddy had yet to master.

Then, "I might as well give you mine." Reciting her number, she paused on the last digit. "You're not going to turn out to be some pervert, are you?" He must've blanched at this, because she made another face and said, again in her mother's voice, "I'm fucking *kidding*, Teddy. Jesus Christ."

"Oh," he said. "Gotcha."

"Did he tell you about his heart murmur?"

"Your father? No."

"Then neither did I."

"ABOUT MICKEY'S STORY?" Lincoln said. Vehicles and foot passengers were still streaming off the ferry. "How much of it do you think is true?"

"Every word," Teddy told him. "He was pretty clear about being all done lying."

"Oh, I don't think he was lying," Lincoln said. "I'm just trying to understand. I mean, think about it. Jacy's mother did everything she could to keep Andy's existence a secret from her, and look at how that worked out. Why would Jacy turn around and do the same thing by putting her own daughter up for adoption and keeping her a secret from Mickey?"

"Maybe for some of the same reasons her mother did?" Teddy ventured, even though the same question had bedeviled him. "To keep her safe? To give her the best chance at a good life? She had to figure that she herself probably wasn't going to be around to watch her daughter grow up. The alternative to adoption would be entrusting her infant daughter to a father who would probably continue being a hand-to-mouth musician playing in crummy bars like Rockers because that was the only life he knew or wanted."

"You don't think Mickey would've risen to the occasion if he knew he had a kid?"

"Actually, I do," Teddy said. "I'm not saying she did the right thing, or was even thinking clearly. But she wasn't just sick, she was desperate. She probably thought she was witnessing not just her own decline but Mickey's as well. He told us himself that he was a complete mess."

Lincoln didn't dispute any of this, but he didn't look convinced.

"Also," Teddy said, "it might be argued that doing to your children what was done to you is the oldest story in the world."

"Oh, I understand it in the abstract," Lincoln conceded. "But the Jacy we knew wasn't cruel. I've tried to, but I just can't quite hear her ever telling Mickey that she wished she'd let him go to Vietnam."

"Maybe what made it conceivable was knowing she'd prevented any such thing," Teddy offered, straining to provide the kind of explanation that a man like Lincoln, who was uncomfortable with mystery, might find satisfying. He came from a family where questions had clear, obvious answers, delivered with breathtaking confidence. At Minerva, he'd felt cheated when Tom Ford declined to provide a clear-cut answer to the Civil War question they'd spent all semester debating. Even now, at sixty-six, he sought transparency in all things, even the human soul.

The last of the vehicles had rolled off the ferry now, and the drivers of those heading on board were starting their engines.

"Here's something else that's hard to imagine," Lincoln said, climbing in behind the wheel and pulling the door shut behind him. "Us never meeting. Can you picture that?"

"No," Teddy admitted. "Not really."

"It *is* weird, though," Lincoln said, turning the key in the ignition, "because what were the odds?"

Indeed. They all might've gone to different colleges and spent their lives in—how had Jacy's mother put it?—"blissful ignorance" of one another's existence.

"Kind of makes you wonder. If there was such a thing as do-overs, if we all had a bunch of chances at life, would they all be different?" When the car in front of him began inching forward, Lincoln put his in gear. "Or would they play out exactly the same?"

To Teddy's way of thinking—and he'd thought about it a lot—this depended on which end of the telescope you were looking through. The older you got, the more likely you'd be looking at your life through the wrong end, because it stripped away life's clutter, providing a sharper image, as well as the impression of inevitability. Character was destiny. Seen this way, every time Teddy went up for that fateful rebound, Nelson, being Nelson, would undercut him, and Teddy, ever Teddy, would hit the boards precisely how he had back then. Viewed from afar, even chance appeared to be an illusion. Mickey's number in the draft lottery would always be 9, Teddy's always 322. Why? Because . . . well, that's just how the story went. Nor, as the ancient Greeks understood, was it possible to interrupt or meaningfully alter this chain of events once the story was under-way. If Teddy had been the man Jacy thought he was when she tried to seduce him at Gay Head, not much would've changed, because she was already Jacy. The ataxia, part of her DNA from conception, would've found her even if she hadn't been living a life of sex and drugs and rock and roll. Maybe this was the unstated purpose of education, to get young people to see the world through the tired eyes of age: disappointment and exhaustion and defeat masquerad-ing as wisdom. That's what it had felt like when Teddy picked up the Minerva alumni magazine and learned of Tom Ford's death— like the fix was in, right from the start. *Of course* Tom would move to San Francisco when he retired, and there, free for the first time to be himself, would contract AIDS and die, Teddy feared, alone.

But this was the *wrong* end of the telescope. Okay, sure, maybe looking at things through the proper end also resulted in distortion by making distant things seem closer than they really were, but at least you were looking in the direction your life was heading. It wasn't in fact possible to strip life of its clutter for the simple reason that life *was* clutter. If free will turned out to be an illusion, wasn't it a necessary one, if life was to have any meaning at all? More to the point, what if it wasn't? What if you *were* presented with meaningful choices, maybe even a few that were capable of altering your trajectory? Okay, say that sometimes it *did* feel like the fix was in, but what if that fix was only partial? What made the contest between fate and free will so lopsided was that human beings invariably mistook one for the other, hurling themselves furiously against that which is fixed and immutable while ignoring the very things over which they actually had some control. Forty-four years ago, on this very island, with mountains of evidence to the contrary staring them in the face, Teddy and his friends had all agreed that their chances were awfully good. Sure they were fools, by any objective measure, but hadn't they also been courageous that night? What were people supposed to do when confronted with a world that couldn't care less whether they lived or died? Cower? Genuflect? If there was a God, he had to be choking with laughter. Stack the deck against them, and instead of blaming him, these damned fools that he'd created, supposedly in his own image, would rather blame themselves.

By the time Lincoln's ferry was out of sight, Teddy had the pier pretty much to himself. It was almost lunchtime, and he realized he was hungry. There was no need to rush back to Chilmark, so he strolled up the street to the tavern where he and Lincoln drank beer when he'd arrived on the island only four days ago. It *felt* like an eternity. Out on the deck, he ordered a bowl of chowder. It was too early to drink beer, but being in no hurry he ordered one anyway. When he finished, he would drive up island to where several months' worth of tasks awaited him. He was looking forward, he realized, to every single one of them. Maybe, before getting started, he'd call Theresa. Let her know what had happened and that he'd not only survived but was feeling better about things than he had in a very long while. He might even tell her he was thinking about starting that book Tom Ford advised him not to write until he had to. It probably wouldn't be any good, but if it wasn't, perhaps he'd be able to fix it. He'd spent the last decade fixing other people's botched jobs, so why not one of his own? For years now he'd believed he had no further urgent business with this world, or it with him. But it could be he was wrong.

Acknowledgments

Thanks to Howard and the "Choir Practice" crew at Off-shore Ale, as well as to Susan Catling and Hilary Wall at the *Vineyard Gazette*. And, as always, thanks to Nat and Judith, to Emily and Kate, to Gary and everyone at Knopf. And, need I say it, none of these books gets written without Barbara.

A NOTE ABOUT THE AUTHOR

Richard Russo lives with his wife, Barbara, in Portland, Maine.

A NOTE ON THE TYPE

This book was set in Janson, a typeface long thought to have been made by the Dutchman Anton Janson, who was a practicing typefounder in Leipzig during the years 1668–1687. However, it has been conclusively demonstrated that these types are actually the work of Nicholas Kis (1650–1702), a Hungarian, who most probably learned his trade from the master Dutch typefounder Dirk Voskens. The type is an excellent example of the influential and sturdy Dutch types that prevailed in England up to the time William Caslon (1692–1766) developed his own incomparable designs from them.

Typeset by Scribe,
Philadelphia, Pennsylvania

Printed and bound by Berryville Graphics,
Berryville, Virginia

Designed by Cassandra J. Pappas